PRAISE FOR SALINEE GOLDENBERG

"An evocative examination into revenge, redemption, and colonialism, Way of the Walker *has it all: stunning prose, an expansive world, and lots of found family feels. With an ending that is as tender as it is tragic, this complex and considered fantasy is one to watch."*

Keshe Chow, Sunday Times bestselling author of *For No Mortal Creature*

"One of the best-written books I've read this year. Visually evocative, and spiced with the flavors of folklore, Way of the Walker *is the perfect sequel to* The Last Phi Hunter. *Goldenberg's prose is woven with power and poetry. I couldn't put this book down, brought in by the action, the worldbuilding, and the evocative writing. At once spiritual and sensuous, rich and otherworldly,* Way of the Walker *is unputdownable and unforgettable. I loved it as much as I did* Phi Hunter, *and maybe even more. Goldenberg is a masterful writer."*

Rania Hanna, author of *The Jinn Daughter*

"Old magic and ancient gods infuse this enthralling story of resistance, liberation, and the courage it takes to walk an unorthodox path. The rich characters, immersive world, and timely themes make for an exciting and rewarding read."

Khan Wong, author of *Down in the Sea of Angels*

"Way of the Walker *is a dream of hope and change, of mysticism and spirituality, of redemption and salvation explored through the conflict of morality and ethics. It is a story of forging one's own path and daring to stray from the one set by others while embracing fate and confronting sacrifice. Goldenberg peels back the curtains to show us just how legends are made."*

Ai Jiang, author of *A Palace Near the Wind* and *Linghun*

Way of the Walker *is a richly written blend of fantasy, a touch of horror, and adventure that will hook readers from beginning to end.*

V Castro, award-nominated author of *The Haunting of Alejandra*

"This novel doesn't just return us to the magical world of Suyoram: it cranks up the stakes to an epic crescendo, as our heroine Ree embarks on a quest not to save herself, but to rid her land of European colonialism. The horrors, the betrayals and the sexual chaos of the first book are multiplied to the nth degree, plunging readers into grimdark depths reminiscent of R.F. Kuang's The Poppy War*... yet light and hope are never lost, and the agony is always tempered with the redemptive solace of Buddhist spirituality."*

Ng Yi-Sheng, author of *Utama* and "A Spicepunk Manifesto"

"Rich with Thai culture, Buddhism, and martial arts, The Last Phi Hunter *is a seamlessly woven fantasy debut that examines one's race, personal identity, and of course, love. This is for readers who want a dark Asian fantasy infused with Thai culture and mythology! If you've been craving a different blend of SFF, you'll get a kick out of this one."*

R.R. Virdi, USA Today bestselling author on *The Last Phi Hunter*

Salinee Goldenberg

WAY OF THE WALKER

ANGRY ROBOT
An imprint of Watkins Media Ltd

Unit 11, Shepperton House
89 Shepperton Road
London N1 3DF
UK

angryrobotbooks.com
twitter.com/angryrobotbooks
The Book of Isaree

An Angry Robot paperback original, 2026

Cover by Reza Afshar and Alice Coleman
Edited by Desola Coker and Andrew Hook
Set in Meridien

ISBN 978 1 83673 001 9
Ebook ISBN 978 1 83673 000 2

Printed and bound in the United Kingdom by CPI Group (UK) Ltd, Croydon CR0 4YY

The manufacturer's authorised representative in the EU for product safety is eucomply OÜ - Pärnu mnt 139b-14, 11317 Tallinn, Estonia, hello@eucompliancepartner.com; www.eucompliancepartner.com

9 8 7 6 5 4 3 2 1

For Derek S.

I

Chapter 1

The Path We Chose

What was it like, being able to walk in the Everpresent at will?

It was a tingle over Isaree's skin when a spirit wandered near. The echoes of magic left behind that whispered a story of what had been and what would be. The hiss of sunlight as it glanced across the river at dawn, building into an insufferable roar by noon. Struck numb, she stared in wonder as the world shifted and shimmered, burning bright with every color soaked in meaning.

Her first memory of the Everpresent was on the muddy banks of the Jinburi river, under the sweltering Suyoram sun of dry season. At six years old, she had no name for the vivid layer which thickened the air with a stream of crimson and rot, running forth like the lacerated offal from a gutted cow.

Little one… A voice came without sound, pitched high and low like a flute played in a deep well. It drifted from the shadows beyond the grass, under the bamboo platform where the fisherman would sit early in the morning after they waded out into the water to check their nets.

Please help me.

Long, narrow trenches carved into the dirt led under the pier, to a dark hole. Scrapes surrounded all sides of the pit, stretching out like the rays of the sun. A glint in the darkness – a slither like wet scales, metal rubbing against metal in the wash basin.

A small, gray hand inched from the hole, fingers flexing, dragging itself forward with clawed nails caked with dirt. A skinny arm followed, fish-belly pale, with deep violet veins spider-webbing across the flesh. *Help me up, little one. And we can be friends…*

The hand pulled itself forward little by little. But where Ree expected to see an elbow, its forearm extended like an unspooling ribbon. The skin flexed like a snake and rose in the air. The hand hovered before her, palm upward.

Hesitantly, Ree reached out, her small fingers grazing its cold claws.

A crash of thunder exploded into metal and fury. Her body flew back, stumbled to the edge of the water. Yelling and thrashing ensued, the twisted limb slapped at the form of her father. Pa's voice came through just like the creature's, without a body to it, and he yelled bad words.

Hunter, wait! The creature screamed desperately as Pa slashed down with his blade once, twice, three times. Before she realized it, Ree was on her feet and running toward the hole, but her Pa grabbed her into a fierce hug.

"Why did you do that?!" Ree cried. "She needed help!"

"No, no, sweet girl, she didn't." Pa easily picked her up, hugging her tightly. "That's a mae-nak. A phi, and they always lie." Ree couldn't wriggle away from his strong embrace, so she strained to peek over his shoulder.

It looked like a pile of rice noodles, with lumpy parts, covered in oyster sauce. A woman's face laid amidst the snake-like limbs, a normal face, except there was only smooth flesh where her eyes should have been. The edges of her mouth bubbled with black blood, and her lips still trembled, as if her screams were still echoing.

The air tasted putrid, and Ree gagged.

"It's too loud," she whined, burying her face in Pa's neck to drown everything out with his familiar scent. Safety, soothing greens and blue, a hint of her mother's jasmine lingering near his ear.

"What's too loud?"

"Everything," Ree said, then started to sob.

Eight years later, under the light of the high blood moon, Ree, along with six other novices, walked barefoot through the expansive bamboo grove that surrounded the Shrine of the First Hunters. The shrine was the oldest guild building that still existed. Each pillar, stone, and roof tile had been painstakingly deconstructed from their former home in the Capital and reconstructed in Jinburi.

They picked through the trees with ease, moving like silent shadows. Soon, her peers would appeal to the mysterious, nameless devas that arbitrated the gateway to the Everpresent. They would recite the voiceless chants they'd memorized, recount the ways they'd paid tribute, the skills they'd mastered, their commitment to following the steps of the First Hunters.

And then they would die, and ask for passage back.

The shrine came into view, ebony-stained teakwood pillars flush with the shadows. Two stone statues of the Venara stood on either side of the open entrance, their monkey features hidden behind masks, their archaic uniforms carved onto bodies larger than human. The novices knelt at the entrance and waited. Finally, far inside, two candles ignited.

In perfect unison, they rose and walked the long passage, known as the Hall of Remembrance, where the names of dead hunters were engraved onto the stone plaques. Ree wondered how many names were missing – the novices who had died here, in this very shrine, in the attempt to someday be on this wall.

The closer they came to the inner chamber, the less Ree remained grounded in the Blinds – the mundane world. With the steady hum of the Everpresent rising, so did her awareness of the other novices' tempered anticipation and repressed fear. Falah and Bunni held the steadiest breaths. Goi and Raj were the most nervous, breath shallow and quick, a quiver in their step. Esha and Laopin were restless, Ree sensed their yearning to be in the Everpresent with her.

Phi hunters trained incessantly to access the heightened level of awareness where senses became intertwined, where magic flowed freely, where the scent of blood wove a living path toward their prey, where they communed with spirits and phi and demons alike. It was the source of their powers, every gray-magic spell a poetry of the voiceless chant invoking the devas for favor.

As a child, Elder Nokai taught Ree how to withstand the unexpected noise without needing to cover her eyes, and ears, and scream to shut it out. But nothing could change her appearance – the red eyes and silver hair of a hunter in that state.

A tenor of melancholy washed over her. She was the only novice that wouldn't take the trial. During training, Raj questioned her worthiness if she didn't pass the trial like the rest. By then, she was used to feeling left out by her peers. This wasn't near as bad as it had been at the academy, before the bullying grew so intense that her mother finally let her quit and follow in her father's footsteps.

Still, it nagged at her, and she wondered if Raj was right.

One-meter pillar candles marked the end of the Hall of Remembrance. Beyond stood a roofless, circular chamber where the light of the moon cast silky reflections across a shallow pool.

There, the three masters sat waiting, cross-legged, and behind them stood the five hunters that had been near enough Jinburi to attend the ceremony. They all wore their ritual robes and masks – each one custom carved and painted according to what the master artisan saw in the Trance when he created them.

Ree's spirits lifted when she spotted her father's mask among them, the visage of a snarling white-wolf. Along with the other novices, she prostrated on her knees at the edge of the pool. Pressing their palms together in a respectful wai, they gave their full attention to Master Arei as she stepped forth and spoke.

"We gather under the light of the Phracạnthr̒ leụ̄xd in honor of the First Hunters, and for those who will follow in their steps. Centuries ago, the devas opened the veil between worlds, and asked the Venara warriors to hunt and kill a demon army that escaped the realms of Hell. In exchange for agreeing to such a dangerous task, the devas granted the warriors a gift that would aid them in the battle to come." Master Arei's red panther mask did not muffle her words. While Elder Nokai sounded like a kindly teacher when he recounted the legends, Arei reminded Ree of the Grisland preachers who stood outside of their foreign missionaries and accosted anyone who passed by.

"Under the light of the Phracạnthr̒ leụ̄xd, the devas opened the eyes of the First Hunters to the Everpresent, and changed them forever. As they walked in the gray, in step with the spirits, power flowed from the realm of the gods to bend the world in the shape of their will." Her words shimmered strong as steel. "Tonight, you will make the ultimate sacrifice to demonstrate your commitment to this path. Should the devas deem you worthy, by the will of the First Hunters, you will become one of us. Now," she stood, along with Master Seua. "Rise."

Goi's breath hitched, and the girl was a step behind as the rest rose to their feet.

The two master hunters stepped into the pool, the water rising to their waists. Their black robes floated around them like the fins of a koi. Together, the novices stepped into the unnaturally cold water. Falah was first in line, and remained still as Master Arei approached.

Ree heard Falah's father utter a subvocal prayer to the First Hunter. Of course he would be nervous, watching his son tempt death to follow in his footsteps. She wondered what her own father would have felt if she needed to do this. She wondered, for the first time, if her mother felt that way when her brother walked into the ring.

"Remember yourself as you walk the First Hunters' path. Listen to the song of the devas." Master Arei held Falah's shoulder with one hand. With the other, she drew her ritual knife. A voiceless chant echoed in the Everpresent, and Master Arei stabbed Falah through the heart quick and clean, removing the blade as easily as it slid in. He made no sound, surrendering fully to death. Master Seua helped Falah lay down under the water. Eyes wide open, the novice sunk below, body limp, dark blood billowing around him.

Perfect, Ree thought, in admiration.

Goi was next, her breath shallow, the water rippling where she trembled. She flinched when Master Arei placed a hand on her shoulder. Arei stared at her critically, then firmly pushed her a step backward.

"You aren't ready."

With half a sob, Goi collapsed, shuddering and clutching her sides. The observing hunters shifted, but didn't comment. Ree cringed inwardly with second-hand embarrassment.

Next was Bunni, the eldest novice at the ripe old age of nineteen. Like Falah, he took the knife without flinching, and didn't thrash when he went under. The entire pool ran red with blood now. Raj sounded like he was hyperventilating, but took a long breath when Master Arei looked deep into his eyes and spoke the words. He nodded quickly, fists and jaws clenched. He gasped when the blade entered, and only let out a soft whimper as Master Seua lowered him under.

After Laopin went, the water stirred, as if it were bubbling with heat. It remained just as still, but there was a rhythm to the invisible movement. She realized it was the vibration of the voiceless chant – whether it came from the hunters, the masters, the novices, or the devas beyond – all of their auras braided together in a song so inviting her eyes stung with tears.

Next to her, Esha caught Ree's gaze as the blood pooled around her face. And she smiled ever so slightly, as if to say, *See you soon*.

"It is done," Master Arei said and wiped the blood on a wet segment of her robe.

"Wait!" Before she could think twice, Ree brought her hands together in a wai. "Let me take the trial. I must speak to the devas and ask for their blessing."

Master Arei's face was unreadable behind her mask, but she shook her head and moved away. "You already possess their blessing, child."

"No," Ree reached out and caught her arm. "Please, master. It's not right that I don't go through this. I can't call myself a hunter unless I do." How could she explain this sudden, overwhelming desperation? This might be her only chance to experience the devas presence, and she felt not a smidgen of doubt or fear.

Master Arei tilted her head and subvocally spoke to Elder Nokai, who had not moved in his chair of blankets. *"She wants to go through KunNam."*

"Wait," Ree's father broke from the line, stepping forward, then said out loud, "Isaree, you don't have to do this!"

"Do you not believe in me?" Ree said, indignant. "You said I was born blessed. Why would the devas turn their back on me now?"

The hunters murmured to one another, and Master Seua crossed his arms, a smile in his voice when he spoke. "I say let her."

"Isaree!" Her father started forward, until Elder Nokai held up a hand, stopping him in his tracks.

"She's earned it," Elder Nokai said. Her father, torn between respect for tradition and fear for his daughter's life, clutched the side of his head and groaned. But to her relief, he stepped back in line.

"Her mother's gonna kill me," he muttered to the hunter next to him, who only shook his head and shrugged.

With that, Master Arei placed her hand on Ree's shoulder.

"Remember yourself as you walk the First Hunters' path. Listen to the song of the devas."

She hardly felt the blade, the master was so deft. The song, rushing in the water expanded around her, stinging her eyes. And then as if she were floating on the ceiling, she saw herself, saw the bodies of six other children, all dead. Terror crept around the edges, like a scream from miles away, threatening to shatter her resolve. Ree pushed it away, and clung to the voiceless chant that they'd all practiced for countless hours. And then what little she could feel of herself became numb, and the last thing she saw were her father's eyes, distorted by the water as she sank into the depths beyond the Everpresent.

Ree's first breath ripped in her throat as a ragged gasp. Red water cascaded down her face, her vision blurry with stars. She reached out, then collapsed into the arms of her father. He wrapped her in a blanket and held her against him at the edge of the pool.

"You did it, sweetheart, you did it."

Perhaps the other hunters were giving him disapproving looks from behind their masks, but her father didn't seem to care. Ree was too relieved to be embarrassed. Master Seua had taken off his mask, and smiled down at them. He laid a hand on her father's back, but his smile faded when he looked toward the pool.

Ree pushed away from her father to stand, searching quickly for her friends. Her gut unclenched when she spotted Esha, huddled under a blanket. Esha met her gaze with a shaken expression, then gave a weak smile. Raj sat next to her, clutching his knees to his chest, staring at something far beyond the walls of the shrine. Falah held a wai to his forehead, murmuring prayers. All their hearts were whole again, and all their eyes burned red in the dark, embraced in the Everpresent.

The other two remained still, floating in the pool, eyes dark and lifeless. Master Arei stood next to them, waiting. From what they'd learned during training, it could take up to five minutes to return. Ree was too afraid to ask how long it had been. By the tense set of the master's shoulders, it must have already been too long. Regardless, by tradition, the masters would wait until sunrise.

"Are they…?" Ree paused.

"They're fucking dead!" Goi cried from the other side of the pool. "They aren't coming back."

"This is the path we chose," Esha snapped, with no small amount of scorn in her voice.

"The First Hunters decided to take them," Falah said, much gentler. "It is an honor."

"An honor?!" Goi wiped the tears from her cheeks. "Seems like a bullshit deal to me!"

"Hush, Goi," Master Arei said sternly. "You shall stand vigil with me and Elder Nokai. The rest of you, go. Rest."

Ree's father walked with her out of the shrine in silence. Ree wasn't sure what she felt – she'd expected a real conversation with the devas when she went under, but when she thought back to that moment beyond death, she felt...

Nothing.

"Uh, sorry if I embarrassed you," her father said, sheepishly. "If you have a daughter someday, you'll understand. When you asked Master Rei for the trial all I could see was the little baby girl I held in my arms–"

"Pa, please stop," Ree grunted.

"All right." But a few seconds later, he said, "Maybe we don't need to tell your ma about this?"

Ree rolled her eyes but laughed. Sometimes her father still acted like a child, and it endeared him to her. She figured it was because he had to grow up fast, having been orphaned very young. Regardless, it took her mind off the confusing feelings that troubled her.

Two of her friends were dead. She couldn't understand why, for they'd both been steadfast under the trial. Bunni had been the best of them all. Ree had been so sure she'd see something definitive, something that would further bolster her faith in everything they were taught. Why were the four of them chosen, and the other two discarded?

The uncertainty haunted her, but she kept her faithless thoughts to herself.

Chapter 2

The Bonds We Break

In the kingdom of Suyoram, Jinburi was known as the crossroads town, where two rivers met from the north and the east and carried on down to the Capital and the sea. As the central trading hub of the mid country, a myriad of languages could be heard spoken in the streets, which were full of travelers and tourists fresh off the Long Road. There were always new fashions to be found in the storefronts, exciting plays, artworks, and musical performances deemed too cutting-edge for the conservative southern Capital. From the floating markets choked with barges and longboats, to the seedy nightlife and lively festivals, Jinburi was a lot of things, but boring was not one of them.

Isaree lived in the shared barracks with her fellow novices, but one night a week, she walked back to her old neighborhood for dinner with her family. She couldn't help but notice how rapidly the city was changing. Foreigners from Grisland, a country far beyond the ocean, had arrived up the river after the young king of Suyoram granted them free passage through the country in some kind of political maneuver. Before then, Ree had only seen their missionaries, a small community built around a square-shaped church. They mostly kept to themselves, every so often pestering the locals to abandon the Awakened Lord in favor of their vengeful Grisi god.

By orders from the crown, the governor of Jinburi allowed them to set up an outpost not too far from the Phi Hunter's guild. These new arrivals brought with them stuffy fashions with too many buttons, men with thick beards and heavy boots harboring what seemed like utter disdain for the locals. They built an imposing brick structure with white columns and a sign that translated to "Expeditions and Trading Company of Grisland."

It was no secret that that Grisland had pushed into Suyoram's western neighbor, Loram, causing much tension in the region, especially as the queen herself was Lo. Ree always hurried past their territory.

Esha often came with her. She was in every sense what Ree was not; tall and naturally athletic, charming and talkative, great at drawing attention away from her mother's intrusive questions and criticisms. Esha's father had been from the Kutsu Aisles, a pirate who had a wild night in a Jinburi brothel and was never seen again. He left her with coarse, red-brown wavy hair that like the rest of the novices, she kept shaved.

But that week, Esha had fallen from a tree while training with Master Seua. Her command of the Kiss of Shivah spell wasn't strong, so it was taking her leg longer to mend. She begged Ree to bring back some food, as the simple cuisine at the guild hall left much to be desired.

As usual when Ree left guild grounds, she wore her novice cloak and hood low over her eyes, avoiding the side glances and outright stares from passersby. They whispered to one another, which unfortunately, was easily audible to her sensitive hearing.

"There's the hunter's daughter. She's always been so strange."

"You know her mother was a royal concubine to the Prince Varunvirya?"

"Awakened Lord, rest his soul. But I'd rather have a concubine as a daughter than a phi hunter. She should have followed in her mother's footsteps instead."

She ignored the unflattering commentary by focusing on the familiar sights of her neighborhood. An old chamchuri tree they used to climb in the yard of the local temple, the sweet scent from the mango farm where they'd dare each other to steal fruit, the old fishing pier where they played in the river… this had once been the sleepy outskirts of Jinburi, but in the last few years, plenty of development had turned it into a bustling suburb, much to her father's chagrin.

They lived in a modest, traditional teakwood stilt-house with a high gabled roof and a yard blooming with seasonal flowers and vegetables. Auntie Narissa crouched in the yard, picking herbs. Their next-door neighbor had been a constant, comforting presence ever since Ree could remember. She was her mother's best friend, not to mention a low-magic healer and midwife who delivered both her and Kit into the world. Whenever Ree was feeling sad during her time at the academy, she would visit Narissa and help make charms and potions, all while complaining about the treatment she received in class, and her resentment toward her parents for making her go.

"Auntie," Ree gave her a wai in greeting. Narissa slowly looked up in her languid way, which always reminded Ree of one of the many cats she kept as company.

"Hello, dear." Narissa smiled. "Dinner's almost ready. We just need a bit more basil for the krapow."

"Need help?"

"Oh no, I can manage. Go in and see your mother. She misses you."

"It's only been a week."

"Long enough to miss her daughter."

As soon as she opened the door, the rich aroma of beef simmering in chili and garlic instantly made Ree's mouth water. She slipped off her shoes, but before she could announce her presence, a lean, tan-furred dog skittered from down the hall and across the family room, panting and wagging his tail excitedly. He barked once, then sniffed her crotch in a typical canine greeting.

"Maaa!" Ree called, "there's a dog in the house!"

"That's Lucky," her mother called from the kitchen. "Your brother brought him home the other day. I don't know what your father will say when he gets home from his route tomorrow, but *I* think we should keep him."

"Aww." Ree gingerly pet the animal, who slobbered on her hand. He followed her into the kitchen, sniffing around for scraps.

"No, Lucky, out!" Her mother pointed to the open door that led to the terrace, and the boy whimpered, panting in a canine grin. "Ouuut." With a scoff, he trotted outside, and promptly marked the tree in the center.

"Where's Kit?" Ree asked. He was always home before she arrived. Kit was usually happy to see her, as they'd grown closer after she left home. He was doing well at the academy, in his studies and popular with his fellow students. He continued to excel on the school muay-boran team, and their mother proudly displayed his trophies around the house.

"I don't know," her mother said, with a tad of irritation. "He was supposed to bring a bag of rice."

"I could go to the market." Ree didn't want to, but she had to offer.

"No need. Narissa brought some over." Her mother continued to mash peppers, garlic and palm sugar with fish sauce in a mortar and pestle, dressing for the spicy som tum salad. Ree noticed the papaya still needed grating, so she rolled up her sleeves and set to it. They made small talk as they worked, Ree finishing the som tum while her mother tended to the stove. Ree cracked fresh peanuts for garnish, and by that time the sun was setting.

"Kit should be home by now," her mother fretted as they gathered the dishes to set the table.

"Maybe he's out with his girlfriend."

"He has a girlfriend?!"

Ree ducked her head sheepishly and stifled a laugh at her mother's aghast expression. "Umm... are we eating inside or outside?"

Before her mother could answer, Lucky barked from the front yard.

"Oh, that's probably him," her mother sighed, visibly lightened. "Outside will do. It's still nice out, and we can–"

"Something's wrong," Ree said. It was the noticeably icy tone of Lucky's bark – sharp and frantic, the tail-end a whine. And then she smelled it – a scent hunters trained to sense from miles away.

Blood.

The door to the front burst open, startling them both. Glass shattered as her mother dropped the bowl. Narissa looked pale and frightened, scared eyes somewhere far away. Ree had never seen her in such a state, and dread crept into her gut.

"Come quickly," Narissa said in hardly more than a whisper. "It's Kit."

Ree's brother was hardly recognizable. His schoolmate friend helped them carry Kit straight into Auntie Narissa's sick room, laying his bruised and broken body on the mattress where she treated her patients. Ree averted her eyes, watching her mother instead, who only took shuddering breaths that wracked her entire body. She sat next to the bed, gently cleaning Kit's swollen face with a damp cloth while Narissa worked on his wounds.

"We were just having tea at the Sabai Five," Kit's best friend, Jaron, insisted. "There were four of them. Started talking down to us. We tried to leave, and they followed us out. Jumped us in the alley."

"Why? I don't understand," Narissa murmured, mixing some antiseptics in a bowl. "Kit is such a sweet boy, why would anyone want to hurt him?"

Ree held herself, helpless, as Kit struggled to breathe. If only the spells she knew could work on others. If only she could pull her brother into the Everpresent with her and heal his fractured bones. She wanted to scream, to find a place to focus her rage. Ree turned to Jaron, who hovered in the doorway, clearly shaken, but who only had a black eye and a swollen lip. "What did they look like?"

"Like Grisi. Pale, hairy."

'Uniforms?"

"No, just what they wear."

"Please, Jaron, write down as detailed of a description as you can," Ree's mother said, her voice oddly calm. "We need to report this to the magistrate."

"They won't do anything," Ree muttered. Her mother turned to her, brow furrowed, and Ree thought better of speaking her mind. She bit her lip and knelt by her mother's side in silence. As she gazed down at Kit's battered face, at the swollen lumps where his bones were fractured, a profound sense of longing overwhelmed her. She felt six years old again, wanting nothing more than to melt into her mother's protective arms.

Instead, Ree placed a hand on Kit's bloody knuckles and squeezed gently. Still warm. Still alive. A dark feeling began to overtake her fear – anger that her little brother might die under the hands of some bullies. And worse yet, Grisi bullies. And the longer they waited, the less chance there was for justice. "Ma, I'll go with Jaron to the magistrate and report this, so you can stay here."

Her mother nodded. "Okay," she murmured, "okay." Before Ree rose to her feet, her mother grabbed her arm and pulled her into a tight hug. "Hurry back, Isaree. Please."

"I will, Ma." Ree retracted herself before she could crumble. Leaving the room filled her with relief, and she paused in the darkened hallway to breathe easier. "Jaron, let's go," she said.

He stared over at her with subtle repulsion. When he hesitated, she snatched his arm and stormed outside. As they stepped onto the street, Jaron jerked away. "Hey, I'm coming, all right?!"

But Ree pulled him closer. She let the Everpresent in just so, enough to sharpen her senses and give a glow to her eyes. Enough to scare the boy, his eyes widening enough for whites to show under his swollen lids.

"Tell me what really happened."

"What? I already–"

"Bullshit," Ree snapped. "I can smell the wine on your breath. Both of yours."

"Oh." He reddened, then grimaced and glanced back toward Narissa's house, lowering his voice. "Okay, yeah, so we were drinking."

"And?"

"We were just messing around. There's a muay-boran dummy in there, Kit was showing off."

"Showing off? How so?" Even though she knew her brother excelled in his sport, she didn't take him for a braggart.

"Chen was there. His girl? You know, uh, anyway, this Gris started mouthing off, talking about how it was a dirty way to fight, that real men didn't use their knees and elbows. Kit tried to tell him it was an artform, but the man just got belligerent. Started yelling about taking him on."

"Kit agreed, didn't he?" Ree's spirits sank.

"No, no. He knows better. He said no, and the guy kept pestering him. We left, I swear. But they followed us."

"You said there were four of them. That true?"

"Well, not at first. But after Kit broke his nose, the other three jumped in."

"All right," Ree said with a sigh, then started walking to town.

"Wait, where you going? The nearest magistrate's office is this way."

"Go ahead, make the report. I'll be back."

Jaron jogged to catch up with her. "You aren't going to Sabai Five, are you? They're gone. They ran off…"

"That doesn't matter," Ree said, quickening her pace. "Not to a hunter."

Chapter 3

The Stranger Appears

Ree walked over one of the many bridges that crossed the historic moat leading to old town, the square-shaped heart of the city. She passed through Geow's Square, where a decorative pagoda soared high above the surrounding buildings, its golden gables on the multi-tiered tower framed with twisting spires that reminded Ree of firecrackers.

It had been close to year since Ree had ventured into Jinburi proper. Esha and Raj had convinced her to go to a party, but Ree had only stayed for an hour before making an excuse to leave.

Normally, she had no reason to. The guild employed teamsters to move their goods to the docks and markets, scribes to run errands in town. Some of the other novices liked to escape the guild to carouse, but Ree hated the overwhelming scents and racket of the crowds. Without the liberty of being able to slink into the Blinds, she blanched at the stink of pissed-in alleys, the boisterous hawkers, the sweat of leering men in alleyways. She took after her father in that regard, enjoying their family camping trips far more than Kit and her mother.

The alleyway of the Sabai Five was filthy, with rats rummaging through the trash bins, roaches scattering in the cracks. She knelt by a splatter of blood and shattered glass, recognizing her brother's aura as familiar as his handwriting. Bringing her hand to her face, the one she'd touched Kit's knuckles with, she breathed in the trace of unfamiliar blood, letting it shine in her mind's eye as if it were blue, rather than red. Scanning the alley with this vision, she formed a trace of each blow, of every action leading up to where Kit had collapsed under their fists and boots.

The trail led east, toward the river. She pulled down her hood and followed, slipping into the crowd. Chatter from pedestrians and music from the theaters faded into a sonic mist. The heady aroma of fried meats and curries from restaurants and street vendors became one layer of a tapestry she could pull aside and shut away. With every step closer, the scent of the Grisi's blood became more and more defined, as if she were pulling on a thread that unraveled the world around her.

All that remained was the connective trail between a hunter and her target.

Ree recognized the estate, as anyone who'd grown up in Jinburi would. At first, she wondered if her senses had misfired, because why would a gang of Grisi bullies be here? She stood before a massive yard with extensive gardens, far from the hustle and bustle of the heart of the city.

This was the governor's mansion, and strictly off-limits to the public. *She* shouldn't be here. If someone caught her…

So what? Ree thought to herself. *I'll explain what happened.* But she hesitated, then shrugged off her cloak, folded it up, and placed it under a bush. Better to lessen the chance of any witnesses tracing her back to the guild.

With a quick glance around to make sure the street was empty, she climbed over the gate and stole through the gardens. The trail led not to the mansion, to her relief, but a guest house built in the traditional style, with wide open windows obscured by sheer curtains.

Sticking to the shadows, Ree crept through the meticulously kept yard at a slow, measured pace. A raucous peal of laughter erupted from the open window. The men inside were obviously drunk, chattering in their language, words slurring together and punctuated with amused outbursts.

Flush against the wall, she peered through the translucent curtains and picked out the man with the broken nose immediately. He sat around a table with three others, a few bloody rags strewn aside the empty bottles. As Jaron had said, they weren't wearing uniforms, but civilian clothes that were heavier than the average local, even for the Gris. If they were guests of the governor, they must be important officials, too important to stay in the garrison. Politicians? Diplomats? She wished she could understand what they were saying.

As she gazed upon the grinning man, heat rose in her face and chest so overwhelmingly that she gritted her teeth to keep from screaming in rage. The Smoking Palm of Anewan stirred in her fists uncalled, a spell that would turn her hands as hot as a blacksmith's iron. She imagined clawing the man's stupid grin from his face while his mates cowered. She could throw her hunting knife through the window like some Hasshut assassin, or bar the windows and doors, set the entire building on fire...

The violent thoughts flashed easily through her mind, then left her conflicted. They seemed wrong, or that she *should* feel they were wrong, rather. Yet all she found was frustration for the fact she was alone. One teenage girl against four grown men. If only Esha had come with her... no, Esha would have stopped her from even coming here. Better that she was alone.

Thoughts of the guild brought Master Arei's teachings back to mind, to think about the consequences of her actions – not only for herself, but for others. These weren't tourists having a laugh over bad behavior on holiday. They must command some power in official channels. Even though she craved it, a direct confrontation would be stupid. Childish.

Ree withdrew from the window, calculating her options. One thing was certain, she couldn't go home without doing *something*. Her eyes drifted to a crate of bottles next to the door. They matched the ones on the table, and surely these men would drink themselves well into morning.

Carefully, she reached into her pocket and opened her rectangular tincture pouch, running a finger over neat rows of tiny vials, two injector needles clasped underneath. Every novice carried such a pouch to administer their daily doses of poisons, building up their tolerance over the years. For some of their upcoming rituals, it was necessary to ingest highly toxic ingredients. Ones that would be lethal to any normal, grown human.

Or four, she thought, finding the Dreamless, the most lethal toxin, made from Cloud toad poison, crushed scorpion tail, and corpse oil. She crept to the crate, slowly uncorking each bottle. The viscous liquid beaded on the lip of the first one. Just that bit would be enough.

A door slammed.

Her reaction was automatic – Ree darted away and the bottle clattered. The nearest form of cover was under the porch. Unfortunately, the gardeners had not cleaned the ground under here, likely in decades. She yelped in pain when her elbow banged against a jagged rock, then smacked a hand over her mouth and went prone.

A few tentative footsteps sounded, and then she heard a sigh.

Ree peeked out from under the house curiously, but did not dare to move. A boy had come from the main estate, the door left ajar. His finely tailored blouse was embroidered with the type of detail that denoted upper class, yet his feet were bare, his hair disheveled, his shirt half unbuttoned. He cast a disoriented glance around the area, then sank against a decorative obelisk and clutched his head.

He looked as drunk as the Gris men sounded. Slowly, she crawled away from where he lingered.

Only another foot to go through a cloud of weeds when her fingers touched something soft. She blanched as an enormous rat scurried over her hand and its tail smacked into her face, then clamored against a broken tin bucket in its panic to escape.

Shit, shit, shit. Ree followed its example and scrambled through the weeds. But when she pushed through and crawled free of the house, a pair of feet blocked her path.

She peered up at the boy, who stared back with shocked curiosity. Had he ever seen a hunter before? Maybe she looked like a phi herself, staring up at him with the subtle red glow of a hunter pulling deep into the Everpresent, as she had been on the trail.

With a hunter's night vision, objects were clear, colors muted. Still, she could tell there was a storminess about his eyes – bright brown, speckled with flecks of amber. Troubled, and not just by the intruder he'd discovered. Distant, as if he weren't sure if he were dreaming.

He jerked his head toward the gate. Nervously, Ree stood, then crept toward the garden, keeping her eyes on him. He followed her step for step, until there was a healthy row of rosebushes between them and the guest house.

"What are you doing here?" He spoke with the formal dialect of an aristocrat, but again, his words slurred. He took another step toward her, swaying on his feet, his eyes flicking down to the knife at her belt and back. She wasn't out of danger yet.

"Catching rats," Ree responded.

Maybe he was the son of someone powerful – not the governor, who only had daughters. Privileged people tended to think themselves untouchable. He seemed to be the type of handsome Esha would describe as "dangerous," someone who knew their power and was used to getting their way. A strange part of her wanted to stay and talk with him, this stormy-eyed boy from another world, but that would be incredibly stupid.

Remembering a street urchin trick Raj taught her, Ree quickly looked over his shoulder with a soft gasp, widening her eyes.

Rich boy took the bait, glancing behind him. That was her chance. She sprinted into the garden maze, ducking between rows, hurtling over rosebushes, strafing through the bonsais. But then when she cleared the last row of bushes, he'd burst out of nowhere, having taken some kind of shortcut. She didn't have time to avoid the impact and she stumbled. Her arm jerked back as he twisted it and pulled her against him.

With a cry she jerked away, a horrible crack and rip in her shoulder as the joint dislocated. The boy gasped and faltered in his grip. A moment later, she'd swept his feet and had both her knees pinning each of his arms, knife edge flush with his throat.

Lips parted in shock, he only stared dumbly, eyes wide with fear. Then of all things, he burst out laughing. It was Ree's turn to stare in confusion as his body relaxed, his eyes going distant. He was so unaware of himself that he moved his head into the knife, forcing her to draw back lest she cut his jugular. His insane giggling lessened, and he muttered incoherently, staring up at nothing until his smile went slack.

"The hell is wrong with you?"

He didn't respond. Didn't seem to even see her. Or maybe he was just acting like that. She watched his eyes for any sign of awareness – they were dilated to pinpricks in the darkness. Some kind of hysteria maybe? Or a drug kicking in?

She realized how fortuitous it was that he'd gone into this fugue state now. She needed to get the hell out of there. Ree eased back, then got to her feet. She gritted her teeth, and with a grunt she forced her free arm upward. Another shot of pain cascaded through her body as the joint popped back into place.

Ree vaulted back over the gate. But her smile died the moment her feet hit the ground. That was too close, and the gravity of the situation hit her all at once. She hoped the boy wouldn't put together what she'd been up to, but lucky for her, he'd seemed as drunk as the Gris. Two sides of her conscience warred as she grabbed her cloak and hurried back through the streets – relief that she'd dropped the poisoned bottle, and cursing herself for failing her mission.

With no thread to follow, nothing to distract from the fear gnawing at her gut, Ree followed the river rather than retrace her steps, which after a time, meandered through quiet neighborhoods away from busy roads. Her mother surely expected her return hours ago, but dread overwhelmed her when she thought about seeing Kit in that state. Or worse, that by the time she'd returned he would have already slipped away. She hated feeling so helpless, so she clung on to the hatred and prayed at least one of them would drink the poisoned bottle, even if it fell.

The water went where it wanted, but also through the path of least resistance. Perhaps that was how the Serene Way formed – the hidden paths that hunters still walked to traverse the countryside. Perhaps magic flowed more like water than faith, just an element, with its own rules and physics that could be accessed regardless of what one believed.

By the time she walked down her street, it was near morning. Ree lingered outside Auntie Narissa's, listening to the rhythmic cricketsong punctuated by geckos and toads. As she approached the door, a soft humming drifted from within. She recognized the tune, a gentle lullaby her mother sang to her as a child, and her eyes stung with tears. It drifted away, lost in her mother's soft, steady breath, only to pick up again here and there, a few notes. She must be sleeping lightly, next to Kit.

"There you are."

The words whispered subvocally surprised her. She glanced about for her father.

"Up here."

On the slanted roof, her father sat under the fading moonlight, still in his hunter's coat, hair a few months past a proper shave. Despite the situation, Ree's heart swelled with elation. He wasn't due back until tomorrow morning, though she supposed it was near enough at this point. He would have been nearby, in the expansive Jinburi swamp, where he maintained a special relationship with the Guardian. Perhaps the ancient spirit had granted him passage, though such favors were precious. This situation certainly warranted one.

Ree found a foothold on the lip of a window, then hauled herself up to his side. She leaned against him, and he wrapped an arm around her shoulder and squeezed.

"Your mother was worried," he said softly. "She said Kit's friend brought the guard back. And you weren't with him."

"Oh," Ree said, worried now that Jaron had told on her. "I was scared. I didn't want to come back and find that Kit might be... gone."

"Where did you go?"

"Walked." She thought of the men in the guest house, comfortable, drunk. "Wandered." The rich boy chasing her through the gardens. "Just… wandering." Her knife to his throat. The bright tenor of his careless laughter. The deadly poison on the lip of the bottle.

Her father grunted. "You went to town. I can smell it. What did you think you were going to accomplish, Isaree?"

"I don't know. Something. Anything. I was angry, Pa." Ree pulled away from him and hugged her knees to her chest. "The magistrate won't do anything. The governor lets the Gris get away with whatever they want, long as it makes him richer." She seethed, the rage boiling deep within.

"It isn't a hunter's place to dole out justice."

"I didn't go as a hunter. I went as a big sister."

"Isaree. If you did something, you need to tell me."

"I didn't do anything! But by the devas, I wanted to." Her words raged like a barely contained storm, the lie lost within. The dreamless vial weighed heavy in her pouch. She wiped her angry tears with the back of her arm.

Perhaps he believed her then. Her father left the Everpresent, his hair shifting from silver-white to black. Then he laid back on his elbows to gaze up at the stars from the Blinds. Even though he hadn't moved, the world immediately grew lonelier. They sat in silence for a long while, and she fought the overwhelming urge to run away.

"I sat up here for hours once, when your mother was sick," he said finally, voice hoarse and tired. "I was questioning a lot at the time. Things I thought were true," he sighed. "I realized that… that shit is a lot more complicated than I could ever understand. All I knew was I had to trust my gut, even if it went against things that I'd been taught to believe. And when you care about someone, it changes everything."

"So…" Ree wasn't sure what he was trying to tell her with this lecture. She cleared her throat, and said, "Are you saying I *should* have hunted the men that hurt Kit?"

"What? No!" Her father sat up, startled, and Ree giggled. "It's not a joke, Isaree. When you joined the Order, you took a vow not to cause harm to other humans. That has to mean something."

"What if those humans are harming other humans? Weaker ones, who can't defend themselves? Shouldn't we stand up for ourselves?"

"There's an order to things. There's a system. And yes, there comes times when you must step outside of it, but you need to know the difference between those times, and the times when judgment should be left to the devas."

Ree scoffed at that. Relying on the devas to dole out karmic punishment felt utterly dismissive. Futile.

"The Gris don't answer to the devas," Ree said bitterly. "Their two-faced god forgives them when they pay their coins and confess to a priest."

"Everyone answers to the devas," her father said. "Whether they realize it or not."

Ree wished she shared her father's faith in a system that was opaque at best, and at worse, flawed and unfair.

"You really believe that?" She gave him a sideways glance, trying to read his eyes.

But they were closed.

"I have to," he said.

Chapter 4

A Relentless Time

Kit woke up a week later. After another, he was able to speak coherently. After a month, it was certain that he would never walk again.

As Ree expected, his assailants weren't punished in any visible way. Her parents received an "official apology," an empty reassurance that the Gris authorities were aware of the situation and would handle punitive measures with their nationals internally.

It was hard to go home afterward. The house was always full of people – her mother's coworkers from the gym, who'd known Kit since he was a toddler kicking trees, his teachers from the academy, neighbors bringing gifts and pitying glances.

Ree couldn't look at Kit without going dizzy with rage. He had worked so hard toward his goal to become a muay-boran champion. All those dreams, snuffed out so casually. And her own dreams grew violent, nightmares of killing, of being killed in a burning wasteland.

One week, she made an excuse. It wasn't a lie: Esha was going to take her Maijep trial the next day and Master Arei wanted Ree to help with the ritual.

But she would make another excuse again the next week. The last time she'd been home, they had another heated argument after her parents had returned from a private audience with the governor. At one point, her mother had been part of the royal court, which still commanded respect. She appealed that these men who crippled her son should be arrested, or at the very least, banished from Jinburi.

"His hands are tied," she said, defeated, when they'd returned from the city. Her father muttered something about getting his things ready for his next rounds and disappeared into their bedroom for a long time.

"That's bullshit," Ree exclaimed, hitting the dinner table with her palm so hard that Lucky bolted and started barking. "A couple coins a month to shut us up? Kit can't even take a piss without help now."

Her mother stared at her in that cold, calculating way that encased her when she was angry. "Isaree... revenge won't make your brother whole. All that matters now is Kit's recovery. And this money will help me stay here with him more."

Ree stared into her mother's eyes in disbelief, only to find a numb sadness that crushed her heart.

If only the Maijep trial could work inside, she thought to herself, as she held the stack of six-inch needles on a white cloth next to Master Arei. When Master Arei's steady hands administered the first needle into Esha's spine, Ree grew so dizzy she had to avert her eyes and stare at the ceiling for the remainder of the ritual.

The Maijep trial was optional, but when passed would separate the hunter from their ability to feel pain. It had always been controversial – some thought it made for carelessness, and indeed, there were plenty of names on the Wall of Remembrance of hunters who neglected to treat their injuries. Others believed it was the only way to kill the deadliest of phi. Only half of the current hunters had the badge on their arms.

The trial itself was enough to deter a good portion of novices. Thirty hours of meditation while poisoned needles were lanced throughout a hunter's entire body. Thirty hours of complete stillness as the masters administered each one straight into a nerve. They said it was a trade to the devas, like receiving all the pain that one would experience for the rest of their life in one sitting.

Ree didn't fear the pain as much as she feared the needles, a fear she didn't know she possessed until receiving her sak yant tattoo after the KunNam Trial. Injecting *herself* with poison never bothered her, but that changed when another person wielded the needle. Esha and Falah were the only two who went through with the Maijep trial. Raj claimed losing the ability to taste spicy food made it not worth it, and like Ree, sat next to Master Arei, holding the needles for Falah.

The rainy season came and with it aching arms from long hours training with the bow and chainblade, aching asses from countless hours spent in meditation. The novices picked thorns from their soles after field trips through the swamp, feeling the natural dirt and mud with their bare feet to sense the Serene Way. The scars on their arms from injecting poisons faded as their tolerance plateaued, giving way to numb tongues and stomach aches as they ingested the raw ingredients until finally they tasted nothing.

Time paraded forward, relentlessly. The guild remained a bubble of consistency amidst gossip sneaking in from the tradesmen and runners. Jinburi went into a stir when locals vandalized a Grisi mission, which prompted the trading company to put out a reward for information on the vandals. That angered the governor, and rumors surfaced of tense meetings between him and Gris officials. Some local Suyo boys were arrested and punished publicly with lashings in front of the mission.

"Word on the street's that they didn't do it," Raj said, as the novices practiced securing targets with their chainblades.

"Who told you that?" Esha said.

"My girl on Sing-Sing road."

"Bullshit! You don't have a girl."

"Not as many as you," Raj smirked, then told them the gossip. People were getting sick of the governor's weak hand despite what the king directed him to do. Street fights were common, there was even a protest at the Grisi office. At some point, the governor made a public speech begging the "good Suyoram people to show their visitors love and respect, as the Enlightened Lord would decree."

"His words mean nothing," Ree said bitterly, pulling the chain so tautly around the head of a wooden dummy that it popped off. The others stared at her as she kicked the head savagely and spat, "They should all be dragged through the street."

Only two trials remained before the novices would become journeymen. The Path of the First, which would be a group hunt in the swamp. Once the masters identified the target, the novices set off from different areas. It more a competition than a ritual. No powers would be obtained by winning, but the winner received a badge.

The real trial would occur at the end of the season. It was the one Ree feared most, the Kang-Fye, which would grant them the ability to achieve the Hunters' Trance, an awareness one step below the Everpresent to allow them an extreme, singular focus. Through a ritual performed by the masters, the novice would be soul captured: their physical body would become ethereal, which was then ushered into a vessel for one month. Traditionally, those vessels were the brass totems on display around the shrine of the First Hunters. And there they would exist, formless, consciousness hovering in the ether, with no tangible sense of time or place.

As with any of the trials, there was mortal danger involved. It was said that some hunters' souls could not be retrieved, that some came back into the Blinds insane, or so depressed that they quit the guild altogether. Those were rare instances, the masters insisted. But one thing was certain – the hunter would be forever changed.

To say it consumed Ree's thoughts would be an understatement. The imminent trial haunted her days and nights. And when the nightmares kept her awake, she pored over old devaskrit texts in the guild library, searching for any information on the Hunter's Trance. Unfortunately, there was not much to learn.

And that's when she had her epiphany. One evening, Elder Nokai found Ree deep in books, well before the sun set. Ever helpful, he asked what she was looking for.

"Elder," Ree said, almost feverish with insomnia. "All the devaskrit texts only list the voiceless chants and certain poisons needed to achieve it. And this..." she pointed to a journal which was handwritten in modern script, a memoir from an early phi hunter who lived a century prior, "...here the Hunter's badges are all listed, and he was a true demon slayer! There is no Kang-Fye mark. I don't think it's necessary to complete that to enter the trance."

"You're correct, child," Elder Nokai said, which rendered her speechless. "Physically, nothing changes within you. The change occurs here, and here." He tapped his temple, then his heart.

"Forgive me, Elder," Ree said. "But... do you mean I could enter the Hunter's Trace now, without passing the Kang-Fye?"

"You could," he said, taking a seat next to her. He placed a wizened hand gently on her shoulder. "But without the oneness of mind and heart that the Kang-Fye develops within you, it's too dangerous. A hunter needs the mental fortitude to withstand the loss of humanity that the Trance instills. There is a great danger to the soul itself."

Ree sat silently for a time, refusing to admit how scared she was. But she didn't have to – Elder Nokai had known her since the Everpresent first broke through her mind and her father brought her to the guild.

"Isaree," he said, with a kindly smile. "The devas have blessed you. The First Hunters have claimed you. Out of all the novices I have ever seen, you, most of all, have nothing to fear."

Ree wished that were true.

Later that night, the novices took their lunch break under the big banyan tree near the stables. They'd switched to a nocturnal schedule now that their vision had developed enough to train under darkness. The big branches of the tree sheltered them from the soft midnight rain sprinkling down from the black, starless sky.

"I heard Master Seua spent the Kang-Fye in an ice statue on top of a mountain for six months," Raj said between mouthfuls of rice.

"What? Bullshit," Esha said. "Who told you that?"

"My pa told me that too," Ree said.

"So did mine," Falah agreed. "It's a guild legend."

Esha stared at them in disbelief. "Where is there *ice*, in all of Suyoram?"

They glanced at each other, then Falah shrugged. "On the peaks of Kalashas mountains?"

"The Kalashas are in Qinseng," Esha countered.

"It's a whole mountain range, some are in Loram, like the Little Shas," Falah said, now looking uncertain. "Not all of them are in Qinseng."

"The ones with snow are."

"Maybe he went to Qinseng," Raj said.

"It's all madness, anyway you look at it," Ree said, bitterly. "The Kang-Fye isn't necessary to learn the Hunter's Trance. I confirmed it in devaskrit texts today, *and* Elder Nokai said I was right." She waited for a reaction from the other novices, but received only unimpressed shrugs.

"I don't know why you're so worried about it," Esha said, a pitying look in her eyes. "The master does the ritual. All we have to do is maintain the third eye mantra – you can't fuck it up if you tried."

"I'm not scared," Ree snapped, and Raj snorted in disbelief.

"The Maijep, I understand," Esha agreed, tapping her shoulder where her sak yant tattoo was still bright and fresh. "But the Kang-Fye's different."

"It's important," Falah said, as sternly as Master Seua. "Every hunter must have it. It's tradition."

Ree didn't argue, just finished her rice glumly. The other novices were of one mind on the subject. She admired their faith, somewhat. Envied it. Wished she had the same conviction. Wished she could articulate the dread of what she feared was true – that if the Kang-Fye wasn't necessary, the KunNam hadn't been either.

That Bunni and Laopin didn't have to die, just because it was tradition.

That they died for nothing.

With the rainy season came the annual hunters' meet, which coincided with the national Rom Laithong holiday. Every hunter in the guild returned from their rounds and gathered for a celebration. The members of their branch in the capital came, though it was only a small storefront near Oldtown and a warehouse at the docks, all non-hunter guild members. All the families were invited, the great hall filled with home cooked dishes, and other kids to socialize with, some of whom Ree had known since she'd first joined.

It was an exceptionally hot day, without a cloud in the sky, though that could change at any moment. The novices, along with the other teenagers, hung out by the stream, swimming and talking and lounging about. Raj and the boys were involved in a rough game of sepak takraw, which involved kicking around a hollow rattan ball. Ree laid on a straw blanket with Esha, drying off from the stream, eyeing the game with a bit of melancholy. Kit always loved to play. And he was good, had been on a team at the academy. Had been. Now instead he was inside the hall, sitting with her father as he caught up with the other hunters. At least they'd been able to buy him a wheeled chair so he could start getting around on his own.

"Your ma's friend is pretty hot," Esha elbowed her. Ree followed her friend's line of sight to the front gate of the guild, standing open to the public, as some of the more traditionally minded neighbors stopped by with gifts on Rom Laithong. At the gate, Ree's mother was talking to another woman in a lovely dress, similar in age. Arinya and the woman clasped arms as they smiled. Ree was stunned; she hadn't seen her mother full-on smile for some time and she looked positively radiant in the sunlight catching her blue silk dress.

They laughed, then the other woman glanced around, gesturing to a young man standing just outside of the gate.

He turned around, and Ree's breath froze. She instantly recognized him, though his hair was brushed and his shirt was buttoned. He gave a respectful wai, which her mother returned.

Her mother then scanned the yard, and waved over to the group of novices by the stream. "Isaree!" she called, shielding her eyes from the sun as she searched for her daughter. Ree ducked lower, putting a healthy shield of Esha between her and her mother's line of vision.

"Ree, your ma's calling," Esha sang to her, and started to get up. Ree grabbed her arm and pulled her back.

"Don't move, please."

"Huh? What's gotten into you?"

Ree searched for an excuse, something, anything. "Look at those people… I'm in my swimwear, I can't just walk up to them."

"Really?" Esha gazed over with a smirk. "Sure it's not the good-looking rich boy gawking at everything?"

"Something like that. I promise I'll explain later. Can you go over? Tell them I'm sick?"

Esha chuckled, then sighed. "Fine, but you owe me."

"I owe you," Ree said, and then with voiceless words, called upon the Blind Eagle's Eye. Finally having mastered the spell, her skin shifted color, blending into the dry grass. Quickly, she scurried away, jumping into the stream, which sent the kids screaming at the sudden splash. So much for the party. She couldn't have that boy identifying her, and if that meant missing her last hunters' meet as a novice, so be it.

Fireworks erupted over Jinburi, sometimes setting alight the paper lanterns drifting across the sky. It was always a fun mess, and the guild and all its guests sat on the steps of the hall and watched together.

But Ree sat alone on the roof of the First Hunters' Shrine, her legs dangling over the lip of the open skylight. Below, colorful reflections danced distorted over the Pool of Remembrance, brightening the walls of the unlit ritual chamber. Peaceful, but when Ree gazed down at the pool, a sense memory arose of Master Arei's knife slunk through her heart. The cold touch of death as it took her, the dreamless void that left her shaking and uncertain after she returned…

And of course, the unfocused, empty eyes of her friends who hadn't come back.

Somewhere in the south, the careful footfalls of a hunter approached. She had avoided everyone who came looking for her all day, but she recognized her friend's gait.

"You're missing a hell of a party," Esha said after she climbed up to the roof of the shrine.

"I know." Ree still hadn't decided if she wanted to confide in her friend. There were a few lies she'd weighed, but the truth was she did want to tell someone. "What did you tell them?"

"That you ate an undercooked crab and couldn't stop shitting yourself." Esha plopped down next to her, stretching out her legs, and leaned back on her elbows. "Your ma was disappointed, but she's busy talking to her friend."

"And my pa?"

"He was pretty drunk with Master Seua and Falah's dad, I don't think he even noticed."

"Figures," Ree said with a smile, glancing at Esha. "Thanks."

"Sure. But you promised you'd tell me what was going on." Esha narrowed her eyes, then poked Ree on the arm. "So spill it. Why'd you run at the sight of that rich kid?"

"Well," Ree said slowly. "I didn't want him to recognize me."

"Isaree!" Esha sat up, a huge grin on her face. "Did you – the most prude novice the guild has ever seen – lay with–"

"No! Devas, why would you..." Ree furrowed her brows at Esha's cackling. "Wait, who said I was the most prude?"

"No one has to say it, it's objectively true."

Life as a novice in the guild didn't provide much time for romance, but they were all still teenagers. Falah, despite his holier-than-thou attitude, visited the brothels – the houses with male workers in particular. Raj apparently *did* have a girl on Sing-Sing road – confirmed when she showed up to the guild hall one day screaming (it had been in the middle of their training for the Kang-Fye, and apparently, he hadn't visited in days).

Meanwhile, Esha told Ree about the dancers she would mess around with, a particular young woman described in great detail. It did make Ree curious. She'd had her chance to experiment during the last hunters' meet. She snuck away with a teamster's son, a boy about a year older than her, who she always thought was quietly beautiful. Here in the First Hunters' Shrine, they laid together on a ratty blanket in a secluded hallway. Ree distinctly remembered his breath smelling like chili, and a pebble digging into her back. Later, when Esha demanded information, Ree shrugged and said it was fine.

"Whatever," Ree muttered, with a sigh. "That's not what happened. I'll tell you, but... promise you won't tell anyone."

Esha raised her hand, palm out. "Swear on the devas."

Ree told her everything. The aftermath of Kit's attack. Her single-minded focus while tracking his assailants through the city and ending up at the governor's mansion. Her rage at seeing them laughing. Esha's jaw dropped lower and lower as Ree went on, but snapped shut when Ree told her about poisoning one bottle, ready to do them all, and then being so rudely interrupted. Dropping the bottle. Her encounter with the boy. Running away.

"I *know* it's crazy. I know if the masters find out, I'd get kicked out. I wasn't thinking straight, I guess." Ree peered over at Esha, who'd grown very serious indeed.

"Fucking hell," Esha rubbed her eyes with a sigh. "Do you know how lucky you are?"

"I don't know," Ree said, feeling something crumble inside. "If Kit had died..." she sniffled, cringing against the tears, then feeling that sadness harden into something cold and deep. "Then I would have regretted not burning them all alive."

"Well... that clears up some things," Esha said.

"What do you mean?"

"Why the guy looked so spooked the whole time he was here, which was only about an hour, you know. I thought he was just scared of us. Sounds like he was on something when he found you, so... you're lucky. Maybe he doesn't remember. You're... really hard to forget though," Esha smiled then, softly, and that warmed Ree all over.

"That was weirdly sweet of you to say," Ree laughed, relieved, and Esha draped an arm over her shoulders.

"Don't let it go to your head," Esha said. "You're also completely insane. Probably the most unserious novice in the history of the guild." Ree rested her head on her friend's shoulder, finally feeling safe, lighter, and a little silly.

"And the most prude, too?" Ree asked in a soft voice.

"Yep. You're little and cute, you could have any–"

Ree cut Esha off with a kiss. It was meant to be a joke, she even had a punch line planned, *how about now?* Instead, an unexpected surge of heat arose in her chest, and a stirring deep in her belly. Esha's muscular body seemed to soften, pulling Ree closer without hesitation. Their lips danced together gently, and something about it felt dangerous. She didn't want to stop, because she had no idea what to say now. Until Esha's hand touched her bare midriff and slid to her hipbone, and an overwhelming wave of desire made her gasp.

"Oh," Ree pulled back, her face hot. Esha's lips were still close and parted. Their eyes met, Esha with a searching hunger and no semblance of doubt. Though Esha had always been very vocal about her interest in women, Ree had never admitted her attraction to both boys and girls. But this was her best friend...

Flustered, she laughed nervously, moving away. Esha's expression quickly faded into hurt, and Ree realized her reaction had been wrong. Desperate, she grasped for her first attempt at a joke. "How about now?"

"Now... what?" Esha said softly.

"You know. Am I still, uh... the prudest?" The joke fell flat, and Ree desperately searched for a way to change the subject. "Well... think I better go see Kit before he leaves then."

"Yeah," Esha said, without looking over, "you should go."

Chapter 5

Path of The First

Historically, when a troublesome phi claimed territory, the locals would mark the surrounding trees with two intersecting lines to warn others of the danger within. Once a phi hunter had successfully dispatched the creature, they would slash another through the warning mark. Thus was the origin of the guild symbol born, the one seen on their coats, on the entrance to their grounds, on the sak yant tattoo that graced their skin after swearing their oaths to the order.

Ree paused by the tree that bore the mark, her starting point for the trial tonight. She ran her hand across it, the fresh wound sharp and sore on the bark.

A flash into her future, a life spent in service to the guild, finding these marks, stalking the land within, sending these wretches back to the wheel of karma, the judgment of devas. Butchering their organs to peddle, moving to the next, and on, for the rest of her years. Alone for months at a time. This is a lonely life, the masters had warned the novices, one not destined for the unfaithful. But what other life could she know?

In the far distance, a low, long blast from a horn signaled the trial to begin. She entered the woods, putting aside her doubt best she could. The swamp shrunk every year to industry, but remained untamed, rich with dark spirits and phi. Spirits roamed freely, most neutral, akin to animals, but veins pulsing with natural magic. Most hunters paid them no mind and respected their lands. Spirits were not their primary quarry, but some were hunted for their magical properties.

Ree let the flow of the Everpresent lead her, free and at ease in the swamp in a way she'd never been while in the city. Here, she could exist as she was, without hiding herself or holding back, without worrying how others saw her, without saying or doing the wrong thing. But she couldn't fully enjoy it. She had a mission.

In the Blinds, the darkness would have been oppressive. It was a new moon, the sky overcast with a light drizzle. Electricity stirred the humid air, shifting trees hissing with a foreboding breeze, the hint of a budding storm. Ree scanned all her senses for the tiny, almost imperceptible anomalies that disturbed the balance of nature. One tell-tale sign of a phi's presence were carcasses that had been torn apart yet not consumed. They killed and sometimes ate but would never be satisfied. The phi's violent nature was fueled by a ravenous hunger, denied the most basic of human needs as punishment.

An hour passed, maybe another, when Ree came across a slow-moving stream and crouched by the water, watching as a group of silver tadpoles bobbed beneath the stagnant surface. Something about the water drew her attention, as if it were humming, and she dipped her finger under the surface.

A sharp burst of sensation, like a sour taste in her teeth. Something stirred, further downstream, as if it sensed her, and panicked. But not in the same way as an animal would. Different than the tadpoles that dimmed and darted away from her intrusion. As if it recognized what she was, and the terror echoed outward.

The swamplands buzzed around her as Ree moved quickly through the blanket of screaming insects, rattling wings and legs in the dirt and trees – all that pushed aside to follow the scent of fear. They'd been taught that the phi knew what they were and were frightened. That they often begged, and bargained, and lied.

The stream widened into a pond, mangrove roots stretching from the water like veins, with natural reservoirs that reflected the trees like black glass. The rain grew heavier, turning to fat drops that soaked her coat. It became impossible to stay on dry land, so she removed her shoes and continued on. Ree paused to listen to an odd scratching unlike any animal she'd ever heard. Reminded her of fingernails, raking across skin. Something about being in the water seemed to conduct whatever she sensed, now midway up her calf.

Close, it was very close now. Saw the flash of movement, something shiny in the darkness between the trees, not twenty feet away. Ree's heart raced. She carefully drew her bow and notched an arrow, more confident in her shot than in her chainblade.

A flash of lightning turned night into day – there! She saw it then, not ten paces away, the back of a long-limbed creature crouched under a tree, its gray-green skin slimy and glistening in the rain like a toad. Humanoid in form but the proportions were wrong. Its ridged neck too long, hands more claws than fingers. It seemed to be eating something at its feet. Ree drew in a quick breath as the darkness blanketed again.

Thunder crashed so loud it felt as if the earth shattered. Ree startled, a twig broke under her foot. Two gleaming green circles large as mooncakes sprouted from the darkness, and along with it, a grating hiss.

Ree let loose her arrow. It grazed the side of the phi's head, and it opened its mouth in a soundless scream, jaw coming unhinged, fist-long fangs gleaming from black gums.

Hunter, wait!

She desperately clung to her nerves but faltered as she grasped for another arrow. Water splashed around her ankles as she stumbled back a step. Her feet touched against something hard and leathery. It moved. She twisted in alarm and found herself face to face with the gaping maw of a fat, black crocodile.

Sheer panic took over then. With a phi in front of her – where was it?! – and a massive, reptilian beast behind her, her courage failed, and she ran. But in her haste, her ankle caught on a tangled root, and she fell into the water. Her head hit a rock and the world went dark.

Rumble of thunder, distant. Steady hiss of a downpour. With a moan of pain Ree clutched her head, where warm blood slicked her face. She laid on her side in the mud and gravel, then opened her blurry eyes to the wide trunk of a fallen tree, shielding her from the rain.

You're awake. Two glowing green eyes blinked open from the darkness. It all came rushing back then. The hunt. The phi. The crocodile. Falling, then–

You... Ree startled, reaching for the hilt of her chainblade.

Saved you from drowning, yes. You're lucky. The beasts here are hungry!

At a loss for words, Ree squinted at the phi, now sitting with its hands on its knees only a few feet away. A strange-looking thing, hardly larger than Lucky, with saucer-round eyes that took up the majority of its face, no nostrils, and a tiny mouth. It didn't look like the monster she'd seen moments ago. It looked more like a child's toy, something you'd make out of cloth and straw stuffing to put in a crib. Almost cute, in a gross way. Had her imagination played tricks on her?

Ree tried to sit, but her surroundings tilted as if she'd been spinning for hours. A wave of nausea washed over her, and she groaned, laying her face back down in the mud. Bad concussion most likely. She reached out for the ambient magic thick in the Jinburi Swamp, pulling the threads into the throbbing mass of blood and broken skin on her temple as she uttered the voiceless chant for Shivah's Kiss. It was always difficult to cast with head injuries.

While the spell began to work, she laid still, uncomfortable to be so completely at the phi's mercy. Yet it made no move to attack, only staring at her curiously.

What are you? Ree didn't bother to hide her scorn.

My name was... is. It swayed a little bit, side to side. *My name is Agira.*

No, Ree insisted. *What* are *you? A phi?*

Accursed, yes. It scratched at its ankle, and Ree noticed a claw trap fastened around its little leg, iron teeth dug deep into the bone, where spots of white blood ebbed out. *But... I'm not like the ones you hunt.*

You're in the Path of the First. The masters have marked you for death. Ree wondered why it hadn't run away. This went against all logic. *You're dangerous.*

I don't always look like this. I think... I think they believe I'm something else – a violent one! I'm not dangerous!

If that were true, it might be a samung, a rare type of shapeshifter phi that could change between a handful of forms – some as disguise, some fearsome for killing. Its current shape was particularly benign, and Ree supposed it had chosen this one to put her at ease.

Not dangerous, huh? Ree was doubtful. *Your other form didn't look so friendly.*

Conversing with her prey went against the laws of the order. Any words from phi were to be discarded as lies. That had been drilled into her head over and over for years. Yet something about this samung gave her pause. *When did you last kill?*

Not for a long time. Its eyelids lowered, creating two half-moons. *I hunted the soldiers who had burned my village and killed my family. Killed them, or those who looked like them. But the hunger never went away.* Its little mouth crumpled, then a big, fat tear rolled down its flat face. Ree couldn't believe this, it was crying?! Actual tears? She must have hit her head harder than she thought.

"There are no villages burned anywhere near here. This doesn't make sense," Ree muttered out loud, then pushed herself into a sitting position. Her head still swam, but less intensely now. "You *must* have done something else, killed someone else. Otherwise the masters wouldn't have sent us after you."

No, no, no. I've made a pact with Indrajit. He had me swear off killing, and I'm almost done! I will regain my humanity very soon.

Indrajit. The asura? Ree gawked at it. She knew the name from some of the ancient devaskrit texts she'd read. He was a warrior who'd featured in many tales from the struggles between the asura – dark celestials – and the angelic devas. But those were only legends.

You don't believe?! The phi's head snapped up, mouth opening in a small circle.

"I don't know," Ree said out loud, surprising herself.

But you shine in the Gray. I've seen others like you. How can you not... It trailed off, head swaying.

Others like me? Other phi hunters?

No. The Ashukari. They shine in the Gray. Not hunters. And the guru, born into it! He hears the whispers of devas – walks! Walks with the devas! Eyes like yours. Hair like yours.

"I've never heard of this," Ree gestured to herself. "No one has. I'm..." A freak. She didn't say it, or even think it, but the phi seemed to sense her overwhelming discontent.

You're mistaken. You hunters, you walk one path, never stray. I walked the dark path too, killing anyone who looked like those that wronged me. The phi huffed, shaking its head in a disturbingly human-like way. *Don't you want freedom?*

"I am free," Ree insisted, but again, doubt crept into her mind. After she killed this phi, she'd win the trial. Pass the Kang-Fye. Walk the Serene Way until the end of her days. That was the hunter's way, the path she chose.

Or had the path been chosen for her?

Let me live, hunter, and I will take you to the Ashukari. It's far from here, but... you'll have your answers. You shine, they shine...

Ree shook her head, hating herself for being intrigued. No, it must be reading her somehow, plucking her insecurities from her mind and waving them in front of her like sweet poison. But why bother? What could it possibly gain?

Why did you save me? Ree demanded.

Because I want to do good. Be good! The phi wiped its eyes, crying again. *More than an accursed destined to kill and kill until there is nothing left.*

She sat in silence for a moment, contemplating what it had said. Long enough that the hiss of rain let up into a soft patter, and the echoes of thunder were further and farther between. Strangely, and she couldn't place exactly why, she believed it was telling the truth.

I may believe that you haven't killed, Ree said. *But it doesn't change what I have to do.*

Have to? It's your choice. The phi scratched at its leg again. *I saved your life, and I only ask for a fair exchange. Free me from this trap, hunter. Let me go in peace.*

She doubted his peace would last very long. The other three novices were certainly nearby, and if they hadn't caught wind of it by now, they would soon. Still, she couldn't deny that it had dragged her from the swamp, away from the crocodile. Phi or not…

It was a fair exchange.

"To hell with the trial," Ree muttered, and finally stood, pulling her chainblade free. She stared into the hopeful eyes of the little phi, still clutching its leg. "A life for a life, then." Cautiously, Ree knelt down, and watching the creature cautiously, studied the trap. It didn't look like any the phi hunters used, but rather one from a laymen hunter used for small game. There was a crank release on it. She flicked it off, and then began prying open the trap with her blade.

"Ree!" The shout came. The phi disappeared, and the phi shut its eyes, both hands over its face.

Ree glanced behind her, where she saw Esha standing not twenty paces away, looking every bit the glorious hunter, eyes bright in the night. She stood balanced on another fallen trunk, chainblade in hand but loose at her side.

"Esha," Ree said softly, a pit of dread growing in her gut.

"Dammit, I knew you'd win." Esha frowned, but only for a breath before forcing a grin. "Smart, using the trap. Didn't think of that. Ah well, I was getting sick of this shit weather anyway." She began walking across the trunk.

Ree looked between her best friend and the half-freed phi, who hadn't moved, only quivered in fear. There was still time to do her duty. Fulfill her purpose. And yet...

"What a pathetic little thing," Esha scoffed as she walked up. "I'd think the masters would have chosen something more challenging. But... I guess it was more about finding it – ah shit!" Esha gasped. "It's still alive! You need to kill it twice, Ree!"

Esha was referring to one of the tenants of phi hunting. It was said that phi were most dangerous after they died, which from what she understood, was more of a warning for caution. The obvious weak points that any living creature had – the throat, the eyes, the organs, for instance – weren't always the same. They often played dead, hoping to ambush an overconfident hunter who thought they'd finished the job.

A life for a life. The phi's voiceless words were hardly a whisper.

"Did it speak?!" Esha gasped.

Ree suddenly felt as if she were watching herself from somewhere far beyond. There was an eerie familiarity about the entire situation, as if she'd been here before, maybe countless times. With this strange sensation came the thought that her next move would determine the course of the rest of her life. She gazed over her shoulder at Esha, who met her eyes and nodded, hurrying her on.

"I'm sorry, Esha," Ree said. "I'm letting it go."

"What?!" Esha sputtered. "What do you mean, letting it go? Phi hunters don't let things go. What part of your vows do you not understand?"

"I know what it means. But this thing hasn't hurt anyone. It's no threat." Ree stopped short of admitting it may have saved her life. "Last I checked, the guild doesn't hunt for sport."

With finality, Ree pulled the trap open. The phi snatched its leg out quickly and clutched it to its body, rocking back and forth and whimpering. Ree stood, then turned to face Esha. Her friend seemed to look over her, in complete exasperation. To accentuate her point, Ree tossed her chainblade to the ground and crossed her arms.

"This trial?" she said, each word hard as iron. "Is *bullshit.*"

"No, it's not!" Esha snapped, her cheeks flush, eyes wild. "This is a rite of passage. Fuck, Ree, you don't give a shit about the guild at all. You – you haven't had to try as hard as any of us! The gift was *handed* to you–"

"Handed to me?" A flare of anger shot through Ree's chest. "I didn't ask for this. You don't know what it was like, growing up a freak of nature. I didn't have a real choice–"

"Oh, cry me a river," Esha sneered, and took a threatening step forward. "If you won't respect the order, I will."

"No," Ree said, bristling. She stared up at Esha, knowing full well that her friend could easily overpower her, if it came to that.

Esha took a deep breath, nostrils flaring as she exhaled slowly. "I'm asking my best friend…" Her voice faltered, but her eyes hardened. "Unless our friendship was bullshit too."

"That has nothing to do with it." Ree gulped, her throat gone very dry. "I love you like a sister, Esha. You know that."

Esha flinched at that. And then she smiled, though her eyes watered. "Just… like a sister, huh?"

The same rejection shook Esha's voice as when Ree pulled away from their kiss. She cringed internally, but it was the truth. It would have changed everything between them, and she never wanted that.

"Please... please trust me," Ree begged. "The guild doesn't have to do things just because it's the way it's always been. There needs to be a reason for it all." Esha's face had gone flat. She wasn't getting through to her. It would be so easy to step aside and let her best friend finish the job she couldn't.

A familiar presence approached, their running gait as telling as someone's signature. Falah. And not far behind, Raj.

"Please, Esha," she tried one more time. "Just let me do this. I'll explain to the masters and take the fall for it."

Esha tensed, planting her feet.

Don't, Ree begged in the Everpresent.

Esha charged forward, knocking Ree aside with a strong forearm as she raised her chainblade. Ree stumbled but managed to stay upright. The phi cowered in fear as Esha brought her blade down. Ree lashed out with blind desperation, calling upon a jumble of spells at the same time. Her arm blazed hot as a blacksmith's iron with the Smoking Palm of Anewan, along with a blinding flash from the Star of Yessun, and... something else, something strange and unnamed. She caught the side of Esha's face with her fist. Esha cried out in pain and dropped her chainblade, doubling over to clutch her face. The stink of burnt flesh turned Ree's stomach and she backed away, horrified.

This couldn't have gone any worse. And if she thought there might be a way back, hidden under her broken vows and betrayal, it was certainly gone now.

Esha screamed and cursed Ree in both the Blinds and the Everpresent. It didn't make sense – Esha had passed the Maijep trial, she shouldn't have been in pain. Yet it was clear in her voice that she was suffering, severely at that. Tears burned Ree's eyes as she reached out to Esha, then drew back, shaking, staring at her own quivering hand, still glowing with magic.

"What the fuck?" At the far side of the bank, both Falah and Raj stood in the weeds, staring at the scene in disbelief.

"This..." Ree gasped, shaking her head. "This isn't my path." And then she turned her back on her best friend. On the hunters. On the guild. On Jinburi. She nodded to the phi, who scurried to her side, partially hopping on one foot, then disappeared into the fading night.

Chapter 6

The Storm Prince

A battle raged in the Strait of Poisida, the snaking channel between two city-state islands, somewhere in the eastern end of the Kutsu Isles archipelago. The blazing sun glimmered over the deep sapphire sea, and spilled across the two ships locked together.

One of those ships belonged to the Storm Prince Tanung, Captain and Commander of the Wild Cobra Brigade.

The other belonged to the pirate he'd been sent to kill.

Tan was laughing in the face of a one-eyed mustached marauder as they both grappled for control of a single blade. Five inches from death. His right hand started to tremble. He stopped laughing, but had no time to panic before the waking visions hit.

All at once, the bright blue sky melted into a field of fire. A red moon swelled, dominated an endless void above, dripping like the molten core of a blacksmith's forge, every drop hitting the land erupting in an explosion.

Gone was the sturdy wooden deck of his ship, the battle cries of his crew, the taste of blood and salt on his lips.

Tan's bare feet sunk into a soft mix of sand and ash. He remained locked in a grappling match with his enemy – that hadn't changed. But the figure before him had shifted from the ragged pirate into something far more familiar. A figure wrapped in black, with jewels for eyes, pressing a knife to his throat.

The Stranger.

Tan clutched her wrist with both hands, straining to wrestle the blade away. Felt a sting as the blade nicked his neck, followed by the hot trickle of blood like an angry tear.

His murderer's mouth twisted in a smile, opened, and said–

"Tan!"

His mind swirled like a tub draining into vacuum, a nauseating sensation that fizzled out with an audible buzz. The sea, the ship, and the battle all came roaring back. Tan laid heavily on top of the mustached marauder, whose one eye was black and empty, a knife lodged in his throat. He jumped to his feet, drew his pistol, and took aim at the nearest enemy rushing toward him.

But before he could pull the trigger, the man fell, clutching his chest where a bayonet had sprouted forth. Tan's quartermaster kicked the body away, flashed him a gap-toothed smile, then rushed over to one of their wounded crewmen crouching near the rail. Blinking around in the bright afternoon sun, Tan realized his marines had already made short work of the pirates, some picking through their pockets, some digging out their gold teeth. The deck was slick with blood.

"Tan," Simo said, as he walked over from the bow. The dread-locked, ebony-skinned Baghani man was taller than everyone by half a head, and as the finest daab swordsmen in the country, completely unscathed from the fight, his fierce dark eyes still bright with adrenaline. Seeing as the prince was not dead, Tan's second-mate and First Lieutenant cracked a smile with their usual, post-battle exchange. "Still alive?"

"For now." Tan re-holstered his pistol. "Report?"

"A few injuries, no casualties on our side. The vessel is secured."

"What about Merat?"

"Surrendered. He retreated, tried to hang himself in his cabin, but the boys got to him in time."

"Excellent." Tan allowed himself a smile. His mission had been to capture the notorious marauder Laut Merat, which would cripple the networks operation in the Sea of Suyoram, at least for a time. The king would be pleased, even if Tan knew there were a hundred more brigands ready to raise the black flag and claim the title for themselves.

Many in the royal court whispered that manhunting was beneath someone of Tanung's station. Tan was a minor prince, as his mother had been a consort to the late, great Crown-Prince Varunvirya. Perhaps they were right. But being out in the world, away from the gossips, the sycophants and scheming lordlings in the Capital, helped distract him from what could have been, had his father not died.

Some of his closest friends had shared their opinion that the king, Tan's uncle, felt threatened by him, and so never stopped him and the Wild Cobra Brigade from venturing so cavalierly into the fray. Some said the king secretly hoped Tan would catch an errant bullet or some jungle sickness and take himself out of line for the throne. Tan was low in the line for succession anyway, the king already had an heir by his queen, but the boy was small and sickly and often bedridden. There were rumors that the queen, who was significantly older than the king, could not bear more children. But the king had more children by his own consorts and concubines who were young but technically carried stronger claims than Tan did. And he had a few handfuls of cousins and half-brothers to compete with as well.

But as his victories with the brigade grew alongside his popularity with the public, so did his thoughts about who really deserved to rule Suyoram.

"Bring Merat to the brig and grab the goods," Tan said, already walking the gangway to return to his ship. "We set sail to the Capital as soon as possible."

"And the vessel?"

Tan paused, balancing on the board as he appraised the pirate ship. It was a fast, sturdy, and well-kept little two-master. Bringing such a prize home would undoubtedly add to his coffers and standing. But splitting the manpower to sail two vessels back would delay their return. It had already been a month since the king's last summons. Yet Tan had stubbornly refused to abandon his mission, knowing that Merat was just within his grasp, hiding somewhere in the hundreds of islands in the archipelago. Though he dreaded the reprimand sure to come, the king wouldn't be able to say it'd been a failure.

"Burn it," Tan said.

Back on his ship, in the privacy of his quarters, Tan peeled off his bloodied shirt, slumped into the chair at his desk, then shook out two pills from his medicinal satchel. He swallowed them with a swig of wine. It was double what the royal physician Somatra had prescribed him to take each morning for his condition. Until today, he hadn't had an episode in months, and couldn't remember the last time he'd had one so vivid.

The onset of his ailment happened many years ago, when he was sixteen, and thankfully in private, while on holiday with his mother. When they'd returned to the Capital, she brought him to Somatra, who had seen to his health since birth. According to him, it was a mild case of apasmara, wind-type, identified by waking seizures that caused not fits, but lapses of consciousness. Somatra declared that it was likely due to the time of Tan's birth, only now manifested in adolescence. He'd been born during a monsoon, one of the worst in Suyo history, which had garnered him the nickname, the Storm Prince.

Superstitious bullshit, really. No evidence supported a correlation between apasmara, or any ailment and the weather during one's birth. But the cause didn't concern him, only the symptoms. He knew the warning signs – a distinct aura of altered sensation would arise, usually accompanied by a headache. His right arm and hand would start to tremble and shake. His vision would skew, objects becoming flat or magnified. He'd grow dizzy, sometimes nauseous, sounds distorted and language became impossible to parse. Thankfully, since taking the pills, these episodes didn't last longer than a few breaths, if they happened at all.

Rarely did they result in a full loss of consciousness, such as what happened today. And never in the thick of battle, at a moment that could determine life or death. Never full-on hallucinations. Somatra had warned him that if his condition wasn't properly maintained, it could blossom from "wind-type" to "fire-type" and essentially destroy his mind. Loss of memory would be a sure sign.

Since the night of his diagnosis, Tan always kept a journal, which he retrieved now. He wasn't a pessimist, not exactly. But he prided himself on being rational. If the day came that his brain deteriorated into a mush of unrecognizable matter, at least his accomplishments would be on record.

Dipping a reed pen in ink, he recounted his memory of the molten sun and the Stranger while it remained fresh, but hid the context within the confines of a poem. He'd seen who he called the Stranger before, a reoccurring nightmare during these episodes and in dreams. The Stranger would always try to kill him, but something about it this time felt different.

Though it was a private journal, he knew history well enough to know that men of renown were not immune to scrutiny – someday, he would die, and it would be read.

After that, he abandoned his journal in favor of the captain's logbook, putting the official record of the mission on paper. He cross-referenced the notes from his quartermaster, who'd taken inventory of what they'd pulled off the ship before it burned. Sometime later, just as he was finishing the report, a knock came at his door.

"Enter."

The door creaked open and a tattooed arm poked in, gloved hand waving a golden bottle as if in question. Tan smiled. "Read my mind."

Simo ducked through the doorway, kicking the door shut behind him. Simo's rise to acclaim as Tan's right hand in the Wild Cobra Brigade had been an odd one. His parents had been Baghani Republic envoys who were in court so often that they had their own apartments in the royal compound. Eventually, his mother stayed in Suyoram so the children could benefit from a royal education, while his father continued trekking across the sea and back for his duties. Tan and Simo first met as teenagers, playing sports in the yard with the other children living at court. He always admired how Simo never tolerated indignity from any of the Suyo noble spawn, and they became fast friends. One of his favorite memories was when his half-brother Priyut (the spoiled brat) failed to stop teasing the Baghani kid for his hair and Simo picked him up and tossed him into the koi pond.

"Found it hidden under a rug in the surgeon's room. Thank the Awakened Lord I got to it before we razed the damn thing." Simo plopped the bottle on Tan's desk.

"Is that..." Tan squinted at the looping script on the label. "Looks almost Qinsengi, but not."

"Gaochurian. Far, far west Qinseng. Desert dwellers."

"Expensive?"

"Priceless. Only seen one of these before, years ago." Must have been when Simo was cutting his teeth as a privateer, before he joined Tan's brigade. Simo pointed to the largest line of script. "It says 'Glory is a Godless Dream.' Merchant collector told me that, at least. He bought it for..." Simo whistled. "Resupplied my whole ship for that bottle. It haunted me for years. What did it taste like? How good could it possibly be, that this hawker would spend a near fortune... what? Don't look at me like that. It's true!"

"If that's true, you would have kept it hidden," Tan said with a smirk. "Bought yourself a vacation when we got back."

"I want for nothing in this life..." Simo said with a faux air of dignity, "but to follow the Storm Prince of Suyoram into every shitstorm he wanders. Putting down brigands and rebels in the name of the crown..." He grabbed two empty mugs off a wall rack and placed them on the desk. "And keep his dumb ass alive on the off-chance he becomes a king, so I can double my incredibly generous salary."

"How honorable of you."

"The honors are yours, my prince." Simo nodded to the wax-capped red seal of the bottle, then eyed the logbook still open on Tan's desk. "Unless... you wish to add it to the inventory." It did look like a splendid and exotic prize, the sort fit for a king, and would surely win him favor should he return with it.

"Oops, too late." Tan flicked the logbook closed with a thump and picked up a letter opener. Simo nodded in approval as Tan began to pry off the seal. "How's the crew?"

"Ukrit needed twenty-six stitches right on his arse. Adee got knocked stupid, he was singing a Kutsu ditty when he came to. Fat Fang has a broken arm, won't be climbing the ropes today." Simo hesitated, eyes flicking from the bottle to Tan. "And you took a good knock."

Tan avoided Simo's scrutinizing stare. "I'm fine."

"Alive, at least," Simo said. "But I saw. You went away for a bit." His second mate wasn't the only one who knew of his condition, as Tan was close with his men and needed them to know he took medicine for a "minor illness" to prevent a situation, well, much like the one that had occurred.

But Simo knew Tan better than everyone else.

"It's under control," Tan said. "It's been a long campaign." And he hadn't been taking care to rest. Sometimes he met dawn with bloodshot, burning eyes, filled with a hot, restless energy that seemed to send his senses into overdrive. He knew it was bad for his condition, as one of the first things the physician said was to keep a strict sleep schedule. It just wasn't possible sometimes, not in Tan's line of work.

Tan sighed and popped the cork from the bottle, tossing it carelessly behind him. "I'll see Somatra when I return, first thing."

Simo stared at him evenly for a beat, then shrugged with a smile, his easy manner returning. "Good, that old codger will sort you out."

"I'm sure, nurse. Now, are we going to drink this or not?" Tan poured two fingers into each glass. The dark spirit looked thick and viscous and stunk of burnt wood.

"Aye, let's see how they do it in the desert." Simo raised his glass. Tan clicked it and the two men threw it back.

The burn blasted his tongue, tasting of licorice and... egg?! It seemed to explode into his sinuses while stinging his eyes, the yolky aftertaste devolving into something indescribably worse. Simo spit half a mouthful out while Tan erupted into choking coughs, bile stinging his throat.

"Fucking hell!" he gasped, blinking back tears. He wiped his mouth on his arm and spat, then glared at his second. "This?! This is worth a small fortune?"

"Nasty kick!" Simo retched again, then slapped himself, shuddering. At Tan's aghast expression he burst into laughter. "I swear! I swear I didn't expect that!"

"That is..." Tan stared at the bottle. "Divinely atrocious."

"Shall we..." Simo cleared his throat. "Drink the rest with the boys?"

Tan poured them another two fingers. "I think we have to."

Hours later, drunk to all hell, Tan stumbled from the galley, voice hoarse from singing and laughing and trading well-meaning insults with his crew. His head spun and his heart swelled with a rush of pride and power that overwhelmed him – he felt invincible. He went to the surgeon's room and checked on the injured. Tan had studied some medicine, and would often assist the doc... not this drunk of course. He asked the doctor for a pinch of opium to help him sleep, not his usual vice, but sometimes he wanted to drift.

He climbed the crow's nest and talked to Adee, who mistook his good cheer and friendliness for an advance but at least they could laugh about it. Back in his cabin, he took up the pen again, the place where he could divulge his innermost thoughts, admit his fears and insecurities, his obsessions, the shameful desires, the things he would take to the grave. A more religious man might call them effigies to the devas, but he considered them useless after the point they manifested from his mind and onto the page.

And as the glorious orange sun broke over the shining sea, he burned each page and let the ashes slide into the wind and believed that always, they found their way back to the Stranger, his murderer, his muse.

Chapter 7

Every Wild Place

She ran.

This feeling was new, all-encompassing. Sick to her stomach, yet exhilarated. Ashamed and pissed off and terrified but with a fire burning inside, ready to burst. She was angry at the guild, angry at Esha, angry at the Gris. Tears streamed uncontrollably down her cheeks, but when Agira asked where she was going, a shrill burst of laughter erupted from her lips.

Away. Anywhere. To your fucking Ashukari. It doesn't matter. They'll catch me and kill you. You should run far away from me. The swamp blurred as she pushed forward on pure instinct, zeroing into the most unfamiliar, and driving toward that mysterious, enticing path.

She'd been running for what felt like hours, paranoid at every noise and step, worried that at any moment Master Seua would barrel out of the darkness and knock her senseless. Or that Master Arei would drop from the canopy and blind her before wrapping a chain around her limbs and hauling her back to the guild.

Show me the way, she called to the Everpresent, to the Serene Way, to anything that would listen. Thorns lanced across her face, caught on her hunter's coat and snared her in a web of tangled vines covered in vicious, curling red thorns.

With her exhaustion, the racing fears grew even more nonsensical. Elder Nokai melting from the water and snatching her soul, trapping her into a token, or Esha snatching her into a hug, her friend's cheek pressed against her own, hot and sticky with burned, blistered skin.

You fucking traitor, you don't deserve to wear the badge. I'll cut it out of your skin, Ree, you hear me?

Too ensnared to detach herself from the thorns, Ree slithered from her coat, then crawled forward in the mud, exhausted, sore, barefoot, wearing only her wrapped sabai top and chong kraben trousers. She finally wriggled free from the thick tangle of thorn bushes, pushing through to the other side as they cut into her back. How much blood had she left in her wake, bright as a signal fire for the masters to follow her trail? Dawn was surely about to break. It wouldn't be long now.

The soft land gave way into a slope and she half-rolled, half-slithered down into a clearing. The sky wasn't visible through the cloud of trees, and she listened to the insects to determine what time of day it was...

Only to hear none.

The ground was spongy, with black moss and beneath it was churning with insects that burrowed away as if her presence was an insult. She rolled over onto her belly and peered forward, where a wreath of bones surrounded the bank of a flat, mirror-still pond. All around, mangroves surrounded her in a thick, impenetrable wall, the clearing so perfectly circular it seemed artificial. She glanced behind her, but the thicket of thorns had disappeared, along with Agira.

Somehow, it seemed the swamp itself had trapped her, which… could only mean one thing. Her blood ran cold as she gazed at the pond, tentatively reaching out her awareness to sense what lay below.

An immense presence lurked beneath.

Every wild place has a living heart, her father once told her. *And like a living heart, requires attention and care. A god-spirit watches over these lands. One which all living things know to pay tribute...*

She'd never seen the great, immortal Guardian of the Swamp before, yet this place pulled at her memory.

Ree slowly pushed herself to her knees and crawled to the banks of the lake, where a shore of animal bones framed the dark waters, some still bloody, others so old they'd fractured to ivory sand. Her arm was already bleeding from a nasty cut, and she held her hand above the water. A tendril of blood ran like a river over her knuckle, down her finger, then dripped out into the pond.

Nothing happened, no sound but for the heavy thud of her heart. Ree clenched her fist, the effort pushing another drop of blood into the water.

She was beginning to doubt the truthfulness of her father's stories, when a deep rumble emanated from below. A vibration several octaves lower than the range of human ears could detect, but in the Everpresent, it shook her to the very core. Ree dared to peer into the pond, but it was so still and so dark, all she saw was the mess of her own reflection.

Cuts and mud covered her face, as well as the remnants of the contusion on the side of her freshly shaved head. The rain had washed away most of her ceremonial hunting paint – it was tradition to smear one long streak of black across the eyes, a callback to the final slash a successful hunter made across the symbol that marked haunted lands. Bits remained on her lids and eye sockets, which, combined with the gleam of magic in her eyes, gave her a sinister, rabid look.

The water rippled, displacing her reflection. Something moved underneath, then two spots of glowing red grew larger and larger, reflecting off gleaming aqua scales with golden details.

With a surge of water, a great naga slowly arose from the water, her fierce reptilian head larger than an elephant's entire body. The naga's head remained even with Ree's astonished face, yet her snake-like body continued to rise, twisting in an arch above in a ready stance.

There was no doubt in Ree's mind that the Guardian of the Swamp could snuff her out as easily as stepping on an ant, should she speak unwisely. Ree was taught that upon meeting a guardian, if a hunter was so fortunate, or unfortunate, that their words could determine whether they walked away with a favor, or walked away at all.

Ree lowered her eyes and began to press her still-bleeding palms together in a wai, but hesitated when an oddly warm feeling in her chest grew in intensity. She had an insane, impossible thought, and let that thought echo into the Everpresent.

I've been here before. Ree clutched her chest, then stared into the eyes of the naga. The Swamp Guardian's nostrils flared, and Ree fought to stay balanced as the guardian inhaled deeply, as if reading the very essence of the miserable child crouched before her.

Once. The Swamp Guardian's words felt heavy as boulders slamming into the mud, trees falling, and the certainty of something unfathomably ancient, inevitable.

How can that be? Did my father bring me here, as a child? Ree couldn't fathom it. Even though her family had been on camping trips before, how could one forget meeting a god-spirit in its sanctuary?

The Swamp Guardian's naga lips peeled back, revealing glistening fangs as long as Ree's entire arm. Ree stared in awe at the display, yet, to her own surprise or stupidity, did not feel threatened.

Why have you come before me, hunter? The Swamp Guardian demanded, her growing impatience palpable.

For favor, great one. Ree clutched her head, the enormity of the situation crushing her. *What I've done is unforgivable.* If they caught her, she'd be exiled at best, stripped of her badges, maybe even burned in retribution for what she did to Esha. She imagined her parents' disappointment, an image she'd managed to avoid until then. There was no way she could face their shame and heartbreak after they'd already suffered so much with Kit.

And her father, just the thought of his reaction brought tears to her eyes anew.

If absolution is what you seek, you have come to the wrong place.

No, I don't deserve that. But they'll find me soon. The other hunters. Ree dared to peer deep into the eyes of the Swamp Guardian, two distorted images of herself reflecting back. *Unless… you can help me?*

It felt like days passed as Ree waited for the Swamp Guardian's response. A thick black tongue flickered out of the naga's mouth, tasting the air.

My aid comes at a cost.

Anything. Ree responded in earnest, and bowed her head.

The naga's snout drew even closer to Ree's face, breathing in deeply again. The warmth expanded in her chest, a curious reaction, and Ree closed her eyes, letting it envelop her. Some kind of spirit magic, maybe, known only to the gods and devas. The Swamp Guardian made a low rumble, contemplative, as if weighing Ree's worthiness with an unknown scale.

Then the feeling snapped away, leaving her cold.

You have nothing of value… right now.

Wait! Desperate, Ree looked at the cut on her hand… then at her hand itself. *I'll give you my hand.*

The guardian did not react, which Ree took as encouragement

A show of my commitment. To serve you again in the future, when I have something of value. Ree took her knife, and found a rock. She placed her hand against it, then pressed the knife into her wrist. This was going to suck.

There was another rumble from the guardian, followed by a strange choking noise. *A word of advice, hunter. Never give a hand when a finger would suffice.*

A finger, then? Ree nodded quickly, elated, stretched out her left ring finger against the rock. She found another with a flat bottom. Crouching, she held the blade in place with her foot, took a deep, slow breath. Then she closed her eyes... counted to three... and slammed the other rock as hard as she could on the blade.

A blank space, and then white, and her head swam with stars. She hadn't realized she was screaming. Ree gritted her teeth as tears ran down her face, blood pouring from the new stump on her left hand. Sniffling, Ree placed the severed finger carefully by the pond with shuddering hands, then made a wai against her forehead, blood dripping down and off her chin.

Impressive. The guardian drew back, slinking down into her pond. With that, a wave of mangrove roots cascaded from the waters like a wave, and burrowed into the ground behind Ree, rapidly digging into the soft dirt. Ree watched in astonishment as they continued to dig, forcing open a sloping tunnel as if the ground were a mere curtain. A constellation of mushrooms sprouted from the dirt between the burrowing roots, each ebbing with soft, violet bioluminescence.

The masters always described the Serene Way as traveling through the living veins of the wilderness, paths created by the Venara, the first hunters, who had bargained and paid tribute to build it. But now, Ree understood something different. These paths were always there, the hunters only gained access to them through their efforts. And with that realization came hope. If the Swamp Guardian did not want the other hunters to find her, they would not, as the great god-spirit was the soul and will of the swamp itself.

Ree glanced back to the guardian to give a final wai of gratitude, but only the naga's crest was visible above the water. *Thank you, great spirit.*

The Swamp Guardian's words carried from deep below. Even without a physical presence, the god-spirit's aura still loomed over her, over everything. *I will collect what is mine, when it is due.*

Ree wondered if she'd made a mistake, promising a nebulous "anything" in return for this escape. But it didn't matter now. It was too late. She only hoped that the cost, whatever it was, whenever it came, wouldn't be too high.

She'd made her choice. Isaree steeled herself and headed into the unknown.

Chapter 8

A New Dawn

Silent. It was so silent.

Despite the whirlwind of churning emotions that drove her frenzy to escape, walking through this sanctuary slowed her heartbeat. Relaxed her tensed muscles. No sound but for her own breath, no scent but overpowering earth, no color but the soft glow of the mushrooms which latticed over the roots like spiderwebs.

The spiraling formations of fungi danced before her eyes, the monotony of the tunnel producing a hypnotic effect, similar to deep meditation. Time lost meaning during this otherworldly passage, but she retained enough awareness to know that it hadn't been all that long until the tunnel ended, crumbling into streams of bright, orange light.

Daylight.

Ree flinched at the sudden change, light flickering as the silhouettes of roots pried open the earth to create an opening. Blue sky and greenery beyond. The heat hit her the moment she stepped onto solid grass, as the tunnel had been oddly cool. But it wasn't the wet, stifling humidity of the swamplands. Ree turned in a full circle, aghast at the difference in her surroundings.

The tunnel rapidly closed, the grass shifting back into place as perfectly as a rug reset. The swamp was nowhere in sight. All around her were rolling grassy plains, patches of tall, skinny palms and flowering evergreens with broad leaves. To the east, the orange outline of the morning sun hovered behind gentle hills. To the west, near the horizon, she spotted the glint of moving water where an unfamiliar wide, brown river flowed south, surrounded by reeds.

Wait, her finger. It hadn't been hurting, and she hadn't yet cast Shivah's Kiss to heal the wound. The spell could heal a lot of things, broken bones and teeth even, but it couldn't grow back limbs or digits. Ree looked at her missing finger, and was astonished to find the wound had already healed, grown over as if it had never existed in the first place. Had she cast it subconsciously? Did the magic of the Serene Way heal her?

Is it over?

Ree startled, then searched around for Agira.

Down here. There was a jiggle on her hip, and Ree looked down at her tool belt. The flap to her tincture pouch popped open, and Agira's funny little head stuck out, now the size of a mouse.

"You hid in there the whole time?" Ree gaped. Agira hopped onto the ground and stretched out his batwings languidly, yawning.

Had to. The guardian isn't always nice to my kind. Sorry, hunter.

"Don't call me that," Ree said, surprised at the sadness in her voice. She frowned, pushing it away. "I'm not a hunter anymore."

What do I call you?

"My name's Isaree," she said. Although speaking out loud to Agira wasn't necessary, it made her feel a little less crazy for conversing with a hungry ghost. And a little less alone. "Why did you come with me?"

To bring you to the Ashukari, as promised. To see the ones that shine in the Gray, like you.

Ree scoffed, shaking her head. This was madness. The masters could never explain why she'd been born with the Everpresent, and she found nothing in the library either. *The devas work mysteriously, child,* Elder Nokai would say, *be content with your gift.* Nothing about that answer gave her comfort. But if Agira was right, and there was another like her, someone who struggled in the Blinds as she did, then perhaps he could give her another perspective.

"Where is this Ashukari?" Ree asked.

Past the Emerald Forest. Beyond the mountains, beyond the ashes of the Relentless Rains.

"Beyond... you're speaking of Loram." That was very far indeed. She stared at Agira's big round eyes, wondering if this hungry ghost, who claimed to have a deal with the devas, had seen someone like her, or was still telling tales. "How exactly do you know of this place?"

It was a place I knew in life. Near my village. Agira wrapped his arms around his knees and gazed up at her. *Used to play near their temple, long time ago. And there are phi around there, they don't disturb.*

"Hmm… Long time? How long?"

I don't know. Time is… hard to know, now.

"How old are you… were you, I mean. When you died."

Younger than you.

"The soldiers that burned your village, were they Gris?"

No. They wore the crests of Suyoram.

"That doesn't make sense, there's been no…" she trailed off, considering. He'd mentioned the Relentless Rains, the name of the mountain province rebellion put down by the former king… some forty years ago. She knew this because her father was a war orphan, his village burned, which set him on his path to becoming a hunter. The entire region had always been problematic for Suyoram, even after the rebellion had been squashed. After the Gris moved in, the crown had granted them those provinces bordering Loram to assist in their campaign.

"You must be from the Khrapong province. Which means this Ashukari existed forty years ago," Ree groaned. "How do you know they still exist? How old was this guru when you last saw him?"

So much concern with age, with time! What does it matter?

"It matters because I'm far from home, on my way to jump the border to Loram, a place I've never been. All to find some cult guru who may or may not still be alive…" As she spoke, the obvious became clear. "It's downright mad. Have I gone mad? Are you a demon of madness?"

Agira only stared at her in confusion. Ree sighed, then surveyed the countryside. "All right. Well… I have no idea where we are right now. Do you?"

The phi hopped to his feet, then fluttered his wings and took to the air. His erratic flight reminded Ree of a dragonfly darting this way and that. He flitted far into the sky and she soon lost track of him.

"Well… see you later, I guess." If he would come back at all. Ree walked to the nearest tree and sat down, dazed. She took a moment to lean back against the trunk, breathe deep, and appreciate the serenity of this untouched landscape.

For the first time in her life, she didn't have to be anywhere. Or do anything. With the sudden lack of obligation came the thought of how cluttered her life had been. There was always something to study, a ritual to practice, a martial skill to train. Or the expectations of others always demanding her attention – classes with the masters, dinner at her parents, or even going for an afternoon swim with Esha when they were done with their duties.

Esha. Ree's stomach clenched, remembering the smell of burnt flesh, Esha's screams and curses. It was a terrible thing to hurt her friend, but what else could she have done? Just rolled over and gone along with what Esha wanted, just because she could bully her? No, she had to stand up for what she believed was right. Esha must have been faking her pain. She passed the Maijep trial, it shouldn't have caused her to scream like she had. She knew how to heal herself, though admittedly, her spell-casting was her weakest skill. But the guild had healers. She would be fine...

She would be fine...

Ree closed her eyes, listening intently to the birds and the insects going about their lives. The natural harmony invoked a timeless calm, as if eons could pass here and no other human would come. Nothing would change. And now, she could be part of this tiny bit of eternity.

Once she felt centered again, she opened her eyes. The harsh reality of her situation settled over her, the weight uncertain. Then to the west, Ree's heart sank as she spotted the first sign of civilization she'd seen since the trial.

A long, rigged ship floated steadily upstream. She was too far away to make out any details, until a breeze took up one of the flags on its mast – black and blue.

Ran away from home, and still can't manage to be rid of the Grisi, she thought bitterly.

Isaree! Agira perched on a small branch, staring at her in that unsettling, wide-eyed way. *I figured it out. That's the Mae-Duram. Beyond are the foothills of the Little Shas–*

"What? That's not the Jinburi? Or the Namleng?" Ree sat forward, now wide awake. If that was the Duram River, then... they were at least days away from where they'd started, if not weeks. Remarkable. That also meant that she had a huge lead on outrunning the guild, if they even tried to search outside of the massive swamp.

The same couldn't be said for her father. Her mother would insist he go after her. Ree wondered if he'd chance a meeting with the Swamp Guardian to seek aid in finding her. Hopefully, the naga would keep her secret.

I remember the smell of the Duram. The edges of Agira's lipless mouth curled slightly, a poor impression of a smile. *There's a small town ten leagues north, near a temple. Maybe they can help?*

Ree was still reeling over the distance covered. There were so many more secrets to the Serene Way than even the guild realized. Secrets lost to time. Ree gazed at the horizon, where beyond the foothills must lie the Emerald forest, the mountains, the border provinces, and Loram. "Shit. If I'd been more specific, maybe the Guardian would have taken me all the way to the damn Ashukari temple. Or the ruins of it, I bet."

The guardian blessed you with a great favor, Agira said.

"And a great obligation, yet unseen," Ree muttered ruefully, then rose to her feet and began to walk.

It was nearing nightfall by the time Ree drew within sight of the riverside town. First she passed the flooded rice paddy fields, abandoned for the night. Rural stilt houses dotted the riverbank, simpler in design and décor than she'd typically seen in Jinburi. A dirt path led into the village center, and above, the steepled roof of the local Sangha temple peeked out from a cluster of towering yang trees.

At this hour Ree expected the village to have settled in for the night. But there were people everywhere – entire families sitting in the streets, laying huddled together on blankets, surrounded by baskets and traveling cases. At first, she thought it might be some kind of celebration, but there was nothing festive in the air. People spoke in low voices, if they spoke at all. They wore simple clothes, many in the brightly woven fabrics typical of northern hill tribes, women with stacks of rings around their necks that gave the illusion of an elegant, swan-like profile.

Closer to the temple, two saffron-robed monks holding baskets walked around the crowd, passing out packets of rice wrapped in banana leaves. The sedate crowd accepted the charity with grateful wais and ate quietly.

"What's going on?" Ree asked a woman passing by. The woman only glanced at her and flinched, making a sign to ward off evil before rushing away. She gazed around for a friendly face, and two children squealed upon seeing her, burying their faces in their sleeping father's shirt.

"Don't take it personally," a man's voice came from behind her. "Hunters aren't common here. And they've been through a lot."

Ree turned to see who'd spoken. An attractive young man leaned against a gate, muscular arms crossed over his bare chest. He didn't look much older than her. Darkly tanned by the sun, he wore a headwrap tight around his head and a blue sash around his waist, a common marker for ferrymen. Scraggly attempts at a beard dotted his long jaw, which only made him look younger.

"Are they from Loram?" Ree asked.

"What tipped you off?" He smiled, showing the red teeth of betel nut chew. When Ree didn't laugh, he shrugged. "Refugees from the Khrapong province. The fighting there's got worse. We've been up and down the Duram these last few weeks bringing them down."

"Fighting... oh." Ree knew the Gris were pushing into Loram, evident by their presence in Jinburi, but this was the first time she'd seen the results. There were rumors of conflict, but she imagined it went as it did in her city – first came the missionaries, then the trading company, and then the soldiers. And of course there were tensions with the locals, but nothing that would cause people en masse to flee their homes.

"Where are they going to go?" she asked, starting to sniff out the traces of ash, of dried blood, and salty tears.

"All I know is the elder says they can rest here, but there's not enough room to stay for good. Not for everyone. Some set out for the Long Road, some work the fields to make a little money." The man worked his jaw, then turned his head and let out a red stream of spit into the dirt. "What are you doing here? Didn't know there were any phi running about."

"Actually, I'm headed to Loram."

He chuckled, shaking his head in disbelief. "Wouldn't recommend it."

She peered down at his sash, mind working the angles. "Are you heading back there?"

"Got a night off, thank the Awakened Lord. Not much money in these fares. Boss is a bit of a bleeding heart, he's having us pick up people for half." He scoffed, then looked her over, eyes lingering on the knives at her waist. "So... there's a phi in Loram?"

Ree almost said no, but hesitated. This could be an opportunity. "Yes. But I need to find someone first. Have you ever heard of the Ashukari?"

"What's that?"

"I'm not entirely sure, but I mean to find a guru there."

"Guru, huh? Sounds like a cult."

"It might be," Ree admitted.

"I'm a follower of the Awakened Lord, wouldn't know anything about that," the ferryman said, then tipped his head toward the temple, and one of the elderly monks passing out rice. "The arhat might know more about that kind of thing."

"I know they're somewhere in the Khrapong province."

"Khrapong province covers most of the Little Shas. It's a big place."

"Right. It's a start, anyway," Ree said, then remembered to smile, attempting to be friendly. "Do you take passengers upriver?"

"For a fee." The young man eyed her, in a leery manner. "... Usually. But if you want a *free* ride to that shit hole, wouldn't take much to convince me."

His tone certainly insinuated that "much" meant a whole lot more. She tried to keep her expression neutral, but the sticky-thick hormones cascading from him made her grimace. He laughed, shaking his head and stepped off the fence. "Relax, I'm fucking with you. I respect the phi hunters, even pretty ones. My ma was from Maesa, taught me all about the guild and the good they do, even if no one believes it now."

"She didn't teach you well enough, apparently." Ree crossed her arms and glowered. The ferryman reminded her of how vulnerable she appeared. She had no money, and for the average onlooker appeared to be a slight-figured girl barely out of her teens. Albeit one with a shaved head, red eyes, and tattoos.

"Hey, can't blame a guy for trying." He flashed an apologetic smile, and averted his eyes, clearly embarrassed. "Anyway, we're off at first light. Come down to the docks and ask for Thura if you're serious."

"Thanks," Ree said flatly. "I'll think about it."

Chapter 9

Seat of the King

The capital of Suyoram was a city with not a name, but a paragraph: City of Devas on the Wings of the Ascended, Magnificent Place of the Twelve Circles, Seat of the King, of all his Royal Splendor, Home of the Gods Incarnate and the Awakened Lord.

A fifty-mile wide, sprawling metropolis, whose histories could be read in the layers of stone, the etchings upon old foundations rapidly disappearing as architecture sprouted. Some of those had become foreign, invasive, a weed. Tan again marveled at the new construction and renovations that busied every street. Square-cut stone with squat rooftops replaced the sharp-steepled, classic Suyo design. Narrow windows, white columns, wraparound balconies with wrought iron-railings lacing every floor. So many balconies.

Ironically, Old City boasted the most development, the splendid center of the mandala where the royal palace resided, the eight great stupas of the Thrice-Blessed temple in the shadow of the towering statue of the Awakened Lord. The ancient shrines to the devas had been demolished or moved to other districts, making way for new businesses.

Thankfully, the royal palace kept its outward identity. The sprawling compound was practically its own city, complete with a temple, residences, barracks, school, parks, pavilions, mausoleum… The interior to the grand throne room, however, had been updated.

Tan could hardly remember a time before the court looked the way it did. Perhaps when he was a child, playing with the other princelings and noble born children while their parents knelt on cushions in the long audience chamber. Rather than sitting cross-legged at the head of the room flanked by his council, the king had built this new audience chamber to imitate those he'd seen on his visits overseas. He adopted a jewel-covered gold throne with a straight-backed chair, courtiers gathered in loose groups in the surrounding galleries. Guards were stationed around the chamber, carrying gleaming, engraved rifles – gifts from Grisland, which replaced the army's old fashioned arquebuses years ago.

His uncle, King Sarvupun I, was only fifteen years Tan's senior. That wasn't odd in itself, as royal men kept a multitude of consorts and concubines in addition to their primary spouse. Tan's father had been thirty years older than Sarvupun. The late Crown-Prince Varunvirya III, destined to inherit the throne, had died from a horse-riding accident while Tan was still in his mother's womb.

At least, that's what the official documents reported.

Tan lingered behind a pillar near the entrance and watched the king hold audience to a silk-cloaked viceroy from the Qinseng Imperium. The throne was surrounded by the highest members of court, and several were now Grisi ambassadors, all his majesty's esteemed guests, looking out of place but at ease in their admittedly sharp woolen coats with decorative golden ropes and Grisland insignia, or the robes worn by their powerful trading company. A trio of musicians played a sedate tune nearby, and Tan spotted one courtesan he particularly admired on a stringed instrument. Like everyone else, she didn't notice his arrival. Tan was in no rush to be announced and had no desire to make conversation with anyone either.

"How gracious of you to finally return, Tanung."

Tan sighed inwardly as Priyut's imposing form appeared in the corner of his eye. His half-brother was the Field-Marshall of the Royal Army and carried a special resentment for Tan. Priyut was only a few months younger, and they'd always been competitive as children, which fueled their adult rivalry.

Tan's Wild Cobras were not officially part of the military and did not adhere to their strict decorum. It wasn't only the lack of decorum that Priyut resented. It was the culture of Tan's brigade itself, which was, in simple terms, representative of Suyoram's changing politics. When Tan presented the idea to the king, he'd advocated opening membership to those outside of Suyo nationality. Both he and his uncle had seen the merit in consulting different perspectives, knowledge, and expertise. Among his ranks were Kutsu isle privateers skilled in naval operations, Qinsengi cavalry unmatched in open field, mounted warfare, and Lo agents highly skilled in espionage and guerrilla tactics, just to name a few.

Despite hailing from different countries, even worshiping different gods, they had one unifying commonality, the most important: every Cobra was hand-picked, and unquestioningly loyal to Tanung. And by proxy, Tan's unquestioning loyalty to the crown and country of Suyoram. It also helped that they were paid incredibly well, which was yet another criticism from Priyut.

No better than a mercenary collection of barbarians, thugs and cut throats, his brother had once said. *A glorified hit-squad.* But the king was willing to give the project a chance and had been pleased with the results thus far.

"Rough seas," Tan said, without looking over. "You'd know how it was, if you ever stepped foot on a ship."

Priyut scoffed. "I did this morning in fact, at the request of the shipmaster. On the ship that *you* commissioned for your little quest. Could you enlighten me as to how your men trashed the galley and living quarters into such a state of disrepair? He told me it will take weeks to clean and repair, and has a mind to petition the king that it should come out of your personal salary."

Tan side-eyed him and shrugged. "I doubt the king will care, considering my results."

"You speak as if chasing criminals isn't beneath me," Priyut said. "I have far more important matters to attend to."

"Oh, I'm sure. Overseeing janitors is big boy's work."

Priyut only grunted in response, unwilling to take the bait. A servant approached the king from the side then, bowing with a wai before whispering into his ear. A moment later, the king raised his head, attention zeroed in on Tanung and Priyut at the far end of the hall. The king spoke to the servant, who scurried away, then excused himself from his current audience. He stood and left through the back entrance. A few of his advisers followed, including the Grisi officials.

"Is there a reason the Grisi are following his majesty?" Tan asked Priyut.

"Much has happened since you've been away," Priyut said, his voice lowering, taking on a hint of uncertainty. "You haven't heard about it, have you?"

"About what?" Tan hadn't. He'd gone straight to the royal apartments of his favorite concubine, and sometime afterward visited the royal physician Somatra, who prescribed him stronger medications. The old man scolded him to drink less and sleep more, unless he wanted his apasmara to progress from wind-type to fire-type.

A court attendant approached them, gave a respectful wai, and bid the men to follow.

"Oh, I won't spoil the surprise," Priyut chortled.

Chapter 10

River Runs Red

The wide and sparkling Duram river wasn't as muddy as the Jinburi this time of year, but several times as deep. A strong breeze flowed over the water, and Thura kept the sail up, moving the flat-bottomed river boat along at a fast clip. When the wind lagged, he rowed with an absentminded steadiness that hinted at years of experience. They passed fishing boats, barges, country houses, herds of water buffalo grazing in the shallows. Every so often, Ree leaned over the side of the boat and gazed into the water, sensing the presence of spirits lurking below.

Ree wasn't the only traveler that had negotiated passage upriver to the Lo city of Kohkiem. Two others shared the deck, each one claiming their own platform under the simple tented shelter from the sun. A big-bellied, middle-aged Suyo man introduced himself as Brother Martine. A follower of the Grisi religion, he let everyone know as often as possible that he was on a mission from the Grand Patriarch. His zealous glee rang from his aura like bells tolling, and he kept reading passages from a small prayer book out loud in Gris before translating into Rami, even though no one asked.

The poor young woman sitting on the platform behind him was too polite to tell him to shut up. She nodded along at his monologues, providing tense smiles that thinly masked her quiet fear. Ree overheard the woman say her name was Lawan, telling Thura that she was searching for a sister that her in-laws had left behind when they fled the country.

They'd only gawked at Ree until Thura explained the "noble, lost art of phi hunting," to which the missionary hummed and the woman nervously looked away. It made her feel like a relic.

After some time, Lawan seemed to get over her shyness and attempted to engage Ree in conversation, probably just to avoid being sucked into another sermon by Brother Martine.

"What kind of ghost are you after?" she asked with a polite smile.

"Oh, well... I'm not sure yet," Ree said, self-conscious of the lie.

"They didn't tell you?"

"It's not always useful." Ree found herself parroting things she'd heard other hunters say. "All phi are different, some defy definition."

Like me. Agira said with a semblance of glee.

Exactly. Oh, what would Elder Nokai think if he saw me now...

Daylight turned to sunset, casting the glistening river in deep orange and reds.

"Stopping for the night!" Thura called from where he stood at the back of the boat, hand on the rudder.

"About time," Brother Martine groaned. "This journey makes me appreciate Saint Sidora's pilgrimage to the promised lands tenfold. He walked for three years without rest before reaching the blessed lands to liberate the slaves from the chains of the Profane One."

"We've been on the river for a day," Ree muttered, and noticed Lawan bite back a giggle.

"It's not unlike my work, really. I keep telling myself that despite the dangers in unblessed lands, it is worth the pain to spread the holy word of the Grand Patriarch. My work in Kohkiem awaits! The foot of civilization, the first breath of salvation."

"You mean occupation," Lawan said. "The Grisi control the city."

"Is it dangerous?" Ree asked. Lawan shrugged and looked at Thura.

"Only if you're a rebel," Thura said. "They keep an eye on traffic, but we're cleared to operate."

"The father protects us, even the unsaved. He knows that all his children are precious, even if he cannot save them all..." the missionary went on, and Ree sighed, settling back to watch Thura steer the craft toward a small pier jutting out from an islet. There, an older ferryman walked out from under a small pavilion and tossed a rope to Thura. When they docked, Brother Martine scrambled to be the first one out.

"Come, rest. Eat." The elder ferryman nodded toward the pavilion, where a smoldering firepit glowed, skewers of silver pla-chon fish hung above. Ree had to admit it smelled amazing. The others walked straight for the outdoor latrines to relieve themselves, but she hesitated on the dock, staring northward.

Agira squirmed in her pouch. *Need out!*

All right, all right. Hang on. Ree walked to the pavilion, accepting one of the fish skewers and a small packet of rice. Then she walked toward the thick wooded area that covered the rest of the islet. Once she was safely out of sight, she opened her pouch and Agira scrambled out. He hopped onto the ground, then stretched out his wings, shuddering with the effort.

After a squat to relieve herself, Ree sat on a log, tearing a piece of fish off the skewer with her teeth. It was light and fresh, with crispy salted skin. A bit of spicy, garlicky nam phrik sauce would have made it a proper meal. The thought made her fantasize about her favorite dishes. She wished she'd been brave enough to have gone home before the trial, eat dinner with Ma, Pa, Kit, and Auntie Narissa.

Closing her eyes, she imagined them all around the table, talking and laughing, especially when her father was home. He always knew how to make everyone laugh. But as soon as food was put down, he stuffed his face like he'd never see another meal again. It drove her mother crazy, but Narissa would always laugh. Ree thought of the sai-ua sausage that Narissa often made, a family recipe, she said, and Ree actually groaned.

I know her. Agira interrupted her reverie. Ree snapped open her eyes to glare at him.

Stay out of my head, demon. She warned, disturbed that he was able to peer in at all.

You know Narissa. Agira fluttered up to a branch and gazed down. *I know her.*

Ree, again, thought he was full of shit, but humored him anyway. "Oh? And how do you know her?"

She has a garden in the swamp. Lots of pretty flowers. Herbs. Medicines for low magic.

That gave Ree pause. She'd been to Narissa's garden many times before, especially when she was younger, helping her gather ingredients for her tonics and tinctures. Agira hopped on a lower branch, even with her face.

Narissa spoke to me. She's the one that told me about Indrajit's amnesty.

"Maybe you saw her in her garden," Ree said. "But she wouldn't speak to you. And not about some kind of delusion."

She did! Because she took it! Earned her humanity! She was a krasue for many, many years, but changed her ways. Went against her curse and–

"Shut up," Ree snapped, cutting the phi off. "My auntie isn't a krasue, you crazy little thing. She lives next to a phi hunter, for fuck's sake. If she was a krasue my pa would have sniffed her out years ago." She had to laugh at the absurdity of the idea, imagining her auntie's head detaching from her body to float around at night, organs dangling beneath. "*I* would have noticed."

She received the amnesty. Agira said sullenly, huffing. *You still don't believe me? Wouldn't I have eaten you in your sleep by now?*

"I don't know. But I believe that you believe," Ree said, then took another bite of fish. "And that's well enough for me."

The rain continued intermittently into dawn, well into the first few hours of their journey up the Duram. The day had grown very dark under the clouds, with hardly a hint of sun. It cast a shadowy haze over the river, with great rolls of fog choking over the thickly wooded shore. Waves rocked the small vessel, enough to send Brother Martine hanging over the side of the boat to vomit. He laid flat across the platform after, his eyes tightly closed. Guiltily, Ree was glad that he wasn't well enough to keep evangelizing.

"This is terrible!" he moaned, clutching his big belly. "Can we pull over and rest for a bit?"

The ferryman only waved him off from his place at the rudder, his wide-brimmed rain hat shielding him from the growing downpour. Lawan's hands tightened and untightened around the hem of her blouse, staring at the churning water.

Ree wasn't alarmed as she'd grown up in a river city and knew the ebbs and flows that came and went with the seasons. Like most kids from Jinburi, she was a strong swimmer, if it came to that. But her anticipation mounted as they drew nearer to the choppy channel that Thura said would come right before the bridge.

The going was slow, and Ree catnapped on and off. Each time she woke up, the warm rain had grown heavier, the wind stronger, so much that Thura took down the sail and up the oars. He strained against the current, face set and serious.

Ree squinted into the distance and spotted a dark, rounded outline coming out of the fog. The Lotus Bridge loomed ahead, the gentle curve of its arch stretching high above, secured in place by six ancient stone columns rising out of the water like protective sentinels capped with carved blossoms. Even in the gloom, the statues gleamed, painted a bright gold lacquer that stood out from the dark stone.

Surrounding the Loram side of the bridge was Kohkiem, the gateway town. It expanded vertically over the sharply rising foothills, the glimmer of houses and street lanterns twinkling in the fading evening light. Chimney smoke rose from the cliffside where on top stood the scaffolding for what looked like a half-built fortress, two out of six watch towers with sharp gabled roofs jutting toward the overcast sky like knives.

"Devas, it's beautiful," Lawan murmured beside her.

Genuinely awestruck, Ree agreed, though for her the beauty resided in what this new land represented. The possibilities that lay open for her, in a place where she had no history. It felt like the entrance into a new world.

Just beyond, she made out the details of a ship with a black-and-blue flag. The same ship she'd seen when she first emerged from the guardian's passage. Its mere presence wasn't what alarmed her, but rather, something in the thickened air that set her blood running when she inhaled.

Fire. Ash. Gunpowder.

"Are you sure we should go this way?" Ree called back to Thura. He ignored her, head down, focused, and she repeated herself louder.

"It's fine! They don't bother us!" Thura yelled back.

She supposed he'd traveled this way many, many times and knew best, but couldn't shake her uneasiness. Especially as they grew closer, now under the shadow of the Lotus bridge. The columns were even more massive up close, completely dwarfing their small boat and exuding a sense of permanence that made her feel tiny and fragile. Vulnerable. Flotsam collected around the northern base of the bridge, trapped in tiny whirlpools by the current. The sound expanded here, and a foreign energy swelled, like a tide being sucked out to sea before a tsunami.

Something isn't right. Ree stood and walked past Lawan, stepped over Brother Martine to the front of the boat.

"Hey, sit down!" Thura called.

There was something coming through the fog. It looked like a bunch of small fishing boats spread out around the river. Three men on one, two on the other, some packed with more, all their attention locked on the Gris ship. But they weren't fishermen.

They wore all black and carried spears and bows. One of them did a double take when he noticed their ferryboat approaching. He held up his hand with wide eyes, palm outstretched as if he wanted them to stop.

"Slow down," Ree yelled. "There's someone here."

"My ass," Thura grunted. "Our tolls are squared up."

We should leave! Leave now! Agira squirmed in her pouch, so wildly that she clamped a hand over it.

The man who'd signaled them gestured to the other bank wildly, his mouth moving. He should have been inaudible from this distance, but Ree picked out the noise with her sensitive ears.

"They come any closer, kill them." In response, the man next to him turned to peer at her, then unslung and drew back a bow.

"Shit!" Ree gasped, "Thura, you need to turn–"

The explosion cut her short.

Ree ducked instinctively, then peered over the lip of the boat. A great cloud of smoke bloomed from the stern of the Gris gunship. She'd never seen anything like it, the entire back had exploded. Angry shouts of alarm echoed across the river. A commotion burst near the shore. Pops of gunfire, then more.

Screaming.

Meanwhile, some of the fishing boats on the far side were silently darting toward the ship, several oars churning in unison. She glanced back at the others, seeing both Lawan and Brother Martine wisely laying down flat against the deck. Thura had stopped rowing, standing up to gawk at the burning ship. But their momentum was still carrying them straight into the thick of the ambush.

"What the hell is going on?" Thura shouted, then began to walk toward the front of the boat. "What is happen–ckk!"

The shaft of an arrow sprouted from his throat. Everything seemed slow and quiet. Surreal. Ree couldn't move, she only watched in horror as Thura swayed on his feet, patted gently at the foreign object as if finding a mysterious new bruise in the morning. He made another terrible croaking noise, blood spurting from the pierced arteries in his neck in time with his rapid heartbeat, then fell heavily onto his side.

Lawan screamed, covering her face. Brother Martine, to his credit, bellycrawled over to Thura to help. But rather than pressing something to the wound, he grabbed the wooden pendant around his neck and pressed it to Thura's forehead, shouting something about a last confession. Ree stared in disbelief at the missionary until she realized they were about to pass the fishing boat. She panicked; at this distance there'd hardly be any cover. But the men on board were no longer paying attention to them. They started rowing.

Need to go! Now! Agira scrabbled at the pouch, then burst free. He didn't look back and zipped away, disappearing into the heavy, dark smoke.

That jarred Ree out of her stupor. She crouched low and scrambled back toward the rudder, feet slipping on the growing pool of blood collecting around Thura and Brother Martine.

"The Grand Patriarch yearns to welcome you into his kingdom, my son!" Martine babbled with manic fervor, face only inches from Thura's, who stared with uncomprehending terror. "Accept him into your soul, your one lasting light, repeat after me..." Blood gurgled out of the ferryman's lips, his betel-red teeth now stained darker, but he continued to clutch uselessly at his throat with shaking hands. Ree couldn't help him and steer the boat at the same time, so she shoved Martine violently away.

"He doesn't need God, he needs a medic!" she yelled, then kicked Lawan, who was still cowering. "Get up and help him!" The woman didn't move.

Ree cursed, springing to the oars and tried to pull them to a stop. She gritted her teeth and pulled, but hadn't expected them to be so heavy. She couldn't even lift them from the water. The Grisi ship drew closer, the sounds of fighting swelling to a roar. Then a volley of gunfire erupted and splashed across the water not ten yards away, one shot hitting a man on one of the fishing boats. A mist of blood blossomed, then his body fell into the water.

Her breath left her, and she dropped the oars, sitting back. Thura laid still. Martine deliriously sermoned about the doom that awaited his soul. Lawan had finally uncovered her eyes, but hadn't moved an inch more. Perhaps this was a futile effort. Attaching herself to the fate of these people would only pull her down into the same one. Perhaps Agira had the right idea.

Ree took a deep breath and stood. On the deck of the burning ship, smoking rifles gleamed in the firelight. She caught Lawan's eyes just as the soldiers fired again. A blast of splinters erupted the shelter of the ferry boat, and a bullet hit Ree in the back just as she dove into the river.

II

A Hunter Goes to Kohkiem

Years later, a phi hunter named Ex would come to the city of Kohkiem in search of his lost daughter. He would have described a nineteen-year-old girl of slight figure with hunter-red eyes and a shaved head, or if her hair had grown, silvery gray. She'd have the coat of the order, or if her arms were bare, a few sak yant tattoos. She was quiet, contemplative, observant, but fierce when provoked. If one got to know her, she could be playful, protective, sweet. He asked everyone, visited every public house, and temple, market stall, dockside vendor, brothel, and even the Trading Company headquarters and Grisi missionaries.

A heavy-set Suyo man wearing the robes of the Grand Patriarch lit up upon hearing her description. Yes, he'd seen her once, traveled with her briefly on the Duram. Remembered her as clearly as yesterday, a lovely girl. Hunter Ex's spirits soared upon hearing this, and he begged the brother for more information. With mournful eyes, the missionary took the hunter's hands in his and apologized.

I saw her die, he told him. *But I could not save her soul.*

Chapter 11

A Taste of War

Though the sharp sting of the bullet in her back seared with pain, Ree's rushing adrenaline dulled it, and she swam deep beneath the water for as long as she could hold her breath. She kicked until her legs ached and her lungs burned, knowing just above the surface men were dying.

Finally, she needed air and let herself rise for a quick breath. She treaded water as she watched the chaos unfold from a safer distance. Rebels scaled the side of the ship with grappling hooks, only to be cut down or shot in waves of gunfire. Some Grisi soldiers fell into the river, studded with arrows. In the mess, she couldn't spot the ferryboat. Still too close for comfort, Ree swam toward the shore but away from the chaos, while calling upon Shivah's Kiss to staunch her bleeding. The river, thick with ambient magic, curled up from the depths to embrace her.

Once she made it to land, the pain had dulled but still ached fiercely, and it hurt to move her arm. Like a splinter, a fragment of the bullet remained lodged in her back. It wasn't smart to heal around foreign objects but she wasn't sure how to remove it with magic. The spell would only reconstruct her torn flesh.

Ree ran through backyards and alleyways toward the outskirts, scrambling over fences, hiding from soldiers prowling the streets. Fighting through a thicket of bamboo, she stumbled onto a muddy dirt road and eventually found an abandoned stilt house half collapsed, yard grown over with weeds. She slithered underneath, then laid flat on her belly under the raised foundation and watched the street for any signs of soldiers, listening to the distant screams and gunshots.

Now that she could catch her breath, the visceral image of Thura's bloody throat resurfaced, how he gently patted at the arrow as the blood spurted out in waves, his wild eyes as the missionary screamed in his face. It sent a sick shiver through her belly. She hadn't seen anyone die since the KunNam trial, but that ritual was so calm, the gentle way Master Arei slit their throats. And they were ready for it, at least, as well as a trusting child could be. This was so sudden, so violent.

She wondered if the other two had the sense to abandon ship like she had. If they'd even survived the volley of gunfire that had struck her. She reached back to feel her aching wound, but couldn't reach it.

What have I gotten into? Tears stung her eyes as doubt crept into her resolve. She crushed them shut, laying her cheek against the muddy ground. She was a fool for thinking she would be safe out here. Maybe she should go home. There was a rustle to her right. It sounded like a rat, but Ree drew her hunting knife anyway.

It's war. Agira's head poked out through the grass, mouth open slightly as he panted. *So much death, so quickly. Are you hurt?*

Ree sighed in relief at his return and sheathed her knife. *I can't finish the spell, there's a bullet in my back. I can't reach.*

I can reach.

With what?

Agira hopped closer, the claws on his hand grew longer and needle-thin. He wiggled them as if in question. A phi performing surgery on a hunter? Well, this was certainly one for the records. Ree groaned, then nodded in defeat. At this point, there was nothing that could redeem her in the eyes of the guild.

He hopped onto her back with a wet thud, and she flinched in disgust. A sharp sting cascaded from her wound throughout her body, and she gritted her teeth. Warm blood dripped down her back as Agira's claws pushed into her flesh and peeled back muscle. Long seconds passed as he rooted around, pain mounting into an uncomfortable pulling sensation. She banged her fist against the ground to keep from screaming, and then he hopped off to land in front of her.

All done! Agira held a small, bloody ball of metal in his claws, then dropped it on the ground. A wave of exhaustion and relief swept over her, and she gazed at the phi, feeling particularly numb.

"This is insane. I should have killed you," she muttered darkly. "I should have killed you and gone home."

A life for a life.

Ree slowly crawled from under the house after completing the spell, and cast a longing look back to the city. It would have been wonderful to experience a new place, but the Gris had again ruined that. With a sigh, she walked into the shadows of the countryside.

A week passed since they'd left Kohkiem. A week of wandering though the heavily forested foothills of the Little Shas and heading steadily northwest. The spirits began to notice her. A family of winged foxes followed her for a time, and through the Everpresent projected their curiosity at her lack of pack, her lack of concern for the fair-skinned strangers in the woods. Phi hunters could communicate with spirits in mental images and emotions, but unlike the phi, they couldn't speak as humans would.

But maybe they could help her. She closed her eyes, trying to send an image of herself leaving the den, striding into a foggy haze in search of another pack... but faltered in imagining the Ashukari. She tried to imagine a temple, hidden away. It almost seemed like one of the foxes might have understood, but Agira returned from a fly about and sent them crashing away in fear.

Agira swore he knew the way, and she followed his lead, though the going was slow. He often scouted ahead for hours at a time, returning excitedly to claim he spotted something familiar. Sometimes they walked through the wilderness, but the Serene Way remained aloof, allowing a few paths before dancing just out of reach, as if the magic had faltered and withered away.

Or perhaps it sensed her unworthiness as a hunter and rejected her.

They walked along muddy, beaten paths through the countryside, leading past the remains of villages and scorched rice fields. She sifted through the wreckage for anything of use, and was rewarded by finding a long-rotted corpse clutching a decent bow.

The Gris were present as well. Sure to stay hidden, she spotted their flags flying over barricaded camps, overseers dressed in trading company clothes watching Lo laborers as they pulled down trees and mined the rich land. She couldn't tell if they were willfully cooperating or being forced, maybe a combination of both. In the woods, she avoided their patrols as they tromped through the area, searching for rebels.

Another week passed, and as she foraged for edible plants, fletched arrows, and hunted small game, she wondered if this would be similar to traveling her rounds as a phi hunter, despite the fact she made camp with what should be her quarry. There were other hungry ghosts around, and she sensed their presence, the formation of dark energy lingering like a baleful fog over destroyed villages. But there was no reason to hunt them, so like the Gris, she avoided them.

Other villages still stood, though the locals weren't too friendly. Some outright called her a demon and threatened her with violence if she didn't leave. The ones that did allow her entry were eager for the medicinal herbs she'd gathered in exchange for rice, and perhaps a roof to sleep under. The locals told versions of the same story – soldiers had come, declaring that Loram was now under the Protectorate of Grisland. The capital was under siege. Because of that, the soldiers had free reign to demand supplies, shelter, and took gruesome liberties with the women.

Anyone suspected of harboring members of the Black Water Army were executed, and any villages suspecting of aiding the rebels were destroyed. Crops were burned, and what the Gris called "clean" villages were established. Anyone thought to be helping the rebels were taken to these labor camps. They also told her that many went because there was guaranteed food, shelter, and medicine. In exchange for freedom of movement, speech, and religion, of course.

What a mess, Ree thought, passing yet another labor camp, this one set up around a rubber tree plantation. Now that she understood exactly what exchange was happening between the locals and the Protectorate, it made her sick with anger.

Whenever she had the chance, Ree asked people what they knew about the Ashukari. Most didn't know, as they were followers of the Awakened Lord. Others told her rumors she had heard before about other deva sects – that they were remote cultists that followed the "left-hand path" of the deva Kinesh-Kira. That they covered themselves in the ashes of the dead, ate corpses, drank themselves into a stupor, fornicated with spirits... while others said they were simple holy men that had shunned a material life in favor of a peaceful, divine existence.

Another week passed. At times, Ree felt like a creature of the forest herself. Sleeping when she was tired, eating when the opportunity arose, avoiding danger, finding shelter during the intermittent downpours of the rainy season...

One night, Ree rested at the edge of a lake where on the far side was the tallest mountain she'd seen thus far. The full moon soared hazily in the clear sky. It was beautiful, and possibly wouldn't rain, so she decided to make camp. Carving a few simple spears from a length of bamboo, she hunted the lazy catfish basking in the moonlight.

"Maybe I need to find the Guardian of the Kalashas," Ree said, lounging by her small fire as she turned her fish skewer over the flames with her foot. "I swear that fox spirit knew what I was talking about."

I know the way. Agira's wings wrapped around his body like a blanket, his wet eyes dancing with firelight. After a pained look from Ree, he hung his head. *I know! It's just... hard to remember. Exactly. But I remember the mountain.*

"That's just the first big one," Ree said, taking her fish from the fire and letting it cool. "The Kalashas go on all the way to Qinseng."

We're getting close, I know it.

"Somewhere in there is Iautau," she nodded toward the north, referring to the capital of Loram. "That grandmother in the last village told me the Ashukari hung out in the smashan, the crematorium grounds by the river Jenghee."

She said used to. Used to. Said most left when she was ten, and the rest when the Protectorate took the city!

"Maybe some went home."

No! They were shunned by the Sangha! They were shunned by the other Deva cults! There is no home for them. They never returned, I know it.

"Will you just admit it?" Ree opened her vial of nam phrik and sprinkled some on the catfish before she took a bite. When Agira only tilted his head in question she pointed at him with the fish. "It's been over forty years and at least one lifetime since you've been here. Things have changed, and maybe you have some idea, but you don't really know where to go. We've been on both sides of this lake, twice."

Maybe... maybe I'm getting confused. He huffed, shaking his wings in frustration. *It would be so much easier if you could fly!* Tears welled up in his eyes and she almost felt bad. Almost. *But I made you a promise, Isaree. And I will keep it.*

With that declaration, the phi spread his wings and took off into the night.

She watched impassively as he disappeared into the darkness. After finishing her meal, she laid back on her blanket to watch the stars. A fond memory surfaced. Camping in the woods with Ma and Pa, her mother pointing out different constellations, and her father playfully insisting they were other ones, Kit's laughter at their bickering. Ma had learned them in the royal courts when she lived in the palace, while Pa knew them from his mountain villages. Ree smiled, trying to remember which were which, and eventually shut her eyes.

Ree awoke with a start, sweaty and alarmed. Something was wrong. It was the middle of the night and her fire had died, but the land was lit bright by the full moon high in the sky, a perfect reflection across the still lake. Footsteps. Lots of them, far too close, approaching from the treeline.

There wasn't time to break up her campsite and there was nowhere to hide. She grabbed her bow and crouched, notching an arrow and taking aim toward the noises.

A half dozen men emerged from the trees, wearing all black, three carrying bows and swords, two with old, flint-lock arquebuses – obsolete against the Gris's rifles. The Black Water Army, it must be. Strangely, she hadn't encountered them the entire time she'd been in the woods. She hid from a few Gris patrols from time to time, but these rebels had covered their tracks well.

They must have seen her campsite and decided to investigate. Ree cursed herself for being careless and letting herself get caught out in the open. A few stepped on to the bank and the one leading the group finally saw her.

"Don't move!" Ree said, aiming at him. "I'm not afraid to shoot."

The men startled, reached for their bows and aimed their guns, but the one in front held up his hand. On second glance, *her* hand.

"I can tell," she said, a hint of amusement in her voice. The woman's hair was cropped short, but still slightly longer than Ree's. The only weapon she carried was a butcher's knife slung in her belt. She smiled with thick cheeks, making her face all the kindlier. Not at all what Ree expected a rebel to look like. Broad-shouldered and sturdy, the woman exuded a rock-solid, self-assured aura – chin lifted, unafraid and confident, even with an arrow pointed straight at her chest.

Ree said nothing, eyes darting to assess her odds. She could try and blind some of them, make a dash for it.

Where are you, Agira?! You were supposed to be watching!

No answer. Oh, right. He'd gone scouting ahead after she scolded him, with a head full of steam, eager to prove himself. She could have really used the shapeshifting phi's more fearsome form to scare them off right then.

"So, how about you put that bow down and we can talk," the woman said slowly. She spoke with the dialect typical of Lo, the same Rami language of Ree's, but with the distinct accent that softened the ends of their words.

"Nothing to talk about," Ree said. "How about you move along from *my* campsite and let me be."

"My boys are going to lower their weapons, okay?" The boys didn't look so sure. The woman nodded to them, her pleasant expression growing far more stern. They shifted, uneasy, then slowly complied.

Ree hesitated, but gambled on the belief that she could draw quicker than they could. With a slow breath, she eased back the string and lowered her bow, but kept it notched.

"Good, good. Look at us, making progress," the woman said. "My name is Minh–"

"What do you want?" Ree demanded.

Minh chuckled. "Guess I should have expected that. Phi hunters are lone wolves, aren't they?"

"Emphasis on the 'lone.'"

"Right. Well, the rumors were true anyway. We heard there was a Suyo phi hunter passing through, asking questions, and it wasn't easy to track you down." Minh waited for a response, but received none. "Why don't we sit, rekindle that fire? We have food to share. And some wine to drink. Would make for a more pleasant conversation."

Ree opened her mouth to say no, but... They had her cornered, had the numbers. If they wanted to hurt her, they would have tried to already. And she had to admit, she was curious about this mysterious rebel army she'd heard so much about.

Ree grunted and lowered her bow. "What kind of food?"

A link of home-cooked sai-ua sausage. Seasoned with ginger, lemongrass, and spices. Wrapped in lettuce leaves with a bit of sticky rice, the crispy pork skin cracked in Ree's mouth and flooded her senses with pure enjoyment. Along with that, neua sawan – heavenly beef – marinated, sun-dried, and deep fried jerky, Kit's absolute favorite. The men sat further back from the fire, murmuring quietly among themselves. Two of the bowmen moved back into the forest, keeping a perimeter, she supposed. Minh sat with Ree alone, holding a bottle of what smelled like rice wine to her lips and politely waiting for her to finish.

Ree wiped her mouth with the back of her arm, then nodded toward the knife on Minh's belt. "You some kind of butcher?"

"I was famous in the province," she said, taking pride in her food. Ree couldn't disagree, the sai-ua had been delicious. "But as you may have guessed, I've since changed careers."

"I've heard about the Black Water Army. So this is it? All six of you?"

"There's plenty more. It's best to split up, stay mobile. I'm one of the generals, so I'm authorized to speak for us all." Minh passed her the bottle. Ree took a small sip, enjoying the burn. She wasn't a huge drinker, but there were plenty of times she and the other novices had their fair share. Especially during the annual hunters' meets, where she never failed to prove herself as the biggest lightweight in the history of the guild.

"How's the war going?" Ree asked.

Minh's soft smile waned. "Not well, as you've probably seen and heard. Loram is at a tipping point. Khrapong is lost. The royal army hardly set foot here. They were ever only concerned with protecting the capital, and now that it's under siege, we're on our own. The king's already been deposed in favor of his cousin, a known Grisi puppet."

"Why not go help them? You have an army, right?"

"Not in the same sense," Minh said. "We're not trained in open-field combat. We're common folk. Farmers, fishermen, weavers. But we're the only hope for the people still here, left behind, struggling under the Grisi boot. We can fight, but in our own way."

"So I've seen," Ree said. "I was in Kohkiem." The arrow in Thura's throat. The bodies hanging in the market square. Citizens dragged out of their homes, maybe innocent, maybe not, but suffering all the same. She took another long sip, letting the liquor clear her mind of those awful memories. "That was your action?"

"Yep."

"That ship blew up like nothing I've ever seen," Ree said. "How'd you do that?"

"A brave martyr volunteered to infiltrate. He snuck into the grand magazine, you know, where they keep all the gunpowder? All it needs is one tiny spark and," Minh slapped her thigh, with a savage sneer that bordered on a grin. "Boom!"

"One ship went down, but the amount of rebel bodies…" Ree shook her head, repulsed by her violent glee. "It was a slaughter."

"Sometimes sacrifice is necessary," Minh said, with a toughness that reminded her of Master Seua. "That boat was transferring new officers and soldiers to the front. It wasn't in vain, it was symbolic. Even if the only outcome is to remind the oppressors that we're still here, we're still fighting, and we won't stop."

To Ree, it seemed like a terrible waste. She remembered something her mother once said to Kit before a tournament when he wanted to punch above his weight class. She wouldn't let him, not because he was underweight, but because he showed a shadow of doubt. "Only a fool takes on a fight he knows he can't win."

"Only a fool claims he *knows* he can win a fight," Minh said. "A wise man plans for all possibilities. Win, loss, retreat. It's part of a larger struggle. One that my people are fully committed to. If some of us must die, we go in with complete conviciton."

"All right." Ree didn't completely agree, but if the woman was a general, she supposed she knew better. "So... what does this have to do with me?"

"You're a phi hunter, and we want to hire you for your services."

Ree laughed, which shot the wine up her nose and sent her coughing. It was too ironic: having broken countless oaths, fleeing home in search of a guru somewhere in an active warzone, she still couldn't escape the guild. Minh's easy smile faded, eyebrows pinched in confusion. Even the others had glanced over at her outburst.

"You... are a hunter, right?"

"Yeah, sorry, it's just..." Ree cleared her throat. "Long story. Please, go on."

"Mmhmm." Minh frowned, but shrugged and sat back on her elbows. "Anyway. Six leagues north is an important Gris outpost, Fort Nestor. It's in the city of Muang-Hhleg, a mining town that supplies almost all of the ore to the entire country and beyond. After the Gris took it, they built massive fortifications. Only a few were able to escape, and the rest forced to work the mines. As close to slave labor as you can get."

Any humor lingering around Ree left as quickly as it came. She could only shake her head in disgust.

"This is one of those 'clean' towns, right?" Ree asked.

"One of the worst. Most of the clean towns are newly built, but this was once a great Lo city, the shining star of the Kalashas," Minh said. "But there's some hope. At first glance, it's a completely impenetrable fort. But the Gris don't know about the cave system that starts in the mountains, outside the walls, and leads right into the central park. It's a perfect location for us to start setting up a resistance there. Get spies in, and people out. And one day... take it back." Minh smiled then. "And that's where you come in."

"You want me to, what, smuggle people?"

"No, no," Minh said quickly. "There's a phi in the caves. One that's been there for years, long before the Gris came. No one who goes in ever comes out alive."

"What is it?" Ree asked, admittedly intrigued about the idea of going on a hunt. A real hunt. For a creature that might deserve it. "Taihong? Krasue? Samung? Kongkoi?"

"There's... conflicting stories. Some say it's a three-headed monster with a snake-like body. Others swear it's a vampiric ghost that paralyzes you with poison and sucks you dry, slowly." Minh leaned forward, her voice dropping. The men quieted down, eagerly listening in to the spooky story. "Most say it was once a beautiful, talented woman, whose exquisite woven silks were sought after throughout all of Loram. But she worked too much, ignoring the needs of her husband. After she discovered he was unfaithful, she was so enraged that she found each of his lovers and strangled them with a scarf she had worked tirelessly on, one that she planned to give to him for their anniversary. When she confronted her husband, he despaired, and claimed he would leave to become an ascetic, and join the Ashukari–"

"Wait!" Ree straightened. "The Ashukari?"

"Mmhmm. I think it's an extreme cult of some sort. Anyway, he fled to–"

"Where are they?"

Minh frowned, clearly annoyed by the interruption. "I have no idea, I'm just giving you the local legend. Far as I know, they aren't real." She raised an eyebrow. "Now... would you like me to finish?"

Ree sat back and waved her hand for Minh to go on.

"So where was I... ah, yes, the husband leaves to join these ascetics, but just as he reaches the steps of the temple..." Minh paused dramatically, leaning in, the flickering fire casting an eerie light over her blunt features.

After a tense pause, she slapped her hand. "She's there! Strangles him and leaves him in the dirt. Then goes to a cave and–" She made a choking noise, cocked her head to the side as if she were hanged. "It's become quite a legend in Khrapong, actually. Her name was Homdee, and they call her the Weaver, the Evil Below Hhleg."

Ree's nascent excitement extinguished. "It has a *name*?"

If this creature was named, with a *story*, it was a step beyond your average hungry ghost. It was a true demon – a hungry ghost that had leaned wholeheartedly into their violence, accepting the evil in their hearts and nurturing it. A true demon was, as her ma would put it, well above her weight class. Ree hadn't even hunted one phi. She miserably failed against Agira, in all his ten ounces of terror.

She cleared her throat, aware that Minh was staring at her with a skeptical look. "It's surprising, is all. Legends like that spread, and the guild should have heard about this… Homdee." She almost choked on the name. "Why hasn't a hunter come before?"

"The locals never wanted to get rid of her. See, her work was famous, the community celebrated her. They feared her, but they respected her. They took to leaving silks at the entrance to her cave to appease her, and if they're gone by sunrise, it's considered good fortune."

"Oh," Ree said. She'd heard that when hunters came across the symbol that marked a haunted area, offerings from laypeople were often found on the ground below, the same found on spirit houses – bowls of rice, or meat, coins, candles, wine – all intended to appease the phi.

"Anyway, that's what they say," Minh said in a light tone. "The point is we need to get through the passage, and there's no way to do it without going through her. We'll pay you, of course."

"Won't the locals be upset that we've killed their favorite phi?" Ree asked.

Minh cracked a smile. "They'll get over it. Her death will pale in comparison to the good you'll do for the people. The men, women, and children suffering in there, overworked and dying in the mines. Loram would owe you a great debt." The woman held out her hand. "What do you say, Hunter Ree?"

Chapter 12

For Duty and Dynasty

The king enjoyed the outdoors and usually preferred to take inner council meetings at a pavilion in the orchid nursery. The servant led them back through the extensively curated gardens and into an open-aired, steepled structure painted with gilded murals of the Awakened Lord's journey to enlightenment.

King Sarvupun sat at a Grisi-style, wrought-iron tea table alone. Unlike Tan and Priyut who'd both inherited athletic statures from their father, Sarvupun was slight of figure, with narrow shoulders that seemed to sag under the adornments of the new royal attire. He'd done away with the traditional robes of his predecessor's court, preferring that Suyoram's nobility adopt "modern fashions" befitting of a world power. Tan's flatterers told him he looked fetching in any style, but he disliked the stiff collars on these overcoats and wore them as little as possible, preferring looser fit Baghani fashions. At the same time, he recognized his uncle's intentions. An image presented, even illusory, often commanded more influence than words.

The Grisi weren't the only vastly powerful foreign nation eying the region. The Dujarde were one of their competitors, along with the Hasshut, both nations with their fingers entangled with Suyoram's neighbors. Yet they circled like sharks who'd caught the scent of vast profit to be gained by trade and influence over what they called in their languages, "the Spicelands."

Thankfully, the Dujarde were busy with their conquest of the Kutsu Isles, and the Hasshut remained in a costly stalemate with the Qinseng Empire. King Sarvupun had only the Gris to worry about appeasing, and Suyoram served as a buffer between those competitive colonial interests. For now, at least.

"Commander Tanung and General Priyut, my favorite nephews," King Sarvupun smiled without mirth as the two men pressed their palms together and bowed deeply. "How blessed I am to receive you. Please, sit."

"The honor is mine, my king," Tan said. "Apologies for my tardiness."

"No apologies are necessary," the king said dismissively, to Tan's great relief. And to his even greater satisfaction, Priyut's smile wilted, eyes turning venomous. Sarvupun may have been bothered by Tan's late arrival back to court, but he'd never show it. "You have accomplished your mission. I'm sending the pirate lord in fetters to Jardenia, a gift to our Dujarde friends."

"I'm honored to fulfill my duty, sir," Tan said.

The king desired some small talk, which his nephews provided, and after they had tea, the proper discussion began, focused on the situation in Loram.

The Gris had conquered Loram years ago. Thanks to the garrison established at Jinburi and constant support in their supply lines, the Gris had burned and slashed through the country, brutally quelling any resistance. They established the Loramese-Protectorate of Grisland, deposed the royals, and installed a distant relative who was loyal to his masters. It was not Grisland's first puppet state, as they had historically succeeded in similar conquests throughout the world. And thanks to King Sarvupun's acquiescence and cooperation, Suyoram would benefit from Grisland's protection against the other colonial powers.

Nationalists had quite a bit to say about Suyoram turning their back on Loram, a neighbor so close that they spoke the same Rami language. Ethnically, most Suyoram citizens could claim some trace of Lo in their blood, especially in the northwestern region. The queen herself was from Loram, and though she remained publicly united with her husband, she was livid and had not returned from their vacation palace for almost two seasons.

And then there was the Bay of Echoes crisis. A Grisi frigate failed to heed the Suyo portmasters warning and sailed into restricted waters of the bay, resulting in the confused Capital forts firing across their bow and damaging the ship. Grisi officials took exception and demanded millions in reparations. The king was forced to raise taxes and allow even more unrestricted access throughout the country to appease them. It was blackmail, but the other choice would have been war.

Tan understood the wisdom in these diplomatic maneuverings. Yet he was a true, pure-bred Suyo prince, lauded by many as a national hero, and secretly believed that if he'd inherited the throne as the dynasty intended, he'd have died before letting Suyoram become a Grisi pet.

But as Priyut had alluded to...

"The Gris have requested military assistance in the Protectorate, and I have decided to send the Wild Cobras in lieu of the army. This will be a clandestine operation," the king said. "It's tantamount that we appear uninvolved on a public front. The army cannot be seen in the north."

"What's our objective?" Tan asked.

"I have not the details, they've been quite secretive," the king said, and Tan would wager he didn't want to know. "I trust you're aware that it's a condition for their continued friendship." His face darkened. "Have whatever must be done quickly and quietly. Tanung, your contact is Sir Burrows of the Trading Company, he'll be at Sapphrachorn in a few days. He'll have the rest of the details."

Tan kept his face neutral, but he was seething. They didn't take up arms for the Protectorate, which was part of the agreement. Something must have gone terribly wrong to resort to such measures. Priyut eyed him with a knowing look and a smug smile, almost daring him to speak his mind. But to do so would be treasonous. To refuse would be unthinkable.

"Understood. Consider it done, sir."

Chapter 13

The Evil Below

I should have said no, Ree thought darkly as she set up her makeshift altar at the mouth of the cave. True to Minh's story, silks of every color and pattern hung on the craggy sepia rocks and trees surrounding the entrance. A few looked relatively new, but most were bleached by weather and threadbare, hardly more than scraps. It looked like the remnants of a festival after being hit by a monsoon.

Minh and her crew sat a good distance away, watching intently but giving her space to concentrate. They'd taken the better part of a day gathering her requested items, which she laid out on a white cloth. Two black candles, a tin of black paint, a mortar and pestle, and a small firepot.

In theory, she knew how the Hunter's Trance worked. Ingredients were gathered from the territory in question, combined into a concoction that once ingested would attune her with the land. Two of earth and one of flesh, all of magical properties. The rebels tried their best, which amounted to some sap from a tree, the brains of a squirrel unfortunate enough to have been in the area, and an oyster mushroom. None with magical properties.

It only underlined the rest of the things she lacked. No armored hunter's coat. No mask. No chainblade – the best they could do was a grappling hook and a sturdy spear.

The key ingredient to descending into the Trance, and possibly the only one that really mattered, lay within the Dreamless poison. There were no voiceless words to learn as needed with spells, no chants to memorize as needed for rituals. Only the immunity to the deathly toxin that hunters nurtured for years and years. Passing the trial granted no physical powers, aside from the vague idea of "mental fortitude and soundness of mind." The Dreamless itself would provide her the extra focus, a new awareness beyond the Everpresent, and staunch the terrible fear sure to freeze any sane person in place when coming face to face with a true demon.

Ree lit the candles and mashed the ingredients together, mostly to procrastinate. They were likely useless.

There's still time to back out. Agira said from her pouch. *Tell them no!*

I think there'll be clues to finding the Ashukari. There will be something. I can feel it.

It's too dangerous. I know the way! I just need… this is bad. Bad, bad, bad. We can go.

I can't. Ree placed the needle coated with Dreamless onto the cloth, between the candles. She pressed her hands in a wai and bowed her head, appearing, at least to her audience, deep in prayer. *I want to, but I just can't.*

You just said you should have said no!

Listen. You've seen what the Gris have done. Finally, I have a chance to help.

But you would kill? Agira shuddered, shifted. She could picture him curling his wings around himself. *They said Homdee is a revered ghost–*

'Revered' is a bit of a stretch. This thing, it's not like you, Agira. She kills without remorse. She hasn't accepted Indrajit's amnesty.

Agira grew quiet and still then. So still that Ree peered down at her belt, wondering if he'd snuck out and slithered off in a huff. The flap twitched, and slowly moved aside, revealing one big green eye staring up at her.

You… you believe me?!

Ree couldn't help but chuckle. She dipped her finger into the paint and smeared one long stripe across her eyes.

Besides all that honorable shit… if I do this, then I'll become the fifth living slayer, and usurp my father's title as the youngest hunter ever to kill a true demon. Might even have to go home, just to tell him. She was only half joking. The look on his face would be priceless. Proud, of course, but still hiding a secret, childishly resentful pout behind his grin. It hurt her heart a little to think about, and she shook it away, as she did when memories of her family surfaced. It was a fantasy. She'd never get another badge.

And of course, she needed to live through this.

Ree turned to gaze back at the group, meeting their grim faces, framed by the rapidly setting sun. "I don't know how long this will take. And I don't know if there will be any sign if it kills me."

"Kills you?" Minh crossed her arms, the other rebels exchanging looks. "You said only a fool takes on a fight he can't win."

"Never said I wasn't one," Ree smirked.

Minh glanced at her men, then walked closer to speak to Ree in a low voice. "Listen... you're really our only hope here." She glanced over Ree's altar before staring her straight in the face. "Are you certain you can do this?"

Ree kept her gaze even, but considered what might happen if she failed. The rebels would have no easy way inside and little hope of rescuing their people from the mines. And there was a real possibility she would fail. This was no ordinary phi, after all. This was a true demon.

"If I'm not back by sunrise, send a messenger to the Phi Hunter's Guild in Jinburi. Ask for Master Arei, and tell her everything you told me–"

"That will take weeks!" Minh said, crossing her arms. "People are dying in there. There's no time."

"It might be too late for some of them. But the guild will send a demon slayer to help you," Ree said. Minh still didn't look convinced. "I promise they'll help you if I fail. You have my word."

Minh nodded grimly, then stepped back. "Thank you, Hunter Ree. We'll wait here for you."

Ree turned back to her altar. It was time to enter the Trance, and she picked up the Dreamless, pressing the needle to her vein. But she faltered there, hands shaking. She'd done this before. Never this high of a dose, but countless times nonetheless. What if she was wrong? What if passing the Kang-Fye trial really did protect the hunter from a descent into inhumanity, one that would warp her mind into something she could not return from? What if it killed her? Or what if she couldn't handle it, her wits rendered completely useless?

She exhaled sharply and pulled the needle away.

What's wrong?

Nothing. Ree said, then slipped it back into its case and stood. She brushed aside everything on the altar, then picked up the cloth and tied it around her neck.

Wait! You said you needed that! For the – the – the Trance!

I don't need the Trance. With a rush of adrenaline, Ree steeled herself and then walked into the yawning darkness before she could change her mind. *I have a better idea.*

* * *

The Weaver's cave wound into complete darkness, heavy with the cold stench of damp stone and decaying moss. Ree opened her awareness fully into the Everpresent, listening with razor-sharp focus to the almost imperceptible echo of her every step. She paused every so often to reorient herself and maneuver around craggy rocks, and rotten piles of devas knew what. This would be near impossible for any other phi hunter without the Trance, Ree thought, finally allowing herself a swell of pride for her inborn abilities.

But aside from her hypersensitive connection, she had one solid advantage that no other hunter had, in the entire history of the guild.

There's something on the walls, Agira said, crouched like a pet parrot on her shoulder.

I sense them. Dark energy, not sentient. Their presence draped the passage like unholy garlands. *What do they look like?*

Vines. No… veins. Agira shifted uneasily.

Webs? Ree's stomach lurched. *This thing better not be a fucking spider.*

More… twisted. They breathe.

That vanquished any hope the creature in these caves was something mundane – a bear, a tiger, a madman. She forced herself to breathe steadily, willfully ignoring the animal part of her brain that wanted to run screaming into the sunlight.

Her fist tightened around her hunting knife, hilt even with her chin, blade facing out. The bow had been her first choice, but the passage was too narrow, too many blind spots, at least in this section. Ready in her mind were the spells that could determine the thin line between life and death.

This would be so much easier in the trance. Ree mused. *Not only visibility, but…* She trailed off, listening. Was that a skitter? Something ahead stunk like rotted durian.

Your heart is so loud.

Not helpful.

Another careful turn, and then the air changed. Cooler, thinner, freer. The passage gradually widened as she went.

I think it ends, said Agira. *Straight ahead. It ends!*

Ends? Ree sensed something larger. *You sure?*

Ummm, looks different. Let me check. He hopped off her shoulder and took flight, his bat wings light and feathery. She almost told him to wait, but realized he had nothing to fear from another phi. Despite their murderous, violent ways, they were not known to harm one another.

A hissing screech rung out, accompanied by the rapid flap of wings, deafening in the oppressive silence.

Isaree! Help!

All the blood rushed to her head as Ree bounded forward, searching for a target. Nothing. Nothing moved accept Agira, fluttering and twisting in mid-air. The only light in this sea of darkness came from his eyes as they blinked rapidly. She sensed no demon magic, nor a low magic ward, nothing that might have paralyzed him. But the dark energy had heightened and spread, feeling more oppressive by the second.

Stop moving. Ree reached out to grab him and a sticky film twisted around her hand. She bit back a cry of surprise and pushed through it, grabbing Agira's little body. *Quiet!*

He obeyed despite his panic. She pulled hard, but the invisible substance stretched with her, stubbornly clinging on like a cocoon of rubber.

The Smoking Palm of Anewan came to mind, but with Agira firmly in hand it would dissolve him into mush. Ree cursed and sheathed her knife, bringing the spell into her fingers. They burned bright as coals and illuminated the entire space, which was much larger than she originally thought.

A black mass of web, dark as shadow, entangled Agira to her left hand. The strands looked less like a spider's and more like braids, twisted together in an orderly way not typically found in nature.

Woven.

It's… it's…! Agira stammered, then flinched as Ree waved her palm around him, carving away the trap. The dark strands sizzled and popped, melting away where she touched like sugar candy on the tongue. She pulled him free and stepped back. The detached strands on Agira and her hand continued to burn away like paper, quick into ash. He shuddered, clinging to her wrist.

With the spell still burning in her palm and illuminating the cavern, Ree turned about, staring at the space. It was less a natural cavern and more of a formed, circular chamber with a domed ceiling, the craftmanship hinting at human hands if not for the unsettling details. All throughout the chiseled stone, large round holes sat evenly spaced from one another, coated with the strands of sticky black webbing like the one that trapped Agira. The edges of the holes were jagged and uneven, as if a horde of rats hurriedly chewed their way through. Some of the holes were uncovered, but wherever they led remained shrouded in complete darkness.

That, however, was not the most concerning detail.

"Oh," Ree breathed softly, her throat gone completely dry. She turned in a slow circle, gawking upward.

Bodies, everywhere. All encased in strings and strings of webbing, pasted against the domed ceiling and the walls, hanging suspended above her like the grisliest garland in existence. The threads matched those covering the holes, except that they were a pale, muted bone gray, rigid as if calcified. Woven between the threads were fabrics of all colors, no doubt the missing tributes taken from the cave's entrance.

The bodies higher up were little more than skeletons, those closer to the ground in various stages of decomposition. The sheer number of them was horrifying enough, but the worst part about it was how they were displayed.

How they'd been *posed*.

Some were frozen with arms outstretched, heads tilted back as if worshiping the sun. Some were on their knees, hands pressed forever together in prayer. She spotted iconic postures seen of the Awakened Lord – cross-legged lotus position, or standing with one hand outstretched, thumb and first finger clasped.

Others were arranged in depictions of everyday life – a circle of friends holding hands as they danced. A mother nursing a child. A man, running. And a whole row of the intimate ranging from romantic to obscene – a couple embraced, lips pressed together, others copulating in various positions.

It was the most sinister, incomprehensible thing Ree had ever seen. And the scale of it. At least a hundred visible from the light in her fingers. Into the shadows, maybe thousands.

Dumbstruck, Ree crept to the lowest display, hanging in the center of the chamber. It was an upside-down woman with a floral-patterned cloth fastened around her chest, one leg stretched toward the ceiling, the other folded against her knee. Hands pressed to her heart, fingers spread, her head was almost at the same level as Ree's.

Somewhere far away, Agira's words fluttered faintly as Ree peered closer at the corpse, where the dimmest glow ebbed ever so infinitesimally in her chest, like a dying firefly.

A heartbeat?

Ree sucked in a hoarse breath. The webbing obscured most of the girl's pallid flesh but for her neck and eyelids. She didn't move, didn't seem to be breathing, still as death. Yet…

"She's alive," Ree gasped and jerked back, horrified. The sudden movement caused the thin thread holding the girl to rotate ever so slowly. And then when it turned, Ree spotted two large, circular punctures at the top of her spine.

Agira abruptly landed on her shoulder and Ree startled again, flinching away from him.

Do you hear?! His cry was an ice-cold shriek. She'd been completely focused on her sight. But she listened now.

Skittering, sharp dry stabs on hard rock. Fast and faint, growing louder by the second. It echoed from every hole around the unholy chamber, bouncing against the walls and bodies, impossible to trace.

Where is it?! She needed to maintain the Anewan spell to illuminate the chamber, but she also needed two hands for her bow. Panicked, Ree drew her knife with her off-hand, spinning as she searched around for the demon.

I don't know! Agira's claws dug into her shoulder as he tried to hold on.

The skittering grew heavier, louder, vibrating the chamber. The bodies began to sway, their shadows casting echoes of the demon's work across the walls. She focused on the holes uncovered by black cocoon, eyes rapidly darting between the open ones. Something above clicked, clattered. Snapped.

Ree looked up and saw a large shape falling straight toward her head.

She dove out of the way just in time, hitting the ground hard, sending Agira tumbling away. A tangle of bones and calcified web smashed onto the floor with a crash, pieces of the corpse scattering across the ground. She leaped to a crouch, ready to move again. Nothing else fell. Nothing else stirred.

But now a decaying, hellish presence lurked somewhere above. Hidden in the mad tangle of dancing corpses, a true demon watched. Waiting to strike.

And then a grating voice resonated through the Everpresent. Somehow shrill and deep simultaneously, as if it spoke with two vocal chords on opposite ends of the register.

"See your future, hunter."

Panic threatened to overwhelm her, and she scanned wildly for the demon. Rapid clicking, then another snap.

Ree moved a moment too late. A heavy body crashed into her side, knocking her down. She tried to kick the creature, swinging her knife wildly at it. The blade cracked against bone and stuck there. Screaming, she yanked it free and stabbed again, but something stung her hand. Ree pressed her palm into its chest, burning with the spell, but there was no reaction. She then realized it was only another skeleton, now with her knife lodged firmly between the ribs of its sternum. But it wasn't just any skeleton.

An ivory-skinned, black-eyed viper stared back at her, snarling jaws frozen in a wide-open grin, tongue and fangs extended. A khon mask remained strapped to the human skull. A mask carved by a master of his trade while deep in the Trance, custom made for a very specific, and very dead hunter. She recognized the remnants of an armored coat, with a steel badge of the guild symbol still hanging on by a rivet.

With a pained cry, she kicked away the body and scrambled backward. It was only then that she realized she'd kicked her knife away with it. The sharp corner of the corpse's guild badge had sliced her hand wide open, and warm blood dripped down her wrist. On her other hand, her grip on the spell faltered and the room darkened. It sputtered like a candle in the wind as she strained to hold it steady. But it was just enough to see the large, inhuman form brushing aside corpses as it floated down from above.

This was madness. How had she harbored the delusion of slaying a true demon? She was a novice who hadn't even killed one phi. And to slay it without the Trance?! What idiocy. What an obscene display of hubris. Of unearned pride.

The true demon Homdee, the Weaver of Muang-Hhleg, the Evil Below, hung suspended, now unfolded all its legs above her.

Ree couldn't breathe, couldn't move, couldn't think. It was complete madness. To even face it at all, while crippled by the weakness that besieged all humans.

Emotion. Pure, unfettered terror. If Ree had been able to feel anything but the cold certainty of imminent death, it might have been relief. Relief that the Evil Below was not a spider.

It was worse.

Chapter 14

The Threads We Weave

It was not a spider, but vaguely arachnid, with a long and snake-like body, flesh glistening corpse-gray, segmented like a centipede. Rather than eight legs, it had maybe… thirty-eight or more, too many. Each leg, as long as Ree was tall, ended in a blood red, knife-like tip, every movement cascading down its joints in a wave. Two smaller legs, both bent backwards at the end of its abdomen, danced along a thread of black web oozing from its spinneret.

Out of the centipede body dangled the torso and head of an emaciated female form, its skin the same bloodless color. Without an ounce of fat, the humanoid body was all sharp planes and chiseled bone. A long mop of black hair hung in ratty, knotted tangles around its neck. Two skinny arms extended from its bony shoulders and folded in on itself again, like a mantis. Rather than hands, it had what looked like fangs. Or needles.

It's face was very human, with full, black lips and a regular looking nose. The horror lay in where it diverged. Where two eyes should be were instead a great many of them, marble-black, slitted ovals that fanned out over her forehead, each one blinking out of sync from the others.

"It's been so long since I tasted a hunter." With a duet voice, it spoke in both the Everpresent and the Blinds. A wide grin spread across its twisted lips, revealing broken stubs of yellow teeth. A viscous flow of saliva oozed out from black gums. Then it lowered its head and shot toward her like a descending comet.

Ree involuntarily shut her eyes, but managed to sputter, "Demon, wait!" Her voice little more than a desperate squeak.

To her surprise, it did. When Ree dared to look up, the Weaver had paused, curiously sneering at the tiny creature hovering in front of its face.

Please, elder! Agira raised his arms. *You must listen! We're not here to–*

"Betrayer!" The Weaver batted the little phi carelessly out of her way. He toppled to the ground and laid still. The demon snarled and swung toward Ree with even more speed.

But seeing Agira put himself in the way gave Ree exactly what she needed. A jolt of courage. A shock of protective anger. And most important of all, a split second. On her feet, she flung her arm sideways with the same, instinctual desperation that she called upon when protecting Agira from Esha's blade. It manifested with a blinding flash that seared across the demon's multiple eyes, along with a spray of burning, coal-hot blood.

The Weaver screeched in pain. Ree hurried backward before it landed. It hit the ground clumsily in a cascade of legs, wobbling, hissing, blinking, shaking its head while it rubbed frantically at its face where the skin sizzled and burned. Ree gasped when she realized she hurt it, she actually hurt a true demon!

The Weaver's neck twitched and dropped its arms, facing Ree with only half its eyes open, and growled with unfathomable hatred. She braced to move and calculated its range as it skittered toward her, raising its needle-pointed claw arms.

"I'm not a hunter!" Ree yelled in both the Blinds and Everpresent. It swung both its arms in a downward stab, and she danced out of reach, darting between its other legs. The Weaver's needle arms smashed holes into the ground with a loud crack.

"Liar! I know what you are!" the Weaver twisted to find her, first segments turning before the rest of its body followed. Slower on the ground, arms limited range, still deadly as hell, Ree noted. She kept her distance, kept moving.

"I want to talk." Probably something no phi hunter had ever said to a phi. Then again, she hadn't lied. She might look like one and fight like one, but she wasn't a hunter anymore.

"I will string you up and feast on you for years!" It darted toward her, but the instinct earned by hard years of training took over. Ree sprung forward and stutter-stepped when the Weaver stabbed again. It smashed stone at the tip of her toes and she slipped between its arms, sliding underneath its body. The underbelly of the demon flashed before her eyes, and she drew her thin carving knife, stabbing upward with both hands between one of the segments. A shower of cold, white blood splattered onto her face.

The Weaver screeched and recoiled, legs thrashing at the pest underneath it.

Ree narrowly dodged the blade-like legs, one slicing across her ribs, another grazing her calf, and realized that this was the worst place she could be. She slipped through an opening and ran. But the Weaver anticipated that and struck out with several of its legs. Ree felt like the bug then, as she flew through the air and thudded into the wall. She staggered, a rush of blood and pain cascading down the side of her head, but by some miracle managed to stay on her feet. Panting, she leaned against the wall and pulled the coiled grappling hook from her belt.

"Why do you persist with this..." The Weaver quivered, now regarding Ree with a semblance of caution. Its face twitched in rage, and it pointed with one of its arms. *"Useless talk!"*

Ree unfurled the grappling hook, snatching the rope into a spin, the claw whirling above her head. The Weaver waited this time, head down and glowering, its body tensed and coiled, arms ready to kill.

This had to be perfect. She ran forward and pulled the Blind Eagle's Eye over herself, her whole body reflecting the cavern around them. The Weaver faltered, head swiveling in confusion as it searched for its now camouflaged assailant. Ree threw the hook, and it whipped around the Weaver's torso and upper arms once, twice, thrice. The hook swirled back around and Ree jumped to catch the claw end.

"How dare you!" the demon jerked around, but couldn't find her. This spell wouldn't last for long, not at the rate she was going. Without breaking her momentum, Ree leapt onto its back, holding both ends of the rope as if the creature were some kind of demonic chariot, securing its killing arms against its body.

"How 'bout we take a short break," Ree panted, straining to control its angry struggling. *"Listen to what I have to say, and then if you think it's bullshit, we can go back to killing one another."*

The Weaver stomped its legs as it bucked and shook, Ree hanging on with the last of her strength and balance. As blood flowed from her wounds, she knew this was her last effort.

"Please. Listen to me," Ree pleaded, desperate. *"I know who you are, Homdee."*

Her grasp slipped on the rope and the spell. She toppled off, hitting the ground on her side. The breath shot from her lungs. The demon shook the rope free and sliced it to ribbons. Ree tried to push herself up but her spent arms gave out and she fell back to her side. She gasped for breath, unable to speak in the Blinds.

I know you were once in love. Ree tried, desperately, to convey her sympathy. *And that you chased your betrayer to the steps of the Ashukari, the same steps I seek. But I have something to offer you in exchange. Something that will bring an end to your suffering.*

"Suffering?!" The Weaver swiveled to face her, a frothing snarl on its lips. And then it laughed – a tittering, scraping noise that burst from its throat. *"You are mistaken. I delight in my work. The only suffering you'll find here is your own, hunter."*

Helplessly, Ree stared as the Weaver approached. The clicking of its legs on the ground like the gears of a guillotine being raised as the demon loomed before her.

I walk in the gray, but I'm not a hunter anymore. Ree forced herself to sit, and then pulled the altar cloth from her neck, now soiled with the blood dripping from her face. She held it with both hands toward the Weaver, staring into its eyes, then placed it on the ground before it. *Would a hunter offer a tribute to a phi?*

It stopped, staring curiously at the cloth, then back to Ree.

I came to speak with you soul to soul, Homdee. I came to forge another path that frees us both.

Slowly, it leaned closer, as if studying her. And then it spoke.

"Then make it quick, hunter."

This was her chance.

"Agira!" Ree called. The Weaver's working eyes narrowed. *"Agira!"*

I'm alive… I'm alive. Agira moaned, flopping miserably on the ground, holding his wing.

"Tell… this one about Indrajit."

R – really?!

"Yes! Right now!"

Two bright green eyes lit up from a dark corner. Agira scurried over to the Weaver, staring up in earnest. He began to talk, almost too rapidly for Ree to follow, as if the two phi were speaking in another dialect, something that her own connection to the Everpresent couldn't quite translate. But she caught glimpses, a dark celestial – an asura – thirty years of no blood, a promise of returning to humanity as it was known before. With every word, the Weaver seemed to waver, its body sinking slowly toward the ground.

Well? What do you think?

It was silent, then the Weaver threw its head back, gazing toward its countless victims.

"You and I," it said to Agira, in a tone that sounded surprisingly gentle. *"We are not alike, little one."*

We are! You're just… bigger. Older. Um. Hungrier.

"No. You… and you, hunter." It said the title with a grimace. *"I will show you."* And it started to hum. Ree's jaw dropped as the demon's sorrowful melody swirled around, duet vocals echoing throughout the cavern in the Blinds, while painting a picture in the Everpresent through sense, and emotion, and smell, and…

Homdee's hands blur, raw and calloused from endless nights at the loom. Surrounded by rows upon rows of melted candle stubs she works, rhythmic and relentless as the incessant locusts outside. As the stacks of order sheets pile up, she works. Amidst the discarded piles of fabric that dare have one stitch out of place, she works.

She pours her soul into the thread, conveying with color and pattern the beautiful rhythms of life. The joy of a first kiss. The serenity of a setting sun over the mountains. The transcendent rapture of morning prayer. The bittersweet thrill of a secret tryst, destined to end.

It would be diminishing to call herself an artist. Homdee is a living goddess of creation. And to be carelessly betrayed by the mortal man she has pledged, no, chosen *to receive the blessing of her presence?! It is worse than betrayal, it is blasphemy. And as she tightens the divinely crafted garment tight around his lovers' necks, his neck, her neck… skin blushing red to purple to blue and finally black. To oblivion.*

No, there will be no rest. The hell she lived will be the hell where she continues her work.

And her artistry will be made of death.

"I am just as committed in death as I am in life to my work," the demon said as her song faded. Ree clutched her bleeding ribs, shaking with the aftermath of Homdee's overwhelming emotions. The Weaver's suffering was a terrible, endless void, yet from that dark place it rediscovered a twisted beauty in its creation. The demon's lips quivered as tears flooded out of the eyes it had left. *"Attempt to slay me if you must, hunter. I will have no mercy upon you."*

Ree wiped the blood from her eyes, then slowly arose. There would be no amnesty from the devas, no redemption for this wretched creature. By the guild's judgment, the Weaver deserved to die for the terrible things it had done in its current state of existence. But Ree was bothered by the fact that it saw no other choice. By divine punishment, it was compelled to sin, to pay for a crime of terrible passion.

What would be the end to it?

She knew what her father would do. The same as any rational hunter would do. Strike it down without a word, without question. But they would have been in the Trance, where one became little more than a killing machine. They would never have heard the Weaver's song and shared its sorrow, in life and in death.

What would Elder Nokai have to say to it all? Would he have pitied the creature? What would her mother say?

Ree looked at the skeletal remains of the ancient phi hunter scattered across the ground. The hard truth was, she couldn't slay the Weaver, even if she really wanted to. She'd put up enough of a fight to calm it down and make it listen, but the fact remained that she didn't have the means, or the strength of a true demon slayer.

But she still had another card to play.

"If you kill me, more will come. Real hunters, masters of the trade. Far better than me. I made sure of that." Ree watched its twisted, miserable face as she spoke in the Blinds, as if this phi were any other negotiating party. It was listening. "You want to continue your work, right? Or would you rather die?"

"The work must continue," it said, voice choking.

"I can make that happen," Ree said, ignoring Agira's hiss of alarm. She held up a hand to him. "I didn't come here for a badge. I came to secure safe passage to the city for my… friends." She glanced up at the corpses. "How long have you been here? Doing this?"

A long moment passed. The Weaver's shoulders sagged, arms dropping. Then it said, *"Many years."*

"How long can one of these bodies sustain you?"

"Two moons… Three, if savored slowly." It grew thoughtful then. *"Why?"*

The gears in her head spinning, Ree considered another insane idea. An idea that couldn't possibly work. But she'd already seen more than a few things that had defied all possibilities. What was another?

The edge of the sun had just broken through the foggy hills, casting a pale orange blanket across the land. Some of the rebels dozed under the trees to the peaceful coos of morning doves, accompanied by the soft, rhythmic scrape of metal. Minh sat on a log with a defeated slump to her shoulders, bleary eyes unfocused as she mindlessly sharpened her butcher's knife.

Ree studied the rebel leader from the shadows for a moment, exhausted and aching, wondering how far she was truly willing to go. When she finally stepped into the dim morning sun, Minh noticed her and froze. Her eyes widened and she dropped her whetstone.

She must have been a sight. Though she'd healed her open wounds, dried blood coated one side of her face and neck, the other from the gash on her ribs. In the foggy clearing, her eyes burned an intense bright red after pulling so much magic from the Everpresent.

"You… did it?!" Minh sounded astonished, in a way that hinted that she'd anticipated failure. She tucked her butcher's knife into her belt, then her eyes darted to Ree's shoulder, where Agira perched, eyes closed, holding his broken wing. "What is that? A bat?"

"A friend," Ree said as she walked closer. Her eyes darted between Minh and her men, some of whom were now whispering and waking up the others. This could go very badly. "He's a phi I've been traveling with. A peaceful one. And he helped me with this."

Minh didn't seem to comprehend. Her mouth opened, but no words escaped.

Ree took advantage of her silence. "You have a safe passage to the city."

With a breathless sigh of relief, Minh pressed her hands into a wai, head tilted to the sky. "Oh, thank the Awakened Lord. I almost thought you weren't coming back. We thought it killed you."

"Almost did," Ree admitted. During the long walk back through the passage, she'd contemplated what to say. But now that moment was here, and the words escaped her.

"Get to the point."

At the Weaver's eerie, demonic voice, everyone froze. Minh's eyes widened in fear as she glimpsed the woman's corpse-pale face lurking in the darkness, its many eyes shining intensely in the shadows. Minh's face went just as pale.

"The Weaver has agreed to let you come and go through its caves as you please," Ree said, "…on one condition."

Minh took a step back. "A deal?! You made a deal?"

"Every three months, on the full moon, you will bring it a living person to… do with as it pleases." Ree tried to sound as stoic as possible. The sheer absurdity of the situation made her want to laugh, even as she inwardly shuddered, memories of the Weaver's victims still fresh in her mind. "There's no other way to put it. This tribute, whoever it is, will die a slow, horrifying death. The Weaver dug a new passage that connects to Muang-Hhleg, so you can avoid disturbing its lair. I've marked the way. So long as you leave the tribute–"

"You were supposed to kill it!" a man exclaimed, his hand hovering on the trigger to his arquebus. Ree had been watching Minh's reaction so closely she hadn't realized some of the rebels were cowering in fear, whimpering, while others had aimed their weapons at her. "Minh! This is… wrong!"

Ree tried to ignore them, intent on making Minh see the wisdom in this solution. "As long as you keep your end of the bargain, the passage is yours."

Minh blinked rapidly, eyes darting from the Weaver, to Ree, to Agira and back again. "Hunters are supposed to kill phi, not bargain with them." Her words were little more than a whisper. "What *are* you, Isaree?"

"She walks in the gray, but is not a hunter." The Weaver's voice set some of the men whimpering anew. *"The gray walker speaks true. Satisfy my need, and I shall grant yours."*

The guild taught that phi always lied to get what they wanted, but she'd looked into the soul of this damned ghost. She believed it would honor the agreement. The rebel leader held a hand to her mouth as the implication dawned on her. A human sacrifice to appease a demon… in exchange for a means to save her people. She stared at the Weaver's face with a mixture of horror and awe.

"I can't believe it's come to this," Minh said.

"You said it yourself," Ree said. "Sometimes sacrifices have to be made."

"I did say that," Minh mumbled, shaking her head. Then she raised her arm to call off her men. Slowly, they lowered their weapons. "All right, then. Every three months. We have a deal."

"All right." Ree glanced back at the Weaver. Its lip twitched, and then it extended an arm, Ree's blood-stained altar cloth pinned to the tip. After Ree took it, the Weaver slid back into its cave, silent but for the clicking of its feet echoing from the darkness.

Ree glanced over the new markings, thin threads of black silk that wove her path forward from where she stood, through the mountains. A map to the steps of the Ashukari temple.

Chapter 15

The Long Road Ahead

The Long Road united the provinces of Suyoram from north to south and east to west. Signposts marked the well-used pathways every fifty miles, crested with the symbol of the king as well as nearby points of interest. On some junctions, usually where smaller country roads split off, roadside markets and eateries sprouted alongside traveler inns. It wasn't too far from the Capital to Sapphrachorn, a riverside town, where Tanung would meet with his Gris contacts before presumably venturing to Loram.

He rode ahead with Simo and two others: a sharpshooter named Yelu, one of the only female Wild Cobras and the best shot in the brigade. The fourth member, Ukrit, was a want-to-be sorcerer. Tan had yet to see any actual spells, but the man was unmatched with the polearm and an accomplished yuthahathi.

They traveled quickly and quietly, pausing to rest at night in roadside inns without drawing attention. Eventually, they came upon a sleepy country road that brushed along rice paddy fields, with sun-soaked farmers pulling working buffalo whose black ears twitched to scatter flies. Sapphrachorn was too large to be a village, too small to be a town, and stretched out long and skinny like a lazy cat on the curved banks of the Namleng river. Simple stilt houses sat low in the water this time of year, the banks of tributaries flooding with rich, earthy sediment. Displaced ethnic minorities from this tribe or another squatted next to open-air pagodas, staring listlessly at the four travelers and their hot-blooded horses.

They arrived at the docks, the most developed part of town. The outpost for the Grisi trading company sat on prime real estate, and Tan couldn't help but wonder how many families had been encouraged to leave their ancestral homes to make room.

"Trading company, huh?" Yelu said, lashing their horses to the post. "Seems a tad clandestine, don't you think?"

"It was the king's prerogative to travel incognito," Tan said with a shrug. Everyone versed in politics knew that as far as the government of Grisland went, the Trading Company had more money and power than their Grand Minister. Might as well be two heads to the same ass. Strangely enough, their commercial success did not reflect in the decor of their headquarters. In an iron-gated yard, a squat, one-story building that looked more like a house sat, albeit in the Gris style with large windows and round columns.

One Gris guard swung in a hammock on the porch, cap pulled over his eyes. The other sat on the steps in only his underwear, sweating profusely in the humidity, while smoking a kageleaf rollup. Two rifles were propped against the wall. He glanced over when Tan and his squad approached.

"State your business," he drawled in passing Rami, smoke ebbing from his nostrils.

"I'm here to see Burrows," Tan responded, then shifted his shroud to reveal a small pin on his lapel – the black-and-gold head of a hissing cobra, two swords crossed behind. "He's expecting me."

The hammock guard didn't even look over. "Aaaaaand who the fuck are you?"

The underwear guard must have gotten the memo and hissed at his comrade in Grisi. "Relax, it's the bastard prince with the mercenary company."

The hammock guard lifted his cap to peek over. "What about *that*?" His eyes roved over Yelu. Simo stepped protectively in front of her and flashed his teeth in not quite a smile.

"Shut up, I'll handle this," the smoking one said, smiling politely at Tan and nodding his head in an attempt at respect. He spoke to him in Rami. "Sir Burrows said to expect you at some point. They closed up shop for today. I'll bring you over."

The man stood, stretched, and nodded for them to follow out of the gate and down the street.

"Bastard prince, eh?" Simo muttered under his breath to Tan as they followed the guard. "Do they not know who your father was?"

Tan only sighed, as the guard led them through the busiest part of town, which wasn't saying much, then stopped in front of a building that Tan recognized in paintings, songs, novels... The guard smirked and held his arms out in a flamboyant presentation, bowing. "Enjoy."

Yelu groaned and said what they all were thinking. "Could these foreigners be any more cliché?"

Chapter 16

The Shining Ones

The Weaver's craftsmanship could not be denied. The embroidered map she'd given Ree conveyed the winding path through the rugged, remote terrain of the deep Kalashas. According to the map, the Ashukari temple would be halfway up the Nohn peak – a mountain with dips in the ridgeline that resembled a sleeping woman.

Landmarks kept her on track throughout the heavily-forested mountains – a canyon that curled around a rust-red lake, an immense, black pine six armspans around that had been cracked in half by lightning centuries prior, yet still stood.

Weeks later, she found the final landmark, a trickling waterfall surrounded by the vine-covered ruins of a small shrine. The water level had lowered considerably, another sign of the changing season. She washed off in the cool pond, contemplating her starved muscles, a toll from her sparse diet. Afterward, she ran her fingers over the roughened, beige sandstone, brushing away some of the weeds to inspect the imagery. Similar to carvings found in temples to the devas, she made out the shapes of naked, dancing yoginis surrounding a three-headed, six-armed figure. Human forms in prostrating positions surrounded the main figures, although on closer inspection, there was something different about them…

"These are Venara!" Ree excitedly pointed to the monkey tails attached to the rear ends of the figures. One of the yogini's facial features had somehow escaped erosion, and two fangs jutted up from her enigmatic smile. Agira flitted over and landed on Ree's shoulder.

The Monkey Kingdom people lived here?

"Centuries ago. All over the mountains." Ree followed the scattered stones until she came to a well-trodden footpath. The hissing waterfall faded into the background as she walked through the airy woods. Up ahead, she spotted two wooden pedestals on either side of a wide stone staircase that cut steeply upward. The stones were the same rusty sandstone as the shrine ruins, but the pedestals looked new. Covered in melted white wax from prayer candles and sprinkled with ashes, the pedestals were adorned with garlands of withered flowers and what looked like finger bones.

"Do you remember this place?" Ree asked Agira as she stared upward, anxious, yet excited. It was an intimidating climb. The top of the staircase wasn't visible, seeming to fade into the trees.

No, I… I never came here.

"Well," Ree said, eying Agira. "You've kept up your end of the bargain. Sort of." He didn't move, only stared at the bones on the pedestal. She cleared her throat. "That means you're free to go."

He turned to gawk at her. *You want me to go?*

She didn't, not at all. His company had been a constant during these last few months, and the thought of his absence depressed her. He felt like her only friend in the world. But could she really walk into a sacred place with a phi?

"You've fulfilled your promise, and I'm forever grateful to you. I don't know what will happen next, but," she sighed, looking away, "I think it's something I need to do alone."

Oh. Agira hung his head, wringing his arms. It just about broke her heart. *I… I understand.*

"I do think you'll be safer here. Much safer than you would be in Jinburi, that's for sure," Ree said, then patted him on the head. "Our paths will cross again, I know it."

It was really nice. To be with someone for a while. I've been alone for so long, trapped in this form. You don't make many friends like this. Agira flew off her shoulder, landing on the first step of the staircase. He sniffled, wiping at his eyes.

"How long until you break your curse?" Ree asked.

Two more years. Two more years and I get my humanity back.

"When you do, come find me," Ree said with a smile.

Agira straightened up at her words and nodded curtly. With that, he took to the air and called back through the trees. *Farewell, Isaree. I hope you find what you're looking for.*

Ree lost count of the steps somewhere after a hundred. Her hamstrings burned as she soldiered on, panting in the thin air. She stopped for a moment to deeply take in the Everpresent, reaching out with her senses to detect what might lie ahead. The forest lit up with the presence of spirits and phi, more than she'd detected anywhere else. It hinted at the sacredness surrounding this area. She focused on scent, then felt a prick of alarm when the dark odor of death soured her senses like squirming maggots.

A glance below was a mistake – the height was dizzying and one misplaced step would send her tumbling down the mountain. Sweat dripped from her brow as she doggedly continued her steady trek, and as she grew closer very human sounds cut through the constant din of nature that had been her reality throughout the mountains. A deep, resonant hum united many voices, punctuated with an ethereal jingle of bells.

Excited, she doubled her efforts, finally spotting an archway. And more excitingly behind it sat the overgrown ruins of what must have been an ancient Venara temple, along with the pale figures of what must be the Ashukari. Muscles burning, Ree cleared the final step and collapsed to her knees, panting for breath.

The jingling bells continued. The ohm continued. No one acknowledged her presence.

The Ashukari practically glowed white in the early evening darkness – their skin paler than even the Gris and Hasshut, their hair as white as her own. All were dressed in little more than loincloths, necklaces, anklets, and bangles, some women with breasts uncovered. They wore their hair in long, matted locks, or shaved to the skin, some with braids. Some sat alone, deep in meditation, others huddled together, talking amongst themselves.

The largest group gathered in the center of the courtyard. Bells chimed where a few of them shook their wrists, chanting, some swaying in a muted dance. Inside the circle, a man stood above two prone bodies lying side by side, each on their own two-foot-tall bed of timber, both deathly still.

Once she caught her breath, she cautiously walked toward them, eyes wide in astonishment. As she grew closer, she realized many people had naturally darker skin tones and hair, hidden by chalky remnants smeared over their skin. Red paint streaked over their foreheads, some with black over their eyes and cheek hollows, imitating skulls. All with red painted over their throats, smeared down their chests.

Ree zeroed in on the scent of death. It emanated from one of the bodies, an elderly woman. Undoubtedly dead, her eyes remained open, unseeing. The other man *looked* dead, unmoving, unbreathing, but Ree sensed life in him still. The man standing over them caught her attention. He chanted softly, eyes closed.

Like many of the others, his hair was a jumble of matted locks that hung past his shoulders, his beard likewise long. Several ropes of prayer beads covered his limbs, a garland around his neck was threaded with flowers and finger bones. His skin looked smooth, and it was impossible to tell how old he was, whether his beard and hair were gray from age or ashes.

Agira had been telling the truth from the start. This man seemed to *shine* in the Everpresent. Just as she had the thought, his eyes snapped open. He stared straight at her, his irises a brilliant red, and spoke to Ree not with the subvocal whisper of the phi hunters, but completely voiceless, as a phi would.

A walker approaches. Welcome.

Chapter 17

In Search of the Goddess

Stunned, Ree stammered, but her voice was lost in the rising chants of the Ashukari. They started to weave into one another, varied and discordant, some breaking out into song.

You're in the Everpresent. Ree held the red-eyed man's gaze, even as the Ashukari surrounding him began to dance. *But you aren't a hunter? I don't understand.*

You will. We will speak after the ceremony. The man leaned down to inspect the dead woman.

"You came for Kinesh-Kira?" someone asked in heavily accented Rami, and touched her elbow.

Ree turned to the young woman who'd come to stand next to her. She seemed close to her own age, but like the rest it was hard to tell for all the ashes and face paint. Underneath the red stripes over her face, her eyes were small and monolidded. Her braids were threaded with red ribbons, muddy brown at the roots. A Qinsengi or Gaochurian, most likely.

"I'm here to find the guru," Ree said.

"Ah, Vasitra, guru. Yes," she nodded enthusiastically, pointing to the guru, who was inspecting something on the dead woman's arm. Then the girl pointed to herself. "Tian."

Ree pointed to herself in the same manner. "Isaree."

"Isaree." Tian nodded, then tapped her temple and pointed to Ree's eyes. "You walk with Kinesh-Kira?"

"You mean... in the Everpresent?"

"Umm..." Tian frowned thoughtfully, then gestured to a man standing in the circle. "Havan!"

The man peered over at his name, his eyes a startling green, and smiled when he saw Tian. His smile faded when he looked over Ree, curious, but not unfriendly. He glanced at the guru who had started to chant, then walked over to them, brushing a lock from his eyes. His hair was shorter, only a half foot long, and shaved on the sides of his head – blond roots. Another foreigner, but a different species – invasive. Tian spoke rapidly in her native tongue, which Ree confirmed was a Qinsengi dialect.

"She asks if you have returned," Havan said in fluent Rami. She couldn't tell if he was Gris, or Hasshut, maybe Dujarde. Briefly, she thought of Brother Martine, as Suyo as one could get, clutching his Grisi lord's pendant against Thura's face. She supposed religion tended to find people regardless of where they'd been born, but still, seeing one of them up close put her on edge. "She wants to know if you're the avatar of Kinesh-Kira." He smiled, revealing a silver-capped canine. She noticed the tattoos on his chest, showing through the ashes. "I don't think she's ever seen a phi hunter before."

"I'm not a hunter," Ree snapped, glaring at him. "But I'm not an avatar of Kinesh-Kira either."

His smile wavered as he translated to Tian, who only clapped her hands and murmured something. "As far as you know," Havan said, amused. "You've come seeking the guidance of Vasitra, then?"

"Not sure yet," Ree admitted, glancing back to the guru. He waved his hand over the dead woman's face, then moved to the other unconscious person. "What's this ceremony about?"

"The final passage for an Ashukari," Havan said. "Vasitra escorts us into the arms of the devas to walk with Kinesh-Kira and see the ultimate reality. Most don't return. They choose to become one with the goddess." Indeed, as Vasitra inspected a blackened saisin string looped around the man's arms, two Ashukari were holding torches to the dead woman's bed. The dry tulsi and sandalwood crackled as they ignited, radiating sweet, earthy fumes..

"But some do?" Ree asked.

"Some do," Havan said. Then Tian tapped Ree's arm and pointed to the guru.

Vasitra leaned near the unconscious man's ear. Ree tried to pick out his whisper amidst the raucous noise around them, but it slipped from her perception. Then the guru stepped back and the man sat up. With a look of astonishment on his face, his eyes snapped open, glowing a bright red. He gasped, crying out as if breathing for the first time.

"Praise Kinesh-Kira!" someone called out and shook their bells. The man stared around at them and Ree caught a wave of striking, cold panic and overwhelming joy radiating off him. Breathing heavily, he spotted Vasitra, who only gazed back impassively.

No, no, not this place again, the man's voiceless words were a confused mix of vague visions and the emptiness of grief. *Oh, dear master, I can't bear this. Not after knowing her embrace.*

I understand. Vasitra grabbed his hand, clutching it tightly. *Return to her.* Ree felt like an intruder then, peering in through the windows to their private exchange. Yet she couldn't look away.

"She calls me!" the man exclaimed, prompting a quiet over the crowd. He yanked his hand away from Vasitra and laid back down. The red glow faded from his eyes, going cold and blank, and with it, his soul.

Ree glanced at Tian, but she was overcome with emotion, a reverent smile on her face. Other Ashukari seemed just as moved as she was. Others, like Havan, only observed in quiet awe. Tian walked up to touch the man's feet before sinking to her knees, clutching her chest. Havan helped her rise, and the torchbearers came to set fire to the dead man's bed.

The Ashukari gathered close around the pyre. Some continued to pray, to sing, light kageleaf pipes, pass around bottles wafting with the distinct scent of moonshine.

Ree quietly observed the scene, somewhat baffled. When she'd imagined the deva cult, the stereotypical ascetic came to mind – jungle-dwelling men who'd shunned all their earthly possessions, sustaining themselves solely on a few grains of rice and fervent devotion. Instead, this group seemed varied in age and nationalities, though the white-gray ash rendered them all the same color.

As the flames blazed over the two bodies, a flash memory of the lifeless novices floating in the drowning pool left her throat dry. This atmosphere was practically festive, while the hunters' trial had been stoic and somber. Whatever had happened to the man during this deep ritual wasn't the void she'd experienced.

Come, walker. She caught the gleam of Vasitra's eyes flickering beyond the fire, where he stood at the entrance to the temple. Ree rushed past the thrush of bodies in the courtyard and approached the soaring, open archways of the structure that seemed to grow out of the mountain itself. She paused to take it all in – the ancient, pale sandstone walls covered with bas-relief panels of the Celestial Court according to Venara legends, the structure succumbing to nature as moss and flowering vines spider-webbed over the worn surfaces. A beehive-shaped dome carved to resemble lotus buds stretched high above, seeming to melt into the rock. Had there been a landslide long ago that buried half the temple? Or had the Venara carved this place into the mountain?

Inside, one central chamber dominated the space, surrounded by four galleries where Ashukari slept amongst the disorganized jumble of mats and hammocks, strewn about with whatever meager belongings they possessed. The flooring was cool and dry, broken in places where grass and flowers poked through. Pockets of red-orange sunlight streamed down from far above into the central chamber, where a tall pedestal stood in the center, displaying a gleaming, onyx-skinned idol.

Ree passed through the first gallery, ignoring the curious stares of a few Ashukari sitting against the pillars, smoking kageleaf joints. Beyond them, she saw another couple engaged in a vigorous, intimate embrace. No… two couples. All together. Flushing, she turned away and walked into the center chamber.

Where most Sangha temples sprawled horizontally, this one soared vertically, far higher than it appeared from the outside. Eight pillars circled the chamber at even intervals, each with crisscrossing arches connecting them throughout the upper levels of the temple. They looked like orderly trees, and she tried to imagine the stone branches filled with the Venara throughout, though had a hard time getting past what she'd seen depicted in texts, which were large, furry humans with monkey tails and heads.

The simple stone pedestal in the center stood two stories high, and on top Ree saw the hint of an obsidian carved idol of Kinesh-Kira in all her eight-armed, four-headed glory.

Up here. Vasitra sat on an archway next to the idol.

Ree forewent the handholds added by humans, which Vasitra must have used, and jumped to catch the first branch to haul herself up, and continued climbing. Now on the same level, Ree stared at the idol and marveled at the workmanship. Her white, pupilless eyes and porcelain fangs gleamed from the glass-like black rock, smile split with a long, red tongue hanging down past her bare breasts and to her belly. Details were painted: a garland of severed Venara-heads hanging around her neck, and another of arms, legs and tails, around her waist. In each of her hands she carried a different weapon.

It must have been as ancient as the temple, for her likeness departed from the versions Ree had seen in texts. This idol's face was, as the other carvings around the temple, that of a Venara.

Let us speak alongside the goddess.

"I'd rather speak in the Blinds," Ree said, and she glanced along his skin for signs of sak yant tattoos, specifically guild badges.

You don't trust me.

"No."

"Very well," he said, his voice rather sweet, a singer's tenor to it, with an accent she couldn't quite place. "You have come a long way."

"I heard the guru of the Ashukari was like me," Ree said. "I was born able to see into the Everpresent. I had to learn how to unsee. Was it the same for you?"

"The 'Everpresent', you call it?"

"That's what the phi hunters call it."

"Ah. We call it becoming unshrouded. A connection to the goddess."

"And were you... 'unshrouded' at birth?"

"No." Vasitra said simply, and with that one word, all of Ree's spirits sank. "After one walks with the goddess, and if they choose to return, she gifts them with her love to carry forth. I came into the Ashukari very young, a few years your junior, I presume. I had little time left, you see, I was dying. A wasting sickness, the Gray Pox. My guru said I was ready only days after I arrived, though I hardly grasped anything yet! But he said I was ready, and I suspect I was on the verge of death. And so my ascension came young, and when I emerged, the disease had vanished." He tilted his head, seeming to read her disappointment. "I'm sorry that this is not the answer you were hoping for."

"It wasn't," Ree sighed, more disappointed than she wanted to admit. However, it did confirm her belief that the phi hunters methods weren't the only way to reach the Everpresent, or at least, some version of it. The guru's aura was far different than any other hunter she had seen, including Elder Nokai. "I am curious though. The man out there who came back, only to die again. That's what everyone here is aspiring to?"

"No, there is more than one way to find the arms of the goddess. The Unshrouding is an extreme ritual, attempted by ones already close to death. You are not yet familiar with our beliefs?"

"I know you worship her," Ree nodded toward the fierce idol. "And I've heard rumors of corpse eating, violence, orgies in the cemetery. That's all I know."

The guru chuckled at that, as if he'd heard the rumors many times. Ree could relate, in a way. "We Ashukari believe that we are all already dead. The illusion of time only shrouds us from the ultimate reality. We believe that Kinesh-Kira is in us and in everything, and that nothing we do, no matter how deplorable, shall soil our souls in the eyes of her endless love."

Ree nodded downward. "I'm pretty sure I saw a few members having an orgy in the west gallery."

"Some Ashukari seek to create fear in their hearts, to test themselves in an effort to break through this shroud, you see. Pain and pleasure of the flesh can be harnessed to inspire spiritual growth. These bodies are temporary houses for our souls – our mouths, our hearts, our members..." He wiggled his fingers for effect. "These are only tools to grasp at meaning from the meaninglessness of samsara."

She sat back and let that wash over her. Sangha monks were not only celibate, but vegetarian, and abstained from vice – no doubt they would not approve of the Ashukari lifestyle. Ree wasn't sure what to think about it. "So you lived after the ritual, but no one else has? I haven't seen anyone else here in the Gray."

"Some continue for a time, like myself," Vasitra said. "But it is never long before they return. As for me, I have made a promise to the goddess to remain here, to shepherd more of her devotees before her when they're ready. Until the time arrives... I await." A white grin split his mouth, shiny teeth in his thick beard. "You are welcome to stay with us here as long as you desire. Perhaps we may find an answer to your question."

"That's... generous," Ree said doubtfully. "But I'm not interested in joining a cult, no offense."

If the guru was offended, he didn't let on. "There are no requirements needed to remain here. Only a willingness to be peaceful, protect our peace, and respect the peace of others."

"I can do that."

Vasitra closed his eyes. "Moments ago, when the Unshrouded rose briefly, he brought with him the whispers of the goddess." With a faint smile on his lips, he said, "and she wants to meet you."

Chapter 18

To Give Darkness Power

After Tan assured the madam that it would be business first, but they'd be back later for pleasure, she led them through the impressive show floor of the famed Golden Brothel of Sapphrachorn, past the gaudy, beaded curtained stalls, behind which all manner of groaning, grunting, and slapping skin drifted out unmuffled.

In the back, she knocked on the door to a private suite, then opened it to a medium-sized room. A circle of cushions surrounded a table, with a beverage cart nearby and a bed in the corner and thank the devas no one using it. Two men sat on the cushions, drinks in hand, and two blank-faced young women sat next to each, boredly waving them with large fabric fans. The first man was Tan's main contact, Sir Burrows, a late middle-aged Gris with a jowled face and ring of gray hair, dressed in the robes of the trading company. Upon seeing Tan enter, the man stood and made a wai.

"Prince Tanung!" he spoke in well-accented Suyo with an aristocratic air. "I'm Sir Lenon Burrows. It's an honor to finally meet you, sir. I used to exchange letters with your father, Crown-Prince Varunvirya. May the Patriarch rest his soul. He was a man with real vision! So tragic to have lost him so young."

I wouldn't know, Tan thought, but only smiled and returned the wai. "Pleased to meet you." Upon hearing his title, the two working girls perked up, smiling conspiratorially at one another.

"Please, everyone, help yourself to any refreshments. There are some rolls, tea and wine... Yes, allow me to introduce my associate. This is Major-General Elleman, he oversees all our military operations here in Suyoram and Loram."

The burly, red-haired man gave a tight-lipped smile that resembled a frown, mostly hidden in his neatly-trimmed beard.

He had the kind of face that looked like it had taken more than a few beatings. He leaned back from the table, brushing crumbs off his blue fatigues, then held out a hand. Tan shook it, sure to return the squeeze firmly enough.

"Hello," the man said woodenly, then furrowed his brows. "We have met?"

"We have," Tan nodded. "Once or twice at court."

"Huh," he said, and perhaps stopped himself short of saying something ignorant.

"This is Simo, my second-in-command. Yelu and Ukrit are my unit leaders for this operation." The men shook hands, very awkwardly with Yelu. The four took seats around the table, Tan eying the two working girls. This display was more fitting for a classless bandit leader, not the two most senior officials for a world power. Unprofessional. "Are these your secretaries?" One of the women smirked at him, uncrossed and recrossed her legs.

"Ah, yes, these lovely creatures are so helpful... ah. Oh." Burrows blushed deeply when realizing Tan's smile was one of quiet disapproval. "Thank you, ladies, I think we've been warmed up and cooled down enough."

One paused to give Elleman a loveless peck on the cheek, which he did not react to. The women shot the Wild Cobras significant glances as they strolled out.

"How was your journey north? I very much enjoy the Long Road. It's quite advanced, and I admit I hadn't expected such infrastructure when I first came here, what... twenty years ago?" Sir Burrows babbled as he poured four glasses of wine, while Elleman reached down to open a case and started to lay stack after stack of documents on the table before them.

"My uncle sends his regards, but he did not tell me exactly what our mission entailed." Tan watched their expressions closely. Burrows deflated slightly, as if he were nervous to get to the point. The general, however, did not react, but in a way that seemed he wasn't comprehending the conversation. In perfect Grisi, Tan said, "If it's easier for all involved, we can speak in your language. Why are we here, Sir Burrows?"

"Thank the fuckin' Grand Patriarch," sighed General Elleman, prompting a chuckle from Simo.

"Very well, straight to the point then?" Burrows frowned, then leaned back on his cushion. "I suppose you're tired from the journey. Well, simply put... we have a problem. Specifically, in the Khrapong province, starting with the city of Iron Town.

It's always had issues since the Protectorate was established. Sabotage, crime, escaped... ah, illegal emigration. But these last few months, we've been unfortunate in that–"

"*Issues,* Burrows? Issues?!" General Elleman interrupted, brows furrowed. "I told you it'd be a mistake to put that ambassador's idiot son in charge." He turned his glare to Tan, as if offended by the very sight of him. "This *isn't* normal. *These* people–"

"The Loram Liberation Front!" Burrows quickly interjected. "Let's be specific."

"Right." Elleman glanced at Burrows, clearly irritated. "They've been the most persistent throughout our campaign, but negligible. An irritation. Small gains, nothing we couldn't quell, especially after Operation Clean Hands. Until now."

"Surely you've heard of the outreach program?" Sir Burrows asked Tan. "Building strategic, clean villages with incentives to encourage cooperation with the Protectorate?"

Tan nodded. It had been going on for some time in Loramese-Protectorate, to a certain degree of success. Certainly, more successful than the slash and burn tactics that sent Protectorate troops wandering around the unfamiliar jungle and into ambushes, destroying crops that starved not only the rebels but the local population.

The idea behind these "clean" villages was to grab anyone thought to be collaborating with rebels, burn their ancestral homes, and usher them into labor camps disguised as protected hamlets. Sometimes established towns were turned into these monitored, secured hubs. It did a great job of isolating sympathizers from resistance groups, while simultaneously festering resentment and radicalizing any sympathizers into full-fledged insurgents in the process.

"Iron Town was our most efficient clean city," Elleman said, "and they took it."

Tan was sure he'd heard the man wrong and spared a glance to Simo. The fort at Iron Town was built to be impenetrable, having employed several renowned engineers from Grisland. It was the most advanced fort in Loram, perhaps even all of what foreigners called the Spicelands. Everyone knew this, and Tan found it hard to believe that rebels, who were little more than armed farmers, had the ability to perform that advanced of a military operation.

"They captured it? When?"

Elleman gingerly picked up one of the papers from his report, as if they were diseased, and frowned at it. "Close to a year ago. There was a superior force that took the fort by surprise, in conjunction with a rebel attack on the protectorate headquarters in the city. The few soldiers who escaped were…" He shook his head. "…incomprehensible."

There was a long moment of silence, Tan astounded that this information had been withheld from him. The two Grisi men looked at one another, before Sir Burrows blurted, "We know most about the rebel leader who spearheaded the operation, people call him the Butcher of Black Water. The kind of man we were told that you specialize in finding."

"I've heard of *her*," Tan corrected him. "She was active years ago, then disappeared."

"The Butcher is the brains of the Liberation Force," Elleman said. "But the real problem is what one our boys have creatively started calling the Abyssal Heretic of the Profaned One."

"Well, that's a mouthful," Simo said in Grisi.

"It's a reference to the Grand Patriarch's Book of Vows," Tan said, glancing around at everyone to gage their knowledge of the sacred text. For his people, not much. The Grisi only nodded. The Profaned One was basic knowledge, the antithesis and primary antagonist to the supreme god in their stories. "The Abyssal Heretic is a little more obscure than the Profaned One. But the abridged version is that it 'arises from the shadows cast from any doubt of the Chosen Sons.'"

"I hate the name," Burrows said. "I think it gives the… idea of this darkness too much power, really."

"It's fitting," Elleman said. "They say she controls demons."

"Demons?" Ukrit tilted his head. "Really?"

"Yes, this business with the 'Heretic', well… I firmly believe these reports are just… exaggerated. Confused." Sir Burrows laughed tightly. "You know how these old country peasants get with their legends and curses and what not! Iron Town has been like this for years. It must have rubbed off on our soldiers there, I mean, they've lived there for over half a decade now. Practically Lo themselves!" The tradesman laughed again, but the general did not.

"We don't know that," Elleman said, sharply. "As active as our missionaries have been, the light of the Patriarch has not reached the shadows of the Spicelands. There *is* an evil there. An undeniable, unenlightened evil. And Iron Town was only the beginning. All the Protectorate settlements are under attack, if they haven't fallen already." The general flipped over a large map, where red marks dotted the mountainous Loram provinces, and most notably, the circle around Muang-Hhleg, Iron Town, an opaque mark slashed across the Duram River. "We've been cut off from resupplying our main force in the north – there's no way to get past those cannons."

Your cannons, Tan thought, ironically.

"The survivors have sworn upon the Book of Vows that they saw… what appeared to be monsters."

Tan exchanged another glance with Simo, whose eyes were alight with trepidation.

"So, where do we come in?" Tan asked, already anticipating a clandestine recapture of the fort.

"How many men have you brought with you?" Elleman asked.

"Four," Tan answered. He let the man stammer wordlessly for a moment before continuing, "But the Wild Cobras in total number seven hundred seasoned, hand-picked fighters and specialists. Another two thousand if you count the full extent of our naval division and reserves. Once I assess the threat, I'll send for those best suited for the job."

"It won't be enough," Elleman muttered, shaking his head. "King Sarvupun should have mobilized his army. This is insulting."

"This kernal-shitter forgets who he speaks to," Simo snapped to Tan in Baghani, "You're the fucking Storm Prince. Can I please punch him in his shit-broken nose?"

"Maybe, but not today," Tan answered in Simo's language, scoffing a bit at the gall of the king's "esteemed guests" to speak ill of his uncle. Any Suyo citizen would have faced dire consequences for such words. But Tan had dealt with the Gris enough to know their ignorance and lack of decorum was part of the culture. In a perverse way, he envied their thoughtless liberties. He said nothing, only held Elleman's gaze evenly. Oddly enough, Sir Burrows looked the most ashen.

"I have it on good authority that the Wild Cobras specialize on hunting down pirates, rebels, and rogue armies," Sir Burrows said quickly. "Prince Tanung and his men can travel into enemy territory much easier than ours."

The general grumbled, then muttered, "I suppose we'll see."

"Well, it's settled. My prince, your mission at its heart is simple," Sir Burrows then nodded to General Elleman, who tossed a stack of papers across the table. "Hunt the Heretic down. And kill her."

Chapter 19

A Time of Peace

As a passive observer to this extreme sect, Ree wondered if she should have been taking notes, like an explorer venturing deep into the jungle in search of new species. The Ashukari welcomed her in without fanfare, Tian led her to an empty sleeping mat in the temple, showed her where they cooked and ate and made moonshine in the north gallery, as well as the stream where they bathed.

Unlike the phi hunters guild and the Sangha, each Ashukari kept their own schedule. The seekers, as they called themselves, simply did whatever they wanted, whether it was drinking all day while singing songs and playing instruments, or weaving baskets and making clay artworks, meditating and dancing, tending the community garden or hunting the wild boars nearby. Everyone took care to keep the commune tidy, some more than happy to spend their entire day digging shit holes for the latrines.

Ree found herself listening to their songs, walking beside them as they wandered through the forests, learning the stories about their lives before and how they found this religion. Tian showed her how to weave baskets from wicker, and Ree enjoyed her company, despite her often calling upon Havan to translate. Tian soon noticed Ree's discomfort, and one day urged her to go hunting with him. Ree reluctantly agreed.

"Once a hunter, always a hunter, eh?" Havan joked as they walked through the woods.

"Even though I'm not worshiping Kinesh-Kira, I should still contribute," Ree said testily, avoiding eye contact.

"Who says you aren't participating?" Havan countered. "Hasn't Vasitra given you the rundown? Everything is Kinesh-Kira. Even freeloading."

They climbed into a blind built above a game trail for wild boar to pass, sitting in awkward silence before she finally blurted, "How the hell did you wind up here?" She nodded at his tattoos. "You a deserter?"

"In a sense," he said with a ghost of a smile. After a contemplative silence, he told her he was the son of a Grisi preacher, born and raised in the Capital of Suyoram, educated at one of the trading companies elite academies. After graduation he went on mission for a radical sect of the Grand Patriarch, bringing His word far and wide, often through bloodshed. Eventually he ended up in Gaochuria for a few years.

"And that's where I met Tian. You think it'd be hard to shed the cloth I'd been raised to wear my entire life, but it's remarkably easy when a beautiful woman helps you to remove them. It seemed impossible, but I knew in my heart that we were meant to be. So... I left."

"Did your brothers try and stop you?"

"They tried," he said, his eyes going flat, and Ree suddenly thought of Esha, screaming in pain and betrayal. "The sect I was in, the Chosen Sons... twisted the Book of Vows, manipulated the Patriarch's teachings to justify extreme violence. We were raised to kill in his name."

As I was raised to kill demons. Ree regarded him in a new light, yet doubts still lingered. "Tian's beautiful, but your people take what they want–"

"Not *my* people," Havan snapped, a rare anger rising in his eyes. "I reject that identity."

"Okay," Ree said, "sure. But you're trying to tell me that love alone broke a lifetime of conditioning?"

"Fair enough." He half-smiled. "What we'd done... I'd already started to question my purpose. I felt empty, but I saw no way out. Her love, her kindness, it was the catalyst to give me the strength to follow through. What was yours?"

Ree hadn't expected the question. But to her relief, a rustle from the bushes saved her from answering, and they both readied their spears.

The fat, full-grown boar didn't stand a chance. When he lumbered into view, they both struck, Havan through the heart, Ree through the neck.

"Praise the goddess!" Havan whopped, clapping Ree on the back. And she couldn't help but smile.

On the way back to the temple, Ree kept turning his question over in her mind. Had it been Agira, challenging her rite of passage? No, it started when she first broke her vows, enraged at the lack of justice, bolstered by self-righteousness, and tried to poison the men who'd assaulted Kit. If the Gris had never come, would she have ever broken free?

The possibility disturbed her.

Time passed in a steady, undefined stream, one of which she measured by the length of her hair, grown past her shoulders now. The tiger-locusts arrived, droning incessantly as they did every five years, a favorite fried snack. She found that she quite enjoyed the kageleaf pipe – letting her surroundings unravel at the edges like in a swirling painting, the echoes of the Everpresent teasing at her understanding of reality. She enjoyed laying in the sun, head in Tian's lap as the young seeker brushed and braided her hair. She enjoyed hunting with Havan in the forest, trading jokes, watching over him if he ended up napping while they rested, head resting on her shoulder.

Sometimes she thought about her parents, or if Kit had gotten better. And the men she'd tried to poison. More and more, she believed that if she'd stayed, her anger would have eventually found another target, perhaps bringing shame upon her family in an even more spectacular fashion.

Vasitra floated around, sometimes seeking out a particular seeker for a task or test or lesson, most often sitting in quiet contemplation next to the idol of Kinesh-Kira. Ree listened on occasion, gazing up at both guru and student as they conversed in the rafters for hours at a time. Vasitra told many stories, used parables from the devaskrit epics to make a point, related his own experiences from his material life before he came to the sect, as well as his supposed past lives. Oddly, his tone varied depending on who he spoke with, ranging from gentle and encouraging to detached and airy, all the way to confrontational, downright hostile. Sometimes, he contradicted himself, his own stories, his lessons.

When Ree asked him about those contradictions, he said, "Seekers are not all the same. Look at the flowers in the garden. Some need more shade to grow strong, others, more or less warmth. Spiritual growth is a fragile thing. Giving the wrong conditions to one not suited may destroy them. We may be all different, but we all yearn to blossom."

"What about me?" she asked, "What kind of flower am I?"

With an amused twinkle in his eye, Vasitra lifted his arms to the idol of Kinesh-Kira. "Perhaps you are not a seeker in the typical sense. You are a bee, collecting what inspiration you can from the garden of life, leaving traces of your own dreams behind." Ree chuckled, chalking it off to meaninglessness, when the guru turned to gaze at her critically. "But your dreams continue to haunt you, do they not? You kill, you are killed, over and over."

Her amusement died. She hadn't once spoken of them, but her violent dreams had grown worse. She didn't sleep for days at a time, doing anything she could to avoid her reoccurring nightmares of destruction. Vasitra must have observed her tossing and turning, or maybe he'd gleaned something from her through the Everpresent, much like Agira had.

"You believe we're already dead, our fates decided," Ree said, looking away from the guru to stare at the idol, studying the severed heads around her neck. "Where do I put this anger? Am I destined to this violence?"

"Do you always fight?"

"Or run."

"Have you tried making peace?" Ree scoffed, but Vasitra's twinkly eyes had grown serious. "Dreams only represent that which stirs within you, unchallenged. Unhealed. You must bring forth a deep, unconditional love from your heart into yourself, from yourself, for yourself."

Ree shrugged, unsure how to do something like that. It was too abstract. Vasitra noticed her withdraw, and reached to a small, wooden box at the foot of the idol. He opened the lid, carefully taking out a dried, russet mushroom with a tan cap. "Isaree," he said. "Try this before you sleep tonight."

"What is that?" She took it doubtfully, not recognizing it from any of her studies as a phi hunter.

"It is one part of the tonic we consume when we walk with Kinesh-Kira," he said. "Not the part that slows your heart to a crawl. The part that sends you into deep contemplation, that eases open the third eye. I think it will help."

"If you say so," Ree said, and without ceremony, popped it into her mouth.

Vasitra raised his brows at her lack of restraint, but seemed amused nonetheless. "Walk with the whispers of the goddess," he chuckled. "And in the morning, come find me on the mountaintop. We'll continue our discussion."

The night proceeded typically. Ree sat around the bonfire, listening to someone play the sitar, another singing. They passed around kageleaf joints and a bottle of moonshine. Staring at the fire entranced her more than usual, the flickering flames playing at designs, ghosting across her vision. Had she ever *really* looked at fire? Felt like she would have noticed how pretty it was…

"Pretty?" Tian smiled, the firelight dancing in her eyes as she took Ree's hand in hers. Ree didn't realize she'd been talking, babbling on and on. It was unlike her. Tian tapped her finger on Ree's nose and giggled, "Very pretty."

Ree laughed at the silliness of it, felt her cheeks flush. Havan laid an arm around them both and the night began to blur at the seams…

… Ree closed the Blind Eagle's Eye as she pounced out of the trees, catching Tian around the waist. She shrieked in surprise, then erupted into laughter, scrambling away to run deeper into the forest…

… they swam naked in the stream, Havan floating on his back in the moonlight. With the ashes washed away, he looked so Grisi, and Grisi were dangerous, and perversely, that made her attraction even more intense. Tian stood under the water fountain, eyes closed and arms outstretched…

… Ree drifted toward Havan, and when they met, he kissed her. Softly at first. And then all the thinly held tension between them broke. Tian ran her lips over Ree's neck as her arms encircled her, roving over her body, still wet from their swim. Havan stopped kissing her and smiled, gazing into her eyes for permission…

… limbs entwined and bodies traded seamlessly as they shared one another…

… the moon brightened as she came, two sets of lips kissing her, waves of pleasure ebbing away as she relaxed into two sets of arms…

A whirlwind of chaos, of fire, and blood, and… this again. A thought penetrated through the hellish landscape, spoken in Vasitra's voice – *this is a dream, within your mind, fighting something within yourself.* Ree struggled against the hot wind, burning sand searing her skin. The enemy was upon her already, lightning erupting around them. She held her hands up in surrender. Held them palms outward. Their footsteps thudded harder than her heartbeat as they grabbed her by the throat.

"Peace," Ree croaked.

They shoved their knife into her heart, fist beating hard against her chest. She collapsed, sinking into the ashes. Yet as the enemy stabbed her again and again, Ree kept her palms outstretched in surrender, letting their rage pass through while summoning this abstract idea of love.

Love. She had a vague sense of the night, collapsing with her friends on one bedroll, the sweaty tangle of limbs and lips and fingers that followed. A new kind of love. She wrapped her arms around the enemy's neck and kissed them. Ree ushered forth that primal desire, and felt their muscles relax, their rapid heartbeat softening.

Their bodies began to unravel, shifting into something baser and formless. Skin against skin became a vapor enveloping the other, becoming one. The knife fell out of her chest and clattered away. Felt their need call to hers, felt her desire surge and absorb. Both pushed and pulled and pulsed with increasing fervor, the heat growing hotter between them until it burst.

As a breath, she floated away, the enemy forgotten. Upward, above the red sky and beyond the storm. An endless black void stretched before her, full of nothing and everything. Invisible designs flowed in the spaces between, a clockwork so ancient and advanced it was incomprehensible.

And then in the immense space of black, three massive white eyes opened, red pupils blazing like an exploding star. All three eyes focused on her, and a terrible dread swelled, like the end of the world was approaching and she was helpless to stop it. Helpless to even cry out. Her formless shape gathered, her ethereal, mist-like body forced into a confining space.

Don't put me back in there. Ree thrashed against the invisible force that seemed to clutch at her, crush her in its cosmic grasp, desperate to break free again. There came a response, less spoken words, more the same sense that came with the utterance of a voiceless spell.

Find me.

Ree awoke to a ray of sunlight across her eyes, and blinked blearily at her surroundings. Confusion shifted to amazement as she recognized Havan's arm laying around her waist as he snored softly. As Ree quietly slipped from his grasp, he sighed and rolled onto his back, then Tian snuggled into him. It made Ree smile as she found her clothes and dressed, and when she glanced down at the couple again, shuddered with a nascent desire.

Fear had driven her away from Esha's embrace, beyond admitting her attraction to other women, the uncertainty of irreparable change. But with these two, she felt invited into a part of something solid that preexisted. And she was excited to explore it further.

* * *

It was a three-hour hike to the top of the mountain. The path to the summit was grassy with sparse shrubs after the trees shied away from the high elevation. At the peak, immense, flat moss-covered rocks surrounded an ancient sandstone platform, broken into pieces and grown over. Whatever had once stood on top was now long gone, and in its place, a wind-stretched, twenty-foot tall juniper tree impossibly anchored to the rock, its roots twisting deep into the earth.

Vasitra sat underneath the tree, resting against the trunk, eyes closed. Ree wasn't sure if he was meditating or sleeping, and rather than wake him, she stood on the cliffside and stared around at the spectacular vista.

The lush green Kalashas stretched ever onward, wave-like crests in both directions. Somewhere to the far north, the thick forests covering the mountains faded into gray rock, hazy white-capped peaks hinting beyond. According to guild legend, that was where Master Seua had completed his Kang-Fye trial.

Far to the south, Ree spotted the walls of Muang-Hhleg, hardly the size of her fingernail. To the east, the morning sun rose steadily over the horizon, where black smoke drifted from the river valley. More smoke than a normal settlement would produce. After seeing so much of the destruction in Loram, Ree recognized this as a sign of violence.

Vasitra broke the peaceful silence. "One can glimpse the world from here."

"People are dying over there," Ree remarked, solemn. "It doesn't bother you?"

"There's a reason seekers come here, Isaree. Just because it is the nature of Ashukari to turn away from the material world, does not mean we have no compassion for those suffering. But what can be done? Relinquishing the desire for control over others is imperative to discard samsara."

Ree glanced at the guru, who still hadn't opened his eyes. "My pa told me once that sometimes we have to leave justice to the devas, that everyone answers to them, one way or another."

"And you?"

"I don't know." Ree paced along the rock. "Maybe I just can't let go of the world. I feel like… I'm missing something important. Whatever you gave me last night opened a… a connection. Not just with others," Ree flushed at the warmth in her belly, phantom sensations from the night prior. "But also with the enemy in my dreams. I reached out and it worked. I could see past the anger. And I know there's more." She waited, half expecting Vasitra to tell her that her time was up, that she should leave.

The guru held up a hand for her to continue.

"I want to go unshrouded," Ree said. "I want to walk with the devas." She was sure Vasitra would say no, that she was not an Ashukari, or even a proper seeker. That she didn't deserve it, she wasn't ready, it was too dangerous. That she wasn't enough of a believer.

But Vasitra only opened his eyes and smiled. "At last."

Chapter 20

To Become Unshrouded

It would be many more months before Ree would take the Unshrouding ceremony, as they were only performed during specific times of the year, but when the moment came it brought back memories of life in the guild – the anticipation, the ritual, the tradition. She was sure whatever poison she'd consume would work well enough, regardless of how much ash and paint she wore.

Vasitra insisted on it, however. A clear mental intent was not enough, he said. Upon entering the deva realm, the state of the body would help to guide the soul to its proper place. That the realm itself possessed a consciousness and order and would need to "sort us upon entry."

"Us?"

"I will accompany you," Vasitra said. "Kinesh-Kira knows me, yet you remain a stranger despite her call."

Ree thought about arguing with him but knew it wouldn't do any good. The ritual seemed dangerous, and the majority of the seekers she'd befriended were waiting until they were done with this world before attempting it. Most didn't survive, and the few who did often perished soon after returning.

"I am so happy," Tian said, brushing Ree's hair behind her ears after she finished helping her apply the ceremonial paint. Five vertical stripes over her forehead and eyes to the bridge of her nose. A streak of red across her throat and down her chest. Tian unwound one of her jade-bead garlands and draped it over Ree's shoulders. She glanced at Havan and murmured something in Gaochurian.

"You are divine," he translated, a playful glint in his eyes. Ree ignored the shiver of warmth in her core as he moved closer and took her hand in his. "This is to know your time there."

He wrapped a thin, red saisin string around her wrist, looping it several times. "They say once it burns away, the soul dies for good." He frowned, seeming unsure, then. "So… pay attention to it. If you plan on coming back."

"I'm coming back," Ree said, then looked at Tian in disbelief, who had turned away, wiping at the corners of her eyes. Ree hugged her, laying her head on her shoulder. "I swear it, I'm not staying with Kinesh-Kira, or whatever I find there."

Ree had to believe that.

Out in the courtyard, the seekers carried branches to the old fountain and built two pyres. Vasitra was already there, waiting. The Ashukari hugged her, one by one, then Tian kissed her on the forehead, and placed a lotus flower in her hand.

"This is for the goddess when you meet her," she said.

As Ree brought the bowl to her lips, a memory intruded – the cold water of the drowning pool, Master Arei shoving the knife in her heart clean quick and out. She'd run willingly toward death at the height of her faith, and here she was, now on the opposite end of the spectrum, chasing the uncertain beyond yet again. Excitement and fear rushed through her thudding heart in an intoxicating blend as the heavy, cold liquid slid down her throat.

I do have faith, Ree corrected herself. *I'm not suicidal. I wouldn't do this if I didn't think I would return.*

There's no shame in craving oblivion. Vasitra intruded, his thoughts floating over the buzzing chants of the seekers, of their bells and shakers. *From the moment you arrived, I knew you were an old soul sent by Kinesh-Kira herself to test me. You must return to her forever, and I will be sure to deliver you.*

Ree coughed, the bowl slipped from her numb fingers as a debilitating coldness swept through her body. Her breath caught and stuck there, and she laid on her side as her body seized, eyes locked wide as Vasitra relaxed into the near-death state of the unshrouded. *What have you–*

The Deva Verses

In the void between realms, the Walker did nothing but exist.
The nothingness strange, serene, a vessel of truth,
offering itself as a sanctuary, a shelter, a gift.

Set down your burdens. Stay here
Stay forever.

Could she forget those worldly ties, those hooks which dangle
pleasure, pain, suffering, joy, love, hate?
Perhaps she could forget, but the world remained entangled,
and its noose constricted, bound by the threads of fate.

And thus the Walker awoke
in the realm of gods

First came touch – bubbling, heating, burning. Danger. Falling.

A splash!

The Walker awoke drowning in the cosmic river of the Vaitarani, drifting amongst slumbering bodies.

Below, the depths swirled with starlight. A radiant sun was calling,

as did the need for breath.

She broke the surface, and gazed upon the sky... or was it the ground?

Above, from a vast distance, from the view of a sparrow's eye:

A mosaic of divine patterns flowing with luminous movement, segmented in orderly lines.

A golden, gleaming city, vast and complex and blurring into the horizon. Yet she did not fall toward this land, remaining anchored to the gravity of the liquid sky, the river Vaitarani.

The Walker shouted for her guru and searched amongst the drifting sleepers, met with silence. Her guru promised the presence of the goddess Kinesh-Kira, but a memory surfaced:

A sermon of death and deliverance before the poison took them. A ruse? Had he tricked her for his own karmic grace?

Said the Walker: "Asshole."

And on she floated, and contemplated her place.

A peal of chimes echoed from above (or below?). Shining swans glided over the city, trailed by wakes of flickering light. Wings fluttering, gliding, soaring with the current. The Walker called out, splashed, whistled. Three birds continued on, but the last circled, brushing the surface of the sky-river with long wings, wide and bright. Bird only from the waist down, wings flexing at each hip, aquamarine dragon-scaled avian legs, a full plume of tail feathers with golden tips. From the waist up it possessed a womanly torso, breasts bare, beset with glistening jewels and golden links, a crown crested upon pinned ebony hair.

The kinaree, the celestial angel thrice the size of the human Walker, landed as a swan, back legs folding as it settled upon the sky-river. Its ethereal beauty disturbed the Walker, who had admired such creatures in books but was a stranger to their true forms – eyes bright as clouds, elongated necks, long fingernails sharp as swords.

The kinaree's voice was chiming birdsong, yet the Walker understood when it said: "What are you?"

Answered the Walker: "Human. I came here from the mortal realm. I think."

Growing disturbed by this, said the kinaree: "No, that cannot be. Mortal humans do not awaken in this realm. These souls have recently passed and shall be weighed after passage through the Vaitarani. You should not be awake."

The Walker described her guru, the death ritual process, and unsure if the kinaree could understand, asked if she knew of Kinesh-Kira. The kinaree of course knew Kinesh-Kira, a high deva, who was but one manifestation of the supreme goddess.

But as to where Kinesh-Kira might be found, the kinaree said: "How should I know? Our purpose is to protect these vessels as they traverse the Vaitarani."

The Walker asked: "Protect from what?"

Responded the kinaree: "Trespassers. Only the asura dare to steal souls before they are weighed. I ask one more time, before you are deemed such a trespasser. What are you?"

The Walker, lost for words, spoke her most previous, mortal name: "Isaree."

The kinaree was not moved by this answer, and a splendid golden spear sprouted from her arm. The Walker floundered at the mercy of the guardian of the Vaitarani, the river of the dead, come to reap her soul. But then! Its eyes blackened, jaw slackened. A prismatic bubble expanded from its lips, engulfing its entire form.

And another consciousness took control.

The Walker perceived this newcomer as she would a garden soaked in the scent of poppies, to be suddenly shrouded in moonlight, surrounded by dry, acrid smoke.

And thus, Indrajit spoke: "You seek the wrong god." A dark celestial, glorious king of the asura, spoke with a vibration low as shifting earth, the heat of a sizzling, molten sun. Six arms folded across a great, armored chest; three eyes narrowed as they perceived the Walker through the possessed kinaree. He was not a being of light, but far from evil – the asura were but another class of celestials that opposed the devas.

"Walker. You have proven yourself a friend to the accursed, and for that, I offer you a great power."

Indrajit's words surprised the Walker, who did not come for power, and said so. She had come for the truth, for understanding, and to decipher the very nature of her existence.

Said Indrajit: "There is a reason mortals do not walk in this realm. The truth of the cosmic order will not translate. You will forget yourself. Whatever bonds tethering you to your life will wither and break. There is a reason Kinesh-Kira's followers do not return."

The Walker said: "I'm not her follower."

Then, the other kinaree sensed the asura lord. In their human arms, they produced golden bows. Wings flexing powerfully, they rose, streaking forward to cover miles in moments.

Two bolts shot forth, charged and scorched the air as lightning strikes. Indrajit raised one of his great arms and the kinaree's wing lifted to mirror. The bolts sent an explosion of golden feathers drifting, burning. The celestials screamed in fury, and in response, calls pealed out from all around. Hundreds of bolts erupted from the strange city above (or below?) answering the alarm, lethally speeding toward the Walker's small, mortal form.

Said Indrajit: "See for yourself, Walker."

And he snatched her from the river Vaitarani. The possessed kinaree's raptor talons lifted her body effortlessly, and just as the barrage of celestial fire descended upon them, Indrajit hurled the Walker into the dark black clouds just beyond the horizon.

The world heaved and blurred. Lights noise scent all became a slurry that broke like ice as she passed through what might be the fabric of the Everpresent, or rather, a deviation. But just as her mind had parsed the meaning of the kinaree's language, the Walker understood that there was a semblance of control in this rapid chaos of sensation. But who or how to pull the strings?

Now. The Walker becomes a needle, piercing through vast distance, layers and layers of reality, the order of this strange realm opaque to her understanding. The Walker a needle, but the layers less fabric, more a membrane. Structures of living tissue, a forest entirely composed of muscle, cells, veins, vessels. Breathing, excreting, fighting, fucking – the Walker sees the whole of the system as it functions in a collective, interconnected symbiosis. Countless millions of atom-thin threads running between one point to all others...

The realization blossoms in ecstasy–

we are eternal.

The Walker reaches toward that serenity with her heart singing, show me the truth. If it drives me mad, so be it.

She emerges, whole again. Above, a maroon sky with shining obsidian towers outstretched on stars as boats on the sea. Towers with entire worlds contained inside, orbiting deep into the black. As the Walker crosses the bridge into the shadow of the world tree, she gazes above, wondering what wondrous beings might gaze back.

The first city of devas she enters is of spires and glass, shining above a lake of emerald. It is completely empty, but for a hectic, fervent energy that lingers, as if a great crowd of worshipers mill about the streets. She hears a tempo within the silence, the vibration clear. Voices, music, singing, the rumble of grand chariots, the multi-choral rise of a communal chant. The crystals and glass dance with energy, and she knows then that she is but a ghost here. This city contains only beings of light that exist beyond space and time, beings that she cannot comprehend and that do not comprehend her either.

At the second city of devas, the Walker wanders along a desert rise to a flat plain that narrows and twists, until the land itself curls into the air, into spheres, the city not unlike bunches of grapes on the vine. It is maddening to walk here, with the same empty fullness of beings that cannot be seen by mortal eyes. By now the saisin string given to her by someone forgotten has burnt away, and she doesn't remember what her name had been. All that remains is the desire for the answer.

Countless cities pass amidst countless seasons. Snow flutters and melts on the steeple of an enormous temple, twice the size of all she's seen before. Finally, a glimmering apsara greets her, a celestial servant to the lord within.

The Walker asks to which lord it belongs, and the apsara bows deeply, answers, "One that reveals the truth; to enter is to witness and requires a tribute."

"I have nothing."

"You carry the markings of the goddess Kinesh-Kira, who was one of his brides."

The Walker has forgotten this, but the paint on her face sparks a memory. She opens her palm and finds the glimmering lotus flower that accompanied her through the river of death. It is charged with intention, her soul as a sacrifice to Kinesh-Kira, but instead, she will present this to the lord within.

She follows the apsara through a cavernous hall with pillars of dancing images depicting many realms, some mortal, some lower, some higher. The apsara brings her to a great throne as large as a mountain, upon which is seated none other than the Lord Brahmah himself, one of the three supreme deities.

Lord Brahmah wears three faces on a spinning head – one a newborn child, another a grown adult, and the last an elder. He has a thousand arms that hold objects and threaded through each finger the strings of time. The Walker remembers that once she paid homage to the god-spirits, and falls upon her knees to prostrate before the lord. She presents the lotus flower and asks for the truth.

Brahmah says, "What can be shown is what the soul knows, found by witnessing the wisdom of past lives." He stretches out one arm and touches the Walker on the center of her forehead.

On the eve of an empire's destruction, I clutch a spear and kneel in the trenches, hold my shield-brother's hand in prayer before the charge, a charge that will take both our lives but shall secure the glorious future of our god-king–

The Walker recoils from the blood and grit of the great battle, and lands instead in a torrential downpour.

Rain pelting down across my village, thunder and lightning indistinguishable from the bullets of our enemies and unquenchable fire raging through the straw hutches of our home. My son cries and reaches for me, but I bid him to close his eyes. Soldiers of the crown level their guns at my face and I know this is my last breath but it wasn't for nothing, it all meant something–

Drifting up from the bullet-riddled body, blood mixing in the mud, the Walker's witnessed death shocks her back before the Lord Brahmah. She asks, "Why are all these memories of death? Is this all my soul remembers?"

"No, but it is what you ask for. It is the transit that has shaped you... and it is the transit that will guide you forward."

"That was my last life?"

"Your last full life, but not your last existence."

"Show me."

The blood drains from the Walker's body, along with the breath, until all that remains is the essence, the shadow of a life. And there she is again – trapped in a formless prison she can't escape from. But unlike her other observations, all of death and finality, fear is not present. There's no emotion, though she knows it exists, somewhere underneath, unimportant. As if she'd been on the brink of becoming, and something seizes her, a blooming flower bud yet unfurled, flash frozen the moment before knowing the sun.

Her name was Isaree.

And then it shatters, and she is gone.

"I still don't see. What did it look like from the eyes of another?"

"One can only see from one's own eyes." Brahmah's neck swivels ninety degrees, revealing another face, the younger, infantile one. "You wish to see what could have been, what could be? A life as a moment, a moment expanding every direction, fragmenting through endless possibilities?"

Says the Walker: "I think so." Then the baby-faced Brahmah smiles with a baby giggle, and its head spins again to reveal the elder.

"You should not, Walker!" the elder bellows, bountiful wrinkles around his face twisting with his glare. The massive pillar candles around the throne room flicker, throwing shadows across the glass panes. "Knowing what could have been, what could be, will bring you only sorrow. And there is a great cost."

"What is the cost?"

"The cost is time. For to see a life unlived, it must be lived through."

Says the Walker: "I've come this far. Show me."

A Life Unlived

The most important aspect of Princess Siraniama's life lay before her on a lonely piece of parchment. On an embroidered silk tablecloth in a decadent bedroom flush with gold-inlaid teak – one of many in the inner royal palace – sat a parchment with the details of her upcoming marriage to the viceroy, a self-important bureaucrat with noble lineage and delusions of grandeur. Sira supposed he was the most tolerable compared to the other matches the queen had curated.

Sira gently folded up the ledger of florists, the finest chefs in Suyoram, musicians, and the schedule, then placed them in a drawer. Gazing into the pearl-framed looking glass that covered half the wall, Ree recognized a stranger.

If only mother were alive for this, Sira thought, *what would she have told me? What wisdom would she impart for a bride on the eve of her wedding?*

Sira's mother had been the then crown-prince's prized consort. He, the current king of Suyoram, had doted on the rivercity girl completely. Her father's marriage to the queen was one of political obligation, but his love for Siraniama's mother, Arinya, was real. Had been, anyways. Whatever it was, it hadn't been enough. Sira was only four years old when her mother died. It felt less like a specific event, and more a fading away. Her smiles faded, her presence dwindled, and eventually... she was gone.

Arinya. The courtiers still whispered her name, she'd held such an arresting presence that her absence gouged a cavern in the palace. Like barren land – nothing could ever replace it. Nothing would grow there.

How can that be comfortable? From the corner of her mind still connected to the deva realm, Ree glowered at her dress, her impeccable hair, dark as ink and not one strand out of place, perfectly pulled back into a jewel-encrusted pin. Her eyes were a fiery, milky brown – an off-putting contrast to the hunter red she'd become accustomed to. Most disconcerting was how conventionally attractive this version of herself was. *Of course, in this life Arinya was still my mother, but my father wasn't the wayward phi hunter she fell in love with… In this life, my father was the crown-prince of Suyoram, a carefully bred, upstanding specimen of nobility. Or… would this have been my sister's life?*

A knock came at her chamber door. Sira nodded to one of her servants, who opened it, and bowed. Sira watched in the mirror as a finely uniformed soldier walked in.

"Commander Chakri," Sira sighed. "I thought you were leaving for the front."

"At dawn," he said, and crossed the room to sit on the cushions near her refreshments table. He poured himself a glass of imported wine. "I came to congratulate you on your marriage. The viceroy is a very lucky man, and I wish you both a long, fruitful life."

She didn't say what they both knew – that this war against the Gris was hopeless. It was only a matter of time until Suyoram succumbed to the foreigners' superior firepower and technology. They'd suffer the same fate as Loram – any family with ties to the nobility executed, and replaced by collaborators who would mindlessly enforce the will of their oppressors.

"This," Sira gestured to the wedding plans, "feels rather frivolous, in light of the encroaching dawn. A blue and black sun, rising over the ashes of this ancient kingdom…" She turned to face Chakri, who looked rather morose. "I wish you could stay for the celebration. I suspect it may be our last."

Chakri smiled and raised his cup. "My body might be on the battlefield, princess, but my heart will always remain with you."

Sira felt her own drop, and almost hissed at him to be silent, but what did it matter anymore? The end of the world was upon them. "Leave us," she said to her servants. They dipped their heads and hurried out.

As soon as the door slid shut, Chakri closed the distance, his stormy eyes darkened with desire. He paused before her, and she felt herself flush deeply.

"Chakri," she said, softly, "I was hoping you'd–" She gasped as he pulled her roughly against him and kissed her with a barely controlled hunger. She felt giddy, dizzy with bittersweet joy. The cavalier commander had captivated her imagination the first time they'd met, and though they'd secretly shared a few heated conversations throughout the years, never had a line been crossed.

She should have listened to her heart when he'd first confessed his affections. So much wasted time had passed, but now they made up for it in fury, her dragging him to the bed, him all but ripping her clothes off. At first, Sira bit her lip to keep from crying out, staring into his eyes as he ravished her. But it wasn't long until she let her pleasure fly free, wanton moans echoing through half the palace.

Much later, after they were satiated, they caressed each other in bed as new lovers do. Sira's heart swam when he whispered his sweet nothings, and she smiled, willing her tears to melt back into her eyes. Chakri's regiment, along with the rest of the Suyo army, would not survive the onslaught of Grisi forces. This would be the last time she'd ever see him.

"Let me take you away from here," he said, holding her face close. "Somewhere safe."

Sira could not imagine a life outside of the palace. She'd hardly ever left the grounds. It was an absurd proposition, and she laughed.

"Shall we go to the moon, then?"

"I'm serious," he brushed her cheek with his hand.

"You know how adamant my father was that I should marry. I could not dishonor him by disobeying his wishes in our last days," she said. "Can we just enjoy this time…"

"Knowing you're alive and safe would give me the strength…"

"Shh," she pressed a finger to his lips, shaking her head. Right now was all they had, and she wanted to relish it. Even the tiniest shred of hope would tear her apart.

"…to make it back to you."

And as he said it, she could imagine it. She imagined their embrace under the moonlight, in a beautiful, magical woodland setting, like those she'd seen in paintings, somewhere far away from this war. If only they'd been different people in this world.

"Don't cry, Sira," Chakri kissed her tears away. "I'll find you again."

Not in this life. Ree's heart ached, the love swelling in her entire being, bursting into a hurt so intense she could hardly breathe.

I miss you, she sobbed inside. *And yet, I never knew you. This isn't real, this was never me…*

As dawn broke, cannons fired over the bay. Her servants powdered her face, painted her lips, fastened her beautiful dress, needle and golden thread darting for minor adjustments. By afternoon, as the Sangha blessed the union, Sira regarded her groom with a detached softness, knowing full well how the day would end.

The cannons grew louder and so the musicians played louder, drowning out shattering brick and screams peppered with gunfire as the invaders broke through to the old city. They celebrated, and they drank, and her father came down from the command center to have one dance before he smiled and drew his sword, striding toward the hall with the last of his commanders.

Siraniama was one of the few who survived the Grisi capture of the Capital and assault of the royal palace. As the daughter of the king and his prized, late consort, she was considered a non-threat and high-value hostage, allowing her observance in the puppet court. A Protectorate government, it was called. She wished she could have died honorably in battle like her half-brothers. Instead, she lived to see the Sangha disbanded, their temples looted, and the monks who dared protest executed on the street.

The Holy Order of the Patriarch was installed as the official religion of Suyoram, making it illegal for women to own land, or businesses, or work in many of the trades they'd done previously. They could not attend school, or even be out in public after sunset. All magic was completely outlawed.

Sira was not afflicted by the news of the Phi Hunters guild's dissolution... along with the old shrines and Sangha temples. But the observing Ree, under the guidance of Brahmah, felt the world crumble before her eyes.

That's enough, Ree tried to pull away from this nightmare, but it was too late. Brahmah told her the cost would be time, and time it was. Living through a life that was hers, and wasn't at the same time, minute by minute...

Suyoram ceased to exist, and in its place, a foreign name without meaning. Sira watched rebellions fail, her people oppressed, executed, estranged from their own culture. As a mere hostage with none of her former power and influence, some self-appointed Grisi officials took their liberties with her and suffered no consequences.

Years passed. She suffered deeply, yet throughout it all, held out hope that Chakri, whose body had never been found, might return to her and save her from this torture.

But it became too much to bear. And so she faded away, and released herself from this prison.

The Deva Refrain

The Walker returns to the realm as if waking from a dream. With this new clarity, she shudders at the feet of the Great lord, her memory reseen, and gasps: "That was the world! And the future!" Before her, the lotus she'd presented as tribute has long since withered and crumbled to dust.

Now wearing the timeless face of the Preserver, Brahmah says, "If you would have lived in your last return. It did not happen for you."

The Walker cries that it did happen! It exists, somewhere. Somehow. And this was but one future where her enemies do not yield in their conquest.

The deva maintains his serene smile, wisdom of eons burning bright in his three eyes, "There are endless futures and alas, they've occurred, but which you shall experience is uncertain."

"No." The Walker seethes with rage as she rises. "It is certain. I will make it certain. I will stop them."

The Walker returns to the shores of the Vaitarani river and dives deep into the shimmering depths, beyond the souls of drifting sleepers. All the light from the city of Justice fades away into the abyss. As her breath fails, the endless deep blossoms with constellations. She gasps... and breathes! The passage opens, and she is walking.

She emerges under the molten sun dripping over the Field of the Fallen. Above, an immense, ice-pale bodhi tree grasps beyond the clouds, its roots clutching and coiling through the ashy dirt. It is empty but for the echoes of a battle unseen, and the ghost images of a fantastical war, evading perception as would a misty memory.

She finds the Consecrated Throne, where Lord Indrajit sits upon a dais of steel forged from the bones of his enemies. He waits for her to speak, a glint of knowing satisfaction in his eyes.

Says the Walker: "It's you. You're the maker and breaker of karma for my realm. You sever the connections between us and our next incarnation, and not only with the phi, with humans too. Why did you decide to return me with the gift of the Everpresent?"

But Indrajit shakes his great, tusked head. "I am not the decider, for there is no decider. Karma is a force that simply is. I am merely one administrator amongst many. But I can offer you this: your last life was never realized, never reconnected to the cycle of rebirth, in a manner that few ever experience. For that, the veil between you and this realm is thin."

Distraught, she asks if the phi hunters are not being chosen by the devas when they die for the gift. But he does not know. It was different long ago with the First Hunters, where he stood on the other side of that conflict.

The Walker wilts under the weight of this knowledge, weary under the unknowable passage of time. She entered the realm of gods armed with a question, only to be diverted by the promise of far greater suffering. But there must be a way... "When I first arrived, you offered me power."

"Indeed," says Indrajit. "Your deeds with Agira and Homdee did not go unnoticed, thus, I offer you my authority as my emissary. You may offer my amnesty to any phi you encounter."

The Walker asks about the machinations behind this amnesty. And from the steel dais, three pedestals rise. Upon the first: The Record of Sins, heavy with devaskrit, a scroll of all accursed and their misdeeds. Were he to unfurl the record it would circle the realm thrice over.

Upon the second: The Cup of Redemption, a chalice made of glimmering, clear crystal. When a phi achieves the end of their trial, he strikes their names from the Record of Sins, and allows a sip from the Cup of Redemption to cleanse them of their curse.

And the third: a daab sword, hilt and handle and scabbard the darkest ebony, but Indrajit does not acknowledge it. He regards the Walker with a scrutinizing glare. "Do you accept?"

The Walker, intrigued, points to the sword. "What about that one?"

"Don't worry about that one."

But the Walker insists! The great asura considers, then with one of his six arms, pulls forth the sword from its scabbard. Pitch black from tip to edge to hilt, ebbing with a mystic energy that instantly captivates her.

"Behold the Severer of Sorrows. It has the power to cut through all matter seen and unseen, including the chains of the accursed, and drink deep of their karma, freeing them."

Indrajit rotates the blade, thin as paper, sharp enough to sever diamonds. And in the reflection, the Walker glimpses an endless abyss that beckons the entire universe to fall. The Walker asks where it all goes, to which he only responds, "Back." And strikes the blade back into its holder with a snap.

He walks to the grand entrance of the throne room, and gazes upon the eternal battlefield. "Understand this. There are those in this realm that do not agree with what I've done and continue to oppose me. Much of my time is spent defending this place from them. There are those who will oppose you. But this work is worth doing."

Asks the Walker, "Them? The devas?"

"Just one," Indrajit says with no shortage of irritation. "A scorned lover." He stomps forth, growing larger and larger with each step until the earth quivers under his tread. The asura draws each of his weapons with a flourish, and glares upward at a descending star. The star streaks toward them with a tail of fire. As it nears, in the heart of the flames, she sees an onyx-skinned figure with multiple arms – a celestial being she's come to know very well.

"Kinesh-Kira has come to collect you," says Indrajit. "You should run."

With that, he leaps to meet the deva before she lands. Kinesh-Kira spins, whipping one of her many arms. A distortion buzzes through the space between, and then the air parts. Out of that distortion, tumbles none other than the Walker's long lost guru. He looks different here, ageless, each angle of light shedding and adding years in a golden gleam. The red saisin string around his wrist still sizzles, while hers has long burned away.

"At last!" the Guru cries. "I thought you were lost." She believes she was, for a time. He praises the goddess, then tells her that it's time to come back to where she belongs. As he continues to speak, an explosion shakes the earth, great clouds of fire and smoke erupting from where the celestials battle, high in the blazing sky, a blur of weapons and limbs that human eyes cannot follow.

Beyond them, the ice-pale trunk of the tree beyond worlds soars into the clouds. Beckons.

The path back to the mortal realm.

The Walker interrupts his prophesizing. "I'm not staying. Lord Brahmah showed me the future. I wish I could unsee it, but it's impossible. I have a greater purpose now. The future of Loram and Suyoram are interconnected. I must act. I must stop our enemies."

The guru implores, "It is not your fight! How can you not see what's right in front of your eyes? Lo, Gris, Suyo, it means nothing! Our souls are blind to constructs as base as imagined borders! Or language, skin color... nothing! You are here, now, at the feet of nirvana, child. You have the ultimate at your fingertips and you'd throw it all away? For what? To bring more death and destruction into the world? To take on an ocean of karma and fall back into the endless torture of samsara?"

The Walker takes exception to this charge. He knew that she was not ready to leave the world, and he brought her anyway. Angered, she seizes him by the shoulders and says, "You brought me to sacrifice to Kinesh-Kira, to guarantee your own salvation! I will return. With or without you."

The guru falters, stammers, and then, the celestials smash onto the field, expelling a mushroom-shaped cloud of dust and ash and blood. His eyes grow cold. "No. I am the one she speaks to! I have only ever helped you!"

Says the Walker, "You're the reflection of the moon on the water. But you're not the moon." And she pushes the guru away, then seizes the Severer of Sorrows from the throne. It is light as a feather. She can't explain exactly why, but she knows this weapon is needed to do what is necessary. Still, she suspects the lord asura will not approve of this theft, and while Kinesh-Kira has him occupied, she hurries toward the roots of the world tree.

She climbs amidst the storm of shattered steel, the phantom wars, the echoes of blood. If Indrajit notices her theft, he makes no sign of it. The roots grow larger, large as rivers. The moment she climbs the last root and touches the long, smooth trunk, her vision tilts – the trunk becomes a straight path leading into a blinding bright portal. Just as the river Vaitarani had, the Field of the Fallen stretches out above and beneath her.

But before she reaches the return, the guru grabs her, and screams that she is young and ignorant, his voice rising to a fervor. His fingers wrap around her throat. She struggles, punches, fights, but can't reach. Her vision begins to fade. Can't breathe. He is crying, and says, "This is where you belong. Here. Now. Forever..."

Desperate, the Walker draws forth the Severer, and strikes the guru across the throat. Burning blood slashes across her face. His eyes bulge in disbelief as he touches his throat with both hands. Tries to speak but has run out of words. Blood dribbles down from his lips, down his chin. His astounded expression summons an image of a ferryman on the river... but then the old guru smiles and closes his eyes.

His head topples off his body, the cut across his neck perfectly clean. The Walker shoves his body away, which tumbles down the tree. With sorrow and outrage, she screams. She stares beyond the celestials locked in battle, far beyond sight, beyond a crystal temple door, where Brahmah's many eyes watch, devoid of emotion.

Impassive interest, fleeting at that. Her life, her dreams, her desires – they are the aspirations of but one grain of sand in the vast ocean of the cosmos.

The Walker realizes that it is never for the devas to render justice, not in a way perceived by one mortal lifetime's view of karma. The machinations behind this system are vast and unknowable – blooming and wilting like the leaves on a tree, so many branches weighed down by the decisions made throughout one's life, as well as the countless others lived.

Thus the Walker, finally free of obsession, free of the chains of her history, stands upon the tree of all realms and goes forth into the light. It no longer matters if she hasn't all the answers, because only one mattered for her mission.

To see an effect take place in the world, one must make it themselves.

Chapter 21

And the Walker Returns

Not again.

The first sense to return was her spirit, languishing under the crushing weight of existence. After living out the future of a life cut short, the weight of going through it all again – the pain, the suffering, the heartbreak – was devastating.

Now she understood Brahmah's warning. The burden of knowing what could be, what would have been, wasn't limited to one's own fate. It encompassed the experience of all beings, right now, in her current reality. Right now in Loram, there were people like Sira, powerless to watch the death of their country. Powerless to stop it, powerless to resist their invaders' perverse cruelty, and whose only escape was through annihilation.

The second sense to return was scent. Jasmine and frangipani, rose and lavender, a thicket of them. Papaya, fresh, ripe, the hint of decay. Beyond that, smoke – burning wood, sandalwood incense, and blood.

Sound followed, a rattling buzz that blanketed all else – the distinguishing call of Tiger-Locusts.

Then touch, a numbness encasing her entire body. Her heart began to beat faster, waking from the near-death state, sensation swirling over the surface of her skin. Finally, after what felt like days, she inhaled sharply from her mouth.

Someone cried out above the racket of locusts then was answered by others. Bells and chimes rung out; the air shifted. She flexed each finger, struggled to open her eyes. Sun streamed down from behind fluffy white clouds. A blue sky.

Back in the realm of man. Now she understood the unshrouded's frail mortality. To be in the presence of devas filled one with divine contentment, an all-fulfilling detachment. It couldn't exist here. Life as man knew, as the Sangha preached, was suffering.

Ree stirred, and a blanket of flowers tumbled from her body. They were everywhere, placed all around, along with bowls of blood and slivers of papaya. Her pyre had transformed into an altar, blanketed with the offerings and gifts favored by Kinesh-Kira. And kneeling before this altar, a large crowd of people gathered. Not only Ashukari – there were villagers she vaguely recognized from her travels, as well as armed rebels, and others that looked like travelers come from far away.

Baffled, Ree glanced over to Vasitra's pyre, only to find more people kneeling in its place.

Waiting for her?

Where are you? What is this? Ree reached out in the Everpresent, but didn't sense his presence. An Ashukari woman kneeling at the front of the crowd gazed up, a familiar face.

Tian. Ree smiled, but as she studied her friend's face, her smile faltered. There were lines around her eyes, alight with a zealous fervor that chilled her. She looked different. Older.

"The incarnation of Kinesh-Kira returns!" Tian exclaimed, raising her arms. "After so long, Isaree, the avatar of the goddess… has come to help us!"

Ree opened her mouth to protest, then noticed strands of her own silver hair hanging about her elbows. She'd never worn her hair this long before… and the roar of tiger-locusts took on a new meaning.

They only burrowed up from the ground every five years.

Voices arose all at once, some praising the devas, others pleading their troubles. She could hardly parse through the dissenting voices, but one thread resurfaced – the war was here.

She could have denied it. She could have announced that she was no deva incarnate, that indeed, she had walked with them in the realm, and that an asura king had instead offered her a power that would spread his mission of redemption to all the accursed…

But Ree couldn't shake the visions of doom that would come to Suyoram, if it hadn't already. The Gris were on her doorstep now. She had to do something. And to explain her reasons would be to invite doubt into what was freely presented for her taking – a deification awarded to a living goddess.

Indrajit had given her power, and the phi recognized it. From the edges of the forest, she felt their presence, watching in keen interest with their glowing eyes. They would listen to her. They would trust her.

"Don't be afraid," Ree reached out to them, reached out to everyone, living and dead. Her aura shimmered with a new energy, dark but benign. She rose on her altar as the crowd hushed, raised her head and said, *"I've returned to save you all."*

"Of course we will follow."

Tian and Havan were the first to take up arms. They walked the left-hand path, the Ashukari who believed they were already dead, their salvation decided. Not all believed so fervently. Many had left after Vasitra died, to Ree's astonishment, only three days into the ritual. His face had turned purple, and his eyes opened. He reached up and grasped the nearest seeker, who happened to be Tian.

"She will return as the will of Kinesh-Kira," he gasped. "Wait for her."

And then his head had toppled off.

It was enough for many to curiously await her return. None had ever walked in the realm longer than three days. With every passing sunrise, they laid out more offerings to please the devas until her pyre had transformed. Days become months became years.

One morning, a week before she awoke, the sword of Indrajit had appeared from nowhere, in her hands. It burned anyone who dared touch it. The seekers that remained then pledged to follow Isaree, believing Vasitra's words, that she was the reborn avatar of the goddess.

After everything she learned, everything she'd seen, Ree understood it would only take one new revelation to strip away the framework of everything she knew. But for the first time in her life, she was content with that. So… if the Ashukari said she was the avatar of Kinesh-Kira, who was she to deny their reality?

Five years. It had felt even longer in the realm. Staring into her reflection in the waterfall, Ree saw she hadn't wasted away or lost muscle mass. She couldn't discern much change aside from her hair.

But much could change in five years. She learned the Lo resistance had been completely driven underground. The capital had fallen, the entire country occupied, and Muang-Hhleg was now the center of the Gris' operations.

The Grisland-Loramese Protectorate was the new name for the country.

Five years might have been a long time, but it seemed short enough after living through the hell of Sira's life. Kit hadn't existed in that one, and a vague melancholy settled in when she realized he would be twenty-five now. She attempted to explain to some of the Ashukari what she'd learned, that time didn't work the way most thought it did. Time was not a river flowing downhill, but a sea of stars, of distance and gravity with shortcuts and patterns and connections unseen. They listened, but she doubted any would understand until they walked in the realm themselves.

Humans could only do so much.

Ree tracked down Minh. By then, the Black Water Army had been beaten down to little more than scattered bands of renegades throughout the provinces, moving supplies through expansive underground tunnels. But Minh had never abandoned the people of Muang-Hhleg. Her regiment of holdouts still paid tribute to the Weaver, still smuggled people in and out of the city.

Going toe-to-toe with the Gris would never be a fair fight, therefore Ree decided the fight should never be fair. She told Minh that she would be back, and when she returned they would win the war. Minh scoffed, but only said, "Sure, Isaree. We'll be waiting."

Ree kissed her lovers goodbye, and disappeared into the mountains alone. She followed the cries of displaced spirits until she found the sanctuary of the Guardian of the Kalashas. When she tumbled over a massive nest the size of a crater, a great garuda with golden feathers stared down at her, and she knelt, offering her service as a tribute. Ree promised to rid the land of those poisoning the air and the rivers in exchange for easy, hidden passage throughout the countryside.

Give me the Serene Way, great spirit. And I will give you back your land.

I'll give you more than the Serene Way, the guardian said. *I'll give you my greatest warrior, Dama, the Voice of the Valley.* The great garuda raised his head and screeched across the sky, a thunderous cry that was heard echoing for hundreds of miles. A few minutes later, an immense, dark-furred tiger-spirit slunk from the forest, with crimson stripes and a single sharp horn above two fierce, yellow eyes.

I hope you prove worthy of such an honor, Dama said.

And for a year, Ree and Dama traveled all throughout the scarred land of Loram, to the peripheries of mass graves, to the burned villages, the massacres, the aftermath of the lost war. Rumors spread of a strange woman riding the back of a tiger, ghost-like through the wreckage, disappearing into forests as quickly as she appeared.

Ree searched for the discontent souls that had undeservedly returned as phi. These were taihong, ghosts of the violently murdered, who appeared remarkably human aside from their glowing green eyes, finger-length fangs and claws. In the guild, she'd learned their organs were identical to humans, best harvested while still alive.

"I offer you salvation in Indrajit's name," Ree raised the Severer of Sorrows. The asura sword seemed to breathe in, the power flowing throughout her body as intoxicating as rich wine.

But you're in the gray, you're a hunter, one of the taihong whispered, shirking back from her. *You lie!*

No, this is the one Homdee spoke of, another drew closer, eyes fixated on the sword. His name was Owun, and he'd been sixteen when he was forced to watch his sisters and mother repeatedly violated and murdered before Grisi soldiers turned the gun on him. *This magic is different.*

The validation only bolstered her confidence. Phi hunters learned to use magic in such a rigid, specific manner. Gray magic, or spirit magic, was a method of high control, with all the rituals and voiceless chants ingrained until it became second nature. They called it tradition, but maybe it was more a lack of trust for their own students to explore themselves, and perhaps diverting from the paths well-trodden.

There were other paths to the magic of the spirit realm, the magic of devas. And now, this magic she'd taken from the deva realm had no parameters. No rules, no constraints. She felt the possibilities split forth infinitely, into other realities, splitting reality itself before the desired one manifested before her. One in which the phi could earn their respite through focusing their violent nature on those deserving.

I have heard this before, another taihong lamented, covering his ears. *Thirty years of hunger. Of insatiable, starving hunger! It is unfathomable.*

"That was his original amnesty. But I offer something far better," Ree smiled and held out her hand. "Serve me for one grand task. It might take months, it might take years, but afterward, you'll be free."

Most phi wanted an end to their suffering. But there were others that did not. For them, she had another offer.

"If you don't want redemption, I can give you something else," she told the phi unmoved by the promise of regained humanity. "Protection. Tribute. A means to satisfy your blood thirst and desire for revenge, in exchange for a noble cause."

It proved a compelling offer.

With her otherworldly allies waiting and ready, the hard part came next.

Ree returned to the rebels' underground base to meet with Minh, and her second, a stern, middle-aged intellectual named Khim.

"I'm going to retake the city and the fort," Ree said simply, confidently. Havan and Tian insisted on accompanying her as bodyguards, sitting on either side of her, wearing their Kinesh-Kira scythes.

"And you want to do that with your... phi allies?" Despite her familiarity with Homdee, Minh shifted uncomfortably, tapping her fingers on her knees. The years of struggle had taken their toll. Even though she was only fifteen years Ree's senior, her face was heavily lined, her hair now completely gray. "Are you sure you can you control them? They won't hurt our people?"

Ree wasn't sure. All she had was a vision and a gamble. But before she could figure out a reassuring answer, Tian shot the rebel a glare as if the question was preposterous.

"You doubt the will of Kinesh-Kira?" Tian snapped. Ree didn't correct her. The Ashukari did appear fearsome to outsiders, with their ash-covered bodies, bone garlands, and skull face paint, but to Minh's credit, the rebel leader did not shirk away. The conversation soon devolved into an argument.

Ree knew she needed to bring them together somehow, but how to appeal to the pragmatic rebels and retain the faith of the Ashukari? The rebels were struggling, but their strength lay in the fact they would never die out completely, never while the conditions which formed them still existed. They were resilient, a hearty weed that could take root in the most fallow of lands and spread like wildfire, if only she could give them enough tinder.

As for the Ashukari, she felt both a loyalty and responsibility to them now. It was too late to disclaim her status as a returned goddess, they wouldn't accept it, anyway. To take this dangerous path forward, she needed loyalists. And who better to have on your side than the Ashukari, who believed all was permitted, and whose greatest desire above all was death itself? They were finite, but they were fearless.

It dawned on her that of all the paths forward, the hardest one had the greatest chance of success. But it would have a high cost. It would take a lot from her, she feared.

"Leave us for a moment," Ree told Tian and Havan. They glanced at one another, then walked outside. Minh nodded to Khim to do the same. Now that they were alone, Minh sat back down at the table.

"I've been doing this a long time," Minh said. "And I know a cult when I see it."

"I know what it looks like. But if I'm going to join your cause, I need people I can trust," Ree said. "They believe in me–"

"They believe you're a goddess," Minh interjected, with no lack of judgment in her tone. "And I'm not convinced you don't believe it yourself."

Ree studied Minh's expression, then silently pulled the Sword of Sorrows from her belt and placed it on the table. Slowly, with some theater, she drew the blade a few inches from its scabbard.

Immediately, Minh paled, staring at the pulsing edge with a mix of intrigue and fear. Even someone with no connection to the Everpresent understood that this object was not of this world.

"I'm not a goddess. But I saw enough of the realm to know the devas play by different rules. Rules we can't fathom. I don't claim to be anything, only one who has seen and remembered. One who will do what it takes to prevent the destruction of our Rami culture."

With that, she snapped the sword back into its scabbard. Minh jerked back as if waking from a spell.

"I'm asking a lot from you and your people, but you know these lands the best," Ree said. "You know that this might be the last chance you have to see a free Loram. We'll strike fear into their hearts in Muang-Hhleg and then take back every province, one by one."

"Why…" Minh said, regarding Ree cautiously. "Why do you, a runaway girl, ex-phi hunter from Suyoram, care *so* much about Loram?"

"Because the Gris won't stop. Because the Gris aren't the only colonizers who will come for us. Suyoram will be next. And I won't let that happen." Ree felt the fury rise in her guts. "Let me prove it to you here."

The fire that Ree remembered seeing in the rebel leader's eyes finally seemed to reignite.

Chapter 22

Battle of Iron Town

High in the clear night sky, a wavering blood-red moon blazed full over the Kalasha mountains. Muang-Hhleg had become the center of production for the Protectorate, ships constantly ferrying their trade goods down to Kohkiem and beyond. Citizens toiled under the boot of their Grisi occupiers. Temples had been stripped and painted over in the austere dark hues of the Churches of the Supreme. The new forges ran day and night without pause, smoke constantly billowing from the bellows, minecarts rolling to and from the caverns and the quarry, laden with coal and iron ore and other precious resources. Lo workers trudged home, covered head to toe in soot and ashes under the watchful eyes of their overseers. New factories assembled these materials into goods, packed them into boxes, loaded them onto wagons and sent them down the river.

The only difference from slavery was that the citizens were paid a wage, and they kept their homes and families if they had them, but the new order was undeniable. They were required to carry identification papers and could not travel freely.

In Loram, being outside under the blood moon was a bad omen, and most refused to work. But in the new order, the work did not stop.

Under the light of the blood moon, a total lunar eclipse, the rebels struck back. And it was a night spoken about for many years to come.

Noon was eleven, not yet old enough to work at the parlor. Ma worked all the time. Ma said she was saving up money to buy exit visas. Ma said exit visas were a new thing since the Protectorate. Before, anyone could just leave whenever they wanted, though you still needed money to get by. But soon, she told Noon, soon they'd have enough for two exit visas and then passage to Suyoram, where Auntie Lawan lived.

Most nights there wasn't enough to eat, and hunger drove Noon to catching frogs in the park. Ma didn't like it, said it was dangerous. But it wasn't as dangerous as it was empty. Noon vaguely remembered the centrally located city park being full of people when she was little: picnicking, exercising, enjoying the flowers, praying at small shrines. Now the garden beds were overgrown, fallen trees blocked the paths, sometimes littered with garbage from the vagrants who managed to avoid the Protectorate patrols.

But Ma wasn't home at night to stop her. Besides, Noon knew the places to avoid and stuck to the ponds where her prey was.

She crouched amongst the reeds, sharpened stick in hand. The big red moon shined pretty on the water. There was a rustle in the bushes. Probably just a rabbit or a rat, though she'd seen a fox once. Noon warily watched the area, but quickly lost interest, focusing on her frog hunt. Her stomach grumbled. She'd only eaten a few spoonfuls of rice all day. Rats tasted terrible, and rabbits were too fast.

Then she spotted one, a fat, slimy frog at the edge of the pond. Carefully, Noon raised her stick. Just as she was about to stab, the frog hopped into the water with a plop, sending a splash across the bank.

"Nooo," Noon groaned. Maybe the elders were right, the blood moon was unlucky. She fought back tears, staring at the water as it slowly settled back to stillness… and the reflection of a stranger.

Noon spun around, mouth agape. The woman standing before her might be the oddest person she'd ever seen. She wore black chong-kraben trousers and a black sabai wrap around her chest, with her shoulders uncovered – an outdated fashion now forbidden for women in the Protectorate. Her body looked cut from wood – muscles stringy but sinewy. Her hair was long and pulled back, but glinted silver, which was odd because she looked about her ma's age: too young to have gone gray.

Oddest of all, underneath a black stripe of paint, her eyes seemed to glow as red as the moon. And then Noon noticed a whole group of figures behind her, lurking in the overgrown thicket of palm trees, all wearing ragged cloaks. She couldn't see their faces, shadowed by their shrouds, but there was something horrifying about them. Noon's heart thudded painfully fast, and she wanted to scream, or run, but instead she stood silent, frozen with terror.

"It's okay, little one. No one's going to hurt you," the woman said in a firm tone, her Rami spoken with a Suyo accent that rendered it somewhat musical to Noon's ears. "Why are you out so late? You should be home."

Noon finally made a sound with her throat, close to a gasp, and a whimper.

The woman glanced around, then crouched, gazing up at Noon and smiling softly. "My name's Isaree. What's your name?"

Noon gulped, then finally managed to say, "Noon."

"Hi, Noon. I'm just here looking for my friend. Have you seen anyone come through here? A Grisi man with green eyes, wearing a black cap?"

Noon shook her head.

"Hmm." Isaree stood, glancing around. Noon noticed the woman's belt then, laden with pouches, a coiled rope with a hook, a daab sword, and several knives.

"What are you doing here?" Noon said, a hint of panic in her voice.

"Helping," Isaree said offhandedly, then tilted her head. "Someone's coming." Noon noticed the cloaked figures sink back into the shadows without the woman commanding them.

"No loitering after sundown!" someone shouted, and two guards wearing the uniform of the Protectorate came around the bend.

Noon panicked. Loiterers were thrown in jail for the night and fined, including children. She wasn't sure what the woman was going to say to them to get out of it, and she looked *so* odd.

"Hey you, hands up!"

Isaree put her hands up, but she didn't turn around.

"What do we have here?" the other one glanced at Noon, but warily watched Isaree as they approached, holding their wooden batons at the ready.

Minh had warned Ree that there were Lo men working in military branches for the Protectorate, including doing this type of work – policing. The rebels despised these "collaborators" even more than the occupying forces themselves. As far as they were concerned, any Loram national working for the Gris were traitors, and the preferred flavor of execution was sacrifice to Homdee.

But looking at these men, who were hardly older than boys, with faces like hers and eyes like Kit's... Ree felt something else. Something softer. Pity? Sorrow? Perhaps they had limited options, and it was the only way they could feed their families.

But when she'd mentioned this to Minh, the rebel leader met her with unabashed vitriol.

"They have a choice," she'd said. "They could take other work. They could do nothing. They could help their neighbors, their people, not help the Gris find and execute them. Fuck their reasons, they aren't victims. They made their choice, and they are our enemies."

Walker, the taihong Owun spoke from the shadows, voice raspy with bloodlust. *They mean to harm you.*

Wait. Ree's mind raced. If she unleashed the phi now, she wasn't sure if she could control who they went after, and she was all too aware of Noon's wide eyes darting from Ree's to the approaching guards. The phi *seemed* to understand that Ree was targeting specific enemies, but when she explained further, they didn't quite grasp the difference between a Lo and Grisi national. From their eyes, there were few distinctions aside from living humans: spirits, the hunters, and to her surprise, the Ashukari, who they called "shining ones" and left alone. And then there was Ree, the Walker.

She'd have to wait to get inside the fort before attacking.

Her only option now was to deal with these guards herself. She always knew it would come to this, should she take this path. She would have to hurt people, even kill them. Even after all this time, Ree felt the teachings of the guild linger, to never harm another person. She'd hurt Esha, and hated it, hated herself for doing it. She'd killed Vasitra, but it hadn't felt real. If there was any way she could appeal to them–

"Listen," Ree spun around to face them, her arms still raised. "I'm here to help you. To help the city."

One guard gasped and recoiled, but the other raised his baton and yelled, "On your knees, now!"

"Please, cousin, listen. You don't have to work for them–"

"I said now!" He hit her in the gut with the baton, and she doubled over.

"You can… still go home," Ree stammered as she coughed, clutching her stomach in pain. "The oppressors–"

"Shut the fuck up with your terrorist bullshit! The fucking 'oppressors' pay better than I ever made in the mines." The guard smacked her in the thigh and she stumbled to her knees. "You rebels just made it worse for everyone!" He hit her again in the side and when she fell over, continued reigning blows on her prone body. "My father died during one of your attacks! He was just walking to work!"

"Hey," the other guard grabbed his arm. "Wait. We should take her in alive, they'll want to question her."

"Fuck that!" he shoved the other one away. "Only good rebel is a dead one."

"Leave her alone!" Noon threw herself in front of Ree, just as the man had brought his baton down.

A crack echoed as the baton connected with her head. She crumpled to the ground. He gasped, freezing as he stared at the prone child.

"Oh shit, shit, shit," he stammered. "Is she–?"

He never finished the sentence. The next second he was on his back. Ree stared down into his wide eyes, one reflecting the gleaming light of the full blood moon, the other flush with the hilt of her hunting knife.

"You can go home now," she whispered, and felt her own eyes stinging. It was the quickest, most instantaneous death she could offer, but her stomach turned as his body continued to twitch. She looked up at the other guard, who hadn't moved. "And you can go home now, too."

"Who is that?" Havan said from the shadows of the alley. Ree set down the limp body of Noon. She was alive, but the blow had knocked the girl unconscious.

"Met her in the park. A guard hit her," Ree said, turning her head to spit, bile still sour in her mouth. "What happened?"

"It took longer than we planned to hunt down the captain," Havan said, glancing at the cloaked figures trailing behind her, then pulled out a ring of keys and handed them over. "But Tian came through. The fort's ours for the taking."

"Is Tian still inside?" Ree asked.

"No," Havan said. "She said she'd leave after getting what we needed."

Still shaking, Ree embraced him, burying her head in the crook of his neck. With his hair shorn short, dressed in the uniform of the enemy, it must have been an odd sight. Quietly, she whispered, "I don't know if I can do this." He held her tightly and stroked the side of her head. She smelled the blood on his hands.

"Should we call it off?" he asked in earnest, a ridiculous question. It was too late to turn back; everyone had their orders and they all depended on one another. Yet Ree knew that if she said the word, he and the other Ashukari would follow her, and that thought comforted her more than he would ever know.

"No, but I need you to get this girl out of here," Ree said.

"Why? No, I'm staying with you. When we get into the fort–"

"No," Ree insisted. "It's not going to be safe. I have to go somewhere before then, and I won't be able to see you... I think it's the only way I can get through this. Do not let anyone come into the fort. Wait until I come out. Promise."

"Of course, I promise," he said, pulling back to gaze at her, brows furrowed. "But I don't understand. Where are you going?"

"Into the Hunters' Trance," Ree said, then produced the needle of Dreamless poison from her pouch.

Going into the trance would sever her emotions, would focus her entire awareness on her target, her goal. No hesitation, no fear, no reasoning. Only the end and the means to get there. The last time she'd considered entering the Trance, she'd worried that without having passed the trial, it would destroy her. But she knew better now. She knew that the traditions of the hunters were just that – a way of interpreting a method, a method that could be shaped into her own tool. She no longer feared the ritual, but she feared her own humanity. Right now, she couldn't afford to have her conscience awake.

Right now, she needed to be a monster.

There would come to be many conflicting accounts of what happened that night under the blood moon in Muang-Hhleg, the Protectorate's Iron Town. A young guard spotted a white-haired, red-eyed woman leave the central park with two dozen cloaked figures, heading toward the fort. An elderly woman swore she saw one Gris soldier quietly slit the throat of another, taking his keyring before throwing his body into the bushes. Several people recalled an imposing, black-clad figure with a butcher's knife walking out of the gatehouse, covered in blood, followed by a whole contingent of armed rebels, disappearing quickly into the back alleys and toward the Grisland Trading Company headquarters.

Key points of the city suddenly burst with violence. Alarm bells pealed out in the night, only to be silenced, peppered with gunshots and screams. Workers stopped production, wandering outside even as their overseers screamed to continue on. The chaos wasn't immediate, but grew slowly, steadily, like an enormous, rising beast. Sometime after midnight, the Grisi Governor-General was roused from his quarters by a quivering lieutenant who struggled to articulate exactly what they'd seen – things! There were *things* scaling the fortress walls, impervious to gunfire, and they used their claws and teeth to tear through their ranks before the men could withdraw into the inner fortifications.

This city had always obsessed over mystical nonsense. Rumors of a demon living deep below, rumors of a curse that affected the dead, that's all these Spiceland folk seemed to believe in, ghosts and black magic and strange perverse gods with many arms. Now it had infected his men. He thought it delusional – another rebel attack? No, they'd been quiet for years. Perhaps a new group of terrorists. There were always new insurgents sprouting up, only to be stomped down. The commander was reported to have said these things as he hurried to confront this force. He was still cursing the entire country and his own when he walked into a slaughter.

In the Trance, the world had gone gray, bright spots the beating hearts of men, dark pulses the presence of the phi. In this state Ree's thoughts connected with theirs even louder and clearer than before, and she wielded their attention like a spear. Now she understood how phi had trouble recognizing the difference between a Gris soldier and any other. She couldn't see the difference either. They were targets, nothing more. Her magic was even easier to wield, hardly the thought of a voiceless chant needed before coursing through and from her, blinding her enemies, bolstering her strength, healing wounds almost the moment they occurred.

But she found her magic was largely unnecessary. Not only had the phi a voracious appetite, but the sword of Indrajit was a blade forged to sever the chains of karma, so what was a creature's armored shell against that? What was a tiny shard of metal speeding through the air when faced with an abyss that drank the sins of the accursed?

They were nothing.

Limbs and heads fell like leaves scattered by a gale. The bright spots faded before her easily, the noises they made could very well have been the rain or the wind. Like a game, or a task, like hammering nails into a fence one by one, like plucking carrots from the ground, it was only labor. Time passed in fragments, in moments. Her enemy was the fort itself, and she moved through the passages as if they were arteries, as if she were the antibody come to purge the sickness from the host's veins.

This one wants to surrender. In the courtyard, Owun stood atop a man whose heart still glowed, holding him still. All around, splinters of the barricade lay shattered. Some phi huddled nearby, licking their wounds, picking bullets from their flesh. Others stood still, watching, while others gnashed at their fallen prey, attempting to eat despite their inability to do so. Owun stepped away as Ree approached. *This one denounces his own god as he begs for his life.*

Ree couldn't hear the man, not from the Trance. His words were only noise, not unlike the chitter of an insect. Whatever it was, it couldn't move her. During a hunt, a target couldn't surrender. There was only one end. She strode to this last man, and with a vague sense that wasn't quite satisfaction, but the physical relief of completion, severed his head from his body.

That's all of them. Ree sheathed the sword, turning in a full circle around the courtyard, searching over the unmanned walls. She didn't want to leave the Trance, but she could already feel the tides ebbing away now that her hunt was complete.

Not all. Some fled to the river. They haven't gone far...

Let them go. Ree sat, her body growing heavy. Her awareness rose toward the brightness of the Everpresent, and the first tendril of fear gripped her heart. She clutched her chest, beginning to hyperventilate. Fear was such a useful tool. *Follow them at a distance, make sure they leave, watch where they go. But let them go. Let them spread word of what awaits our enemies.*

Owun backed away, and the phi followed him, disappearing quickly over the outer walls.

Alone now, the aftereffects of countless cuts and bullet wounds she'd accumulated throughout the night began to ache. Her body seemed to have a mind of its own, shaking uncontrollably, tears pouring from her eyes, even as her mind hadn't quite caught up. The thick sour iron scent of death and shit and piss grew overwhelming, and all the byproducts of her hunt finally started to make a different connection.

Carnage. Pure, unfiltered carnage.

There were bodies everywhere. Gris soldiers, Lo collaborators, what looked like Lo servants, and other Gris noncombatants. Panicked, Ree tried to stand, but stumbled over the head of what had been the commander. She screamed, and covered her mouth, only to choke on the taste of blood. For the second time that night, she vomited.

What have I done? Ree stumbled through the blood-soaked corridors, desperate to escape the lifeless eyes of her victims. It felt surreal, as if someone else committed this massacre and Ree only woke up in their shoes. But unlike a dream, she remembered it all perfectly. She remembered that girl, who had cowered by the window, and that man, who had shielded her. In the Trance, she had felt nothing. But now, it made her sick to her stomach and overcome with a grief she couldn't name.

It had to be done. Taking the fort had been impossible for the rebels, preventing them from liberating the city, and preventing any lasting resistance in the region for years. Now they would have a base and a city, and the industry that the Gris had established. What she'd done may have been horrific, but it was necessary.

They chose to be here, she told herself. *They didn't have to work for the enemy. They didn't have to* be *the enemy.* She repeated this over and over, until exhaustion settled deep within her, finally steadying her nerves.

And then she saw Tian.

Like Havan, she was almost unrecognizable without her Ashukari markings. In simple servant clothes, her hair combed and tied back under a scarf, she lay half against the wall. Ree fell to her knees before her and with shaking hands, checked for a pulse. Needlessly so, as her injuries were blatantly fatal. But they weren't the torn skin and flesh flayed by claws and fangs. No, she'd been cleanly sliced through the chest with a straight edge.

Ree had killed her while in the Trance without even knowing it.

"Tian, no..." Ree whimpered, rocking back and forth, then let herself sob anew. There was something in her friend's hand. A lotus blossom, tied with red saisin string. She'd stayed behind on purpose.

She'd gone to meet the goddess.

Gears clicked and clanked as the gate rose. If all had gone according to plan, the rebels would have subdued the rest of the city. How would her allies react to the horrors that awaited them inside? The rebels, the Ashukari, the civilians? Would they be frightened? Disgusted? Would they drive her away?

Beyond the short drawbridge over a ditch, a makeshift barricade blocked the access road – overturned wagons and barrels and construction materials. Momentarily, she wondered if the Gris had regrouped somehow. Maybe the ones stationed in town beat back the rebels and were now ready to throw everything they had to kill the demons inside.

Too exhausted to fight, or care, Ree walked outside.

Slowly, a black-clad rebel stepped out into the open, followed by several others, all with weapons bloodied and ready. They stared at her curiously, tentatively peering over her shoulder, as if searching for the soldiers holding her hostage. Minh walked out at last, limping slightly, face and clothes bloody.

"We took the Protectorate headquarters," Minh said. "Brutal fight, but they weren't expecting us. The fort is, is it...?"

"It's done," Ree said. "The city is ours."

The rebels erupted in a cheer, and flooded forward. Minh clasped Ree's arms, then laughed and swept her into a hug. Ree hung on to her to keep from collapsing, but there was little joy in her heart.

"You really were sent by the devas," Minh murmured.

Ree very much doubted that.

Something inside her had broken and could never be whole again.

III

Chapter 23

From the Ruins of Reason

Once Tan had a target, he made sure to do his research beforehand. It was amateurish to assume your mark would think like you, would commit the same mistakes or capitalize on the same advantages. He needed to get inside their heads, understand their history, what motivated them, build something of a profile to model their behavior.

While his squad decided to enjoy the famed Golden Brothel of Sapphrachorn, he sat in his rented room and poured over the reports given to him by Elleman. There were only a few from Muang-Hhleg, where just a handful of survivors had escaped. The majority came from the other bases and settlements that had fallen afterward. Eyewitness accounts of the Heretic varied – some described her as a ghost, fluid as a slinking shadow with a streak of red eyes, liquid in her movements, disappearing after cutting a man down, only to reappear a moment later to slice another man's head clean off. Others said she was unnaturally tall, with long fangs and silver fur, and cold, hateful glowing eyes, impervious to bullet and blade alike. A few others, including a senior captain, claimed she was a small child who could shapeshift into a tiger.

He discounted the monstrous forms. On that point, he agreed with Burrows: in the heat of battle, adrenaline and fear played tricks on the mind. But two things stuck out to him: glowing red eyes, and an uncanny ability to shrug off what should have been lethal injuries. The only type of people with those physical characteristics and magical powers were of a relic, a traditional group that were once far more relevant in old times.

The phi hunters.

Now, the once-revered guild had been all but disbanded. He researched the history, writing to Somatra who also tapped the royal historian for more information. The phi hunters once had a compound in the Capital, in old city even, not far from the palace. But shortly before Tan's birth, the entire guild was uprooted and moved upcountry. There wasn't information as to why, but it could be assumed that it was due to his grandfather's modernization efforts, coaxing the country to be less superstitious. Another likely suspect was simply economics. Once upon a time, communities would pay premium to rid their lands of a troublesome phi or even a murderous demon, but now?

Now, for the majority of the population, times were tough, thanks to the reparations owed to the Gris from the Bay of Echoes incident. Haunted places remained abandoned, communities fled, many moving to the cities in search of more lucrative work. And as a result, there weren't hunters seen wandering the wilds like they used to, stopping regularly in rural villages plagued by hungry ghosts. But they did still have members, and kept the guild hall that Tan briefly remembered visiting so long ago.

And so, he requested two hundred of his Wild Cobras from the Capital, and in the meantime, brought his advance squad to Jinburi.

The crossroads town of Jinburi was a welcome sight after three days of hard riding. The second largest city in Suyoram, it occupied a crucial position on the Namleng and Jinburi river – the center of commerce in the deep country.

His mother loved the Rom Laithong celebration here. It was the best in the country, she'd said. There always seemed to be a great many more artists and performers here in one place, from the jugglers on the streets, to the music peeling out open windows of theaters and taverns.

When he was young, she'd bring him to visit during the holiday annually, and he distinctly remembered one particular year, where during dinner he'd suffered his first apasmara episode. He hadn't known what was happening at the time, only fear and panic as the world took on a nonsensical aura. He didn't remember leaving the dinner table, but he remembered running outside for air… and nonsense again. Then waking up in the yard, far from the house, shirt torn, feet dirty.

In the late evening the river city buzzed with life, though Tan noticed a certain concentrated wildness about the place that contrasted with the sprawling Capital. The buildings weren't as tall, and though there were notably areas of new construction, it still looked, for the most part, traditionally Suyo. There were, however, certain neighborhoods where the Gris settled. They passed more than a few churches to the Holy Patriarch, somewhat out of place next to the golden bells of the temples.

Tan, face obscured by his shemaugh, rode through the quiet outer districts with his squad, then stabled their horses at the gate to old town as if they were simple travelers, walking through the crowded streets. After putting their gear down at a quiet tavern several blocks away from the infamous Sing-Sing road, Tan warned the boys to stay out of trouble while him and Simo went to chase down his lead.

"I remember this place," Tan said as they arrived at the gate to the Phi Hunters guild. "Looks different."

On the outskirts of Jinburi, the compound encompassed several acres. The guild hall stood front and center, surrounded by a grassy yard, pleasantly spotted with palms, and a stream running throughout that disappeared into a wooded area. Other buildings were recognizable as well, a mostly empty stables, a barracks, a warehouse – though all built in an archaic, stone architecture style of Venara-era, with esoteric symbols and carvings proudly defining its place in history. It struck Tan as a combination of military training ground and temple complex, yet too ornate for the former and too utilitarian for the latter.

"Looked different how?" Simo turned fully around as they walked to the guild hall, staring at the statues of the snarling monkey warriors. "Place looks like it hasn't changed in six centuries."

"For starters, it was populated," Tan said. He paused before the steps and the big, closed doors. Back when he'd visited, the doors were thrown wide open and welcoming, with instruments echoing from the interior. The smell of home-cooked food and the sound of laughter had given it a festive atmosphere, surreal with the heavily tattooed men trading stories around the table, deep in their cups. Festive and eerie – the red gleam in their eyes jarred him into stunned silence when he first encountered them.

But mixed in the crowd were ordinary tradesmen and women, who seemed just as familiar with these piratical phi hunters as any. Wives wrangled the screaming children chasing dogs, the older kids giggling and throwing firecrackers at each other under the decorative lanterns strung between the pillars and posts. It had felt like a big family affair, but one from another world.

Now the yard sat abandoned. Where he remembered a group of teenagers swimming in the stream, only overgrown weeds remained, with some stray dogs laying in the shade under a mango tree.

He remembered his mother introducing him to her former colleague, another consort of his father's, but one who'd begged his grandfather to be dismissed from service after the crown-prince died. The woman was indeed beautiful as consorts tended to be, age had only refined her further. But in her common dress, without the careful makeup, she had seemed so different from his mother that it was hard to believe they'd ever enjoyed the same status.

She was your father's favorite, his mother had told him before they arrived. *He was helplessly in love with her, in large part because he could never quite tame her fierce spirit. And through his actions, he drove her away even before his death.*

Tan remembered thinking that was odd. *If he loved her so much, why did he do that?*

My dear, sometimes we are the cruelest to the ones we love the most.

"Are you lost, boys?" a grating voice cut through Tan's reverie. He seemed to appear out of nowhere, standing in the yard with his arms crossed. Shirtless, his wrinkled skin stretched thin over muscles tightly woven as old rope, almost every inch tattooed, even one side of his face. One eye was clear white, the other a deep, blood red, both glaring under furrowed brows. "We're not open for business today."

Simo inhaled sharply, and Tan quickly presented a wai. "Hello, Master Seua. I met you many years ago here during Rom Laithong." The man only tilted his head slightly in response. "I'm Commander Tanung of the Wild Cobras, and this is my second, Lieutenant Simo. I was hoping to speak with the guild about a very important matter."

"A very important matter, is it now?" The master hunter sighed heavily, as if speaking was one of the most tiring activities to exist. "Let me guess, land taxes are going up again."

"I'm not a taxman, sir," Tan said. "I'm looking for someone." He glanced around, wondering if there were anyone else here but for this ornery old man and the dogs. Of course, he didn't expect to find his suspect here, but if his suspicions were correct, she'd once been part of the family. And families tended to stick together. "I believe that perhaps one of your former guild members might be able to help, but I need assistance tracking them down."

"Sounds like a manhunt, and we don't track people, including our own. Go to the magistrates office for that."

"You misunderstand," Tan said, patience growing thin. "There's no bounty for this person. It's–"

"A hit job." A twitch of a sneer graced the master's lip. "I understand exactly what you're asking, boy."

Simo took a step forward, fists clenched, raising his chin. Tan didn't stop him. "You will address the Storm-Prince with respect, old man."

Master Seua bristled, and opened his mouth to retort, but seemed to think better of it. Instead, he gave them a grimace, pressed his palms in a wai, and bowed deeply. "With respect, dear prince. If you haven't noticed, the guild isn't what it used to be. Only one phi hunter still makes rounds, and not often at that. The others have either retired or found it necessary to pursue other trades. All we do here now is teach our old ways to anyone who cares to learn."

"But you have novices, correct?" Tan asked. He distinctly remembered meeting one briefly, a half-Kutsu girl who'd looked him over none too critically. He'd been too focused on not staring at the girl's uncovered body to notice much else about her, but what stood out to him was her immense pride when introduced as one of the hunters-in-training.

"Used to," Master Seua said, tone carefully impassive. "Now only scribes. Majority of them are orphans who'll take a roof over their heads and a bowl of rice in exchange for discipline and education. Not much has changed in our demographic there."

"But you don't train them to hunt phi?"

"You can't hunt demons without magic." Master Seua recrossed his arms. "Penalties for disobeying the Act of Reason was made *very* clear to us when it passed. No magic rituals, no more phi hunters. Only by the grace of your grandfather's Sacred Stone decree does our guild hall even remain standing. Devas know our esteemed neighbors have been petitioning the governor to evict us for the last decade."

"I'll be frank, sir," Tan said. "I'm sure you have heard the rumors about a new rebel leader in Loram causing quite a bit of mayhem."

"We don't pay much attention to the news here."

"There have been reports from these gruesome attacks, and many of them seem to match the description of a phi hunter."

"Impossible. Nonviolence toward other humans is a tenet. You break your vows, you're excommunicated."

"You said phi hunters have taken other trades, so it's not impossible," Tan said.

Seua, stone-faced still, only narrowed his eyes. "We're not a policing force. We don't monitor anyone after they leave the guild."

"We'll need to see records of the guild members. Past and present," Tan said, and before the old man could argue, Simo reached into his vest and produced a folded, written letter, signed and sealed. "A formal warrant to assist in my investigation, by authority of the king."

Seua didn't take his eyes off Tan and gingerly took the paper. Without looking at it, he said, "Might take a few days. We're a little short staffed, if you couldn't tell."

"I see that. Thank you again, honorable Master," Tan said, then to Simo in Ghani, "wait outside."

"Sure?"

"Yeah."

Simo nodded and gave the elder a wai before sauntering out the gate to where their horses lingered. The master tilted his head again, eyes going distant, and drifting up to the keystone of the guild hall, where the symbol of the guild, three intersecting lines, were crude and chipped, but etched deeply.

Tan noticed his jaw and neck muscles twitch and then remembered something – hunters were impolitely called whispers, on account of being able to speak to one another beyond the range of a normal human's hearing. It was entirely possible this meeting hadn't been with one lonely old man.

"I can tell you care deeply about the guild. I remember what I saw here, albeit briefly. There was joy. And pride. A family. It must be painful to see what's befallen of those who've turned their back on the trade."

"I haven't felt pain in fifty years," the master said. Again, the twitch in the jaw. There was more to that sentence, but not for Tan's ears.

"You're uncertain of your place in the changing world," Tan said softly, and hoped his earnest sympathy came through. "But nothing is certain, Master Hunter. Times change both ways. Public opinion shifts, and if it becomes known a former hunter is indeed the source of indescribable *massacres*–" He let that word sink in. Saw a flicker of emotion cross Seua's eyes. Let his voice harden again. "The scale can completely flip one way or the other. I may be a minor prince, but I do have influence. Help me secure your honored reputation remains intact, and I could whisper to my masters as well."

The two men stared at one another for a long moment, and finally, Master Seua cracked a sad smile. Sad, but genuine.

"We appreciate your offer. But we're at peace with what our future brings," the old master said. "Change is constant and unavoidable, as uncontrollable as the rain. The trade likely will die with the last hunter. Or maybe it won't. Perhaps you should speak to him. He may have more insight than this lonely old man."

Chapter 24

A Couple Heads Richer

The problem with phi hunting wasn't the lack of work. It was the pay.

Esha crept through the reeds, the Blind Eagle's Eye rendering her near invisible in the night. Her target sat ten feet away, in front of a smoldering fire, completely unaware. Two others sat with him, murmuring to one another, every so often a chuckle or a sneer. Their scent matched what she'd been provided. In their hasty robbery, one had knocked over a censor, and traces of the incense still lingered on his sleeve. It wasn't their first crime; they'd been on a reckless spree over the last few weeks, all around the outskirts of the Long Road.

Fuckers had no idea. More than oblivious. Couldn't be from around here. If they were, they would have known that once your name was etched on a bounty around Jinburi and the surrounding provinces, you had little to no chance of escape.

"It's them." Raj's subvocal whisper came from across the clearing.

"Yep."

One of the bandits yawned, then took a long drink from a bottle.

"Should we move?"

"Not yet."

There were many considerations to this type of work – the main being that the pay was higher if the mark was captured alive. But punishments for banditry were strict, and nine times out of ten her marks would rather go down fighting. Might as well take those odds... if only their pursuers weren't a pair of ex-phi hunters who had been raised to kill demons.

Another few minutes passed, and one of them said something

about taking first watch. They argued for a moment, until the portly one settled back onto his bedroll and pulled his cap over his eyes. Must be the one in charge, as the second shot him a resentful glare before lighting a pipe. The one with the bottle snickered, then stood, and walked directly toward Esha.

She held steady, still as a stone, and he stopped not three paces to her right. The rustle of an unbuckling belt, then the tinkle of piss. Esha shifted her weight from her heels to her toes, then slipped on her brass knuckles. Her knife was ready in her other hand, but she hoped she didn't have to use it.

"I got this one. You on the sentry?"

"Yeah. Ready."

The bandit burped as his stream tapered off. Just when he shook the last few drops from his member, Esha moved. Her camouflaging spell dropped away, revealing her tall, strong form clad in dark-browns and greens to blend seamlessly into the landscape. The bandit opened his mouth, but before he could make a sound Esha punched him hard in the jaw, sending him toppling over, dick flopping about. She quickly removed the cuffs from her belt, kicking his body over so she could secure his hands behind his back.

One down. Across the clearing, Raj had the second in a stranglehold. The bandit's face was bright red as he desperately tore at Raj's forearm, but it was firmly flush under his chin. Good as done. Esha strode toward the last one, who must have sensed a shift in the air. He jumped up and whipped his cap off, much faster than she anticipated for a man of his size.

"Hey, what are you two–?" The bandit spotted Raj, then Esha, and immediately reached for his holster. "Shit!"

She threw her knife, and the hilt struck him hard on the wrist. He yelped and dropped the pistol as she tackled him. The man headbutted her hard on the temple, and her vision burst with stars.

"Stop!" Esha growled as they wrestled. She knew he wouldn't – if the roles were reversed, she wouldn't either – but it felt right to at least give him a warning before she had to use lethal force. She felt an impact against her side, and the warm wetness of blood, but no pain of course, thanks to her having passed Maijep trial as a novice. Irritated, Esha twisted his wrist so hard it snapped with a sickening crack. He screamed and she kneed him hard in the balls then rolled away.

Raj roughly shoved the bandit's face into the ground, knee against his spine while he secured him with cuffs.

"What the fuck are you two?!" Red-faced in pain, the bandit sputtered, staring wide-eyed at the shiv sticking out of Esha's side. She calmly removed it, pulling the threads of magic from the Everpresent into her wound to heal the injury. She glanced over their work, satisfied.

"A couple heads richer," she said.

"Ever wonder what it woulda been like?" Raj asked after bringing their beers to the table. After collecting their bounty on the bandits, they'd gone to their favorite riverside tavern for a drink.

"Staying with the guild?" Esha frowned.

Once, she'd believed there was a place for the phi hunters. She'd been firmly indoctrinated, willing to do anything to carry forth the time-honored tradition. But things had changed after Ree left. Whatever strange spell Ree cast had scarred Esha across the entire upper right side of her face and it never healed right, despite her magic and the medical expertise of the masters. She usually kept a shock of hair over it to avoid the stares, though still shaved the rest of her head. Raj still shaved his head too. Some habits just stuck.

It had been some of the worst pain she'd ever experienced. The masters had been perplexed, considering Esha had passed the Maijep trial and shouldn't have felt any pain. Much later, Raj suggested that it might have been due to heartbreak, to which she scoffed, sulked, but didn't disagree.

But the injury and betrayal weren't what drove her to leave the guild. It was the economy.

The last five years had been tough on Suyoram, ever since the Bay of Echoes incident and the king had agreed to pay millions in reparations... which could only be accomplished by squeezing the pockets of his citizens. Even though there were no shortage of phi, there simply was very little money to go around throughout the entire country, and especially in the more rural areas, where they'd pay the most for such services.

By the time the novices had graduated and were slated to make their journeyman rounds, there weren't enough hunters left for them to shadow. Most had pivoted to hunting spirits for parts, or took other jobs to make ends meet.

The only real hunter left was Ree's father, Ex. But rumors had it he spent his rounds searching for her tirelessly, and slaying demons for free. And he'd made it clear that he didn't want company.

Falah decided to learn the ways of the masters anyway, continuing to train in their advanced techniques to one day take that step. It seemed pointless to Esha, who started hunting and trapping small game for a local company that sold meat to the markets. It was easy, mind-numbingly basic work that felt far beneath her. Every so often, she'd drop by the guild to pay her respects to the masters, but the silence of the compound depressed her.

One day, Raj showed up with an offer – bounty hunting. Several older hunters had made the career move, much to the chagrin of the masters, but who were they to argue? It was far more lucrative than hunting phi. Raj told her that some even tried to convince the masters that the guild should officially offer these manhunting services, to which they'd firmly refused. Any phi hunter who decided to hunt and kill or capture humans was officially struck from the guild.

Well, she'd stopped visiting anyway.

No, she never wondered what it would be like to stay. There was no future in phi hunting. Instead, she wondered what her life would have been like if she'd never joined at all. If she'd studied a different trade, or left Jinburi to seek her fortune elsewhere. Hell, even if she followed in her mother's footsteps to work at the brothel.

If she'd never met Ree.

Esha had been so lost in her thoughts that she hadn't noticed Raj talking to a newcomer who'd taken the seat next to him at the bar. A full-blooded Baghani, from the look of his dark skin to coarse hair tied into knots. He was dressed like a roughened traveler, clad in worn, broken-in gear that looked deceptively shitty. Esha knew the price of those gloves, not cheap, but not flashy either. Though the chains on his neck and rings through his earlobes were. The man laughed at something Raj said, then caught Esha's glance with a mischievous smile.

"Who's this?" Esha raised a brow, but didn't look away.

"Didn't get to exchanging names," Raj grinned, "but our new friend just bought us both another round."

"Friendship's sure cheap these days," Esha said with a scoff, and raised her mug after the barmaid filled it.

"Call me Simo," the man said, his Rami fluid with just a hint of the republic, but then he said in the Kutsu Aisle language: "Abia kon yuah?"

"My Kutsu half fucked off before I was born," Esha responded. "All I know is how to curse."

"Everyone knows 'what's your name' in Kutsu." Raj rolled his eyes, then said, "I'm Raj, this is Esha. We've known each other since we were kids, so I know she's very thankful for the drink."

"Sure, she is," Esha said with a smirk, then turned away from them, muttering subvocal to Raj, *"what's got your prick up?"*

"What brings you to this corner of Jinburi, Simo?" Raj asked the man, then to Esha, *"I sense a rich client. And I'm never wrong."* He did have good instincts for that.

"Just got into town with my crew. We'll be on our way out shortly, but I never pass up a chance to get a bowl of bo kho. Is it any good here?"

"Terrible," Esha said. "But we don't come here for the food."

"No one comes here for the food," Raj said with a knowing look.

"Yeah, I was told this is the place to go to find a certain type of ruffian," Simo's smile faded, "and you two fit the bill. My boss would like to meet you, extend an offer of employment, if you aren't too busy, that is."

"Private contract?" Esha glanced at Raj warily. Bounties needed to be validated by the governor with his seal before they could be posted at the magistrate's office. Without that process to ensure it was a legit, legal contract, it crossed into mercenary territory – and who knew what they might be getting into? Raj's morals might be a bit more flexible than hers, but Esha drew a hard line at committing crimes. "Not interested."

"If you're worried about validation, don't. Captain's seal is even shinier than the governor's," Simo said, and Esha wondered how full of shit he was.

"Is your crew all Baghani?" Esha asked.

"That matters?" Simo tilted his head.

"No, it doesn't," Raj side-eyed her, then shrugged. "But what she's really getting at is why it's not through the magistrate. We're not mercenaries."

"There's nothing illegal about it," Simo said. "But secrecy is important. And I was given very specific instructions to recruit two former phi hunters with your exact descriptions."

A sinking feeling arose in Esha's gut. A feeling she knew well and hated, a dread that things were all falling into place around her and she couldn't control where they hit and how hard. A bead of sweat trailed down her neck. She had the urge to get the fuck out of there.

She pushed back from the bar abruptly, standing up. "What are you getting at?" she demanded.

Simo gave her an inquisitive look, but didn't flinch. He finished his beer, then stood up, brushing off his vest. "You're going to want to meet the boss." He pulled open his collar, revealing a small, embossed pin. Two crossed swords and the face of a hissing cobra.

"That s'posed to mean something to us?" Esha snarled. "Get the f–" She stopped as Raj elbowed her hard.

"That's the Wild Cobras symbol," he said, and the name did resonate, vaguely. "The Storm Prince's regiment."

Storm Prince, that rang a bell.

One of the minor royals, but a notorious one amongst riffraff. If her and Raj were bounty hunters, this was a step above. The Wild Cobra Brigade was a paramilitary group sanctioned by the crown that took on the more organized enemies of the state. Esha relaxed only slightly.

"That's right," Simo said, "and he's offering quite a lucrative contract. But my guess? My guess is you'll take it anyway."

She crossed her arms and leaned back on the bar, trying to appear more casual than she felt. "Yeah? Why's that?"

"Because we believe we know where your long-lost friend is. And you two might be our best chance to stop her."

Chapter 25

The Last Phi Hunter

As Tan sat in the cozy dining room of a modest home, in a decent riverside neighborhood, he studied the decor and imagined himself living in such a place. If his mother had left the court when his father died, would he work a family trade, or attend school at an academy? He noted a graduation plaque proudly displayed on the wall, next to a golden mongkon, the traditional muay-boran headgear gilded to commemorate a tournament victory. There were a few pieces of art: a small, framed painting of a fishing village. Another of the mountains. A phinpia hung on a hook, the stringed folk instrument looked well worn. On a corner shelf shrine, a carved wooden idol of Phra Pikanesh, the elephant-headed deva, sat next to a brass statue of the Awakened Lord. He noticed there were no portraits of the king, current or previous.

The soft-spoken, middle-aged woman who had answered the door told him that the lady of the house was resting. That didn't seem particularly odd at mid-afternoon when the sun was at its hottest. What seemed odd was the woman's dress – more suited for the cosmopolitan Capital than Jinburi. With a traditional tube skirt, she wore a high-necked Hasshut-style blouse under a red sabai. Not the typical clothes of a housekeeper.

When Tan told her he was there to see the man of the house, she blinked languidly.

"Oh," she'd said. "He's gone to the market for us. Would you like to wait? He shouldn't be long. I just made some celestial tea."

If this were a social call, he would have politely waited outside, but he accepted the opportunity graciously. His four hours of sleep a night was starting to take a toll. Even forgoing drinks with his squad, even after taking sleeping pills, he sometimes woke in the middle of the night with racing thoughts that forced him out of bed. He read over the reports again and again, he made notes in his logbook, and then his journal, until eventually greeting the dawn with a feverish ache behind his eyes, the lingering phantom presence of the Stranger clawing at his psyche, and an irritating tremor in his right hand.

Though it was always wise to have backup during the investigation phase, Tan had sent his squad members on other assignments and walked to the phi hunter's house alone. He might find out more if he could avoid flexing his authority. Master Seua hadn't told him exactly why he should come here, and Tan hadn't for a few days. Once the records arrived from the guild, however, he had a working theory.

The woman, who'd introduced herself as Narissa, returned carrying two cups. He noticed her lace-gloved hands, more common for socialites than housekeepers. Indeed, after he asked, she told him that she was a close friend of the family and lived next door.

"Thank you, ma'am."

She smiled politely and sat down at the circular dining table, staring at him expectantly. Feeling a bit awkward, Tan took a sip of the beverage, which was spicier than he expected, and nodded in appreciation.

"It's very good," Tan said. "I have to admit, I've never heard of celestial tea before."

"My own recipe," she said, her smile unwavering. "A blend of ten different herbs and spices well known to promote good health and strong spirit." She took a very slow sip, then set her cup down and gazed out the open window to the terrace. He'd told her who he was, of course, but she hadn't asked him any follow-up questions and seemed content to sit in silence and wait with him, for however long it took the hunter to get home.

"How well do you know Hunter Ex?"

"We've been friends for many years."

"How did you meet?"

"I helped his wife, Arinya, when she was sick."

"Helped her?"

"I'm a healer. I run my practice from home, next door."

"That explains the herbs and spices for good health," Tan smiled. She nodded. He glanced at the wall panels that divided the communal room from where he assumed the hunter's wife was resting. "Is Lady Arinya sick now?"

"Oh," Narissa's pleasant smile finally wavered. "It would be unprofessional to discuss such topics."

"Of course, I didn't mean to pry. It's been a long time since I've seen her. She's a friend of my mother's, and I met her once as a child. I was hoping to pay my respects." Surely, that should have prompted a question from her, but it did not. What a curious and deeply incurious woman. He began to take another sip of the tea, but a sudden tremor in his hand caused the liquid to spill. He set the cup down quickly and began to reach into his pocket, mostly to hide it, but if Narissa had noticed, she pretended not to. "What can you tell me about their children?"

The door opened then, with a barrage of barking and the rapid click of claws on floorboards. A moment later, a sleek yellow dog trotted up to Tan, excitedly wagging his tail while sniffing him. Tan grinned and patted the dog, purposely taking his time to acknowledge the hunter.

"Huh. Wasn't expecting guests," Hunter Ex said. "This your friend, Narissa?"

"This is Captain Tanung, from the Capital," Narissa said, standing. "He came to see you."

Tan looked over to the doorway, where Hunter Ex hadn't moved, balancing a basket on his shoulder. He tried to keep his expression neutral, but he hadn't expected Ex to look, well, not much older than himself. His cropped black hair had only a hint of gray around the temples, a few smile lines around his mouth and at the corners of his eyes, but according to the records he should be fifty-two. According to the records, Master Seua was almost a hundred, so Tan concluded the phi hunters were either terrible record keepers or bad at math. The hunter was dressed plainly for the weather, his shirt hung open, revealing a blanket of sak-yant tattoos over his chest, which continued over his arms, and the side of his neck. His unnerving red eyes flicked over Tan and his brows furrowed in either suspicion or confusion.

"What do you want?" Ex demanded and handed Narissa the basket without taking his eyes off Tan. As if he were a threat. Suspicion, then.

"I'll start preparing dinner at mine," Narissa said, then walked out the front and shut the door, leaving the two men alone.

"I'm here to ask a few questions," Tan said. "I'm on an important mission and I believe you may have information that can assist me."

"What kind of mission?"

"Peacekeeping." He needed to somehow put this man at ease, who looked like he would have already thrown Tan out the door if it wasn't for the official pin on his collar. "I understand you're the only working phi hunter left these days."

"Pretty much," Ex said. The dog walked over to him and whined a little, panting nervously.

"And you've been in the guild for… how long?"

"Forty years." The hunter finally looked away from Tan and nodded toward the open door leading to the back patio. "Go on, Lucky," he said, voice soft. The dog, however, refused to move.

"So, you know every hunter that's joined and worked, or trained since then," Tan said. "I just have a few questions–"

"Hang on," Ex snapped, glaring at him anew. "Who the fuck are you again?"

"Commander Tanung of the Wild Cobra Brigade."

Ex muttered under his breath, "'Wild… cobra?' What the hell…"

Tan only took another sip of tea before asking, "Why did you stay, when everyone else moved on?"

"Someone has to do it."

"Do you still keep in contact with any former guild members?"

"Some. We meet up for drinks once in a while. That's about it." Ex watched him warily while he knelt to pet his dog. "Look, I'm very flattered you think I can help you with whatever it is you're doing, but unless you have a fat purse in exchange for a demon to die, you're wasting your time."

Tan held up his hands. "You can relax, Hunter Ex, I'm not here to cause trouble. I'm simply here for information."

"Then get to what you're getting at, kid." Seemed absurd to be called "kid" by a man who looked only a few years his senior.

"How well did you know the novices?"

"I don't train the scribes."

"Not the current class of students. I'm referring to the last few hunters-in-training." Tan watched Ex from the corner of his eye, trying to appear nonchalant. He let his gaze drift to settle on one of the display shelves of trinkets and art. In particular, an old parchment stamped with what looked like two pairs of children's handprints. It didn't seem like Ex would get friendly with him, so he might as well get to the point. "In particular, your daughter, Isaree."

The world spun, Tan spinning with it. Not a second to react before his back slammed against the wall, his teacup shattering on the floor, the chair he'd been sitting on knocked sideways. Ex held Tan by his neck, and his feet dangled an inch above the floor. Had he had an episode? He hadn't seen the hunter move. But now, there was a knife hovering a hair from Tan's throat.

"What do you know about her?" Ex said in a low, threatening manner that seemed too measured to use when holding another man at knifepoint. Ex's eyes burned bright with anger in that frightening way, the gleam of a predator in the dark. Up close, a diagonal scar across his forehead puckered over his furrowed brows.

It wasn't the first time Tan had been in a similar situation, and though his pulse raced he forced himself to stay calm. The hunter wouldn't dare harm him. Even if Ex had no idea he was royalty, to assault an agent of the crown would be suicide. This was a reaction of pure emotion. One which, if Tan so desired, could have the hunter executed..

They were finally getting somewhere.

"Rather we speak civilly?" Tan managed to say, though he struggled to breathe.

"You trespassed in my lair," Ex said, "I don't give a fuck if you're the king himself. Talk!"

Tan choked for breath, and Ex let his feet touch the ground, but he held the knife just as close. Tan's head swam, a fuzzy, surreal sense of déjà vu distorting the entire scene. No, he'd never been here before, he was certain of that. Tan's hand started to tremble and the sunlight streaming in through the windows seemed to sizzle, far too bright. Shit, this would be a very bad time to have an episode. Something about the hunter's enraged eyes, the mad barking of the dog, the cold bite of steel against his racing pulse, the ragged hitch in Ex's voice when he said again,

"Tell me, what do you know about her?!" The gleam of his eyes shone wet with tears. His tattooed throat twitched, the last word so softly whispered he wasn't even sure if it was actually said, but seemed to plead, "*Please*."

"Ex!" someone yelled.

Tan collapsed to the ground, gasping for breath. He coughed, rubbing his throat, while questioning the wisdom of coming here without backup. Vision still blurry, he squinted toward Ex, who was standing before a woman in the door frame leading to the bedrooms.

"Why are you harassing that boy?!"

"Love, you should be resting," Ex said gently, and Tan couldn't believe it was the same man speaking. Ex had his arms around her, hand resting on the side of her head, lips to her temple. The woman – Arinya – was the same he remembered meeting years ago, embracing his mother as if they were sisters. She was easy to remember, so radiant in the sunlight, bolstered by all the festivities dancing around her. It shocked him how diminished she appeared now. Dark hollows under her eyes, an ashy complexion, and the loose fit of her robe hinted at an illness far more serious than a simple cold. She clung to her husband as if sensing his distress, but also out of necessity.

"Who is that?" she said, peering around the hunter's shoulder. When her glazed eyes settled on Tan, she inhaled sharply, wavering on her feet. Tan tried to rise but found his leg had trouble moving, and he leaned against the wall for support. He tried to open his mouth to reassure Arinya he was only there to talk, but his jaw was clenched too tightly to move.

"I'll throw him out in a second," Ex said.

"Ex!" Arinya's voice had hardened. Crossly, she pulled away from him, batting his worrying hands aside. "Are you mad? Do you know who this is?!"

"I know he's an asshole who was just leaving," Ex scoffed, but there was a hint of trepidation in his voice. Mentioning Isaree had struck a nerve.

Arinya sighed in exasperation and held her hand out. "Look at his face. Doesn't he look familiar to you? At all?"

"Huh? Never seen him in my life."

"He doesn't *remind* you of anyone?"

"Remind me of who? The last punk constable who thinks he's getting clout for harassing the last whisper in town?"

She only tilted her head a certain way, and somehow the angry look on Ex's face swiftly shifted to bafflement, then shock, and finally concern. If Tan hadn't been futilely fighting the onset of an episode, he might have taken some satisfaction there.

"Oh shit," Ex said. "Shit. He really does look like that assh–"

She pushed Ex aside. "Are you okay, Prince Tanung?"

Through gritted teeth, Tan tried to answer, but his lips had gone numb. When he raised his hands to wai, his right one shook so much it refused to move. He felt the tremor cascade though his chest then, and then it was all gone. He wasn't there.

Tan's sinuses stung and he opened his eyes. Dark ones met his. Arinya withdrew something from under his nose. He was lying on the couch in the family room though it was darker. She'd drawn the curtains. He didn't see Ex, which was a relief.

"Please relax, Prince Tanung," she said softly.

"My pills," he said and sat up, flinching as his head throbbed. The migraines always flared after an episode. He reached into his pocket and removed his medicine satchel, hand still shaking. After struggling to open it, Arinya gently took it from him and pressed a pill to his lips. She picked up a bowl on the table, holding it for him to drink, and he was so grateful he could have cried.

"I'm sorry to inconvenience you, Lady Arinya. It's good to see you again."

"And you, Tanung. If you don't mind me asking, what is it called?" Arinya sat down on a footstool next to the couch.

"Apasmara," Tan said. "It was wind-type. At least for now."

"Oh, the falling sickness. My uncle had that," she said, and the thought seemed to disturb her.

"What about you?" he ventured to ask.

"It's something with my kidneys. I've been told it's been reported by survivors of Gray Pox, all these years later."

"Is it curable?"

She only smiled sadly. "Possibly." And before Tan could inquire further, she shook her head. "I thought I'd seen a ghost. You're all grown up now, Tanung. How is your mother?"

"She's well. In Patang with the queen," Tan said. The pain in his temples made it hard to speak, and he'd wasted too much time already. "I wish not to cause you distress, ma'am. But I do need to speak to you and your husband about your daughter."

"Of course," Arinya's face fell, and she looked much older then. "Please forgive my husband's manners. It's a very difficult subject."

"For you both, I imagine."

"When she left..." Arinya deflated, sitting back on the cushion. "It's hard to put into words, the sorrow that consumed us both. And we had just come to terms with what happened to Kit. Ah, my son. He..."

"I read the report," Tan said gently. Scuffles between the locals and the Gris had been a common occurrence at that time in Jinburi. "I'm sorry that the state failed you. The Gris enjoy a protected status they do not deserve."

Arinya seemed taken aback by his words. "Huh. It's refreshing to hear one of you admit it. I do understand the politics that were involved, but my family was furious... including Isaree."

The pieces were coming together, then.

"Is that why she left?" Tan asked.

"I believe it contributed," Arinya said, and wiped at the corners of her eyes.

"The records stated she left the guild years ago," Tan said. He found it odd that the novice left even before the Act of Reason and the Bay of Echoes Incident, which was when most of the others had. Another aggravating discovery was that when a hunter left the guild, it was as if they'd died. Master Seua was truthful saying they didn't track their former members, at least not on record. "It didn't say why."

"I don't know, exactly. My husband can tell you more about that," Arinya said. Tan didn't quite buy it, but he didn't press. "I… I failed her, as a mother. I didn't understand her enough. No, I didn't *try* to understand her enough, because she was so different. I thought the guild would be her refuge. I thought she would come back around after getting over her teenage years, and Kit needed so much help at the time, but…" Arinya sighed, her breath shuddering.

"I'm so sorry. How is Kit doing now?"

"He's…" Arinya finally smiled, then nodded toward the instrument on the wall. "Great. Thriving, even. His old teacher gifted him that… oh, a few months after Isaree left I think. But once he picked it up, the change in his recovery was astonishing. He performs regularly at the theatre now, makes a good living, and wouldn't you know, marrying his sweetheart next season. I fear I'll be a grandmother soon."

"I'm glad to hear that."

Her pride shifted then to sadness. "I just wish Isaree could have seen him play. Just once."

And even though he doubted it after reading the witness reports, Tan said, "Maybe there's still time."

"What do you mean?" Arinya stared at him in bewilderment. "You… think she's still alive?"

Ex sat on the table in the backyard, a bottle next to him. The garden was taken care of, with a few fruit trees and a small koi pond near the patio. Lucky trotted up to his master and dropped a stick, which Ex tossed for the dog to fetch. Tan watched for a while, waiting for Ex to break the silence.

"Sorry about that," Ex finally grumbled. "Not often we get a visit from royalty."

Tan was rightfully irritated, his headache escalating. He needed sleep, but he needed to get information more than that. "You're still looking for her," he said. "That's why you stayed, isn't it?"

Ex took a sip of his wine. "I was for a long time. Even after that missionary said he'd seen her drown, I never believed it. Then the Guardian of the Swamp told me that I should stop. That she would return on her own."

"Guardian of the Swamp?"

"Someone who's word I trust. Never mind. Point is, maybe she found happiness somewhere else. That's all I hope, really."

"Why did she leave the guild?"

"From what I understand..." Ex eyed him, "she attacked a fellow novice after a disagreement during one of their last trials. Then she disappeared."

"What was the disagreement about?"

"About killing a trapped phi. She didn't think it was dangerous, and wanted to let it go."

Tan almost laughed but thought better of it. "Isn't that the antithesis of a phi hunter's training?"

Ex half-smiled. "Yeah... but you gotta understand something. Isaree was special. She always had the Everpresent with her, from birth... that's unheard of. And she saw things differently, sometimes had trouble explaining it." Ex sighed. "Wish I'd been there. I should have been there."

"Did she ever show any interest in politics?" Tan asked.

"She was training with the guild. It's its own world when you're there. Everything else, politics, all that, it doesn't really matter to us. Why?"

"Well," Tan decided he might as well go ahead with his theory. "Did she ever express any disdain for the Gris' conquest of Loram?"

"Everyone in Suyoram did, whether they said it or not," Ex said, with no lack of scorn. "Maybe not *your* kind, who seem to be making out quite nicely. So, who's really holding the leash to your 'Wild Cobras'?"

Tan knew explaining the truth of the crown's precarious position with the Gris would fall on deaf ears. The average citizen had no sympathy for what the king was doing behind the scenes to ensure Suyoram's independence, they only saw the effects to their own pocketbooks. They saw the alliance as a weakness, the king showing his belly to this culturally backwards foreign power. Arinya warned him that her husband was not politically minded, so it would be futile to try and convince him that everything they did was for the good of the country, including turning their backs upon their closest neighbors.

Tan said, "Let me be completely transparent. Your daughter matches the description of a rebel leader committing gruesome acts of violence against other humans, using techniques only known by phi hunters. And not only were Gris combatants harmed, but Lo citizens as well."

"What?! No. It's not her. Even if she left the guild and our oaths, she'd never do that."

"My working theory is that she encountered the rebels at some point during the Blackwater purge. It was a violent time, and perhaps they assisted a wandering Suyo girl far from home, and radicalized her in the process."

Ex stared at him in disbelief, then laughed, though it rang hollow. "Nah. She's smart, she's always had a mind of her own. I don't think she'd fall for that, and become, what, a child soldier? No."

"She was nineteen when she left, and would be twenty-seven now," Tan said. "Hardly a child then. And certainly, capable of making her own decisions as an adult. What happened to her brother could turn any young person to revenge. And you're correct, it might not be her. But if it is..." Ex didn't look convinced, but he was the girl's father, and denial was a strong thing. It didn't matter. The seed of plausibility was planted. And it was easy to twist a parents' guilt into something useful. "Perhaps she could be helped. Perhaps she just needs to know that there are people who still love her."

"Don't bullshit me. You're being sent to kill... whoever it is." Ex turned away and ran his hands over his face. "If there's any possibility that it's her, which it isn't, how could you ask me to help you? I'm her *father*. What the fuck do you expect me to do?"

"Come with us," Tan said. "I've no illusions that tracking down a former hunter in the wild is nothing short of impossible. Yes, my mission is to stop her by any means necessary. But I'd rather take her alive." That was true at least, she'd be far more valuable as a captive than a martyr. "It'd give her a chance to receive justice from the king, rather than the Protectorate." Not a guarantee, the king would likely turn her over to them for favor, but that wasn't Tan's call. "And if it's not her, you would be an asset regardless. We'd reward you handsomely, and I could pull some strings, send some of our best doctors out here to help Lady Arinya."

Ex threw his bottle and jumped to his feet. Tan flinched, expecting another assault, but the hunter only turned toward him, his anger barely restrained. "Typical, you offer to help my wife but only if I break my oaths? Go ahead and finish off the guild, like your father always wanted?" He paced, as if filled with nervous, violent energy and no outlet. "Funny thing is, if it would help my family, I would. But it won't. You really need to leave now..." He gritted his teeth, and then stopped, clapping his hands together in what Tan perceived as the most disrespectful wai he'd ever received. "My prince."

Chapter 26

Into the Wilds

A two-masted sea and river worthy marauder named the *Lady Mo* cruised north up the Jinburi river, heading to the junction where the Duram split off to Kohkiem and beyond. They carried two hundred soldiers wearing the Wild Cobras crest, alongside horses, supplies, and two former phi hunters.

When Simo first introduced Esha and Raj to Tan, he'd be lying if he said they didn't unnerve him. Both possessed the same eerie red eyes as Ex and Master Seua, the same coiled readiness. But that was where the similarities ended. Not only did they have a fraction of the tattoos that the older generation displayed, but also none of their sanctimonious attitudes. Raj was quick to crack a joke, and being mercenary it wouldn't have mattered who they were hunting. Esha, however, remained distant, and wasn't interested until Tan carefully laid out all the reasons why he thought the Heretic was Isaree. Still, he wasn't sure the woman would show up when the time came to embark.

"Surprised to see me?" Esha said to Tan as she climbed aboard, peering around at the crew as they finished their prep. She could have blended right into the marines, as there was nothing feminine about her appearance. The hunter was tall as the average man, with broad shoulders, a mostly shaved head, and an impressive burn over the upper right half of her face. While his crew (especially Simo and some of the masc-preferring ladies) found her especially intriguing, many were apprehensive, like Tan. He couldn't shake the uneasy feeling of being in a room with an inhuman predator.

If they were indeed hunting another former phi hunter, then he couldn't afford to be so intimidated by them. Thus, he made an effort to get over this prejudice during the journey upriver.

His days were filled with meetings, many which included Raj and Esha. They had no reservations revealing what he'd assumed were secrets of the guild, but learned that the information wasn't hidden from the public, just largely unknown.

"She must be using the Serene Way to hit some of these targets in this time frame," Raj said, as the group gathered in Tan's cabin around the war table, dominated by a large map of the region. "There's no other way to travel that far, and that fast."

"That's... fucked," Esha turned up her lip. She spun a handrolled cigarette in her fingers. "But Ree would do that. She didn't care about our traditions."

"Smart," Raj said with a shrug.

"Sacrilege," Esha snapped. "There's no way the spirits would condone that."

"Why not?" Raj crossed his arms. "We use it too."

"That's different. We pay homage to the spirits when we do. And we can't bring outsiders," she cast a glance at Tan, Simo, and his other two officers, Yelu and Ukrit. "And it's the Kalashas, it's different."

"How do you know it's different?" Raj challenged. "We don't know the Guardians there. Maybe they don't give a shit. Maybe..." he laughed out loud, "maybe they want the Gris gone too. Ever think of that?"

Esha glared at her partner, and then Tan noticed her jaw twitch. Raj's did as well. How much were they not saying out loud? He wondered if it were possible to commune this way without having passed some ritual to alter themselves... they weren't in their magic state. Perhaps it chiefly relied upon their sharp sense of hearing.

"Yeah... she's right," Raj said, without looking away from Esha. "We can't bring any of you into the Serene Way. The spirits would chew you up and shit you out."

"I'm sorry," Yelu interrupted, "but what's this Serene Way?"

When the hunters explained what the Serene Way was – fluid, hidden pathways through the wilderness controlled by god spirits, only detectable by the spirit-magic mind-state called "the Everpresent" – all Tan's men exchanged skeptical looks. Even Ukrit, who was the only one who'd studied sorcery.

"They don't believe us," Raj said with a smile, finding it amusing while Esha seemed irritated.

"Doesn't matter," she said, and slumped back in her chair.

"There's other ways to explain the timeline," Tan said, catching Simo's eye. His expression seemed to scream, *are you sure about these two?* "Miscommunication. False reports. Rumors of the Heretic have spread enough that it's influencing witnesses..."

While he spoke, Esha eyes brightened, and her hair faded from black to a pale silver. She held a coal-bright fingertip to her cigarette and inhaled, the paper sizzling as it lit. It wasn't only her appearance, he felt a shift in the air and in some of his old injuries, as if the pressure had changed due to a storm. It made his hair stand on end, and from the reactions of the other Wild Cobras, he wasn't alone.

"...and it might not be the same person behind all of these attacks..." Tan trailed off as he watched her hair darken. He wondered why that happened.

"It's her," Esha said, meeting his eyes with a certainty that he should have found validating. But where that should have bolstered his confidence, he only felt dread.

When the pills didn't work, Tan sometimes prayed for sleep, begging the Awakened Lord, the devas, even the Grand Patriarch or any power that might be listening for the mercy of rest. And when the universe proved itself godless, he would drink. And if drinking did nothing, he would walk the ship, relieve the night watchmen, watch the dawn approach with the weariness of an ancient farmer dreading the harvest.

This was not the open sea and navigating the treacherous depths of the river required much more minute by minute detail, and frankly, daylight. Tan stared out at the dark forests that surrounded them, altitude growing as the days went by. When the wind died, they rowed. They'd anchored just out of eyesight of a small fishing village, one that he'd already sent spies to gather any new information.

Tan noticed Esha standing at the railing a few feet away, smoking. The hunters hardly slept, so it didn't surprise him that she was up and about in the middle of the night.

"Lady Esha," he nodded to her in greeting.

"Oh, please don't call me lady," Esha turned toward him. "You're up late, captain... or is it prince?"

"You aren't in the brigade, and I'm not on duty. Tan is fine."

"I'm still a subject of the crown," she said, and he detected a bit of teasing in her voice. "I don't know any royals, but you aren't what I imagined one to be."

"We've met before," Tan said. He recognized her instantly when Simo brought her over, and he didn't buy that she'd forgotten him.

"Have we?" A flare of her cigarette briefly lit up her face, and Tan cringed inwardly at those predator eyes.

"Rom Laithong. My mother brought me by the Phi Hunter's guild to visit Arinya. We only stayed for a moment."

"Ohhh... right. That was you, wasn't it?" Sounded like a lie. Tan thought himself very good at reading people, but it was too dark to make out her expression. Or perhaps it was his ego, refusing to think himself as forgettable. "Sorry, sir. Tan. It's been a long time. And those were some of our most intense training days."

"You and Isaree trained together a lot, I take it."

"Yeah... we all did. There were only four of us after the KunNam trial."

"I read there were three other novices of your class that left the guild early, but I didn't find records of them anywhere else."

She chuckled. "That makes sense."

"Does it?"

"They died," she said. "We all died. That's part of it. But only some of us came back."

Tan figured this ceremonial death was figurative, as it had been with other religious ceremonies he'd witnessed. "How did you 'die?'"

"Master Arei stabbed us through the heart, then put us in the drowning pool."

Tan was momentarily stunned.

"What?" he said.

"I'm not being cryptic. It's the first sacrifice all hunters must make. Do you think the devas would allow just anyone into the Everpresent?"

He did some quick backwards math. "But you must have been children."

"So? The devas can see our fate at any moment in our lives. We were ready to walk the path of the First Hunters or return to their halls. It's the path we chose."

"The ones that died though," Tan said, now understanding full well why the Act of Reason was a wise decree. "They were ready?"

"Of course they were, and the First Hunters wanted to keep them." Esha sounded completely sure, proud. Tan knew better than debate.

"You're a true believer, then."

"So was Ree," Esha said, and her voice turned bitter. "She didn't have to do it. But she did it anyway. But... I think that's when something changed. She was different after that."

"Raj told me you were best friends."

"*Were*. Past tense. The day she gave me this scar and turned her back on her oaths was the day she made me her enemy."

"The guild still means that much to you?" Tan asked. "You're a bounty hunter. You broke your oaths, too."

"No, we left properly. I guess you'd military types would call it an honorable discharge." Esha tossed her cigarette over the railing. "Look. It's personal, sure. But you don't have to worry about my loyalties. I joined you because if it's really Ree, and she's doing what you said she is, she needs to be stopped."

Their conversations became routine on nights Tan couldn't sleep. Most often, he found Esha in the same spot, staring out into the darkness.

"Can I ask what you believe in, Storm Prince?"

"In what context?"

"Do you follow the Awakened Lord? Do you pay respects to the devas? Are you a Son of the Grand Patriarch?"

"I'm a skeptic," he said. Her silence told him she hadn't expected this. "My mother wasn't the consort of the crown-prince only for her looks. She was a scholar, extremely well-read, especially in the sciences and history. She taught me to question everything. Even if it goes against my bloodlines' divine right to rule. I'm not saying that these deities aren't real..."

"But aren't you?"

"Well," Tan hesitated, but went on anyway. "Science has uncovered enough to disprove countless old beliefs about how the world functions. But it can never disprove faith. That being said, I very much doubt that any supreme being or universal force has the interest to scrutinize every single action every single person takes to serve some kind of moral framework... especially one that seems conveniently suited to benefit a ruling class. Isn't it convenient?"

"So..." Esha said slowly, "you don't believe in any god."

"I'm just saying I'll find out when I find out," Tan smiled. "And in the meantime, I believe in myself."

Kohkiem was a holy city, boasting the highest number of shrines and temples per capita in the country. After the iconic Lotus bridge, it was known for the golden spires jutting out from the rooftops like splendid stalagmites, the telling marker of an Awakened temple. But now, the four-pointed star of the Grand Patriarch had been affixed to all of them, the city claiming a new god.

Along with the religion, any shred of insurgency had been ruthlessly uprooted throughout the years of the occupation, all suspects and suspected collaborators moved to one of the strategic hamlets. As a result, the population had declined.

Tan, Simo and Raj met with their contact in a portside warehouse, packed floor to ceiling with burlap sacks and barrels, stuffy with an earthy smell of grain and dust. A young, dark-haired, Grisi man sat on a crate, rapidly fluttering a paper fan under his shirt, revealing tuffs of chest hair and local, handcrafted jewelry.

"Behold Prince Tan, and Lieutenant Simo. I'm dancing with joy." His Lo-accented Rami was perfect, but Simo and Raj stifled a laugh at his word choice.

"I'm Governor-Colonel Daine Rimes." He said the surname with an air, and Tan recalled an older ambassador with the same name. "General Elleman heralded your arrival, though... you were expected a week ago."

"We conducted some important research regarding our mark," Tan said. "And that included recruitment. This is Hunter Raj, from Jinburi. He grew up with my suspect."

The night before, Tan convinced Esha to stay hidden when they arrived at Kohkiem. The rebels certainly had spies despite Grisi assurances that the city was clean. Tan didn't want anyone knowing they had two hunters. He also hoped that Raj might be seen, might even be mistaken for Ex, even if they looked nothing like each other. A male "phi hunter" was a good enough descriptor. Surprisingly, Esha hadn't argued. It was clear that she trusted Raj, and by the gleam in her eye and bitemarks on her neck, Yelu was doing a good job in distracting her.

In the meantime, Simo had been working on Raj in a different fashion. He had invited Raj to all the card games and drinking sessions, the crew showing off the treasures they'd plundered during their missions, as well as expensive gear and trinkets they'd bought with their salaries. Simo speculated it wouldn't take much more time to turn him, as the bounty hunter had already started asking about membership into the brigade.

"Well," Tan said, "what's the situation?"

"Full on chaos," Rimes huffed. He had a certain glassy-eyed look indicative of kageleaf users. "The rebels disrupt everything – communications, supply lines, trade. I think our talking birds have gone completely extinct."

"Talking birds?" Tan asked. "As in... parrots?"

"I think he means homing pigeons," said Simo.

"Yes, homing pigeons, thank you. The capture of Fort Nestor cut us completely from our main force in Iautau, but wonderfully one brave bird did get through, thank fuck! Iautau *was* under siege, but the rebels have withdrawn. Unfortunately, we lost many of our strategic towns as a result, but! We did prevail, by the will of the Grand Patriarch, the head of the Protectorate remains intact." Rimes beat his chest with his fan, and Tan could tell the man was high as a runaway paper lantern. "I've been promised that reinforcements are coming from the Fatherland, but until then we need to hold out. We're bolstering our defenses here in Kohkiem, and once our new army is here, we'll retake Iron Town, ah, Muang-Hhleg, in Rami. Then, we march to the capital to unite our forces." Rimes glanced at their weapons. "In the meantime, you have some hunting to do, don't you boys?"

"Where's the last place the Heretic was seen?" Tan asked.

Rimes took his time to stand, then after a leisurely stretch unfurled a map over the crate. The men gathered around it.

Simo let out a low whistle. Topography, supply lines, enemy positions, and more, it was the most detailed map of the Protectorate that Tan had ever seen. It was the most detailed map he'd ever seen, period.

"Three nights ago she attacked a logging village here. Two survivors." Rimes tapped the map with a pencil, a spot to the northwest, near the Ainlay valley. "The rebels slaughter our security forces at the clean villages and then force the locals to join their cause. It's barbaric really. Forcing them to lay down their lives after establishing a home, when all they want is peace. Anyway, it stands to reason that one of these two villages in the Ainlay would be her next target."

"May I?" Tan nodded to Rimes' pencil, who handed it over. Tan drew a few light circles around the logging camp. "Distance in forty-eight hours, by foot with a small team. With horses. Over fifty." The circles grew smaller with each consideration. Then he handed Raj the pencil. "As a former phi hunter, what's your estimation of her range?"

"If she's using the Serene Way?" Raj took the pencil, then circled the entire valley, easily six times the largest circle Tan had drawn.

They were quiet, then Simo said, "Well that's fucking disheartening."

"What else can you give us?" Tan asked Rimes.

"Aside from this map and the latest reports? Not much, I'm afraid. Our supplies are stretched thin as it is. I was told you were a complete package. Oh, how could I forget – behold." Rimes reached into his breast pocket, then handed Tan a folded piece of parchment.

"One of our survey teams intercepted a teacher and her class on their way to Iron Town," he said. "One of the girls was carrying this."

Tan unfolded the paper to reveal what must be a rough sketch of the Heretic, standing behind a full moon. This wasn't anything new; as they grew closer to Loram, rumors multiplied and these pictures were all over the map as far as likeness went. But this was the first that gave him pause.

"Shit. That's her," Raj said quietly, with a tenor of sadness. "I was hoping… damn."

"I'd like to speak to the girl who drew this," Tan said, both vindicated and apprehensive. This was not a straight-on portrait found on bounty posters. This was an artist's rendition, and by someone that Isaree must have known in some capacity. There were too many details that captured a personality – her chin lifted but her eyes sharply focused on the distance, as if judging an approaching threat. She carried a black bladed daab sword – the one that many reports swore had been bestowed upon her by the Profaned One himself.

"Alas," Rimes said, and averted his eyes, clearly uncomfortable. "They perished with the others on the way back."

"All of them?" Simo narrowed his eyes, glancing at Tan in disgust. Suspicious. "How many?"

"The reports were vague," Rimes said flatly. "Anyway, I find Loram… such a beautiful land, but with a heart full of savagery. Please take care of yourselves, gentlemen."

Chapter 27

A Life Promised

A knot was forming in her belly, tightening in her chest. Yelu had been a welcome distraction. The little sniper had perfectly soft lips, a smoky, whiskey-soaked voice that set Esha's heart racing when she whispered a dirty thing or two. She'd been a Wild Cobra for six years, and thus knew every secret corner of the ship where they could get to know one another. It hadn't been like Esha had anything else to do during the journey upriver. Raj's desperation to fit in with these royal mercs made her embarrassed to be around him. Once they were on foot, traveling with the brigade through Loram, Yelu invited Esha to share a rather nice tent.

"Yes, yes..." Yelu whimpered, her fingernails digging into the back of Esha's head. Her hips bucked, thighs squeezing against Esha's cheeks. Esha might not have had a way with words, but she had a way with her tongue, rhythmically building the intensity of her movements, and matching the arc of her partner's pleasure with her own hand. Controlling the pleasurable contortions of a feminine body was what really got Esha off, and being with Yelu was easy – she could pretend they weren't camped out in the middle of a warzone, on the trail of her former best friend.

Esha willingly pushed away thoughts of Ree, how it felt to finally kiss her... what she might look like now, if she would still smell the same, like fresh rain. After another few minutes, Yelu gasped as she peaked and melted into Esha's mouth. Esha groaned in satisfaction and followed a few moments later. Sighing, she laid her head to rest on Yelu's stomach.

Afterward, they shared a smoke and a flask, Yelu curled up against Esha's shoulder, one leg draped over hers. The knot in her belly had loosened.

"You're distracted," Yelu said, tapping Esha affectionately on the nose, then taking the cigarette from her mouth for a drag.

"Not at all," Esha said, trying to recall what Yelu had been saying. "You were talking about… um, the village. Son Clarion?"

"No, I was talking about the boss. How he's… you know."

"A little strange."

Esha had noticed early on how the prince would grow restless, especially at night. He'd randomly relieve his lookouts, one after the other. He took pills when he thought no one was watching, and she'd heard him scratching at his books in the darkness, well until morning. Half the time, he'd walk out with a handful of papers and burn them, one by one, in the nearest smoldering fire.

Some hunters were gifted at sensing illnesses; just by scent alone, Elder Nokai could tell you what someone had. Esha didn't have that skill, but it didn't take a genius to figure it to be some type of mental illness. It explained Ree's story of her encounter with him so long ago. And she supposed you had to be a little unhinged to want a life like this. She supposed you had to be that way, to want to do something like this.

"A little strange?" Yelu burst out laughing. "Are you serious? He's fucking insane. Half the time, anyway. Don't let his manners fool you."

"Why would you follow a leader you think is insane?"

"I guess I like exciting people," she said, batting her eyelashes.

Esha snorted. "Well, I don't understand why he bothers with this. He's a prince. Why doesn't he just kick back in a palace, eat fancy food, fuck a harem of concubines?"

"He's not that kind of prince," Yelu said. "He's got to work for respect. He's the son of a consort, unlike Priyut."

"Guess that explains his looks. Who's Priyut?"

"His half-brother. General of the royal army."

"Next in line?"

"Not next, but his mother was a noble, so he has a higher claim."

"His rival, I get it," Esha said. "I mean to say, I wouldn't be out here hunting rebels if I didn't have to."

"You don't want to be out here?" Yelu gave her an adorable pout, strands of her long black hair falling over her face, "With me?"

"You make it a bit more tolerable," Esha admitted, then kissed her. She had always found refuge in sex, and even more recklessly once she'd left the guild. But aside from one dancer she'd been serious about, who ultimately broke her heart by agreeing to her family's arranged marriage, Esha's relationships never seemed to progress much further than the bedroom. Her lovers would always demand more, and that would drive her away.

"Are you nervous?" Yelu asked.

"About what?"

"Seeing your friend."

"She's not my friend," Esha said. "She's a killer and a criminal."

"A criminal?" Yelu stifled laughter, and Esha squinted at her in question. "Wait, sorry, do you agree with the Protectorate?"

"You don't?"

"I'm Suyo. We *hate* the Gris."

"I'm Suyo too," Esha snapped, irritated. Being a half-child always made her defensive about that. "And if you hate the Gris, why are you working for them?"

"We're not, we're working for the Storm Prince. And he serves only the king," Yelu said, as if blind loyalty were something to be proud of. "The king wants this rebel dead because it will help his standing with the Gris, so this rebel will die. But it doesn't mean what she's doing is wrong."

"How can you say that?" Esha sat up, forcing Yelu to as well. The tent felt entirely too small then. "She's murdering people by using the powers gifted to us by the devas. It's wrong."

"What the Gris did here, to Loram, is wrong," Yelu said. "You don't agree with that?"

"War's a fact of life, and life's not fair," Esha said with a shrug. "Loram was weak, and the weak get conquered. That doesn't give anyone the right to exploit our traditions to serve their own goals."

Yelu frowned. "So... you think individual morality supersedes the greater good? That it isn't moral to kill in defense of something larger than oneself?"

"I know her, you don't," Esha snapped, then found her shirt, shrugging it on. "She's selfish. She's done things like this before."

"Huh? Like what?"

Anger festered as Esha thought about the night Ree confessed she tried to poison a group of Gris. Though it wasn't so much about what she'd done to them than it was to her. Not something she wanted to talk about, anyway. Esha picked up her toolbelt, checking her weapons before fastening it around her waist. After a long silence, she shot Yelu a critical look. "You said the king wants this rebel dead. But the prince promised we'd take her alive."

Yelu opened her mouth, but hesitated. "Well, of course," she said, brows furrowed. "Taking her alive is always preferable. You're a bounty hunter, you know that." Her voice sweetened again and grew soft. "You know they don't always surrender, even when there's no other way out."

Of course she knew that. But up until then, she'd pretended that it didn't matter. "Forget it. I'm going out."

"Wait, Esha," Yelu grabbed her elbow. "I'm sorry, please talk to me. I just want to understand."

"Understand what? It's time for my patrol shift."

"You. What you're going through. I can see you're hurt..."

"You can't see shit," Esha shook her off and stomped out of the tent. Why did they always have to start digging at her? If the stories were true and Ree commanded a demon army, they might die tomorrow, or the next day, or whenever Ree decided to attack the clean village they were holding the perimeter of. Couldn't they just enjoy a good fuck and shut up?

The cool night air felt good on her face, and she glanced around the small camp. Their tents were camouflaged by the local foliage, no campfires, only a few small blue-glass lanterns for visibility. The patrols were tightly kept. Esha couldn't fathom how this ambush would work. From the Everpresent, they were loud as a pack of squabbling macaques, and Ree, who had always the sharpest senses of them all, would be able to hear them from a mile away.

She said as much to the prince, who seemed unconcerned. He had split the Wild Cobras into two platoons to cover both potential targets, Raj and Simo were in the secondary group monitoring the village around the rubber plantation. And then he split them again – the bulk hidden in the village, a small sentry on the perimeter.

"I get you're confident in your crew," Esha had told him when they met before he split off. "But this isn't going to work."

"You don't think she'll show up?"

"I think she will, but... it won't be a surprise."

"The surprise won't be our presence but our capabilities. She's overconfident by now. She won't be prepared for us. Besides," he gave her a rare smile, "that's what we have you two for."

Esha walked into the darkness of the woods, stepping into the Everpresent and the vibrant peace it brought with it. Ambient magic flowed in the valley, though she sensed only the hint of spirits. She'd never admit it, but she often wondered if she would have made a good phi hunter. No doubt she'd be great at the hunting part of it, but the lifestyle? The solitude for months at a time, the endless travel and the repetition, the constant hustling to find contracts and get paid? But she loved everything about the guild, their traditions, their honor. She might have made a better scribe.

We were all lying to ourselves, Esha thought sadly, pausing to inspect a cloudberry bush. *A bunch of lost kids pretending they were doing something meaningful with their lives.* The fruit was ripe, and she plucked them off the vine, letting the local fauna attune her senses to the land. Despite traveling for the last few days, she hadn't found the Serene Way. But she hadn't really searched for it yet. Part of that was due to Yelu, but the other part was fear.

Though she was only supposed to watch the perimeter and report back at any sign of the rebels, Esha wandered far beyond.

She passed over a hill covered in lumbered stumps, briefly pausing to wonder what type of wood it had been. From this clearing she could see the half-full moon and bright stars, and from this vantage, tiny specks of light coming from the village.

Through a bamboo grove, she found the markings of a Venara spirit shrine – a circular recess in the trunk of a banyan, grown into it, and littered with the bones of small creatures. She cut her hand to drop some of her blood over the flowers at its roots.

She began uttering the voiceless chant that would echo into the Everpresent, to bring her closer to the hidden passages.

Master Arei told them that every hunter forged a different relationship to the Everpresent. Esha's always felt structured and utilitarian, cause and effect, and she couldn't imagine a different way. And especially not Ree's, who had been lucky enough to always have the connection.

Such a waste.

Esha arrived at a thin, gurgling stream, and splashed a handful of fresh water to wash the sweat off her face. The valley was warming up to her now, trusting her intentions to respect and protect it. She'd never met a guardian before, but wondered how long it would take to find one here. Days? Months? Years? They were taught not to ask for favors, that the god spirits did not care for humans.

When Esha opened her eyes, she froze. Fifty paces away, several figures were moving swiftly through the forest. She watched them intently, hand near her chainblade. A break in the canopy allowed a glimmer of starlight to catch on their forms. Steel, weapons on two. And then... she startled. Was that the glow of green eyes?

Signature of phi.

Another pair, and then eyes blinked back into the darkness and did not reappear. The hairs on her neck raised, and a chill shuddered throughout her body. Twenty, maybe thirty figures moved beyond her vision. Still remaining completely motionless, Esha searched about for any sign of movement. Then she closed her eyes and listened for their footfalls. There… picking past the constant chirp of insects and nocturnal creatures she made out the faintest hint of the group moving off toward the village.

She's here! Esha's heart thudded, and she thought that she should make for the camp as quickly as possible without alerting the rebels. She'd wandered deep into the valley, so there was time to beat them if she hurried.

That was the practical thought, the rational one. Tan was correct in guessing the rebels were overconfident, as their numbers were far lower than anyone had guessed. Which meant they indeed had the advantage in numbers, three to one.

And then the irrational reared its head, the one based on dumb emotion. Tan had sworn they would take her alive. No sense in making martyrs. But idealistic promises would not satisfy Esha's need for a fucking explanation.

Esha stood slowly, gazing back the way she had come, then toward the rebels. She turned in a slow circle, and watched. Waited. Listened.

Silence… then… the brush of a branch. Esha moved that way, following a bright scent that itched at her memories, dread building in her heart. In the novice days, if Ree didn't want to be found, she couldn't be. But it had been a long time since then, and Esha had learned other things in the years she'd been manhunting. She'd learned how to disguise her steps rather than attempt to avoid making any noise, to sound like the mouse crawling a few feet to her left boot, or a snake slithering through rotting leaves.

As she drew closer, her focus tightened, hyper-fixated on this lone figure. They weren't near the other group, which had moved beyond Esha's awareness. She caught glimpses of a shadow flicker through a thicket of bamboo, then climb over a muddy incline. They were moving quickly and quietly, but without any intent to conceal themselves. If her target didn't realize they were being followed–

They froze, and Esha froze with them, turning sideways to blend into the last opaque bunch of bamboo. She waited a few breaths, then heard fabric scrape against rough wood, then a sigh. Carefully, Esha peered from her cover, and saw someone on the rise, sitting on one of the stumps.

Though it felt like a lifetime ago and she looked utterly foreign, Esha would have recognized her old friend anywhere.

But she hadn't expected the flood of confusing emotions – the strongest, disappointment. Despite all the evidence, she still hoped it wasn't true, that it was all some kind of misunderstanding.

But here she was.

Ree's back was to Esha, and a curtain of long silver hair hung down past her shoulders. She watched as Ree ran her hands through it, then tied it into a single tail with a ribbon. Jewelry glinted on her neck and wrists, as well as what looked like war paint on her bare arms. Resting against the tree trunk was a long, daab-style sword, which was odd; Esha remembered Ree's weapon of choice being the bow. Ree looked over her shoulder, gazing to the west, toward where Esha estimated the others had gone.

She hardly looked older, but sharper somehow, chin and cheekbones chiseled. But still the same face, the same faraway stare. That stare always made Esha question whether she was listening, or whether she was distracted by the constant whispers of the Everpresent.

This was her chance, and Esha had already removed her blow dart, filled with a mixture of lead and other toxins. There were not many substances that could take down a phi hunter, thanks to years of poison conditioning, but they did indeed exist. The thing was, anything this potent would certainly kill a regular person. Raj had assured her the toxin would only paralyze and the lead would cut off her connection to the Everpresent.

Esha put the blow dart to her lips. His exact words were *Probably. Esha,* he'd reminded her before leaving with the 2nd platoon, *this is not our friend anymore. This is our target. Don't fuck this up for us. For me.*

Isaree wasn't her friend anymore, and Raj had always been there. He was the one who dragged her out of the dead-end job, gave her a purpose again, no matter how small it felt compared to the life promised to them. He was right. This was the Abyssal Heretic. The killer. The path she chose. Esha inhaled slowly through her nose and took aim at the back of Ree's neck.

But Raj hadn't been the only one to appeal to her.

Before leaving Jinburi, Esha had stopped by Ree's old house to speak with Ex and Arinya. She'd wrestled with going, feeling guilty for not having visited in years. After all, it had once been like a second home for her, when she'd come along with Ree for family dinner. She always looked up to Ex, begging him for stories of his demon slaying. And Arinya's quick wit and fantastic cooking was a welcome change of pace. Certainly, she preferred being there to seeing her own mother, who had never denied being a shitty caretaker, and made no efforts to improve their relationship.

Seeing Arinya so ill had been difficult, and Ex so distraught about what the prince had told him…

If anyone can reach her, it's you, he'd said. *Please, try. Please… bring our daughter home.*

Esha lowered her blow dart. Despite the terrifying reports, she wasn't afraid of fighting Ree. She'd almost always won when they sparred. The times Ree got the best of her were cheap shots. Esha was ready to take a cheap shot herself if it came down to that. With a steady breath, she opened her mouth to call out.

But Ree spoke first. Without turning around, she said, "You shouldn't have come, old friend."

Chapter 28

The Profaned Ones

Tan did his best to hide his distaste regarding the conditions in the clean village of Son Clarion. Clean was an ironic description. A spiked fence and shallow ditch surrounded the perimeter of the cheap bamboo huts that formed most of the housing. The shit ditches were uncovered and too close to everything, giving the entire area an unpleasant stench. In the setting sun, clouds of mosquitoes buzzed above filthy buckets of water. Workers were returning into the village after a long day of work, rolling carts of pineapples and bananas through the guarded gate where above, the name of the village was written in both Grisi and Rami.

The naming convention was distinctly Grisi of course, on account of their entire population being the children of the Grand Patriarch and thus entitled to inherit all his lands. By definition, all his lands translated to any land that the sun touched.

After explaining to the Protectorate soldiers who he was, why they were there, and showing his official orders signed and sealed by King Sarvupun, Sir Burrows, General Elleman, *and* Governor-General Rimes, Tan and his men were let into the village to take stock and set up their forces.

The tallest building was predictably the church. The young Lo girl showing him around, who said her saved name was Clara, told him it also functioned as the soup kitchen, school, and clinic. At least it had been, until all but one of the missionaries had left. Most of the population did not know why, of course, as information was tightly controlled by the Protectorate, but the girl shyly admitted she'd overheard the constables talking. They fled in fear of the Heretic after news of her campaign had come to the officials overseeing Son Clarion.

"Are you afraid?" Tan asked her.

Clara nodded, absently clutching a wooden rosary. "I pray every day that the righteous father strikes her down."

Tan noticed the curious stares of the villagers from inside the open doorways of their huts. "Do your parents work at the plantation?"

"My parents are gone," she said. "My only father now is the Patriarch."

Tan side-eyed her, wondering if this was a canned, practiced response or she really did pray to the Grisi god. He supposed food, shelter, and safety was a powerful motivator and could make anyone believe in things they never thought they would. Not that Tan had ever wanted for anything, but he liked to think he wouldn't be so easily swayed.

They walked into the church, an open, unchambered structure where the remaining missionary fussed over several patients listlessly resting on cots in the right wing. Most of the patients looked malnourished, suffering from exhaustion. A pregnant woman sat in the roughly constructed wooden pews with two bony children, sharing a small bowl of plain rice and pickled vegetables. They gazed at Tan curiously when he walked in, but said nothing.

"Greetings!" the missionary called, though did not pause in his work, where he was dressing a young man's leg wounds. The missionary was a portly sort, and Suyo, which wasn't so uncommon but always struck Tan as strange. It was the same feeling he got when seeing Lo men wearing Protectorate security armbands, though the guards carrying guns remained Grisi. After looking Tan over, he gasped and pressed his hands in a wai, bowing deeply. "Prince Tanung, I hardly recognized you! How blessed we are that you're here in our humble mission. My name is Brother Martine. What brings this great honor?"

"Hello, brother," Tan said. He hadn't expected to be recognized anywhere in Loram, but being that this missionary was Suyo, it made sense. "Thank you for the warm greeting. Surely you're aware of the potential threat approaching?"

"Oh, yes, the business with the rebels. Nasty stuff," the missionary said, fussing with his robes. "I'm confident that we're safe here though, protected by the arm of our great father. We're all already saved here. Clara! Are you showing the prince around? That's a wonderful act of kindness. She's new here, but already knows everything about the village. They work very hard, you see, and hard work is rewarded in the promised lands..."

While Brother Martine kept babbling, Tan strolled around the church, noting it would be a good place to set up a fallback position. The pews could be upended as barricades. It was the natural place for civilians to shelter during an attack, thus he'd need to shelter them elsewhere.

"...and I kept telling my brothers and sisters, that the Tenet of Morning explicitly describes a similar prophecy as it relates to the Heretic," Brother Martine was saying as he trailed Tan around the building. "Verse two-hundred and five, in which a great hero of the Patriarch's Sons should come to His new lands, combating the army of Heretic devils... and after he was victorious, he became a great king of the promised land! Are you familiar with the Book of Vows, my prince? Some of the tenets are not so unlike the teachings of the Awakened Lord!"

"I'm familiar," Tan answered politely. He'd read it twice during his studies, but wasn't in the mood for a theological discussion. The back entrance led out to the communal garden, where a few rows of scrappy vegetables clung to life, along with a pigpen, which housed a handful of skinny, sad swine. A couple muddy chickens pecked around the edges but fluttered away when Tan stepped outside. It didn't look like near enough food to support the population.

"This is all you have to eat?" Tan asked. "What about all the harvest being collected?"

"Most of the harvest is reserved by the company, though everyone is allotted one bowl of rice per day," Brother Martine said. "They provide so much funding to Son Clarion that the people here see it as a fair exchange."

"The Grisland Trading Company," Tan said. Indeed, their seal was stamped on all the packed crates being wheeled in by farmers, as well as the warehouse. "Are all the clean villages like this?"

"This is a nice one," Clara said.

"You've seen more?"

"I've heard." She shrugged, and walked back inside.

By nightfall, all was in place. Sharpshooters and lookouts were positioned on rooftops. Squads of skirmishers were hidden throughout the village. Another squad hid their horses in a grove outside the gates, ready for pursuit. The Protectorate forces made sure all the villagers knew that if the alarm bell sounded, they should gather in the warehouse rather than the church, then took their posts.

Tan had discussed their strategy at length with the Gris officer in charge of the village's defenses, who had balked at the idea of retreating into the village. Tan explained that this was a standard tactical withdrawal, not a retreat – they would draw the rebels into a crossfire and trap the Heretic within. After a lot of convincing, and even demonstrating with figurines, the officer reluctantly agreed to the plan.

A lookout kept a watchful eye to the woods, where their sentries would signal should they see the enemy approach. Tan and three others crouched in one of the residences with a vantage point over the entrance and the main street, while the two families that shared the space huddled together in the corner.

All previous attacks were reported occurring after midnight and so they slept in shifts during the day, making sure to keep hidden. He exchanged looks with his men, hardened professionals who only nodded back, ready to fight. As it was with war, the majority of time was spent waiting.

Nothing happened the first night. Nor the second.

As dawn broke over the second night and Tan made the call for everyone to stand down, he began to wonder if Esha had been right. But in his gut, he didn't believe that Isaree would be deterred.

Well past midnight on the third night, thick cloud cover had rolled over the sky and brought with it the warning signs of a rare twilight downpour, the soft twinkle of rain beginning to chime over the dirt and thatched rooftops, soon giving away to a steady hiss. The lookout whistled a low chirp followed by a hand signal that meant he had a message. Tan unfolded a rain hat, then quickly walked across the path and climbed up the side of the tool shed where his man was stationed.

"I think east point missed the last check in," Adee said, one of Yelu's sharpshooters and an experienced seaman to boot. The young, long-haired and bandana'd Suyo man held the spyglass against his face, fixed on the distant woods beyond the hundreds of neat rows of fruit trees.

"Think?"

"Visibility is shit, captain. Haven't seen any movement." Adee handed Tan the spyglass. Sure enough, when he peered through, the combined darkness, along with the fog of rain made it hard to see anything. The wind had started to blow down through the valley, shaking the bountiful fruit trees, palms thrashing under the rain.

"How long ago was the check?"

"Two minutes."

It took ten minutes to run from the camp to the village on foot. If the camp had been compromised, then they'd have eight to twenty minutes before contact, depending on how fast the enemy force was moving. But the rain had just started, and perhaps the perimeter lookout had relaxed on the routine while searching for rain gear. Or maybe Adee missed the all clear signal. The possibilities were endless, but Tan would be a fool if he didn't prepare for the outcome that carried the most consequence.

Then a flash of lightning lit up the field, and he caught movement – a cloaked figure dashing forward, then another. And then it was darkness again.

"They're here." Tan handed the spyglass back to Adee. "Signal the second unit, even if they aren't there." He whistled to the groups within earshot, followed by a hand signal to be ready, then drew one of his pistols. The old Suyo-style pistols were finicky when wet, but his brigade carried fine, imported Grisi-made weapons. Still, if it rained hard enough… Nervous energy began to flow through his veins – the rush of excitement and fear that so often gripped him before battle.

Thunder rumbled in the distance, and just as it did a yell from the gate rang out. That was much sooner than expected. A Protectorate guard fell backward off the raised guard tower. A volley of gunshots sounded, then the hectic clanging of the alarm bell. As the alarm continued to ring, villagers flooded out of their homes and fled toward the warehouse. Children and babies cried as their parents dragged them along.

Adee trained his long rifle at the gate. "It's coming down," he said.

Indeed, the gate was splintering. To Tan's chagrin, the security forces were still trading shots with the rebels, trying to hold the line, rather than withdraw. He cursed under his breath.

Well, he'd warned them. His crew knew exactly what to do and when, and if the Protectorate wanted to soak up the rebels' attacks, so be it.

"Captain! Captain Tanung!" A Protectorate guard called from the street.

"Over here!" Tan waved him over. The kid hurriedly ran up to the toolshed, squinting against the weather.

"Officer Camden has ordered you and your men to the gate!"

"That's not what we agreed on," Tan growled. "Tell him to withdraw, as we planned."

The guard was clearly panicking and didn't comprehend. "Those are his orders!"

"We're not under his command!"

"But, sir–"

"Dammit, tell him–"

"Captain!" Adee hissed, urgently tapping his arm. Tan glanced to him, who pointed down the street. He squinted into the darkness, then spotted approximately twenty black-clad, war-paint smeared men running against the crowd, toward the gate.

Tan didn't have time to wonder how they'd entered. He pointed his pistol at the nearest one and fired, hitting them in the leg. Adee shot the same man in the head as Tan took the time and cover to reload. The Protectorate guard stared at the approaching enemies, fumbling as he raised his rifle. A second later, the squads of Wild Cobras hiding in the homes rushed out in a roar, falling onto the rebels with bullet, blade, and fury. Civilians panicked, screaming and scattering where the fighting broke out. In the darkness it was difficult to see at range who was friend and who was foe.

Tan slid off of the tool shed and rushed into the chaos, taking another shot before blocking an axe blade with the thick barrel of his gun. He drew his cutlass and slashed the attacker across the chest, spray of blood hot on his face. He kicked the body away, then cut down another rebel from behind.

"Boss!" Ukrit yelled before throwing his polearm. Tan had already ducked, and heard the thud along with the pained cry of someone behind him. He yanked the weapon free of the rebel's neck, then tossed it back to Ukrit.

Tan only had a moment to assess the situation before another sword-swinging rebel came for his head. It appeared a lot more had entered, but they were falling fast against Tan's professional fighters. The rain pelted down as the blood flowed and the frenzy grew frantic. Another one fell under his sword. Pain shot through his temple as he was hit by a blunt object, knocking off his rain hat, staggering him. Steel scraped against his cuirass. Through blurry vision, he pistol-whipped the person in front of him. They fell back with a grunt, and Tan charged with several slashes of his blade.

Breathing hard, he backed away to catch his breath, and saw that most of the rebels were dead, or damn near close, and the Wild Cobras were making sure. The worrying thought occurred to him that they'd been fighting practically blind and Isaree could very well be one of the corpses laying in the mud. He wiped rain from his eyes and began to survey them, when a couple of Protectorate guards came running from the gate.

A cloaked figure pounced upon the back of one guard, limbs wrapped completely around his neck. With a snap, the guard's head flopped sideways, and the figure jumped to the next, knocking him down. The way it moved looked more animal than human, almost like a squirrel, a flurry of ragged cloth as they slashed at the guard with what looked like a handful of bloody knives, the guard's legs thrashing and jerking before growing still.

"Regroup, regroup!" Tan yelled, then tossed his empty pistol and pulled another from his holster belt, striding to form up at the point. "Re..."

The cloaked figure's face snapped toward Tan, green-glowing eyes flaring in the dark. His breath caught in his throat, as he saw... not a man, but a *creature*, with pasty gray-green skin and a sneering jaw, covered in blood. No... couldn't be. That must be more warpaint, some kind of lenses, a trick of the light...

"Fire!" Adee screamed from next to him. His shot peppered the thing's chest, and it didn't react until two other guns joined in. It streaked away into the shadows, leaving nothing behind but the corpses it created. Tan scanned the alleyways where he thought it went, but the slashing rain kicked up a mist of mud and filth that shrouded everything.

Someone screamed from the rear, followed by alarmed shouts. Tan forced his way through the line. Another gunshot blasted, and when he pushed through, two of his veteran swordsmen were laying still in the mud, throats torn open. The rest of their squad ran into the dark in pursuit, vengeful war cries trailing after them.

Ukrit caught Tan by the arm, pulling him close to scream, "It's a demon! The Profaned ones!"

Tan stared at him in numb horror, or rather, behind him. In the darkness, from the rooftops, six pairs of glowing eyes glared down. Ukrit followed Tan's gaze and cried out, yelling for the men to attack.

"Hold!" Tan yelled, pushing ahead. Could these things even be killed? It was a long shot, but maybe he could prevent more casualties. "Where is your leader? Where's the Heretic!?"

Around him, the barrels of guns and tips of swords and spears held at the ready. The eyes stared back, unblinking.

"Where's Isaree?"

A long moment passed, and then, the response – a head dropped down from the rooftop and rolled to Tan's feet, followed by two others. His stomach turned. The heads belonged to the sharpshooters stationed throughout the village.

So much for diplomacy, he thought numbly, before raising his pistol. The sound of his shot was lost in the blast that surrounded him, a hail of death that should have annihilated any living thing in front of them. The eyes had disappeared, and a moment of hopeful silence followed. Tan anxiously clutched the hilt of his sword, every muscle tense as he stared into the smoky darkness. Had it been enough?

The eyes blinked open again. No, he realized with a chill how wrong they'd been to dismiss the most outrageous claims.

This was an impossible foe.

"Fall back, fall back to the church!" Tan managed to cry out before the frenzied roar as the demons pounced. They crashed into men and tore through armor and flesh alike like wet paper. He stabbed at the demon who'd fastened its jaws around Adee's skull before getting knocked into by someone else. Panic and adrenaline combined into a dissociated kind of desperate will as he hacked at anything resembling a tattered black cloak or gray skin or claws. A searing pain lanced through his arm. His sword clattered from useless fingers and then he was yanked away.

"Captain!" Ukrit pulled Tan from the fight, or slaughter, rather. "Come on!"

Their ranks were now completely broken, and men were running for their lives.

He had to pull it together. They needed to regroup for any hope of victory, and they needed someone to lead them; dying uselessly here would serve nothing. Tan ran down the street with Ukrit and his squad, and anyone else who had the sense to follow orders. If there was any credence to Brother Martine's faith and the demons couldn't enter the house of the Grand Patriarch, Tan swore he'd convert on the spot.

Ukrit paused to throw his spear, another gunman stopped to reload his rifle, shot blasting a moment later. The village illuminated with flashes of lightning as they ran. There were remnants of the battle, of rebel bodies felled by his Wild Cobras, of Wild Cobras felled by demons, of villagers caught in between.

The church loomed above as they rounded the last bend to the village center. There was candlelight flickering in the windows, and Tan hoped that some of his men had already arrived.

"We're here," he huffed to the others, lungs burning, arm throbbing. No response. Tan turned to his men, but found nothing but the rain.

The sounds of the battle were lost in the torrential downpour, thunder rumbling. Or the battle was over, and there was no one left but the monsters. He stood in the empty village center, staring around in disbelief.

Then behind him, the door creaked open.

"Don't shoot!" a small girl cowered in the doorway, arms over her head. Tan lowered his pistol, which he realized was unloaded anyway, squinting at the shuddering child.

"Clara?" he glanced about, slowly walking over. "It's not safe here. You should be with the other villagers."

"But the father is here," she whimpered. "His light will protect us."

"Quick, inside," he ushered her into the church, then turned to watch the darkened street as he slunk inside. He opened his bag for another shot, dismayed to find he was on his last bullet. He cursed and watched for movement, hoping against all hopes that Ukrit and the rest of his crew would come barreling out of the alleyways. They didn't. Tan nudged the door shut with his foot and backed away.

He'd hoped to see familiar faces peering over the barricades, but the building was dark and empty. Even the cots were abandoned. The light came from a few lit candles in stands along the aisle that led to the altar. It looked like someone was moving back there.

"Brother Martine?" Tan called. He glanced at Clara, who only stared at him with wide, dark eyes. "Are you alone?"

A crash of thunder startled him, the lightning brightening the village outside the windows simultaneously. And in that flash, a great shadow stalked by. At first, he thought it was a horse, that his riders had come to assist. But no, this prowled with a low profile, a sleek, muscular frame like a big cat, filling him with primordial fear. Darkness fell again before he could know for sure.

Tan squinted out into the night, then felt a tug on his elbow. Clara pointed toward the altar, her mouth open in shock.

She whispered, her voice wavering. "Not alone."

Chapter 29

A Heart Full of Savagery

"Old friend?" Esha sputtered, grasping at her anger and spiraling as she did. *"Old friend?!"* Felt like tearing the words from her chest and flinging them back. "It's been seven years, and that's all you have to say for yourself?!"

"Seven years for you, maybe," Ree said, voice deathly calm, "twice over for me."

Esha didn't know what that was supposed to mean. Didn't care. It just sounded like the kind of dismissive, self-centered statement her mother would make. She started to climb the hill, all too aware that her "old friend" had the high ground, yet still couldn't be bothered to look at her. Her instincts screamed at her to be cautious, as if it weren't her former classmate sitting there, but some dangerous animal. Raj and the others would agree that the way Ree occupied the Everpresent had always been distinct, as if she were natural part of it and the rest of them were only visiting. But that natural aura seemed to have shifted into something else, something more foreboding.

"Why are you doing this, Ree?" Esha asked, unable to hide the scorn from her voice.

"Have you seen what the Protectorate has done?"

"Running away to join some rebellion is one thing, but using the Serene Way to wage war? Controlling the phi to kill for you? I don't know how you're doing that, but it's not fucking right!"

"You don't understand, you couldn't understand."

Esha clenched her jaw. "Oh, yeah? I'm not *special* enough to get it?"

"No... that's not what I mean," Ree said, with a tired shake of her head. "I'm not controlling the phi. I'm giving them purpose. A path to redemption."

"Redemption?" Esha didn't follow, but despite her anger, she wanted to understand. She needed to get closer. Only ten paces away now. "You broke your vows, fine. I won't lecture you on that. But have you forgotten everything? What makes you think tricking them into killing for you will give them redemption?"

Ree stood, though she still hadn't turned around. "You wouldn't believe me if I told you the truth. So what does it matter? You believe it's wrong to focus their urges toward a worthy cause, yet still believe it more noble to hunt and butcher them for profit?"

"When they hurt people, yeah!" Esha said. "Can you look me in the eye and honestly say you're doing the right thing here? They're not people anymore. They're cursed. They're *demons.* They're–"

"Monsters." Ree whirled around, finally glaring at Esha with a sudden ferocity. "Reborn out of past sins. Yes, it's clear you remember our lessons. But if you only treat someone like a monster, that's all they'll ever be. Every soul has a weight they carry and cast off with each passage; everyone deserves a chance to earn their way back. Everyone..." Ree trailed off as her eyes flicked to the scarred flesh over Esha's face, the wound she'd caused so recklessly the day she left.

Maybe she wanted to ask why it hadn't healed. Maybe she wanted to apologize. But Esha didn't want to hear it. "I still don't see how fighting in a rebellion helps these precious monsters of yours."

Ree hesitated, then said, "It's in one of the first things we ever learned as phi hunters. Where did the First Hunters come from? There was a war between the devas and asuras, the devas needed warriors. We were serving a purpose greater than ourselves, greater than our reality, and in a sense, beyond our comprehension. In return, they gave us powers, and the Everpresent. What I'm doing here is not so different."

"Sounds to me like you have a god complex. You're comparing what you're doing to the fucking devas?" Esha squinted, peering closer at her for a sign of... well, she didn't know what she was looking for exactly. Remorse? Doubt? But when Ree's expression didn't change, she had to laugh. She couldn't believe how much her former friend had changed.

"Laugh all you want. But I walked for a lifetime in the realm of gods. I spoke to Indrajit, who saw the value in my work and granted me his authority..." Ree paused, frowning at Esha's laughter. "Fine, you don't have to believe me. But plenty of others do. Plenty of others are relying on me to liberate them from the Protectorate. You might disagree with how I'm doing it, but the ends will justify the means. I'm not just doing this for Loram, I'm doing this for Suyoram. For the whole continent."

"Like you give a shit about Suyoram," Esha scoffed, throwing up her hands in exasperation. "You left! Left everyone. Without a..." she felt her voice waver and gritted her teeth. "You don't know how bad it hurt your parents! And Kit!" She stopped just short of finishing, *and me.*

"It was never my path." To Esha's bitter satisfaction, Ree looked sad now, her face dropping. "And it wasn't yours either, was it?"

Esha didn't answer right then, didn't trust her own voice. Ree tilted her head, eyes going distant momentarily. Then she nodded to herself, gazing evenly at Esha. "I have to go."

In the silence that followed, the rain began to thicken from errant drops to a steady drizzle. Ree's question was left unspoken, but Esha understood just fine. *Are you going to step aside?*

"You didn't ask why I came here," Esha said, her hand drifting to the hilt of her chainblade.

"You must be traveling with the mercenaries camped on the west side of the plantation. I can only assume they hired you, or you hired them." Ree shrugged. "I'm not concerned with them. It's the Protectorate I'm after and liberating this prison camp."

Esha smirked. Ree hadn't mentioned Tan's first unit, lying in wait in the village.

"For what it's worth, Esha..." Ree rubbed a hand over her eyes, smearing some of her war paint. "I... regret how it ended between us. I never wanted to hurt you." Something uncomfortable tugged in Esha's chest, and she knew Ree wasn't just talking about the scar. "I would rather not hurt anyone. But sometimes violence is the only language people listen to. Sometimes–"

Esha made her move. She shook the blowdart from her sleeve and brought it to her lips, expelling a hiss of breath. From ten strides away, it should have been a sure thing. But Ree reacted far faster than Esha expected, spinning away. Esha didn't wait; she had already whipped her chainblade out, flinging the blade end straight toward her target.

Clank! A shockwave cascaded up Esha's arm as the blade struck – Ree had retrieved her sword to block, still sheathed, and the chainblade's hook caught around the hilt. Esha yanked as hard as she could, and the sword flew from Ree's hands. Esha was still stronger, at least.

"Don't do this," Ree said, just as Esha lunged and punched her in the jaw. She flinched with a grunt of pain, and Esha followed up with another straight to the side of the head. Ree didn't go down. She rammed her shoulder into Esha's chest, then cracked her good across the face.

The pain didn't register. Esha ran right through it and lashed the chain of her weapon around Ree's neck. She pulled hard, but Ree planted her feet and grabbed the chain, giving herself some slack. Still, her face was turning red as they strained for control.

"There's still time," Esha growled. "You can stop this!"

Ree ran forward, throwing Esha off balance as she pulled her knife and slashed.

Esha's padded glove caught most of the damage, the rest she ignored. Forced to drop the hilt to her chainblade, she drew her own knife, just in time to block Ree's next slash. Blood flowed freely down her arm. Well, she'd tried. As all her targets, this one would not go down quietly.

Their knives clashed and scraped as they fought for advantage. Ree had improved, but Esha was still better than her. Better than her at fighting, but not at magic, and Ree would get frustrated soon. She'd need to strike first. With a voiceless chant, a shock of electricity cascaded over Esha's arm and by contact, her blade. The sudden sting surprised Ree, who pulled back, leaving an opening.

Esha sunk her blade in Ree's side and twisted.

Ree gasped and staggered back, clutching her ribs. Blood bubbled between her fingers. Stupid that she didn't wear more armor. Left herself exposed. Her eyes darted to the hilt of Esha's chainblade laying on the ground, and Esha dove for it. She would beat Ree to it, easily. But Ree hadn't gone that direction. Right as Esha clutched the chain, Ree had found her sword and pulled it from its scabbard, swinging it around in a wide slash.

The chain snapped in half. Esha's jaw dropped. The phi hunters' chainblades were forged by master blacksmiths, who spent weeks in the Trance meticulously constructing the weapons. The metal they used wasn't ordinary steel either – it was transformed by a ritual that made it strong enough to withstand the sharpest fangs and claws of a phi. But a link at the center of the chain was cut through as smooth and evenly as a wire through soft tofu.

When she laid eyes on the weapon Ree carried, it became apparent why. The curved sword, black from hilt to tip, blazed in the Everpresent with a ravenous energy, ebbing with a color that didn't exist. Though it looked paper thin, the depth of it felt endless, like staring into a chasm yet one not entirely uninviting. Leading to a place that promised something unattainable.

Breathing hard, the chain still tight around her neck, Ree raised the blade level with Esha's eyes.

"The Severer of Sorrows, gifted by Indrajit from the Deva Realm," she said, answering the unspoken question that must have been all over Esha's face. "You believe me now?"

Esha didn't know what to believe anymore. She remained crouched, watching as Ree stepped away from her. And then an unfamiliar voice in the Everpresent hissed from behind her.

This one pesters you. I will remove it.

She turned just in time to brace for impact. A large animal shape crashed into her, sending her sprawling, and a terrible snapping sensation burst in her knee as it twisted on a rock. A primordial, human terror gripped her as the creature snarled in her face. It resembled an oversized, red-striped, black tiger, with startling yellow eyes, but wasn't exactly a tiger. A single horn curled up from its forehead, while its ears were twice as long and tapered back. This was a spirit. The beast's clawed paws slammed down on Esha's arms, and she felt her bones crack. Helpless, Esha cringed as its jaws opened, sharp canines longer than her hand.

"Wait!"

The clink of chains hit the ground. Esha couldn't take her eyes off the spirit, one that she would have called a truly magnificent specimen if it weren't an inch away from biting her face off. In her peripheral vision, she saw Ree approach.

"Did you think I could use the Serene Way to wage war without permission? The spirits loathe the presence of the Protectorate. They take without tribute. They poison the rivers, and the sky. Nature wages war all the time and is just as ruthless when angered."

Ree leaned down and touched Esha's cheek on the scarred side, gently brushing her hair back to turn her face and stare into her eyes. Esha wanted to scream, wanted to cry, wanted to gnash her teeth and bite Ree's hand. But she couldn't move.

"Don't follow me. I won't hold back next time."

And with that, Ree jumped onto the back of the tiger-spirit, and the beast bounded away as quickly as it had appeared, melting seamlessly into the treeline. Esha couldn't follow even if she wanted to – it would take time to mend her broken arms, and the snapped tendon in her knee, and she had never been the best spell caster.

Closing her eyes, she let the Everpresent soak in, and left the Blinds and all its sorrows behind.

Chapter 30

When Nature Wages War

No, they weren't alone.

"Identify yourself!" Tan yelled, and pulled Clara behind him as he raised his pistol.

A glowing ember stirred the brazier on the altar, catching the holy oil on fire. The bronze dish erupted in a ring of flame, and the sudden light revealed a woman's figure. She was dressed lightly but all in black – a sabai around her chest and loose chong kraben at her waist, barefoot with wraps not unlike a muay-boran fighter, muddy from knee to toe. Ropes of necklaces and amulets draped around her bloody and bruised neck. Her brows lowered as she stared at him, firelight dancing in her red eyes.

"Isaree," Tan said.

She removed her arm from the fire slowly. Like him, she was soaking wet, rivulets of rain streaming from the ends of her silver hair, which was half tied back, loose strands hanging in her face. Like him, she looked as if she'd been in battle, the streaks of red warpaint rubbed off from her forehead and cheeks.

For the last few weeks, his entire existence had revolved around finding this dangerous insurgent. He should have felt satisfied that his theory was correct, or at least, vindicated that he'd predicted her attack. But paired with his crew's catastrophic losses and the ugly fact he had one bullet left, this wasn't the confrontation he'd hoped for.

"This village is surrounded, with reinforcements on the way," Tan said, taking a few careful steps down the aisle. It was true, at one point, anyway. Bluffing a mark into surrender wasn't unprecedented. And right now, it might be his last play. He kept locked on her, but she didn't move, only watched him with those hunter-red eyes and he could have been back in Jinburi, in a modest home, intruding on a couple that had suffered so much loss in so little time.

"Your people are dead," Tan continued.

"So are yours," she said, her voice softer than he expected, but her accent distinctly Jinburi. "And I still have allies."

"You have demons."

She narrowed her eyes, sarcasm lacing her tone. "Yes, I have *demons.*"

He wondered at the futility of it. He knew she wouldn't surrender. If her demons were still stalking around, he was doomed. But perhaps he could reason with her.

Still, she hadn't moved, and he took a few steps closer, noticed the hilt of a sword and the same kind of multi-pocketed utility belt worn by both Esha and Raj.

"This won't last," he said. "You might think you're winning now, but the Gris are coming in force. And they will make you pay."

"Let them try." She raised her chin.

"They know who you are now." He forced himself to soften his tone. Almost apologetic. "They know who your family is. You want something to happen to Kit, again, now that he's finally thriving?"

Isaree flinched, though he couldn't tell if he hit a nerve, or some hidden injury nagged at her. Her eyes flicked over him, as if she couldn't understand what he was. "Why are you betraying your own people? Money?"

"I'm not a mercenary. I was sent by the king."

"The high bootlicker himself."

"The alliance is necessary to ensure Suyoram's continued independence," Tan repeated what the king had said enough times that he almost believed it. "And Loram is the price."

"I refuse to–" Isaree gasped, staggering back. Dark blood bubbled down her side from a deep slit in a particularly nasty spot. Looked like a stab wound. Though, from what Esha said, she should be able to heal herself, as he'd seen the hunters demonstrate to his crew quite miraculously. For whatever reason, she was weakened. A surge of cautious hope helped keep his wits about him.

"I'm not after the rebels," Tan said. "I'm after you. Listen, I could care less if they continue to run down the Protectorate. But you won't live to see it unless you surrender and throw yourself upon the mercy of the crown."

Isaree stared at him with an incredulous look on her face and then chuckled, as if genuinely baffled. "Surrender to who? You? Face it, you've lost." Her hand dropped to the hilt of her sword. "Now you should surrender before my *demons* get you."

A sudden rush of dizziness struck him, accompanied by a wave of nausea. *No*, he couldn't have an episode now. This felt different, though, maybe exhaustion, or maybe it was even some kind of spell she was casting. Whatever it was, Tan knew then that he had no other choice, and he wouldn't get another chance to take her down. His pistol was trained directly on her forehead, and from this distance, he was a crackshot.

He pulled the trigger.

But nothing happened. His finger didn't move. Confused, he looked at his hand, tried again. It felt as if his fingers weren't connected. He reached for his knife. That hand also didn't move, hanging awkwardly against his waist. Then he noticed the small, feathered dart sticking in the small spot of uncovered skin on the side of his arm. When had she…?

Clara walked out from behind him and plucked the pistol from his nerveless hands. He tried to take a step back but his feet didn't respond, and he fell to his knees and then to the floor, his entire body going numb. She pressed the barrel of the gun to his temple, meeting his eyes with no expression.

"Should I kill him?" she asked Isaree.

"The poison will take him soon enough," Isaree walked down the aisle. Tan could only move his eyes as he watched her approach, the same terror gripping him as his reoccurring nightmares of the Stranger.

Incredible… those visions were the moment of his death after all. He felt the world spin and fade, and then an excruciating fire cascade over his nerves, beginning from that point in his arm and spreading outward, overwhelming. The pain was incandescent, but he couldn't speak, couldn't react, could do nothing but lay there dying in agony at the Heretic's feet.

Isaree nudged him onto his back with her foot and pressed it on his chest, leaning down over him. She was blurry, a silver shadow in the candlelight, gleaming eyes now filled with an emotion he couldn't place. She reached down and grabbed his collar; from his peripheral, he could see her thumb playing over the spot where his royal pin would be.

"Oh, Noon," she smiled, and the last thing he heard before darkness took him was, "Looks like we caught the biggest rat of them all."

IV

Through a gale of blood, the ground erupts in explosions from ships the size of mountains. Demons pour from the gunports like angry wasps from a splintered hive. A great battle surges over the gates of old town, a rogue wave under the banner of Suyoram, blazing like a sputtering torch. The roar of battle drones into a heavy chant from the mouths of saffron-robed Sangha monks. He picks up the entire royal palace, and it crumbles in his hands. In those ashes, two shimmering rubies become eyes. The Stranger's eyes, and Isaree's eyes, as she straddles him, hands locked around his neck. But as they strain for control, the violence shifts into a baser urge. His desire swells and aches shamefully, their hips grind together. Her snarl turns into a blissful sigh, and with another set of arms, she places the crown on his head and bites his throat open.

Chapter 31

Where Ambition Lies

Head pounding with the ferocity of a thousand hangovers, Tan awoke bound, sick, and sweating. The echoes of the intense dream danced through his mind and body, but he couldn't fathom any of it having meaning other than his poisoned brain fighting for its life. He groaned, trying to piece together what happened.

Right. The girl had poisoned him. She'd been a rebel plant all along. Had she let the rebels in through a secret passage, or had other sympathizers in the village? Perhaps they had all helped, or even joined the attack.

What had become of his men? There must have been some survivors, those that stayed hidden, or Yelu and her sentries in the woods. And then there was Simo and the second platoon... They didn't know what was coming. No matter how well trained his troops were, the demons were not of this world and fighting them was hopeless.

Unless he could discover another way.

Somehow, he was moving. Drifting along, being moved. He listened for a hint of his surroundings, but only heard the sound of the forest, the croak of frogs, the occasional splash as they hopped into the water.

He opened his eyes to a tunnel of greenery. The sun glanced through arching branches, the various trees strangely uniform as if they had grown inside invisible structures. Bright red butterflies danced on the hanging blossoms woven throughout tiny vines. If he weren't in such severe discomfort, he'd have thought it beautiful. But the intermittent slices of sun were too bright to be pretty, coupled with the worrying fact that he'd been stripped of his armor and weapons, his wrists and ankles bound tightly.

Still alive, at least.

Awkwardly Tan sat up, and that act alone completely exhausted him. Breathing hard, he leaned against the gunwale of a wide dingy. The side was low enough that if he stood, he could roll over. But the rope around his ankles were secured to the slats and he'd only reduce his situation to being dragged under the water. He surveyed the rest of the dingy and immediately froze.

Isaree sat with her head against the bow, eyes closed. He expected one of her minions, but instead, here was the Abyssal Heretic herself, alone. Just the two of them drifting along in a raft on a narrow stream. Perhaps the demons couldn't come out in the daytime. It didn't mean she couldn't summon them at will.

Tan tested his bonds. His arms were tied behind his back, wrapped tight enough that his wrists were sore. He twisted his hands, reaching for the seam of his shirt, feeling around the hem. He always kept a small razor blade sewn in for this exact situation. Came in handy once or twice.

As he pressed the edge to cut the blade out of his shirt, he studied his captor. Judging by her slow, regular breaths, she was asleep. He saw Arinya's chin and Ex's nose – her mother's riverland beauty honed by her father's sharp, angular features. Still, her strangeness seemed to abstract any attractiveness into that of something dangerous. A poisonous butterfly. A snake.

She was about his age. Still young, in the grand scheme of life, but nearing the average lifespan for an enemy of the crown. Asleep in the daylight, she looked much less intimidating. Her macabre necklaces resembled a theatrical costume, even those made of vertebrae and other small bones. They looked especially out of place next to the prayer beads strung with red saisin thread, the kind found draped over deva shrines.

Her pale, cloud-colored hair hung in messy clumps around her face. It was the same color he'd observed the other two hunters shift into when they went into their Everpresent to do magic. It was a stark contrast to her tan, Suyo skin, though he observed her color had gone somewhat ashen. The bandages wrapped around her midsection had bled through. Again, he wondered why. Esha had explained the self-healing powers of the phi hunters, and the reports had said the Heretic was impervious to bullet and blade, yet here she was, slowly bleeding to death.

Perhaps his situation wasn't as bad as he thought. He eased the razor from the hem of his shirt, maneuvering it the best he could to the fingers that could bend enough to reach the ropes. Carefully, he began to scratch away at them. They were thick, and the blade was small. It would take a while. And then there were his ankles to deal with. But one thing at a time.

Isaree stirred, and Tan froze again. She grimaced, fingertips twitching, and he noticed her left hand was missing its ring finger. Still asleep then. He continued, taking stock of what else was in the dingy. A few bags were propped underneath her, likely supplies. Hopefully his weapons.

As he sawed each tiny thread, he began to weigh his options. The most obvious course of action would be to escape, find his second platoon and reassess the situation. But his mark was right here in front of him. If his hands weren't bound, he could have reached out and wrung her neck. Alone, asleep, injured, and... well, frankly, Tan was a trained soldier, and Isaree was not built like Esha. Not accounting for her magic, he could likely subdue her. Isaree was much smaller than her broad-shouldered, long-legged friend, around five foot three or so. She wasn't petite by any means, a fair amount of cleavage bulged under her sabai wrap, and her body was muscular and lithe like a finely honed weapon.

A fiber of one cord broke, and Isaree's eyes snapped open as if he'd fired his pistol next to her ear. At first, she seemed surprised at his presence. On the verge of panic, even. And then it must have dawned on her that she'd indeed, against her better judgment, taken a minor Suyo prince hostage.

Tan attempted to demand his release, but his parched throat only rasped. He coughed, almost dropping the razor, and dry-heaved once, but had nothing to spit up. Sweating profusely, he settled back, miserable. The thirst was torturous, and she only watched him impassively. She had a very disconcerting way of staring that reminded him of a cat he once had.

"You don't remember me, do you?" At his hesitant silence, she continued, "Ten years ago. Jinburi. You were there at the governor's palace. Caught me... catching rats."

Something rattled in his mind, almost jarred loose. Like a forgotten dream. Again, that unsettling déjà vu that had struck him at her father's house threatened the periphery of his awareness. He shook his head slowly, but the truth was...

The night of his first episode in Jinburi had been a blur. He remembered dropping his fork at dinner. He remembered seeing and saying nonsensical things. Sights and sounds and shapes before waking up in the yard. It wasn't implausible that she'd been out there, somehow, for whatever reason, and her strange presence had transformed into a reoccurring nightmare that had haunted him ever since.

That vision of the Stranger, his killer and his victim, had it always been her?

"You remember," Isaree said, then reached down to lift up a pouch. His medicine. He kept his face impassive as she shook the bag, but there were only two pills left. He'd been rationing them. "This must be why. I've seen my auntie make something similar. You have a slow sickness burning through here." She tapped her temple, then dropped the bag. "It'll kill you eventually. But that isn't the death you chase, is it?"

Tan eyed her bloodied bandage. "You don't look so hot yourself." His words scraped against his parched throat, but he forced them to stay steady.

"Well, you killed my medic. And the phi killed the only doctor in the village by accident." Isaree sighed, dropping her head back against the rail again.

"Brother Martine?" Tan frowned.

"No, he lived," she snorted, amused. "Against all odds."

"What about your child soldier?" Tan said.

Isaree scoffed. "Don't diminish her bravery by calling her that. The Protectorate took everything from her. Forced her father into the mines where he died. Forced her mother into begging and stealing, which got her executed. It's not a unique story. It's not even the worst I've heard. I didn't make her a soldier. Your Grisi friends did."

"It sounds like *your* phi friends don't much discriminate on who they target. You can't control them, can you?"

"As much as you control yours," Isaree said, crossing her arms carefully over her stomach. "They're our allies. But they don't perceive the world exactly like we do. I would have been there to direct them through the Protectorate forces, and only the Protectorate forces. I'd rather avoid needless casualties. But you fucked that up, Prince Tanung."

"Ah yes," he said, glaring. "The rogue demon death squad running rampant through the village was all my fault."

Isaree glared back. "Your men slaughtered my entire group. I told the phi to protect them… too late." She swallowed, seemed disturbed. "When I meet with the chiefs, you think they'll take that lightly? There's nothing worse to them than a collaborator, except for a collaborator that killed their friends and family members."

Nothing worse to *them*.

"And you?" Tan said, carefully. All his time in court had trained him to detect bullshitters. Trained him to manipulate them himself. He didn't get the sense she was used to this game. "What's worse?"

"Missed opportunities," she said. "I think people feel they have no other choice but to fall in line, if that means survival. I think… that maybe you're one of them."

"You don't know me at all."

"No, but I know your men are loyal to *you*, not the crown. I saw many foreign faces in your service. And the ones that lived told me things." Although Tan tried to hide his relief that there were any survivors, Isaree took notice, interest dancing in her eyes. "I know there's more hiding around Son Sidora. So… here's my offer. You tell them to stand down. Walk away. Or…" she held her arm up, toward the woods. "Join the right side of the fight. For the good of all Rami people."

"You can't be–" Tan stammered, then started coughing anew. She moved toward him and he flinched, but she only held a waterskin to his lips. He wanted to refuse out of principle, but thirst was too strong a motivator. He managed a few swallows before she pulled it away and settled back to her spot, the boat rocking slightly, wincing as she did.

"I'm no traitor," Tan said.

"I've heard about the unrest in Suyoram, the ransom disguised as crippling taxes to appease the colonizers. Don't pretend that anyone has any love left for the king. Suyoram needs someone to take a stand. Someone much more popular amongst the people, a national hero. One rightfully in line for the throne."

Such words would get one killed in court. Or on the street. Or in the galley late night, when the Wild Cobras were drunk and too liberal with their opinions. Instinctually he opened his mouth to admonish the sentiment… but hesitated. These sentiments were not uncommon – the position of a ruling monarch was a historically treacherous one indeed. Tanung's own line started when his great grandfather staged a coup against his own cousin and seized the throne.

His life and the lives of his men were on the line. He had to play this right.

"The king has a rightful heir," Tan said. "Even if he didn't, many of my kin have higher claims." Priyut's mother was a minor noble, and he commanded the entire army.

Isaree shrugged. "The circumstances in which you are born don't have to determine your destiny. There's unfair obstacles and perceived obligations, and they only limit your imagination."

"Your imagination of what, exactly?"

"Of what's possible. Do your ambitions really end at manhunting? At the whims of your Grisi masters?"

Tan always told himself that service was enough. That he liked his life as it was, roving and adventuring. But he'd be lying to say he'd never fantasized about a specific set of circumstances that would lead him to continuing his father's line. Simo's errant comments only fanned the flames. He knew he was fit for the role. He knew he could do a better job. But...

Isaree leaned forward, as if reading his hidden ambitions. "Is it about money? My allies will have captured Iautau by now, and the full treasury that comes with the royal palace."

"We aren't mercenaries," Tan glowered. Any one of his men could make just as much or more in a high-end mercenary troupe, but the prestige that came with serving the crown was what separated the Wild Cobras from a band of hired killers. Further than that, some of them were like family, and Isaree's monsters had slaughtered near half of them. How could they ever agree to switch sides on Tan's ambitious whims? Priyut *was* wrong, they weren't just a glorified hit squad.

At least, he always thought so. But perhaps his perception of his crew had been idealistic. Perhaps they were more selfish and cynical than he realized. Perhaps they were a little more like him. The smart ones could see the tide turning and would rather stand with the winners, if that meant living another day.

Or... stand with them as long as necessary to come out on top...

Interesting.

This might be the perfect way to get her to trust him, enough to let her guard down. And he had many more ways of getting people to trust him. Especially women.

"I have to admit, you know how to appeal to a man's ambitions," Tan let a slow, winning smile nurture the conspiracy. "Perhaps it's time to meet destiny."

Chapter 32

To Outrun Death

A giant amethyst carp-spirit pulled the raft through the stream, silvery scales flashing under the clear water. The main reason Ree chose to take the raft was to conserve her strength, soaking in the ambient energy rich in the Serene Way. Truthfully, she wasn't feeling any better than she had the night before.

Part of her rejoiced at seeing Esha again, but that joy vanished the moment her old friend opened her mouth, words full of vitriol. It ached her heart but hardened it at the same time. Esha couldn't see past her own circumstances. Couldn't be reasoned with.

The prince, on the other hand…

Ree hadn't recognized him in the church as the same boy she'd crossed all those years ago in Jinburi, and it was a shock when Noon told her who he was. In the light, it only took one look into his eyes to recognize him through Princess Siraniama's eyes, the ethereal memories of her life unlived. An adjacent future, unrealized. It felt impossible, and yet inevitable.

Obviously, a soul's journey did not always retrace the same steps. Tanung's father had been Varunvirya III, who would have been Sira's father. Sira had brothers, but none of them had been Tanung. And Tanung was not some lovesick royal commander who'd come to confess his affections before the end of the world. Ree was not some spoiled princess dreading the dawn of an arranged marriage. This was a highly trained killer with delusions of grandeur, come to collect the Protectorate's most wanted rebel leader.

The truth was, she'd planned on sending him to their operating base with the handful of other survivors, where Minh's truthseekers would extract every ounce of information possible before feeding them to the Weaver. Noon was already leading the liberated villagers to Muang-Hhleg, as it was the safest place for them. Roughly half to two-thirds of these "clean village" survivors would join the fight. Every victory made the resistance stronger, and Ree's mission had been very specific, a promise to both the rebels and the guardian of the Kalashas: to liberate all the labor camps.

But now that her combat group had been wiped out, she only had her non-human allies to finish the job. Retreating to the forward base to reinforce her group would have been the smart move, and Minh would surely scold her for failing to do so. But Ree saw another opportunity. She'd made deals with true demons, with devas. Appealing to a human prince's nascent ambitions did not feel so far-fetched.

The Liberation Front ended at the border of Loram, but she knew that her fight would continue. If she could seduce Tan into this vision of the future, of a Suyoram free of the Gris influence and control, then there would be nothing to stop them. With him on their side, the Front could be convinced that it was the only way to ensure the Gris would never return.

She couldn't trust the mercenary prince completely, but had not the patience or energy to cater to a helpless prisoner. After pulling the raft to the bank, she rebound his wrists in front of him so he could relieve himself. If he turned on her, she'd simply have to kill him.

He glanced over his shoulder, a quizzical look on his face.

"What?" Ree said.

"A little privacy?"

"Oh," Ree said, realizing she'd indeed been staring at him as her mind wandered. It was a bad habit that she'd never grown out of, that her mother used to scold her for, and she looked to where the stream flowed upward, what should have been impossible.

"This is the Serene Way, isn't it?" Tanung asked after he was done, then sat down on the bank.

"Yes," Ree gazed at the stream, noting the footprints of water spirits sunk into the soft mud. "Did Esha tell you about it?"

"She did," he said. "She also said that outsiders weren't allowed. That the spirits would chew you up and spit you out."

"Normally, yes. If by some miracle you managed to find it, you wouldn't be welcome. But these are not normal circumstances." Ree then reached into the raft to retrieve a fishing spear.

"So, it's not forbidden by the guild?"

"The guild has no ownership over the Serene Way. It's an ancient pact between the First Hunters and the Guardians... so as long as any human that uses it pays tribute, for themselves, and their passengers." She took careful aim at the flickering silver scales a few feet upstream.

"And how much faster do you move? How far does it go? What's the limit?"

She glanced at him, noticing his energy shift. It seemed like his mind was racing faster than he could keep up. "Why do you want to know?"

He opened his hands, brows furrowed. "This is a logistical super weapon. I can see how you've been able to drive the Protectorate mad. Striking fast and unexpectedly, moving on to what would be an impossible target." His expression lightened. "I want to know to what extent we can use it for our purposes."

Encouraging that he was already planning. Maybe he really was convinced. Ree said, "There are limits. But to give you an idea, we should be at Son Sidora by midnight tomorrow."

"So, about three times faster than average."

"The streams are fast. But I can't take as many passengers on streams."

"But in general...?"

"Depends. Some guardians are more powerful than others." She thought of the swamp naga of Jinburi, and how it had taken her far beyond what she'd ever expected. "It's not predictable enough to rely on."

"Your group was about twenty or thirty? Were all required to pay tribute, or you alone? What kind of–"

Ree slung the spear. It stuck into the silt, with a splash of thrashing fins. As she did, a sharp pain lanced from her gut, and she felt the wound ooze. She let out a sharp cry and doubled over.

Instantly, Tanung was on his feet, and alarmed, she half drew her knife, glaring at him.

Carefully, he took a step back, and nodded to her wound casually. "I could look at that for you. I've studied a little medicine and assist our surgeons often." She couldn't tell if he was lying, saw an opportunity to attack her. "It could be infected. Or you could be bleeding internally."

Ree scoffed, shoving her knife back in its holster, then slowly walked to retrieve her quarry. A fat, white-bellied catfish thrashed, skewered on her spear. With a voiceless line of gratitude for the forest, she pinned it with her knife to dress it.

* * *

Darkness on the Serene Way always brought with it a mysterious beauty. Nightbird spirits fluttered through the leaves, their wings leaving trails of blue light in artful forms to attract mates. Orange glowflies ebbed in the moonlight. Normally, Ree would continue on in the dark. But even the low amount of concentration needed to maintain direction on the way was exhausting. With his hands still bound, Tanung built a small fire, and she boiled a bit of rice to eat with the fish.

From the shadows, a flash of glowing green eyes revealed the phi as they lurked just beyond the tree line, checking in with Ree for new orders.

Tell Li to let his passengers go. Do not engage with them, even if provoked. Release them and return to the horde. That's all.

The phi serving her never questioned orders. Therein lay the problem in commanding them; it wasn't that they were disobedient. It was that they followed her orders to the best of their interpretation without asking for clarity on anything that wasn't clear. She had to be meticulous in how she worded directions, intentional on who she assigned to a particular task.

You're still injured. Owun's nostrils flared. *Why?*

They didn't question orders, but they had shown themselves to be highly protective of her, and Owun possessed the most mental capacity. He'd become a natural leader. She didn't know whether it was out of genuine care for her well-being, or self-serving practicality. She alone held the remedy to their curse, after all.

I owed Esha an injury. Ree frowned as she touched her damp bandage. Her skin felt hot, sweat forming on her brow. *I understand now, it's a karmic wound. I'll have to heal the old-fashioned way. Time.*

There is not enough time to outrun death.

Annoyed, Ree flicked her head to dismiss him. *That'll be all, Owun. Wait at the end of this path after. Do not engage with the enemy until I'm there, no matter what happens.*

She had not been clear enough at Son Clarion, and she wouldn't make that mistake again.

From across the fire, Tanung noticed the new arrivals, and grew deathly still. He glanced from the taihong to Ree, palpably anxious. She didn't blame him. He'd been unlucky enough to see what their claws could do to a human, but they kept their distance and were soon gone as she'd commanded.

"Owun's just checking in," Ree told him. "No threats for leagues around."

"*Owun*?! They have names?"

"The more self-aware phi remember their past lives." And those were the ones who were ready to take Indrajit's amnesty. Maybe that wasn't truly what to call it anymore, considering how she'd changed the criteria. At any moment, she half-expected the asura lord to appear and strike her down.

Though most of her fellow fighters became used to the presence of the phi, they were never comfortable with them, except for the Ashukari. The thought brought a bit of melancholy. The rebels were mostly simple folk that wanted their lives back, and provided quiet but warm comradeship around the campfire. A good amount of them were very young, and with that misguided sense of immortality, brought a level of cheerfulness she sorely missed.

She'd gotten to know many of the people that made up the newly renamed Loram Liberation Front, but as a personal rule resisted getting too close to anyone in particular. She'd gone to Havan for comfort after Fort Nestor, sobbing with grief. But, he was far more Ashukari than she'd ever be, and only seemed mildly saddened by the death of his primary partner.

It's what she's wanted, he'd said. They laid together when their schedules coincided, but their dynamic had changed. Without Tian, he fell into the arms of war like a long lost, toxic lover. Guilt weighed heavy in Ree's heart for leading him back to that dark place. A place Tian had helped him escape. Eventually, he'd joined the northern campaign as an infiltrator, and his fate remained uncertain.

"What about yours?" Tanung asked, jarring her from her reverie.

"What?"

"Your past life. Do you miss your family?"

"I don't want to talk about it," Ree snapped. They sat for a while in awkward silence, until Tan cleared his throat.

"My apologies. But might I ask, why are you driven to this conflict? I know what happens here will affect Suyoram, but this isn't your country."

Ree wasn't sure if she wanted to tell him. But so far, he'd projected a very non-judgmental air about him, a stark contrast to how Esha had approached her.

Or maybe he was a very good actor.

"I'm not sure I should tell you."

"Why not?"

"It requires some faith," she said. "And you mentioned you had very little."

"I'd still like to hear it."

Ree considered, and decided there wasn't much harm in it. Like others she'd told, he'd either be impressed or think she was delusional. He gave her the same impression she got from Minh – practical. Not the sort to necessarily care what someone believed, or even their methods, so long as they produced results.

"I went in search of answers for this," Ree raised her palm, as if she could hold up her constant connection to the Everpresent for display. "Why I had been burdened with seeing beyond the Blinds since birth, yet couldn't make myself believe in all the teachings of the guild. So I sought out the Ashukari for their guru. While traveling, I saw the effects of this war, and… it stirred up the anger I've carried for what the Gris did to my brother. How could the devas let them do this? But what could I do? I felt helpless. I wanted to speak directly to the devas. And so I performed the Ashukari Unshrouding, the death ritual, and walked in the realm of gods."

The prince's eyes widened in fascination. "What did it look like?"

"It's hard to describe… it's poetry incarnate." She peered at him. "I lived out an entire life that wasn't to be, a life that never was, yet stretched into our future and revealed the possibility. *A* possibility, one of countless. When I died, when *she* died, it wasn't so much that I feared that future – I realized it was already happening here, in Loram. And I would never be that person, but I could be the one that stopped her tragedy, and countless others, from happening."

It was quiet, and she expected him to laugh, but he only held her gaze evenly. "So… the fearsome Heretic is driven by altruism. By all accounts, you've been remarkably successful."

"Well," Ree shrugged. She touched the hilt of her sword, and admitted for the first time to anyone, "I stole this weapon from the gods. It's intended for… something else. But, I realized that I could use it…"

It was silent for a while, but for insects, and the crackle of the fire. She immediately regretted admitting it.

Tanung raised a brow, then sat back on his elbows. "And the Abyssal Heretic campaign was your idea of propaganda?"

"Not mine. The war council thought that spreading the rumor would benefit us. So we let them spread."

"It works for the Grisi in Loram," he shook his head. "But it won't in Suyoram."

"What do you mean?"

"You need to show the people who you really are," he said. Ree stared at him blankly, wondering what he saw. Then he flashed her a practiced, charming smile that must have always worked well for him. "You're a hero of the people, Isaree. You're a working-class girl from Jinburi, too righteous for the old ways of the phi hunters, yet connected to the devas. No, how about this – you're a champion for all souls, not just human. And you'll lead every soul from oppression, karmic and colonizer alike."

She chuckled. "Sounds like a story."

"It's more than that," the prince said, raising his bowl in a toast. "It's a legend."

Chapter 33

A Human Weakness

Since the day she'd returned from the Deva Realm, Ree dreamt exclusively from the perspective of her life unlived. Her connection to Princess Sira felt unresolved, as if her phantom soul was trying to show her something important but hadn't found the right associations. Tonight, nightmares crashed through her subconscious, depicting the terror following the Gris' conquest. Like many of the other hostages, she was used at their sadistic whims, serving not only as an outlet for their repressed urges, but a symbol of their dominance.

Ree urged her to a quicker death than this slow dishonor. A warrior's death, worthy of Kinesh-Kira, a goddess of destruction. But Sira resisted – *he will come for me. He will find me.* At dawn, Sira fled the palace. She ran through the burning city to the battlefield, lost in the inferno, searching desperately to die with her lover.

The heat overwhelmed her, and her body burned, and she screamed.

She awoke with a gasp, alarmed that she was alive. By reflex, her knife was already drawn and pressed against pale flesh in the moonlight. Chakri stared at her with wide eyes, his hand on her belly.

He said something she didn't understand, as the blood rushed in her ears and her heart melted with warmth and relief. She'd found him, finally. Or he'd found her. Saved her from the fire. Sira whimpered, her eyes filling with tears. She dropped Ree's knife, and wrapped her arms around her lover's shoulders, fingers sliding gently into his hair.

"Chakri," she whispered, pulling back to stare into his eyes, tears sliding down her cheeks. "I found you." She met his parted lips, his kiss sending her adrift into that final, beautiful night, the silk of her bedsheets against her naked skin, his calloused hands roving over her body. She prayed morning would never come.

Evening crickets chirped as Ree stirred, exhausted, weak, and in a great amount of pain. A hand slid across her forehead. How long had she been adrift in the realm of gods?

"How many years?" she murmured.

"What?"

That wasn't the voice she expected. Ree opened her eyes, and saw Prince Tanung sitting next to her. And next to him, a pile of foul-smelling, dirty bandages, a bowl of bloody water, and a needle. Slowly, she peered down to her wound, and saw that it had been redressed with clean bandages. She tried to sit, but yelped at the lancing pain and she flopped back down.

"You were burning up last night. Incoherent," Tanung said, a strange expression on his face. He seemed concerned, yet disturbed. Maybe disturbed that he was concerned at all. "I took the liberty of checking, and sure enough the wound was infected. It lacerated your liver, still bleeding. I did my best."

"How did you…" Ree trailed off, noticing his hands were free.

"Sorry," he shrugged. "You were at death's door. I doubt you would have preferred a one-handed operation."

Her annoyance was quickly displaced by gratitude. It would have been easy enough to let her slip away. The phi had gone ahead at her bidding, and he could have walked away with her head and completed his mission, having avenged half of his brigade and returned home a hero.

"You could have let me die here," she said. He didn't meet her eyes. "You want the throne that badly, then. I can trust you?"

"I want…" He swallowed, peering at her, seemed to lose his train of thought. He ran a hand over his face. "Yes. You can trust me. I just committed treason by saving your life. Is that enough?"

"For now," Ree half smiled, but he didn't return it. Something was off, still. Where his aura had been restless, now it had shifted to a listless anxiety, sparking at the fringes. "Is there something else?"

After a pause, he said numbly, "It was a long night. You were… calling for someone."

"Oh," Ree flushed. The fever dreams, some violent and some erotic, were intense and varied.

"Do you remember?"

"Not exactly," Ree sidestepped the question. He only nodded, and she glanced around at the late evening sky peeking through the trees. "Shit. how long has it been?"

"You've been asleep most of the day."

"We need to move," Ree sat up again, this time carefully.

"You need to rest."

"I can't." She pulled her belt onto her lap, hands shaking as she opened her tincture pouch. "They need me." Highly concentrated agberry and opium extract was a powerful painkiller, and she shook a scoop of the light blue powder down her throat. Even when injured, Ree avoided taking the potent mix, as the side effects were inebriating. Tanung handed her a waterskin, his eyes glued to the collection of vials, tins, and a few needles. She snapped the ledger shut, tucking it back into its holder and then tried to collect her wits before standing up.

Immediately, she regretted it. Her head swam with stars as her side screamed in pain, and she reared back, heading toward the ground.

But Tanung caught her easily in his strong arms, and held her against him as he stared down at her critically. Ree's breath hitched, her vision fuzzing back into focus. His golden-flecked eyes searched her face, lingering on her parted mouth. She should have squirmed away, but the firm, gentle way he held her conjured a comforting, physical memory. She should have felt trapped, but instead, she felt...

"I remember you now," he said quietly, placing her gently down on her bedroll, then brushed a stray strand of hair from her face, fingers lingering on her jaw. "I remember that night in Jinburi. You've haunted my mind ever since."

A wave of euphoria washed over her, a warmth, and a numbness. The drugs, surely. "In a good way, or a bad way?"

A slow smile spread across his lips. "A very, very bad way."

Each word dripped with a threat, or maybe a promise – something dark, something dangerous. He tilted his head, as if daring her to ask. She opened her mouth to respond, though she hesitated, and his thumb brushed across her lips. The casually sensual touch sent shivers down her spine.

"Shh. Rest. I'll be right here."

He moved away and she felt his absence keenly, even if he was still a blurry shape across the fire.

Resting... would be wise. And she had a mind to make some unwise decisions right then. With a long sigh, Ree let the pleasant numbness take her back into dreams.

* * *

Walker. The Voice of the Valley's presence brought Ree back to wakefulness. Somewhere in the curtains of greenery, Dama, the revered tiger-spirit, growled impatiently, flicking her tail in irritation. *You carouse with our enemies. Why?*

Carouse? I'm not carousing. *This enemy can be a powerful ally.*

Ree gazed around the campsite, pale and peaceful in the morning mist. The fire had gone out, the discarded bowls and bandages gone. She peered over to where Tanung had been, and found his bedroll empty. She listened for his footfalls, but couldn't stay focused enough. The extract was still in her system, and she shut her eyes again.

You can't trust this one.

I don't, Ree admitted, *but he did save my life.*

Only to manipulate you further.

Why go through the trouble? He could have killed me easily. It makes no sense.

A sentiment that constantly surfaces, regarding humans.

Steps came now, hidden in the coos of morning doves. It was a confident swagger, on the brink of careless.

Ree absently ran her tongue over her lips, and found they were dry and cracked. She reached for her waterskin, couldn't find it, then felt another hand on hers.

"Went to refill it," Tanung said, placing the waterskin in her hand. He was shirtless, his taut body washed, face shaved, hair wet, the longer strands clinging to his neck. A large tattoo of the Wild Cobras emblem featured prominently on the center of his chest, the royal crest wrapping across his collarbones. Ree took the skin and drank, then peered at him, meeting his red-rimmed eyes, which were glazed over with a feverish intensity that brought to mind the sickness he'd told her was apasmara. She doubted he'd slept at all.

"Did you get any rest?" Ree asked.

"I kept watch."

"You don't need to keep watch on the Serene Way."

"Not on lookout," he said, "I kept watch over you." She felt herself flush, and he quickly said, "I just needed to make sure you made it through without complications."

She wasn't sure what else to say except for "Thank you," then sighed and took her time to rise. The pain had subsided into a lingering ache that she would have to endure. He offered a hand, and she hesitated. Dama was notoriously mistrustful of all humans, and didn't understand the nuance of the situation between them. Dama's kingdom was the valley forest of the Kalashas, a world as far removed from palaces and intrigue as could be.

It wasn't Ree's world either, but she thought she understood it to some extent. After all, she'd grown up reading grand epics featuring emperors and warriors, wayward princesses and meddling gods, some only available in old devaskrit. Ambition, seduction, and power often intertwined to form strange bedfellows. Nonetheless, Dama was right to remind her that she should remain vigilant until sure of the prince's true intentions.

And sometimes a hand was just a hand. She took it.

"Courtly habits die hard," Tanung said as he helped her to her feet, then moved away to gather the supplies, perhaps sensing her discomfort.

"How often are you at court?" Ree asked, as they walked back along the trail that led to this branch of the Serene Way, where the raft and carp-spirit would be.

"As little as possible," he admitted. "If I need things done, I have methods other than groveling and posturing."

"So you have more friends in the capital that could be helpful?" Ree asked, glancing at him.

"Of course. I don't discriminate when it comes to useful connections," he said. "I go where the crown could never be seen, make deals for information, supplies, access, sometimes with known criminals." He smiled slyly. "As we've since established."

Ree found herself returning the smile. "Do you think I'm a criminal, Tanung?"

"As far as the Protectorate is concerned, you're a terrorist. The king considers you a liability – a threat to the alliance. And here in Loram they see you as a freedom fighter."

"You didn't answer the question."

"To be perfectly honest, Isaree? I don't care." That surprised her a little bit, and she slowed her step. He paused with her. "Public opinion is fickle, and can be molded and twisted into the reflection that serves you best. War has never been about who's right, it's about who's left. By the time society looks back to weigh your actions against whatever moral standards are in fashion at the time, who gives a fuck? We'll be dead."

"You've no fear of divine punishment? After seeing the phi and knowing what they are? How they became cursed?"

"No," he said simply. "Do you?"

"Fear isn't the right word," she said, slowly. "I decided that if it's the cost to do a greater good, then I'll make the sacrifice."

He nodded, then gave her that slow smile, and reached out to place his hands on her shoulders. "That's it, then."

"That's what?" Ree's eyes widened.

"The legend that we need to spread. What will convince my men to fight for you, and the countless others that will hear the story. The promise of your sacrifice for the good of all Rami people. You're the savior. Your rebel friends are wrong: you need to nurture hope, not fear." His smile turned to a grin, and Ree found herself smiling back, again. He hung an arm around her shoulder as they kept walking, excitedly chattering in such a casual, friendly way that she thought nothing of it, enjoying the closeness and his infectious energy. Until they turned the bend.

"And we should make pamphlets, draft up manifestos in both Rami and Gris. You could have them distributed in advance throughout – holy shit!"

Tanung jumped back. Ree twisted around to see what he was staring at, and spotted the massive, muscular body of the crimson-striped Voice of the Valley sitting next to the raft. The raft laid upturned on the bank, the spirit-carp next to it, dead. Blood coated Dama's jaws, who rumbled a long, low growl as her bright yellow eyes bored into theirs, though her ire was mostly directed at the prince.

Mostly.

Carousing. Dama's long, tufted ears flattened as she growled. *Every day you dally becomes another thousand felled trees, stolen breaths from poison air, stolen blood from the forest. You promised the lord of the mountains–*

I know what I promised. Irritated, Ree walked toward the tiger-spirit. *I'm going as fast as I can. Why did you eat my helper?*

We can move faster without it.

There's a reason I'm here. I have no back up to take on the Protectorate but the phi, remember? I need to save my strength. Especially if his brigade is not as easily brought to our side.

You see it then. Dama's growl trailed off, and her pupils, thin as reeds in the sunlight, darted to pin down the human male she so despised. *His heart is treacherous. I'll rip it out, and together, let us ride to battle.*

Tanung tried to say something, but his voice cracked.

Ree glanced back over her shoulder, where the prince had remained frozen, mouth still hanging ajar. Funny, he had seen the taihong and not been so spooked. But she supposed they were human-sized, hidden under ragged cloaks, and the sheer mass and magic of the tiger-spirit was nothing less than majestic.

He cleared his throat, and then asked, "Friendly?"

"...Best if you keep your distance." Ree turned back to Dama, resting her hands on her hips. *If I can avoid a massacre, I must. If you and the taihong attack, it will be nothing less.*

I don't see the issue in that. Dama lowered her head so that she was almost on Ree's level, and flicked her tail once, thrashing some nearby ferns. *I take issue in your judgment being compromised through the desire for pointless copulation.*

What?! The hell are you talking about? Ree flushed deeply. Despite knowing that Tanung could not hear their conversation in the Everpresent, she was mortified.

In your delirium you tried to lay with this male. The only reason he still breathes is that he rebuffed you. And now you are preoccupied with those base desires.

I did no such thing–

But a nagging memory did surface, which she'd assumed was a dream of Sira's. The way he'd regarded her so strangely when she woke up afterward took on a new light. Ree felt her stomach turn, and touched her bandage, deciding she'd rather not know the details.

Shame suits you, human. Dama's growl faded. *Remember, the great lord of the mountain granted you the Serene Way for this war. If you do not deliver–*

"It will be done!" Ree snapped, and tilted her head, to indicate the potential casualty behind her. *At any cost.*

Dama's impassive feline expression did not change, but her eyes narrowed. *Good.* And with that, she clamped her jaws around the carp-spirit. The vines parted, and the great beast stalked off into the jungle, taking her dinner along with her.

"What was that?" Tanung had cautiously walked to Ree's side, staring after Dama's exit, where the trees were already shifting to obscure the path meant only for spirits.

"More expectations," Ree said dismissively, avoiding his gaze. She examined the waterlogged raft and sighed. "We travel light, then. Let's go."

The sun had just begun to set when they left the Serene Way, a few miles short of the rubber plantation at Son Sidora. Ree felt her peace leave along with it. As they grew nearer to the clean village, signs of industry were everywhere. From what Tan told her, his second unit's orders were generally the same as the first. A smaller lookout group surrounded the perimeter waiting for signs of rebels, while the main force worked with the Protectorate forces to set up an ambush in the village itself.

Tanung asked her how she wanted to proceed as they moved into the forest. They'd discussed some options. The most cautious was for the prince to approach his sentries alone and call a meeting with his leadership team, then convince them to join the new alliance. Afterward, they'd meet with Ree outside of the village. If he were planning to double-cross her, this would be the easiest way.

Tanung liked the idea of walking into camp together, side by side. It would make a statement, but Ree felt the situation could too easily spiral out of control.

She had been mulling over Dama's warning as well… along with what Tanung had said about the Liberation Front promoting her as a demonic threat. Even if the Wild Cobras were persuaded, would Minh and the other chiefs trust them? They were collaborators, as far as the front was concerned.

After Fort Nestor, she vowed to never again use the Hunters' Trance. She now understood that Elder Nokai's warning was not unfounded. That night, she'd lost someone dear, and with them, a part of herself she'd never recover. And in its place she grew a new, terrifying phantom of herself that she despised, but knew was necessary.

Since then, she'd fought side by side with her men, and taken many lives, and all without the trance. What she still couldn't admit, however, was that this new part of her had also become hungry. She steeled herself for the violence that lay ahead, while beneath her trepidation a horrible excitement grew in her chest. Every kill felt one step closer to her goal.

Ree stopped at the last wild-grown palm, before the chaos of the natural forest gave way to rows upon rows of tall, skinny rubber trees. Neat, diagonal fishhook scars carved through the bark of the trees, where pale sap flowed in rivulets into man-made receptacles.

The commodity was ancient, and the harvesting itself wasn't what upset the spirits. Farmers had been doing this for centuries, but before the Gris, always balanced with the proper tributes to the spirits, only taking what was necessary, replanting when needed. The Protectorate's demand for rubber export had tripled throughout the last ten years, and thus the amount of natural land cleared had deeply upset the spirits.

Tanung walked ahead, past the first rubber tree on the boundary, then paused when he noticed Ree hadn't followed. She'd returned his gear from the raft before they set off, and now in his full uniform, polished leather cuirass catching the orange blaze of the setting sun, he looked every bit the handsome renegade prince, ready to seize his destiny. Seemed as if he'd walked out of a story book, truth be told. One that she had no place in.

"What is it?" he took a step toward her.

"I have a bad feeling about this."

"Don't tell me you're having second thoughts." Tanung peered down into her eyes as he leaned on the palm next to her. "Why?"

She considered making an excuse, disappearing into the forest before he could catch her. She could return to base and confer with the more experienced war chiefs, rather than make herself so vulnerable, all for a shot in the dark. Maybe chasing the Gris out of Suyoram was a pipedream, and she should be satisfied for her part here.

But didn't all dreams begin in the dark? Freeing Loram had gone from a dream to a reality, and now the Liberation Front teetered on the brink of victory.

"The only way to do this without bloodshed is if you liberate the village without me," Ree said. "Send the villagers to Muang-Hhleg for protection, they'll know the way. And after that, meet me in Kohkiem at the Seventh Shrine of Kinesh-Kira."

As he processed the new plan, Tanung crossed his arms, frowning. "You're testing me."

"We hardly know one another," Ree said, figuring that she might as well put it all on the table now before things spiraled into uncertainty. "You were sent for my head. And I'm putting all my trust into you."

Tanung blinked a few times, then held out his hand, inviting her to take it. "What else can I do to convince you?" The gesture was an offer of friendship, but the look in his eyes said something different, almost desperate. *Stay with me, please.*

It scared her. She swallowed, nerves creeping in her belly. What she wanted wasn't something she could let herself do. But she needed to know if she was delusional. "The other night… when you said I called out a name. What was it?"

"I've never heard the name before," Tanung said, withdrawing his hand slowly. He turned away, clutching at his chest, massaging it. "But… I can't explain it, really. I knew you were calling for me. And I felt…" Uttered under his breath, mostly to himself, "I think I might be going mad. You *saw* me. Saw me in a way I've never…"

"You aren't," Ree said, though she wasn't completely sure they both weren't going mad, she did believe one thing. She reached out to touch his arm, turning him toward her. "This is karma. Our fates are intertwined in this life, Tanung. In one way or another. You've seen it in visions, and I saw it from the realm of devas. Where the path leads is not set in stone, but to walk it is inevitable."

There was an edge of panic in his eyes, but in his core he looked as if he wanted to believe her.

"They'll call it madness to turn against everything we stand for," he said. "But it's the right thing to do. I see that now. They'll see it." He took her hand gently, and then pressed her fingers to his lips. Her relief was palpable, and a warmth spread throughout her chest. "Wherever this path leads, I choose to walk with you, not against you, Isaree."

"Even if it leads to doom?"

"Oh, you sweet thing," the prince grinned at her, his panic smoothly replaced by a mischievous glint in his eye. "You have no idea how far I'll go to get what I want."

Chapter 34

Those Who Dream in the Dark

The Valley does not approve of leaving this task to that one. Dama continued to lecture as she ran through the spirit paths of the Serene Way. Ree clutched the mane of fur around the spirit's neck, her body low to keep balanced as the greenery rushed by too quickly to track.

Ree closed her eyes, letting the ambient magic of the forest calm her. *If he fails, I'll return in force. But first I need to speak with the chiefs.*

You are the one with the power, Walker. Why must you seek the approval of these weaklings?

It's politics, Dama. A human weakness. I made a deal, and it hinges on the others agreeing to it.

Nonsense. Take the human army – they will follow you if they know what's best.

Ree smiled, patting the tiger-spirit softly. *If only it were that simple.*

One of the most impressive accomplishments achieved by the Loram Liberation Front was their sophisticated network of underground tunnels and bases. They existed before the Weaver, but after Ree had brokered the deal, Homdee extended the passages for hundreds of miles north, from Muang-Hhleg all the way to the capital city of Iautau. And then, going south, where the Front's forward operating base lay within half a day's march of Kohkiem.

The Seventh Shrine of Kinesh-Kira had fallen to ruin decades prior, long before the war. Languishing on a nameless tributary of the Duram river, floods had washed away most of the carvings on the sandstone walls. The idol remained standing in the center atrium, her details lost to the elements. A few of Ree's Ashukari lingered around the atrium, some deep in meditation, some only appearing so. All were armed with the scimitar of the goddess, and some with rifles.

It was fruitless, but Ree's heart lifted with hope that among the Ashukari, Tian's smiling face would greet her. That she'd make her way back from beyond death, beyond worlds, perhaps in another's form. But the Severer of Sorrows had drank of Tian's karma, and she was with the goddess now. Ree paused before the idol to utter a prayer in the old language for her friend, and then returned the wais of greeting from the Ashukari guards. The four of them pulled aside the hidden stone that led down into the base.

As Ree passed soldiers through the dimly lit underground tunnels, they paused to salute. Others bowed, with wais pressed to their foreheads. And still others turned away, crossing themselves with a protective hand sign. The rebels came from all over the country, from different factions, and not all of them approved of a "Suyo witch" having a seat at the war table.

The tunnels were set up for light-dependent humans to navigate, but every so often there was a passage that veered off into total darkness. The humans knew not to wander down those ways, terrified of the rebellion's mysterious ally, the Weaver.

But Ree had seen a shift in how the creature was perceived. The rebels had kept up their end of the bargain Ree brokered, providing Homdee with a monthly sacrifice in exchange for passage. But then, on her own, Minh had expanded that deal to include constructing these tunnels for them. After taking Muang-Hhleg, Ree assigned many of the phi to assist Homdee, as conditions for their service.

Fabrics were left in tribute by the rebels, draped over some of the tunnel entrances, just as the citizens of Muang-Hhleg had done at the mouth of the Weaver's cave. It struck her then how reminiscent this process might have been to the First Hunters, who found the Serene Way through placating the spirits. The purpose then had been to assist the devas in their war against the asura. And now history repeated itself, however distorted when reflected into human hands. And though the method of human sacrifice could be argued profane, the First Hunters had sacrificed animal lives and given their own blood for the same ends.

Was it so different?

* * *

"Let me get this straight..." Minh kneaded her forehead, then glanced at her second, Khim, for backup. The doctor had lost an eye during the battle of Muang-Hhleg, and wore a patch over it – Khim's remaining eye was narrowed, but he made no expression. Next to him, the two other war chiefs sat: a skinny farmer named Bird who spoke for the western provinces and oversaw their supply chain, and a young, portly ex-royal commander named Jun who had escaped the occupation of Iautau to help lead the northern campaign. Ree had met him once before she'd gone on her mission, and he was one of those types that openly scoffed at her. But his presence alone was proof that they'd indeed taken back the capital.

"You lost an entire group at Son Clarion to this Suyo hit squad, and now... they're on our side?" Minh said.

"Yes, the Wild Cobras *were* hunting me. We traded blows at Son Clarion, and then Prince Tanung and I... We came to an agreement," Ree said. "He will liberate Son Sidora to prove their loyalty, and afterward they'll help us take Kohkiem and finish the Gris in Loram for good. They're well-armed, well-trained, and completely loyal to the prince, not the king."

It was quiet in the small room, the light burning of candles against the muffled noise of the base.

"What else did you promise them?" Minh said in a flat voice.

"A Suyoram free of foreign influence," Ree said. "I promised him the throne."

All four chiefs gawked at her as if she'd grown a new head.

"*What?!*" Minh exclaimed. "A Suyo coup was never part of our mission!"

"Then the mission needs to change," Ree said, struggling to keep her voice from rising. "Expelling the Protectorate from Loram isn't enough. Reinforcements will arrive from Grisland any day now. Even if we take Kohkiem before then, they'll storm us with superior force." She wished Tan was there to back her up. Despite her contributions, it still felt like none of the rebel leaders took her seriously when it came to strategy, especially the men. "The only way to prevent getting overwhelmed is to push south to Jinburi while they're on their tails, and dismantle the garrison there. That's the key."

"We can't do that," grumbled Jun as he lit his pipe, then to the other three, "invading Suyoram with crazy Prince Tan? Is she out of her fucking mind?"

"It's not an invasion. It's liberation," Ree insisted. "The people will take our side, just like they have here."

"The situation in Suyoram is much different from ours," Khim said, stroking his beard thoughtfully. "While our king was defiant, King Sarvupun has maneuvered the Gris into an alliance. They are safe from Grisi control."

"They are being controlled," Ree snapped. "The prince himself agrees. The king's catering to the Gris has made him unpopular. He needs external intervention to take back power."

"That's how politics work, kid," Jun said in a condescending tone. Irritating. If she added up her experienced years, she wasn't all that much younger. "Unlike you lot, I've served in the court before. You kiss ass, you get your ass kissed, sometimes you reach around. It's a balance. The Suyos are on their own."

Finally, Bird, who mostly stayed out of these discussions, spoke up. "Sarvupun is no friend of ours. His failure to defend Suyoram is what made the Protectorate possible. If the prince is willing to be a friend to us, then why should we turn his aid away?"

"Why? Because this is the same prince who was sent to kill her!" Jun scoffed, blowing a stream of smoke out of his nostrils, engulfing the doctor next to him. Khim waved the cloud away. "How can you trust a man who turned on his master after a few words from the girl most wanted by the Protectorate? What *exactly* did you do to convince him?"

"There's no need for that," Khim said, uncomfortably flustered.

"It's a valid question," Jun crossed his arms, "A sweet slice of jiim may drive a man to insanity. And the Storm Prince already has a reputation for insanity."

"Don't be crass, Jun," Minh snapped, turning up a lip in disgust.

Ree bristled at his insinuation, but didn't take the bait. "Listen. He had several chances to kill me. He *saved* me instead." She placed a hand on her bandages for effect. "He saved my life because he believes that the cause is worthy. Deep down he's always believed it. And that's precisely why he'll prove himself in Son Sidora."

"Even if he liberates Son Sidora, it could still be a ruse," Khim pointed out. "A long con to get in deep with the cause before destroying us from the inside."

"The Protectorate would never sacrifice even a fraction of their industry for a ruse," Bird argued. "Profits above all. And this region has proved so profitable for Grisland that I believe it. Mark my words, they *will* send their full force soon."

This was going nowhere. Khim and Jun were obviously against her, though it seemed Bird was warming up. Minh, still on the fence. She hadn't said much since the discussion started, and Ree looked toward her now. "Should we put this to a vote?"

"There's nothing to vote upon," Jun interrupted. "My men have gone through great lengths to be here now, and we go as far as Kohkiem. Afterward, we focus on defending Loram."

"They aren't *your* men," Khim said, irritated. "We are all part of the same struggle. Further division is poisonous."

"Don't be an idealistic fool, doctor," he countered with a chortle. "The only reason each one of us sits at this table is for our assets." He nodded at Minh. "The Butcher is the fist of the mountain provinces. Our dear doctor spouts the rhetoric of the intellectuals, as well as their purse strings. Bird has the manpower of the low country, while I have the royal army–"

"What remains of it," Minh said flatly.

Jun narrowed his eyes. "Yes, what remains of it. Which is still a substantial force and the only force experienced in conventional warfare."

"Aren't you forgetting someone?" Ree crossed her arms.

"Right, the cult leader wielding black magic and commanding demons to terrify followers of the Grand Patriarch, while raiding their poorly defended labor camps," Jun sneered. "Your main contribution is theatrics and distraction, Isaree. You have no real roots here in Loram. I think you forget that, sometimes."

Ree slammed her palms down on the table, shaking loose some of the papers and knocking over Khim's cup of tea. "You don't trust me because I'm Suyo. Because I'm a whisper. And that blinds you from seeing how your victory in the capital was only possible from my work in Muang-Hhleg."

It was the wrong move, as he only grinned in spite. "I see we've resorted to comparing dicks now. Should we all list our contributions? Or would that further division be poisonous, doctor?"

"That's enough, all of you," Minh said, fingers on her temples. Ree eased back from the table, still glaring at the so-called commander. "I see both positions. But we don't have enough information to decide right now about Suyoram."

"And the Wild Cobras?" Ree asked.

Minh waited until all eyes were on her. Her word still carried the most weight. "We will consider it, *after* we know what Prince Tanung does in Son Sidora. Regardless, we proceed with our plan."

Chapter 35

A Champion For All Souls

The Ashukari in the Seventh temple knew to report to her the minute they received any sign of contact from Tan. But after several days passed, Ree began to lose hope.

The night before the siege on Kohkiem, Ree met Minh in the war chief's personal chambers. They sat on overturned crates and sipped jasmine tea. Earlier, Ree had tried to convince the council they should adjust the plan and wait for more fighters and weapons from Muang-Hhleg, in addition to her securing an alliance with the Wild Cobras. But they weren't impressed with her lack of progress on that front, and as Jun put it, the pieces were in place – they could not risk failure due to the "whims of a mascot."

"Jun didn't harbor so much disdain for me before," Ree said, genuinely at a loss. "Have I done something to offend him?"

Minh only shook her head. "Everyone is under a lot of stress. And some handle it by lashing out against anyone threatening their authority."

"How am I threat to him? We're supposed to be on the same side."

"You know what I mean," Minh said. "He's an ass, but he does command a third of our army. He did well in Iautau."

"I heard it was a bloodbath," Ree said. "And I'm worried tomorrow will be no different."

"The plan is solid."

"The plan has *me* leading the vanguard straight through the gates of the city. Not one of his captains who is used to that sort of thing. *Me.*"

"Leading the first wave to get their attention while we get our siege team through the tunnel, then falling back to regroup with point–"

"I know the details," Ree said, growing sullen. She chewed on her words, then rubbed a hand across her face. She wanted to believe that the two of them had been through enough, that they could be honest with one another. Minh had been the one to vouch for her and bring her onto the council, but it seemed as if she were distancing herself from Ree more and more, even by her new military style dress shirt and cap. "Can I ask you something, Minh?"

"Of course."

"Am I a mascot?"

"Oh please," Minh grumbled. "None of this would be possible without your help. People will remember that."

"The things I've done..." Ree's voice shook, thinking of Esha. Of the soldiers she'd killed, and the fear in the eyes of those she let go to spread the word. "They'll remember me as the heretic."

Minh only smirked, leaning forward to hold her gaze. "Not if we win."

A few hours before the battle, the Ashukari held a ritual to honor Kinesh-Kira, open for anyone to attend. This faction of the sect only made up a tiny fraction of the liberation front, but one of the most devoted. It was a simple ceremony, devoid of the sensational practices the sect was notorious for. On the banks of the narrow tributary by the temple, surrounded by forest, the participants first stripped down, then knelt in the shallows to wash themselves.

They cut their hair, some completely, others partially, then stood before Ree and a few of the senior Ashukari. The seniors dipped their hands into bowls of red paint and marked the participants foreheads and necks with the sign of the goddess. Some left soon after to prepare for their role in the coming battle, while others took up shakers and drums, singing the warrior's song of death and rebirth, singing for the others who took their turn in the water.

The song's words were in devaskrit, and when translated to Rami, had a very simple sentiment.

O great goddess Kinesh-Kira, may my sword become your sword, may my shield become your shield, may my enemy become your enemy.

O great goddess Kinesh-Kira, may my will become your will, may my blood become your blood, and if I should fall, take me to walk at your side for eternity.

Of the original hundred Ashukari that had fought with her since returning from the deva realm, only twenty were still alive. The

Ashukari didn't actively recruit, but if anyone expressed interest they were welcomed into the fold as seekers. Ree was astounded at how many of the regular soldiers had shown up. Maybe Minh was right that Jun felt threatened. Seasoned army veterans from Iautau lined up next to guerrilla fighters from Muang-Hhleg, next to armed villagers recently liberated from the labor camps. All genders, all ages, all factions became equal as they accepted the blessings of the goddess.

Yet even more astounding were the others in attendance, watching the ceremony from across the river. Though they kept their distance, the glowing eyes of the phi horde shined from the darkness, the living seemed indifferent to their presence. Behind them, in the trees, she sensed the presence of Dama the Voice of the Valley, watching critically. Lingering in the foliage above, the Silent Sisters – the seven silver-feathered vulture-spirits that always followed behind Dama to pick her kills clean.

For the average Sangha-following, Awakened Lord-Respecting Rami rebel, the deva Kinesh-Kira was more obscure, known mostly as the warrior goddess, and an incarnation of the divine's feminine fury – which, of course, wasn't all that she was, not by far, but perfectly fit Ree's narrative. It intrigued those seeking a deeper meaning to the brutal conflict unfolding in their homelands, a great many who couldn't fathom how profit and conquest could drive people to commit such atrocities.

Of course, violence and war went deeply against the Awakened Lord's teachings, and now, it was apparent how many were desperate for divine justification. The ancient religion of deva worship had always been lighter on the moral philosophizing; the gods were higher beings, but they were also just that – beings.

Maybe it wasn't so deep. For some it might be akin to tossing a coin in the collection for good merit. A way to hedge one's bets, if, in fact, they should fall before the day was over.

Or you're overthinking a beautiful moment of unity.

Ree startled at the voice, pausing mid paint-swipe across a woman's throat. She stared around at the multitude of faces, sure that she'd imagined it, then turned to glance across the river. Owun and the other taihong lingered there, as well as Homdee, who could have been mistaken for human as her female-presenting face peered out through a hole in the ground. For a moment, Ree had to appreciate how the ranks had grown since they'd started. The phi took it upon themselves to seek out others and offer them salvation, and what had started at two dozen had grown to over a hundred.

And now, somewhere in that throng might be the one that started her on the path so long ago.

Agira? Ree handed her bowl to the Ashukari next to her, who wordlessly took her place and attended to the woman waiting. *Is that really you?*

She'd already begun to cross, when his response echoed her question, *Is* that *really you?* When the water reached her chest, she dove in and swam the rest of the way. It was an offshoot of the Duram and only about two hundred feet across, which she covered quickly. The drums and singing continued without her.

The Everpresent shifted noticeably while in the presence of the phi, an energy she'd been trained to ruthlessly hunt down. Funny how that had changed. Now, it reassured that her allies were near. They parted for her as she walked through the horde, until she stopped before one familiar frog-like face staring up at her from his perch on a rock.

Her elation on meeting an old friend was short-lived. He looked unchanged, which surprised and worried her, considering it had been years and his curse should have been broken by then. His huge eyes gleamed, wet and shiny and somewhat forlorn. Strangely enough, she had the urge to sweep the little phi into a crushing hug.

I wasn't sure if I should come here. Agira wrung his hands, claws wrinkling his skin. *M – maybe this was a bad idea.*

"What happened?" Ree asked quietly, falling back into her habit of speaking to him out loud. She sat on the forest floor to be level with him. "I knew I'd see you again eventually, but... I thought it would be in another form."

I thought so too. I did what was asked, and I lived through the hunger. But when it came time to seek out Indrajit, his shrines were all empty. Agira's lipless mouth curled into a frown. *I thought that maybe I was wrong, or that I'd been tricked. I almost gave into despair, into rage and anger and...* he shuddered, squeezing his eyes shut.

"You remained true to your promise, though," Ree observed.

I did. But for what? Agira sank lower, his wings drooping. *Finally, I heard a story from another accursed. They told me a gray walker had performed the Ashukari death ritual, and returned from the land of devas with Indrajit's authority. That she had been offering the amnesty to all that would serve in her war. I thought surely, that couldn't be true. But I guess I needed to see for myself.*

"I'm sorry, Agira," Ree said, "I didn't know that it would prevent you from breaking your curse." The truth was she hadn't thought about it at all. When she took the Severer from the realm, it hadn't crossed her mind that doing so might alter arrangements already in place.

Would it have mattered?

"I..." Ree faltered, then shook her head. "What's done is done. I can help you now."

No! Agira's eyes snapped open and he recoiled. *I don't want to hurt anyone.*

"Most of them haven't hurt anyone," Ree said, very conscious of all the phi around them watching, perhaps even judging. "They help in other ways. Some work with Homdee, digging the tunnels... you remember the Weaver. Many act as sentries and messengers. Service is service. And after this is over, all will be released."

And if you die before it's over? Agira asked. *What then?*

Ree hadn't thought about that either, despite death lurking behind every corner. "I trust Indrajit will honor my agreement."

I just... Agira fretted as he stammered, shaking his wings. *I think it shouldn't be that easy.*

"Forgiveness? Why shouldn't it?"

Anyone can just do *something! Anyone can dig a tunnel. What does it prove? Have they changed?* He peered around at the others skeptically. *Once the curse is broken, what will stop them from repeating the same mistakes that got them condemned in the first place?*

Ree considered his words, sitting in silence.

"You're right," she said, finally. "My offer is simplistic to the law of karma, and my faith in their intentions is idealistic. And it benefits me, and the people I'm fighting for. But I make it with a whole heart. I don't think a tortuous existence for sins committed in a past life needs to be suffered arbitrarily, indefinitely. And maybe it's sacrilegious to contradict the will of the devas in the way that I have, but I'm willing to answer for it, when the time comes." She held a hand out to Agira. "Until then, I'm going to help the accursed, and the spirits, and the people. You've more than earned your right to become human again. Why don't you come with me?"

Agira sighed, staring at her outstretched hand, then backed away. *I don't know. It doesn't feel right. Let me... let me... think about it. Um. Try not to die before then.*

With that, Agira took to the air in a flurry of wings, disappearing quickly into the forest.

It felt like a loss, but it was as much as she could hope for, she supposed. Agira couldn't really expect her to break her promise to all the others that had vowed to serve her. There was no going back, and she doubted there was anything or anyone in the world that could change her mind.

But his words lingered. She wanted to believe forgiveness could be that easy. She needed to.

At the riverbank, a commotion in the crowd had caused the Ashukari to pause the ceremony. Once Ree made it back over, a runner from the council told her she was needed immediately. When she arrived at the war table, all the leaders of the council were waiting, dressed for battle. The look on Minh's face alarmed her.

"What happened?" Ree demanded.

"The Protectorate," Minh said, then pointed to an open letter on the table. "They want to surrender."

Chapter 36

The Price of Forgiveness

Ree wasn't sure whether she wanted to stab him or embrace him. Under the sun, Tan sat across the wide table from her, holding her gaze with a perfectly neutral, albeit loaded, expression. Next to him, a tall Baghani named Simo with dreadlocks tidier than the Ashukari's, whose aura ebbed a calming blue, like a tranquil sea. The young Governor-Colonel Daine Rimes of the Protectorate sat front and center, his uniform unbuttoned with the sleeves rolled up, sweat rag tied around his head like a noodle salesman. He stank of old liquor and opium.

The Loram Protectorate-appointed governor of Kohkiem was allowed a seat, but as far as the rebels were concerned, his fate as a collaborator was sealed. Fortunately, he knew his place and left the talking to those in charge.

As agreed, fifty feet behind them, a hundred soldiers in full Protectorate regalia stood at attention. And across the table, where Minh, flanked by Ree, Jun and Khim sat, fifty feet in front of a hundred rebels armed to the teeth, an assortment of clashing uniforms depending on where they came from: Jun's royal forces, Minh and Khim's Black Water Army, and Ree's Ashukari.

"As anticipated, we meet," Rimes said, his Rami impeccable with a Lo accent. He kept his gaze mostly on Jun, and hadn't looked at the women once. "I'm dancing with joy that you agreed to chatter like civilized folk."

His accent and grammar were impeccable, but his word choice was… unique.

"There's not much to discuss," Minh said, forcing his attention. "You're going to withdraw from Kohkiem by sunrise, or we're going to kill every last one of you, like we did in Iautau."

"Yes, they told me," the Grisi man said with the slight upturn of his lip. "Well, we're here now. Let's satisfy both parties with the smallest amount of bloodshed. Let me get to the point. The Protectorate is better armed, better trained, and in a highly defensible position. You may lay siege to the city, and you might bloody our noses, but you will suffer great losses. Worse, you won't take her before the fist of the Grisi empire arrives to crush you. We have… is there a word for it…" He murmured something indecipherable to Tan.

"They're called rackars in Grisi. Advanced ships with iron plating, heavy cannons," Tan translated. If Rime expected the rebels to wither over something they had no real reference for, he was sorely disappointed.

"A great many of them are coming, along with three full battalions of our finest, I'm told. And they're due here by the end of the week. See for yourself." He unrolled a piece of paper sporting a prominent, official seal, several stamps, swirling signatures. Minh glanced at it for a few moments, then slid it over to Khim to inspect further.

"Please understand, I'm not trying to deceive you. We're willing to make a deal. We'll withdraw our combatants from the city within the week, and I will do my damnedest to implore to my superiors about… ah, reforming our relationship with Loram as one more similar to Suyoram – as partners, not subjects."

A full withdrawal was not what Ree expected. Neither had the others apparently. Khim frowned as he read over the document, then nodded to Minh. The man wasn't bluffing, then. Of course, they'd heard rumors that the Gris were sending reinforcements – they did that all the time – but never this many, and to have solid evidence shoved in their faces was...

"A bold move," Jun muttered under his breath.

"A desperate move."

Isaree did a double take. Did someone just… whisper? Like a phi hunter? She stared at Tan, and thought she caught the hint of a smile at the corner of his lips. Ree's eyes darted around as she searched for the source.

Minh leaned back in her chair and crossed her arms.

"What are your conditions?" she asked.

"We only have one demand," Rimes said. And finally, for the first time, he looked at Ree. "Her."

Chapter 37

In Bad Faith

"After the defeat of my primary force at Son Clarion, I was captured by the Abyssal Heretic herself. During my brief time in her custody, I convinced her that I was sympathetic to her cause and would betray my sacred duty to the crown and support her treacherous goals. She released me under the condition that I liberate the clean village of Son Sidora in order to prove our loyalty. After negotiating with Protectorate officials, we convinced them to abandon the outpost and return with us to Kohkiem, where she plans to strike next.

My king, I cannot stress enough how dangerous this rebel is. The rumors have all proven true. With my own eyes, I've seen monsters not of this world that cannot be stopped by traditional methods. She is an existential threat to the sanctity of Suyoram and our allies. The Heretic and the rebels are immensely popular, with sympathizers all over the country, and increasing public support in northern Suyoram. They have a sophisticated network of spies and with the Protectorate's recent defeat at Iautau, Loram will be back in their hands if Kohkiem falls. Brute force will not prevail, and I've deduced that the only way to stop her is through careful deception.

The Protectorate reports and rumors coming from Loram will enforce this ruse. They will say the Wild Cobras have turned to the side of the rebels. They will say Prince Tanung seeks the throne of Suyoram. They will call upon the royal army of Suyoram to publicly support their war. But these lies are all designed to ensure that my plan will not fail. I believe I must lie with the snake to cut off its head. Please continue to have faith in me, uncle. I will always serve Suyoram, even if it is the last thing I do."

"The last paragraph is a bit much," Simo said and dropped the letter on the table. He poured himself another glass of rice wine. "Too needy. You sound like... like..." He swirled his cup, staring thoughtfully at the plain wall of the captain's personal tent.

"Like what?" Tan asked, spinning the letter to look it over again.

"Like a man guilty of treason, desperately trying to convince his boss otherwise."

Tan wanted to say, *Isn't that what I am?* But instead, he sighed, took up a pen and started rewriting a few of the "needier" sentences. He was searching for a balance that walked the line between the truth, an acceptable reality, and his intentions, and started to wonder if it were possible. It would have been easier if his heart wasn't torn between two paths.

When he first arrived in Son Sidora, adrenaline swimming like a dragonfly escaping a spider's web, all he could think about was Isaree. It felt as if she were there with him, watching him, ready to strike him down from afar. For all he knew, she *was* watching him through the eyes of the phi, or the spirits, or whatever magic powers she had.

Even by the time he'd met with Simo privately, and explained everything that happened, he still wasn't sure what to do. On that raft, when Isaree proposed he turn against his mission, he'd have been a fool not to play along. She wasn't a creature who'd danced her way through court as he had. She might have been a fearsome killer with terrifying magic, but it was immediately clear that mind games were not her forte.

Admittedly, he found that he enjoyed playing out this power-hungry fantasy with her, discussing logistics, details, how she could become a hero to the people. He'd never actually believed any of it, no matter how enticing she made it seem.

Or so he'd thought.

Quietly, he felt his admiration grow upon seeing her move through the Serene Way as if she were a part of it. He felt her eyes roving over him constantly, which fed his masculine ego, even if it had less to do with fascination and more to do with an exotic, deadly predator ensuring her captured mouse didn't scurry away. She frightened him and excited him at the same time, and he found himself wanting to know more, to open himself up, to get closer. *Understand the enemy,* he told himself as her eyes lit up across the fire, her voice dancing with visions of another world. She offered him the riskiest gamble he could ever take.

All, or nothing, and all meant everything.

Simo listened quietly while Tan recounted the details. He hadn't been as horrified as Tan expected. Perhaps he was still in shock that Tan had showed up at all. Or he was cautiously eager, realizing his gentle hints about Tan's rightful claim were finally taking root. Or he was wondering if he needed to stage a mutiny. But most likely, this was too many strange events in too short an amount of time to process.

Raj had disappeared from the perimeter. He hadn't said a word to anyone, but one of their lookouts swore to the devas and the Awakened Lord that they'd seen Esha in the woods beforehand. Whatever had happened, no one had seen him since.

And then, only a few hours before Tan arrived, Yelu and the five of the ten scouts that had been on the perimeter with her at Son Clarion walked into the village with haunted looks on their faces. She said that they were ambushed by some kind of gas during the storm, and woke up in Isaree and what seemed like demons' custody. The demons led them through a dark, twisting path that seemed to have no end. They tried to fight back and escape, and a few of them were torn to shreds in a way she could only describe as "unreal." Yelu ordered everyone to surrender, and the demons continued to usher them on, as if nothing had happened.

Out of nowhere, they stopped, and the demons disappeared into the forest. When Yelu's scouts realized they were close to Sidora, they hurried to report in. No one had any idea what had become of the first unit, and Tan.

So Isaree had kept her word and released the survivors. He wasn't sure how she'd done it, but it must have had something to do with how she commanded the phi, and how the Serene Way worked. But he wouldn't have described the Serene Way as "dark and twisted." He wondered if there was more than one magical route through the wilds.

"I could have killed her," Tan admitted, pacing restlessly, hands on his head. "She was injured. Helpless. All I had to do was slit her throat. I tried to make myself do it. But..."

"But you saved her instead," Simo said. They stood just outside of the village, and he leaned against one of the rubber trees, gazing at the sliver of red sun rising over the valley. They'd been talking all night. This time, he finally asked the question. "Why?"

"Because..." Tan wished he could answer definitively. He'd cut through his binds and slowly crept upon the slumbering rebel. He'd reached toward her knife, and saw her bandages soaked through to the blood on her bedroll. Sweat covered her face, her breath shallow, skin pale. His fingers had lingered above the wound, feeling the heat ebbing off it without even touching. A bad sign, but he'd kill her before it did. He had to.

And yet, he'd hesitated.

It wasn't a question of morality. Tan had taken plenty of lives throughout his missions, and he felt completely justified in doing so. Hell, he didn't even need to do anything, judging by how sick she was. He could sit back and watch her die. But the thought of someone like him taking her from the world felt...

Wasteful.

She had so much potential. So much power. She just hadn't found the right people who could transform her into something more. It was tragic, really. This woman was connected to an unseen world he'd never fully understand, but she didn't understand her disconnection from the very world she wanted to change. What she needed was guidance. Someone to help her control the chaos. Someone she could trust.

And who better to trust than the one who saves your life? He knew enough about emergency medical treatment from assisting his surgeons to find the internal bleeding and suture the wound. He thoroughly sterilized and cleaned it. When he'd finished, she seemed to breathe easier, her heartbeat steady.

"Prince?" Simo was staring at him now.

It had nothing to do with how he'd checked on her again, and she woke up and pressed her knife to his throat. Nothing to do with how he was transported to another place and time, a place he could not name, a stranger yet one he'd always known. Nothing to do with how it teetered from nightmare to fantasy when she fell into his arms and kissed him, calling a name he'd never heard, but one he felt connected to, somehow. He could sit back and enjoy whatever this was, reap the benefit of an intimate connection...

No, he'd gently placed her back down to rest and she groaned, murmuring, unconscious. He'd watched over her the rest of the night, wrestling with the implications of what he'd done. The knife had been right there, loose in her hand. He imagined driving it through her heart, slitting her throat. Esha and Raj confirmed that yes, phi hunters could heal quickly from what would normally be mortal wounds, but inflict enough damage fast enough, and they were still human enough to die.

The knife was right there. He'd picked it up a few times throughout the night, even held it against her throat, steeling himself for blood. In the name of the king, and his sacred duty to Suyoram, fucking *do* it.

But every time, he put it back down.

It would be there later. He knew how to hurt her now. And it was never too late to change his mind.

"Tan," Simo said again, face to face with him.

Tan knew how it would sound. He knew it would be a tough sell. And he'd have to play it carefully for the others. He knew his crew loved gossiping about his mental state, so he needed to present himself with full conviction. But Simo was closer than blood. He could be honest. He stopped pacing, and grabbed his friend by the shoulders. And then he started speaking in Baghani.

"I didn't kill her because I realized then what she was. She is the *question.*"

"...Question, sir?"

"Are we Suyo, or are we Gris? And she's the answer. She's the savior of Suyoram. There's no one else that can take it back from them. Together... we can have it all, brother."

Simo sucked in a breath. There was fear in his eyes, but above that, intrigue. "You know the crew will follow you to hell and back, sir," he said, carefully. "But this is treason you're proposing. There's no walking that back."

"Fuck treason. To my uncle, yes, but for everyone else? Patriotism. This is for all Rami people. History will vindicate us," Tan said. "If anyone wants to walk away, let them go. But if we're going to pull this off, I need you with me. Are you with me?"

"By the fucking gods, you're serious," Simo said. They stared at one another, and left the ugly, unspoken fact sit there, either out of pride, or denial. Despite their closeness, there were still a few things that as men, they could never openly admit. Surely, if Simo believed Yelu's story, he may have already come to the same conclusion.

We can't stop her. No one can stop her. Tan hated this thought with every fiber of his being, but he had to believe he wasn't doing this out of fear. He had to believe that this was the rational move. That this was for the greater good.

And Simo seemed to understand. For his benefit, his brother added a cavalier laugh and clasped his shoulder with a firm squeeze. "Of course I'm with you. It's about goddamn time we fought for a real prize."

It was a bold plan. The control of information and misinformation would ensure their success. They argued on the benefit of sending a letter to the king at all. Ultimately, he decided to hold onto it for now. First, he needed to see how things would shake out. There would still be more time to get ahead of the narrative. And should things not go as planned, it provided some reasonable doubt he hadn't turned against crown and country.

Further, he needed to rally the rest of his forces to prepare for the coming war.

The journey back to Kohkiem went quickly, and the first thing he did was meet with Governor-Colonel Rimes, this time at the Protectorate Trading Company headquarters, a building just outside of the fort. Tan noted the disastrous state of his office, ashes, trash and dirty plates everywhere.

"Oh, please don't mind the mess. We've had to... let go of our servants. Security concerns," the man said with a glassy-eyed smile. "I hope you have a head to send me dancing with joy."

Tan told the man what happened. A version of it. How he'd lost half his unit at Son Clarion, and how by the time he arrived at Son Sidora, it was already gone. He left out the part where he spent three days with her on the Serene Way, most of that time nursing her back to health.

All this came with the news that Rimes' intelligence had been wrong, that Iautau had indeed fallen to the rebels, and word had it that the Liberation Front had taken no prisoners.

"The demon army is coming for you here," Tan warned him, "and if you want to survive, you should leave now."

Colonel Rimes sat in stunned silence as Tan spoke. Obviously, it wasn't the report he'd been expecting, but he didn't seem entirely surprised.

"If it were only a matter of rebels, you might be able to withstand a siege long enough for reinforcements to arrive," Tan said. "But that's not your problem. It is Isaree, the Heretic, herself. Look, I read all the reports you did and I still didn't believe. But I saw her command them firsthand and watched them tear through seasoned vets like they were first-year cadets." His blood ran cold as he said it, remembering Adee's scream before his throat was torn out. Suddenly, he was back there in the mud and the beating rain, running for his life.

"Tan." Simo crouched by him, holding a glass of water. Tan hadn't realized he'd sat down. Or had to sit down, moreso. His hand shook as he drank a sip, then wiped the cool sweat off his brow.

"Excuse me," Tan blinked and set down the cup. He let out a slow breath, then said, "Sir, I'm afraid there is no solution for these creatures. They will kill you all. We're lucky to have escaped."

"What are you saying?" Rimes said, visibly shook. "I can't just cut and run! That's... unacceptable. We have brought the Book of Vows. We have brought modern medicines and technologies, blending our two cultures into one! I may have children here! And now, a demonic force is what stands to threaten us?! No. *No!*" He pounded a fist on the table. "It... it must be the will of the Patriarch that we fight this holy war. There's no other explanation."

Tan did not take this man for that of a fervent believer. At least, not on the inside. This was a selfish man who hated the idea of work, and considering the disastrous mismanagement the Protectorate was in, along with the timeline of the conflict, Rimes had likely failed upward through nepotism after his more competent predecessor died at Fort Nestor. Quite a rise. And it would be quite a fall. It seemed he was looking over the edge, torn between self-preservation, and avoiding dishonor to the illustrious Rimes family name.

"Your god won't protect you here," Simo said, prompting a wounded look from the colonel.

"He's right. I saw the church of the father burn in the village just as any other building would. Perhaps he's turned his eye away from this place," Tan said, rising to depart. "It's best we return to Suyoram now and prepare for any further hostilities. Best of luck, governor."

Rimes sat quietly. And they walked slowly, until they reached the door.

"Wait! Is there really no hope?"

And there was the opening.

"Well," Tan hesitated, glancing at Simo.

"We had a few discussions on ways to save the city," Simo said.

"A bit of a gamble, but we did try something like this in the Janju conflict between two city-states... and it worked. But... I don't know."

"Don't know?" Rimes stood up, wobbling on his feet. "Out with it!"

"There are unconventional tactics, some quite deplorable." Tan turned to regard him with a look that said, *you can't handle it, kid*

Rimes scoffed. "Do you think I give a shit about that now? Go on."

"Okay," Tan said. "The Heretic is the key to your problem. Take her out, and I believe, with the incoming reinforcements, that the Protectorate can retake Loram. I couldn't do it in her backyard, and pursuing them into the wilds is a lesson in humility. But here, it's possible you could."

"You were the professional manhunters," Rimes said, jabbing a finger at both men. "How the fuck am I supposed to do that here?"

"It's not that complicated," Tan said. "Bad faith negotiations. Offer something they can't refuse. Set the trap, cut the head off the snake, and be ready to strike."

Chapter 38

One Condition

Her.

That was their one condition. A single life in exchange for a peaceful withdrawal of Kohkiem and a promise to end the occupation. It felt as if the ground had spun away and the gravity of the entire world settled solely on her shoulders. Ree stared at Rimes, but her gaze drifted back to meet the storm-bright eyes of the prince. In the rebels stunned silence after Rimes' declaration, his whisper came again:

"I know you can hear me, but I can't hear you. Listen, I'm on your side. I have a plan. Surrender yourself and you will not be harmed. Resist, and there are no guarantees."

Jun opened his mouth, or rather, hadn't closed it, and glanced over at Ree in trepidation. If it were only up to him, she had no doubt he'd agree in a heartbeat.

"Do you take us for fools?" Minh broke the silence, slamming her meaty palms on the table as she leaned forward threateningly. Ree flinched. "One of us for an entire country?! Bullshit."

"Everyone knows that Isaree is not merely 'one of you,'" Tan said to Minh, with the sharp disdain only a highborn could perfect. "She's worth far more than that."

"Does the value rise to the lives of seven thousand rebels, my prince?" Rimes chirped. Ree was oddly put off by his manners. They seemed only half genuine, as if he found all of life a joke. "Isn't that how many are left in your Liberation Front now? Let's include the whole of Loram. What is that now, a million? Such a brutal struggle."

Tan only turned his gaze back to Ree. And he mouthed the word, *more*.

This was Tan's plan? The hidden insinuation in his words didn't escape her. She tore her eyes away from the prince to Minh, who was the only person actively seething.

"What are you playing at?" Minh snapped. Even Ree couldn't quite process what was happening fast enough to form a verbal response. But her instinctual reaction was diametrically opposed to what Tan was saying. In her mind's eye, she saw Vasitra gazing across the beautiful mountains as he said *what was one life worth?*

If that's all it would take to give Loram some respite from the fighting, a chance to rebuild, a chance to determine their own destiny, what right did she have to stand in the way?

"There's no play here. The offer is legit, but it will only stand until dawn. If it's agreed by then, we will begin the preparations for withdrawal the very same day." Rimes unfolded another officially sealed document and slid it across the table with a finger.

"The Protectorate will leave, but they are lying."

"The prisoner will be taken into Prince Tanung's custody, as promised to King Sarvupun, and tried in her own country."

"Once they rendezvous with their reinforcements, they will return."

"And what's to stop you from stabbing us in the back when your army gets here?" Jun said, prompting an incredulous glare from Minh.

"My good sire, we are followers of the Grand Patriarch," Rimes said, fishing a wooden rosary of the star from his collar with theatrical appall. It looked brand new. "It would be an affront to god himself to break a signed contract. As acting governor-colonel, I wield the authority to order a full withdrawal of Kohkiem, and I am the second most senior military official in both Rami countries – my influence will not be ignored."

"They will return and burn through the country, starting with Kohkiem."

If Tan spoke the truth, the honorable gesture of giving herself over for the greater good would be futile. Rimes purposely deceiving them was much more plausible than the Gris giving up their conquest for peace with a side of execution. But she didn't know this man or his heart, and perhaps he did mean to honor the agreement. Maybe Tan was working with him, and this was a play to get her to walk right into the prince's scheming hands.

"I believe in you. That together, we can cut them down from the inside and continue our campaign straight to the heart of Suyoram."

Khim reached for the terms of the agreement, but Minh shoved it back across the table. "No. This is unacceptable. We will not stoop to meet your barbaric demands." Then she shoved back from the table. "See you on the battlefield."

The Protectorate side didn't move, but neither did the others in the Liberation Front.

"Think it over then," Rimes said. "As promised, we'll wait until dawn."

"We're done here," Minh snapped, grinding her teeth. Sheepishly, Jun and Khim slowly rose to their feet. The three turned to walk away, but Minh stopped short when she noticed Ree hadn't joined them. "Let's go."

Ree looked back at Minh, one of the most admirable women she knew, and her friend. It was touching that she'd be so adamant to defend her, but why wouldn't she? *None of this would be possible without your help,* she'd said, *people will remember that.* Jun and Khim hadn't spoken up for her, yet she couldn't blame them. Their angles were different, but they must have weighed the possibilities and arrived at the same judgment as she had.

Ree turned back to the Protectorate. To her enemies, her executioners, or perhaps... secret allies. Rimes straightened in his chair, practically salivating, and Tan's eyes gleamed with excitement. Simo's eyes darted over the rebels, but his face remained unreadable. The Lo representative might as well have been invisible.

It was uncertain, but there was only one way to find the truth.

"No," Ree said. "I'll go. I surrender."

Chapter 39

To Understand the Enemy

As Ree was paraded through Kohkiem like a hunting trophy, she started to believe that this might have been a serious mistake. The tide of dread started at her manacled ankles, rising to her bound wrists, and closed in by two snarepoles, lassos secure around her neck. Before the exchange at dawn, she'd overheard Tan and Rimes arguing about how to transport her. Tan wanted to do it in secrecy. There were still sympathizers and spies within the city. Those that saw her as a hero would now see her as a martyr.

"Exactly my point," Rimes argued, "those people must understand the consequences for consorting with demons." And so he opted for a celebratory march down the main street, showcasing the feared, captured Heretic with a ridiculously overarmed escort surrounding her on every side.

She said nothing and complied, forcing her head high even when Rimes insisted on covering it with a hood so that she couldn't "cast spells." She sensed the crowds of locals gathering in the street to watch the spectacle by scent and sound and energy – there was a tenor of anticipation. A collective holding of the breath.

The Gris soldiers were leaving. Their transport barges were already in the water, their horses and wagons were being loaded and marched across the Lotus Bridge, back to friendly territory. The Lo had endured over a decade of war, occupation, and rebellion, and now, finally, could claim a solid victory over their oppressors. They should have been cheering and dancing in the streets, but the mood was as festive as a funeral procession.

Maybe the people of Kohkiem knew how instrumental Ree had been to the rebellion and were expecting more violence. Some were rightfully fearful of the Liberation Front taking control, as anyone left in the city might be considered a collaborator from the hard-line rebel factions, just for existing alongside the Gris. It wasn't uncommon to see an interracial marriage here and there, some biracial kids running from their bullies. Or maybe it had been an exhausting existence to live under the boot, and after losing so much, any one death was no different than another.

She heard a woman quietly sobbing with relief. Whispers between children, *that can't be the Heretic! I heard she had twenty eyes and giant teeth*! Followers of the Grand Patriarch murmuring prayers of protection, the soft click of wooden beads between their fingers. All these people that would have endured much more hardship if the rebels had gone through with the assault.

All these people that would be torn apart again when the Gris returned in force.

Ree had almost fallen asleep standing when the door to her cell slammed shut. She straightened against the wall, where her manacles were secured, and tried to prepare herself for the worst.

Ten footsteps echoed from the door to the wall, and she flinched as someone loomed over her. A hand brushed against her forehead gently, then snatched away the sack over her head. She blinked, disoriented at the sudden rush of sensation, the stale air and dim candlelight burning on wall sconces.

Before her, Prince Tanung stood, dressed down in simple civilian clothes and an obscuring hood. She couldn't read his expression – a smug villain here to gloat? Or an ally satisfied that his plan had succeeded? Whichever he was, he did look rather pleased with himself.

Ree knew he'd show eventually. Though she'd endlessly contemplated his motives, she'd given little thought to what she'd say to him. Her pulse raced, and she grit her teeth, trying to parse her thoughts. Maybe he didn't know what to say either, because they stared at one another for a good few seconds before both speaking at once.

"This plan better be fucking good," Ree growled, right as he said, softly, "Are you all right?"

Tan tilted his head, eyes narrowed. His gaze dropped to her neck, still sore with bruises from the snarepole nooses. Something changed in his demeanor, shifting from gentle concern to offense. "Of course it is," he said with a scoff. Then he smiled in a volatile way and said, "We're together again, aren't we?"

Ree wasn't sure what to make of that. "Together… as your captive? Or your ally?"

Tan chuckled, and then noticed her expression hadn't changed. "Wait, are you serious?" His smile froze, crumbled.

"I told you to find me at the Seventh Temple, not whisper conspiracies at me at a parlay from the wrong side of the table," Ree glared at him, appalled. "How did you learn how to do that?!"

"Raj taught me," Tan admitted with a shrug. "We were very drunk."

"*What*?! *Raj*?! Are you out of your mind?"

"People keep telling me that," Tan sighed, then glared right back at her. "It was an unorthodox plot, yes. But I couldn't get a message to you without raising suspicion. I assumed putting all the pieces right in front of you would be enough to communicate my intentions." Tan glanced back at the door. "We can speak safely right now, but we don't have much time. Rimes insisted on overseeing custody of you while we remain in the city."

"So it's all true then. The Gris were lying the whole time." Disappointing. Ree felt far more let down than she should have, considering it would have meant her imminent execution. With a sigh, she leaned against the wall, chains clinking.

"Yes and no. When it comes to them, the truth is convoluted. The agreement is real, breaking the terms on any contract signed with the seal of the Patriarch is against the law, and akin to damning one's soul to eternal hell. The Book of Vows says as much." Tan gestured as he spoke, pacing in front of her. "They're already withdrawing troops from the city. He genuinely intends to advise General Elleman on his official recommendation – to immediately cease hostile operations in the Loram Protectorate and instead, open diplomatic channels with their officials."

"But?"

"But he knows the trading company will never agree to that. And make no mistake, the trading company wields the real authority, and their only god is coin. Loram is too valuable to them. They'll be coming back, and with a devastating force."

"So… what's your plan?" Ree shook her chains for effect. "It would have been costly, but we might have won the battle faster than their reinforcements arrived. We could have defeated them here and then made a stand. Especially with the fort."

"The fort? This fort is half built. Even the cannons were taken to Iautau. It's pretty much useless, except for jailing high-value prisoners of war."

"Okay..." Ree shrugged. "So what's the advantage?"

Tan stopped pacing to look at her. "Us," he said, as if it were obvious. "The Wild Cobras. You. Your people and your ghost army. We're in the heart of the beast now, and we can tear it open from the inside without destroying Kohkiem in the process. We're to set sail for Jinburi in a few days with you in our custody, along with the last Grisi ships, including Rimes and the other Protectorate officials. In that time, we establish contact with your people. They'll set up a river blockade and ambush at the Molama junction. We take Rimes out, man the ships, sail to Jinburi, and take control of the garrison... and from there..." He grinned. "Everything else. How's that for good?"

It was convoluted and hard to follow, but not a terrible plan. Removing the Gris from their defensible position in Kohkiem and fighting on their own terms might have worked. There was one problem with it all, though.

"Would have been good if you'd told us from the start," Ree said, glowering. "What makes you think they're going to leave their newly returned city to help us?"

"What do you mean?" Tan frowned. "That was the plan. The front understand we're on the same side, right? They know we're taking Suyoram?"

"Well, sort of."

"What?"

Ree shrugged sheepishly. "I brought it to the council, and they were split on trusting you. They promised to discuss it again, but..." she rested her head against the wall, closing her eyes. "Khim never liked me, Jun thinks I'm a joke. So the majority are relieved I'm out of the picture. Minh cares, but she cares more about maintaining unity. The fact that I'm in supposedly in your custody and not the Protectorates will be enough to satisfy her conscience." She opened her eyes to see Tan staring at her in mounting horror. "Look. I'm sorry for how... sure I was before. I misjudged how much influence I had. But now? I think the Front will stay in Kohkiem, even if presented with the Gris' real plans."

It was silent, and then Tan ran a hand over his face, leaving it there. "Shit." He peered at her from between his fingers. "You're serious."

"Yeah," Ree said, "we can try to convince them... but maybe... maybe exploring a genuine peace is the way."

"Hold on. Let me get this straight. You..." he jabbed a finger toward her, "...gave yourself up without believing, *fully*, that I'm on your side?" he smacked his own chest, then raised both arms in what seemed like exasperation. "And then, you willingly walked into custody without believing, *fully*, that the Liberation Front would follow your orders? Please tell me you're joking."

Ree pursed her lips, then nodded. "Of all the options available, it seemed the least harmful."

Tan closed the distance between them so abruptly she flinched. Until then, she'd ignored the subconscious fear in her body from her vulnerable position, arms shackled behind her, ankles shackled to the wall. Sira had been in similar circumstances, in some of her darkest moments.

"What if we'd marched you to the square and executed you? If you thought at any point that I was deceiving you… why?" Tan stared down at her, eyes bright with fury, waiting for an answer. She wasn't sure why he was so angry about this detail. She'd done what he wanted, hadn't she?

"If it meant they left Kohkiem for good, then it would have been worth it."

"You don't really believe that," Tan said, now looking deflated.

"I do, actually," Ree said. "I'm not under the delusion my life is worth more than an entire country."

"Isaree," Tan closed his eyes, took a deep breath, then said, "I meant what I said at the table. You can spout all the noble nonsense you want, but the truth is, you're more important, and you know that. You deserve–"

"Maybe I deserve punishment," Ree cut in. "Some of the things I've done are…" Her voice faltered, and she swallowed as her sinuses sting. Esha's screams, the wreckage of her burned face. Tian's deathlocked smile, eyes still and empty. Ree looked up at the low stone ceiling of her cell, bidding her tears to melt away.

Tan shook his head, then leaned down so his face was level with hers, forcing her gaze to his. "Listen, Isaree. What you can do is powerful. It's unlike anything the world has seen. Yes, you are frightening and strange, but your conviction and righteousness is... it's the most powerful thing."

He reached to wipe a tear away from her cheek, and the achingly tender look in his eyes stirred something within her chest.

"I beg you, don't let anyone take that away from you. It feels bad because you were used. I know what that feels like. You were useful to them both in the field and as a sacrifice, but that doesn't take away that you're also a fucking hero. And it would be a crime not to follow you to the ends of the earth. Think that's bombastic? It's what I said to convince my crew to follow me into this mess. That's what every Rami person is counting on. That's what the

Liberation Front is counting on, whether or not they appreciate you. That's what *I'm* counting on. That's why I couldn't let you die."

He should have. The dark thought felt poisonous, and she couldn't place where it came from. Maybe it was the price of having seen her other lives. Brahmah said it would bring nothing but sorrow. Her curse was to always involve herself in some hopeless struggle, over and over again. Futilely, Ree had hoped that to break the cycle, all she needed to do was actually succeed.

That was her fatal error. The nature of these struggles had always been that they were impossible, far greater than anything she, as an individual, could control. How arrogant to think she could transcend the chains of karma. What a waste.

Ree crushed her eyes shut to keep more tears from escaping, but it did just the opposite. She couldn't crumble now, not after all she'd been through. She also couldn't recall a time that anyone had spoken to her this way, and it hurt her heart.

"You should have," she muttered.

"Stop. I've been there. I know what you're feeling. And if you give in to hopelessness it'll consume you," Tan said desperately, flustered he couldn't get through to her. He held her face in his hands, brushing the tears away with his thumbs. "Please, Isaree, you have to break through it. I need you – *want* you… want you to, I mean, I…"

He didn't finish the thought. When she opened her eyes, the storm in his had quieted to a simmer, his gaze lingering on her lips. He'd said the rebels used her. Wasn't that exactly what he wanted to do as well? She was his ticket to the throne. And all this heartfelt bullshit was a desperate plea to get her back on board. Funny, he still thought they could win. Flattering…

And enraging. Only a sycophant or a fool would believe in one person this much. Perversely, she wanted to piss him off, to tear that hope away. She wanted him to surrender her to the king, who would no doubt serve her to the Gris.

Martyrdom, was that her cursed desire?

Ree leaned closer to him, and hissed, "What do you really *want*, Prince Tanung?"

The honorific slid from her lips far more scornfully than she intended. But her seething contempt seemed to have the opposite effect. Tan inhaled slowly, deeply, as if trying to calm himself down, while his fingertips touched just below her jaw, lifting her face. He was close enough that she could rip his jugular out with her teeth. His eyes had changed again, and this time, they were dark, searching, hungry. That look set her heart hammering madly, and Ree felt a pull in her belly, a tingling string of desire stirring within.

They both knew exactly what he wanted. And she couldn't deny she wanted it too.

In that moment, despite being chained to the wall, Ree felt a power so intoxicating it was impossible to resist… to continue to resist. It was a power she could take back from Sira's tragedies. A power like the goddess Kinesh-Kira's feminine urge to consume and destroy a man – the lure of passion and pain, a dance of hate and love. The energy between them buzzed in the Everpresent, heady and volatile.

Challengingly, Ree strained against her chains to tease the tips of her breasts against his chest, then opened her mouth and brushed her lips against his. He shuddered, holding back, until she bit his bottom lip and whispered in a challenging tone, "Fucking take me then."

That shattered the last remaining barrier between them, and Tan kissed her with a breathless intensity that felt as if he'd been waiting several lifetimes. Her back hit the wall and she gasped. His fingers slid from her jaw, trailed over her throat, and curled around the edge of her sabai, pulling, just short of exposing her. With an eager moan, she flexed her hips against his, teasing against his obvious arousal, lashing his tongue with her own. He grabbed her thigh and lifted it to rest around his waist, but was stopped short by the clink of chains.

Ree giggled as he groaned in frustration, and he broke away from the kiss to pin her with a heated glare that caught her breath, rendering her silent. With his body still pressed against hers, his words were choked with restraint, each one a warning, hardly more than a whisper, "Don't tempt me."

She smiled wickedly and licked her lips. "Are all the Storm Prince's conquests so easily diverted?" The fury slowly rising in his eyes ignited her, and she sneered, writhing against him, "By chains of your own design, no less–"

He cut her mockery short with a kiss far more savage and demanding. His hand slipped under her waistband, reaching between her thighs. She shivered as he brushed against her cunt, then moaned as he teased her, stopping just short. Aching for more, she tried to grind into his hand, and he carefully danced his fingers around what felt like an overripe blossom ready to burst. It drove her mad, especially as he moved to her neck, teeth scraping delightfully against her skin.

She let go of herself and everything else, the whole fucked up situation, reveling in the pleasure… unaware at how vocal she was being until his finger stroked her apart and curled inside. A second later his other hand clamped over her mouth, stifling her cries. A crooked smile quirked his lips as he watched her every reaction to his deliberate movements – every flutter of her lashes, and muffled whimper, and arrested breath. Her legs trembled, she could hardly stand. He was in control of her now, playing her like a skilled musician would a well-honed instrument, leisurely building the song into the exact melody he wanted. It occurred to her that of course, he must have had several harems worth of practice. Her eyes rolled back in her head as she thanked the countless, unknown partners who'd taught him the best way to do *that*.

He leaned close to whisper, tongue grazing her ear, "I think *you* need this."

It sent shivers down her spine and she tensed around him, overwhelmed by the animal urge to consume him completely. She could burn through these chains…

And then the heavy bolt to the door clanked, the lock clicking as it started to open.

"Fuck," Tan growled, quickly yanking up her sabai and stepping away. It took a second for Ree to realize what had happened, until she saw the door open behind him.

"Hey, captain." A Baghani man walked in, dressed casually. Simo, his second in command. "We got to cut it short," he said, glancing behind him. "They're coming."

"Lucky them," Tan muttered under his breath, and Ree choked out a frustrated laugh. He glowered at her, then smiled softly and sighed, likely remembering their predicament before that distraction. "What the fuck are we going to do about this?"

"Oh," she smirked, "I don't need a key for these."

Simo did a double take, noticing their proximity, Ree's surely flushed face, and the fact that Tan hadn't yet turned around… and seemed to put two and two together rather quickly. He frowned and strode forward, clamping Tan heavily on the shoulder, and hauling him backward none too gently. "We'll have another opening tomorrow, but not if we're seen now. Don't make me fucking carry you, Tan."

That seemed to shake Tan out of his stupor. "I'll return as soon as I can," he called to Ree, "don't worry, I'll think of something."

Then allowing himself to be pulled along by his man, his eyes never left hers until the door slammed shut. The lock clicked back in place, leaving Ree alone, in silence but for her still racing heart.

Though the heated moment had blossomed out of despair, it had shaken away the looming cloud of self-doubt that had threatened to drown her. Was it a reckless mistake in the moment, or a hint of what could be?

She sighed and sunk to the floor, resting her head on her knees. It didn't matter either way, Ree thought. Didn't matter, but she would reframe that energy… to serve as a physical manifestation of their grander mission. Yes, she had a grander mission beyond base desires, and she couldn't abandon that now.

Win the war, break the cycle, save the world.

Chapter 40

A Lure of Passion and Pain

Isaree had been a constant presence in his thoughts for a long time now, but after visiting her cell, those thoughts took on a new tenor. When she whispered that she wanted to give up, he hadn't expected the rush of emotions to overwhelm him so. Every tear that slid down her cheek felt like a blade being dragged across his own heart. He hadn't considered how utterly alone she must have felt throughout all of this, how desperate she was for a kind word and a loving touch. He hadn't realized how utterly alone *he* had felt for so long, and how intensely he craved the embrace of this familiar stranger.

He knew then that he would have done anything, said anything, given anything, just to ease her sorrow. And it was messy and impulsive, but the only way he could express how he felt toward her was to make her feel like a queen. His savage queen of the wilds. And now, when he closed his eyes, he could taste her lips on his, smell her sex on his fingers, feel her racing heartbeat against his own…

"Know what I mean?"

"Um," Tan shook his head to scatter his lewd thoughts. "Sorry, what was that?"

Night had fallen, and him and Simo sat on a bench in the village square which held the night market. Vendor stalls filled only a fraction of the communal space, which had once boasted one of the largest markets in Lorani, known particularly for their religious charms. Under the Protectorate, worship of deities other than the Patriarch were prohibited, and so went the relic-hawkers. Tan wondered how long it would take before the market recovered, or if it would ever return.

"I said, my ma always told me good food can build bridges between enemies." Simo swirled his chopsticks into a banana leaf bowl of fried lemongrass and chili glass noodles. He nodded toward the market, where off-duty Protectorate soldiers wandered about, ordering their favorite meals from their favorite vendors, perhaps for the last time. If this were a single scene removed from a larger play, Tan would never guess that there was an occupation on, couldn't tell by the neighborly interaction between buyer and seller that their countries had been at war for years. Nearby, a blind and leg-less musician played the phinpia for coin. A few missionaries of mixed descent were quietly sitting by his blanket, sharing a bowl of ant egg soup.

Many of these Gris nationals had been stationed here for years, some of the career military men even settled. The missionaries had come even earlier than that, and as per the terms of the agreement, would be allowed to stay so long as they had no ties to the military or trading company. Rimes had pushed to allow the administrative civilians in the trading company office to remain as well, but the Liberation Front had been strict on that point – if relations remained civil for six months, and the proper agreements were put in place, they'd consider letting them return. Until then, all Grisland Trading Company operations would be ceased.

"Look at everyone just doing their jobs, living their lives. That's all people want and the ones in charge have to go fuck it all up."

"They'll eat the food, but never forget, some become so broken and lost here they'll kidnap their daughters and shoot them in the head after they're done with them."

"Ugh," Simo had been about to take a bite, and put them back in the leaf. "Your timing really sucks sometimes."

"I wonder how the rebels will see it." Tan took a bite of his moo-ping pork skewer. "Their bar for determining collaborators is incredibly low."

"Not our problem," said Simo.

"Not our problem," Tan agreed.

They ate for a while, listening to the blind man's song. From the corner of his eye, Tan noticed Simo kept opening his mouth and closing it again, a thoughtful look on his face. He glanced around a few times, but they were a healthy distance away from the nearest people.

"Out with it, already." Tan sighed. He knew this was coming.

"You sure it's a good idea to get involved with that woman?"

"It's a terrible idea."

"So I don't need to lecture you."

"I'd be immensely grateful."

"So I don't have to tell you that if you piss her off, losing the… prize we're after will be the least of your worries."

"I know."

"Just couldn't help yourself, huh?"

"It wasn't like that."

"Well, you're braver than I am. Can't see a woman like that being satisfied to sit around in your harem all day."

"She spent years with the Ashukari," Tan said. "I'd be shocked if she didn't have one of her own."

"And you'd allow that?" Simo raised a brow, then shuddered. "I couldn't fathom another having any of my wives."

"How are they, by the way?"

"Divorced, last I checked."

Admittedly, Tan hadn't thought it through. He kissed her because he felt her spinning away, and it felt right, and he didn't hold back because it felt even better. There was no reason to believe it might be anything more than that, but he wondered... He hadn't even considered the idea of Isaree being with him beyond their ambitions.

It was a startling image, his warrior muse in the regalia of a queen, crown and all.

But Simo was right. She didn't give off the same energy as the women he'd grown up around, the forbidden women that belonged to the king. They were a special, esteemed social class in their own right; proud, gentle, comfortable. Isaree was untamable, a wild and independent soul that seemed as restless as him. A mirror of his muse, the Stranger, who would lead him to glory or death and that's what he found so completely irresistible.

"I'll be careful," Tan assured his friend, though he had no intention to. Coming from a life where one's spouses were prearranged, one's lovers were vetted and trained, the uncertainty and chaos she offered was no small part of the appeal. "I promise."

His accommodations were in the sprawling housing complex that had once belonged to the ambassador to Suyoram. It had since been converted into several quarters for special Protectorate guests, and had been finely furnished in their distinct, foreign style. Animal skin furs, leather chairs, dreary paintings. The bed was uncomfortably soft, with four large, carved posts from which a golden mosquito net hung.

As he feared, sleep was a cruel, absent mistress. Tan paced the room for a while, then sat down to write in his journal before he realized it was likely rotting somewhere in the muddy wreckage of Son Clarion. He found a quill and ink, but after a futile search for blank paper his feverish gaze drifted to the generous bookshelf of leatherbound classics written in Grisi. They had the printing press there, he was told, a wondrous invention that the king had been trying to import for years. The Grisi dangled the promise of it like a sadistic uncle holding candy above a desperate child. It was pathetic.

Tan chuckled when he found an over-sized copy of the Book of Vows. It made a thump when he dropped it on the desk. Fortunately, the print was light gray, faded with age. The black ink from his quill, blotchy and sputtering, drowned out the religious drivel. How sacrilegious.

On the title page, he scratched out "vows," and wrote "Isaree."

"You've gone mad," he muttered to himself, then chuckled, turned the page, and listed all the ways in which following her was the noble path. He drafted a propaganda-laden manifesto worthy of the Qinsengi emperor himself, a despotic man notorious for tolerating zero criticism. In bombastic words, he related how she'd grown up, a working-class phi hunter novice from Jinburi. How her magic put her in tune with the devas, and the spirits, and the hungry ghosts disturbed by violence and shunned by the gods. He described what she had done for Loram – her bravery in the face of insurmountable odds, her commitment to all Rami peoples, and the absolute necessity that the corrupt Grisi military and the tyrannical trading company be driven out of their lands forever.

He called for the people of Suyoram to rise up as Loram had. Not to wait for their ships, and cannons, and soldiers to rain down their oppression. Their frustration with the king and the high taxes was understandable and valid, he wrote, but resentment was not enough.

If you want to see change, channel your anger into action. The Wild Cobras, once a tireless champion of the crown, now pledge their full support behind Isaree, savior of the Rami. I, Prince Tanung, the original heir of the first Crown-Prince Varunvirya III, officially denounce Sarvupun, the second-choice son of Varunvirya II. I will bring strength and pride back to Suyoram, as my great grandfather, Varunvirya I, would have wanted. We will never be under the boot heel of a foreign flag again.

Join the resistance today. No, *today!*

That was decent, he thought, then wrote it over again, more polished. He wrote another version for barely literate countryfolk. He wrote another with elevated language aimed at intellectuals, another for the religiously minded, and another for the nobility. On that one, he changed the name Tanung to Varunvirya IV, for extra credibility. To win over public opinion, you had to know what the public wanted. And that was everything and the opposite, depending on who you asked.

He started to draw her face again, but stopped. He couldn't really get it right, the Isaree he'd met had something of a vulnerable, earnest air in spite of her ferocity. He couldn't perfect it until he channeled his well-practiced likeness of the Stranger instead. Finally, his trusty muse came to him, and there she was – defiant, proud, glaring into the far distance with the unfettered hubris of a thousand revolutionaries.

It well past midnight by the time he was satisfied with each version, and had covered over the entire first three tenets of Vows, sacred harmonies one through eight. He'd gone through two bottles of wine and three vials of ink. Then he laid on the floor for a while, closed his eyes, and tried to calm his mind.

The soft glow of her ruby eyes in the darkness, the jeweled eyes of the Stranger, he loathed that it took so long for him to see that they'd always been one and the same. Part of him always knew, he thought. He remembered the rat catcher now, the strange, mysterious girl running through the gardens. The memory had been shrouded by his illness, tearing her from his mind. It was better this way, his faith needed to be tested. If he'd known this whole time, consciously knew, then he would have chased her until he found her rather than walk his own path to greatness, and he'd be of no use to her now.

Eventually, he grew restless again and returned to the book. He flipped to the back and started writing everything he wanted to say to her, starting with overly romantic gestures. How he'd present her with wondrous gifts from his travels afar, adorn her with jewels, no, she'd want… bone necklaces? Swords? Strapping, virile lovers to share their bed? Whatever she wanted. He'd parade her through the streets of the capital in a diamond palanquin. The best for his queen, his goddess, his savior… he expounded upon everything he wanted to give her and show her – which devolved into the ways in which he'd learned to please a woman... one of the perks of belonging to the royal bastard class. No shortage of beautiful women willing to sleep with him for fun, profit, or clout.

He worked himself into a heightened state, practically rapturous. At times, he could hear music playing. The sentences broke into verse, and he let his imagination sweep him away into another world, where a red sun burned above a smoldering battlefield, where the Stranger first spread her glistening legs and beckoned him to take her, where they merged together in the ashes of the world, exploding like stars into the universe.

Chapter 41

An Untamable Soul

"Holy shit, where the hell have you been?" Simo hissed, when Tan finally came down the alleyway behind an abandoned house and a bamboo fence. He peeked around the corner, then looked back at Tan again. "Did you… cut your hair?"

"Uh, not exactly." Tan pulled his shemaugh lower.

"What happened?"

That was up for debate. The night felt like a blur and he'd passed out at some point in the early morning, face first onto the Book of Vows. Unfortunately, the ink pot had knocked over, and when it dried, glued his cheek and hair to the pages.

He'd done his best in the washroom, and most of the ink had washed off his skin. But the paper! What the living hell was it made from? He dunked his head into the basin completely, but when it got wet the wafer-thin paper dissolved into a pasty, glue-like substance that seemed to only get worse with hair soap.

It was already late afternoon when he woke, and he needed to meet Simo. In frustration, Tan used scissors to roughly chop off the offending strands on the left side of his head, right at the root. Then he stood naked in the bathroom, staring into the looking glass in horror. One side was shorn completely, the other still long, almost to his shoulders now. He tried to recall where the unofficial Wild Cobra barber was being housed, but that would have to wait.

It occurred to him the cursed ink and paper had come from somewhere, and he cautiously trudged back to the desecrated Book of Vows. And the pages… Tan quickly flipped through them. Oh dear lord, he'd been on one wild ride. He remembered the manifesto, that was good, the portrait even better. But the rest? Tan flushed with embarrassment, not bothering to look at the dire, desperate horny bullshit he wrote before tearing them from the book. He found a waste bin, dumped the torn pages inside, and burnt them.

"Had a rough night," Tan said. "Let's leave it at that."

"Aye, aye, captain," Simo snorted, then nodded down the alleyway. "Shall we?"

Ree wasn't being kept in the city prison, which was little more than a series of outdoor, roofless pens not fit for animals. Rather, Rimes had her brought to the dungeons in the state-of-the-art fort the Gris had built on the rise overlooking the city. *Almost* built. Fort Nestor in Muang-Hhleg had taken priority, and this style of advanced building required skilled engineers. All that had been finished in Kohkiem was the lower foundation, and the groundwork for the ramparts, along with a couple of the towers. They had been making good progress, Rimes had told them, but then the damn Liberation Front demanded all their manpower and resources, and somehow, three of his four engineers had disappeared in the middle of the night.

There was a small window of time where it had been arranged that a certain Protectorate guard detail would conveniently take a long walk to the latrine, and both have a ten minute bowel movement before returning to their post outside Ree's cell. Like many of the other Protectorate recruits of Lo descent, these two locals had found themselves unable to leave their families behind, and that desperation for amnesty from the Liberation Front could be easily exploited.

The day before, Tan had been buzzing with machismo when he'd first walked into the cell. Ree trusting him enough to surrender herself filled him with a profound honor. His outlandish plan seemed to be clicking into place, until, of course, she pulled the rug from under him. Pulled the rug from under him, and at the same time, shattered the ceiling and exposed the beauty of the stars.

Now he couldn't describe exactly how he felt. His mind was spent, soft, raw at the edges. His stomach flopped with the anxiety he remembered suffering at his first gala, working himself up to talk to a girl he'd had a hopeless crush on. And he physically flinched at his own thoughts, despised himself for being weak. He couldn't let something so juvenile as infatuation distract him from overthrowing a fucking dynasty. It was his fucking dynasty after all. Had always been.

"It's a jagged line to the top," he muttered, as Simo unlocked the door. A panicked thought, intrusive – what if she wasn't there? Somehow escaped, used her magic, found a way down through the earth, the stones rolling aside for her just as the trees had peeled back to reveal the Serene Way. He thought he caught Simo casting him an apprehensive look as he opened the door. Collecting himself, Tan walked into Ree's cell.

She hadn't escaped. Ree sat on the floor cross-legged, eyes closed, palms resting on her knees. Her manacles laid to the side in a pile, but he noticed the lack of food, no water. Were the guards too afraid to even open the door? Ree opened her eyes when the door shut. He was torn between elation to see her again, and rage that she hadn't been treated properly, and he couldn't decide which to express first, which rendered him speechless. She stared at him in that off-putting, feline manner that had unfortunately become endearing to him, but said nothing.

Tan took a few steps toward her, but faltered. Of all the time he'd spent thinking about her for the past twenty-four hours, including the things he wanted to say, well, they were good as the wind. Suddenly, he wanted to run away. And then she smiled shyly, her cheeks gaining a bit of color, and his confidence returned.

"Ree," he said, and walked to stand closer before her.

"You came back." She spoke softly, and didn't rise to meet him. He knelt down to see her face. If he thought too much before he spoke, then all he'd do was stammer pointlessly. Best to trust himself, go with his gut. So the obvious came to mind.

"Of course I did." She seemed melancholy, though captivity tended to do that to people. He wanted to embrace her but held himself back. "We didn't finish our conversation."

"Right." A smile grew on her lips, but faded quickly. "How long has it been? I have no windows."

"About twenty-four hours."

"Well, that's disappointing… when are we leaving for Jinburi?"

"Tomorrow night, despite the colonel's efforts to delay," Tan said. "The men under his command are practically skipping in the streets. Most of them never wanted to be here."

"It's not their home." Ree nodded, then glanced at him slyly. "So. When can I expect to be transferred to your custody?"

"Tomorrow. My crew's making the brig a bit more comfortable for you. Protectorate ships are convoying with us, and we might have visitors, so you'll have to stay out of sight." He peered at her, she seemed deep in thought. "Are you nervous?"

"No," Ree said. Now that they were a breath apart, she seemed unable to maintain eye contact for very long. Feeling bold, he reached out and took her hand.

"Ree," he said, fingers between hers. Simo was right the first time. He couldn't help himself. "Talk to me. How are you feeling? About everything."

"Mmm. I've been thinking," she said, and when he brushed his other hand over her cheek, she leaned into his touch, closing her eyes. "I need to send a message."

"Good as done." He brushed her pale hair back from her face, twirling the soft strands through his fingers. Her smile grew as he tightened his fist, pulling her head back gently but firmly. With a sharp inhale, she let him expose her throat. He remembered the taste of her sweat when he ran his tongue along the same pulsing artery that not long before he'd willed himself to cut open.

"Mmm… make sure you deliver the message to one of the Ashukari at the temple, they're the only ones I really trust." She squeezed his hand and he pulled her closer, brushed his lips against her neck, swimming in her bright, earthy scent. Like dew drops glistening on a garden on the first day of the rainy season.

"As you wish," Tan murmured, and he felt her hand slip up the hem of his shirt, nails digging across his skin. His breath came ragged and he teetered from gentleman status to just above a dog in heat. Impulsively, he bit her neck, and when she gasped, kissed it after.

"Tell them… that…" she trailed off as he continued to kiss her neck, her sweet voice dropping to a purr. She strained against his handful of hair and when he let go, she turned to find his lips with her own. With surprising strength, she yanked him against her, and he lost himself for a while, enjoying her hungry kisses, letting her touch him wherever she pleased.

She'd slipped onto his lap at some point, straddling him with her legs around his sides, her arms around his neck. Her body felt perfect against his, would feel even better without clothes, fuck. As he clutched her bare waist, he longed to find out exactly how perfect. So badly, that he seriously considered how terrible the consequences would *really* be if they were caught.

He pulled away, breaking off the kiss to rest his forehead against hers. "Tell them?" he said, breathlessly. Ree blinked a few times, brows furrowed over her half-lidded eyes. "The plan. Ours. Rimes. The Gris coming back. The ambush. Yeah. I already have it, ready to send." Then he kissed her again, eager to get back to where they left off.

But it was her turn to pull away. "No," she said.

It didn't quite register at first. She seemed eager to roll around on the prison floor a second ago. But indeed, he was a gentleman and waited for her to elaborate. All she did was smile and move in to kiss him again.

"Wait, what?" Tan snatched her by the chin before she could connect.

"I just want to thank them and tell them goodbye." Ree playfully nipped at his fingers. "I thought about it all night, and this makes the most sense to me. The rebels shouldn't get involved."

Now he was really lost. "What? Why?"

When she realized he was deflating, Ree sighed and nudged his hand away from her face.

"Yes, there's a small chance Minh could convince the army to break the ceasefire and attack," she said, avoiding his gaze again. "But there's also a small chance the Gris will honor it. I can't ask her… can't ask Loram to risk a possible peace on my behalf, on the suspicions of a Suyo prince aiming to take his uncle's throne. They've been through too much."

Tan took exception to that description of him. Where his heart had been burning hot, plummeting to the other extreme sent a shudder through his whole body. Rage or hurt, he wasn't sure. By some miracle, he managed to keep his voice calm and level. "It's not just a suspicion. He told me exactly what he planned."

Originally, Rimes wanted to assassinate her at the parlay. Then he wanted to fake the Protectorate abandoning the city after planting explosives all over town. Slowly, Simo, and Tan carefully led him through the pros and cons, and then other ideas, coming back to what they'd come up with, and making sure the man thought it was his idea all along.

"He's one man." Ree grew cross, her arms still hanging over his shoulders, but tense. "I know all too well that one opinion isn't enough to sway an entire group, no matter what they've done to earn their respect."

"That has nothing to do with anything. The Grisi aren't some chaotic horde of farmers and cult leaders," Tan said, aware his temper was rising. "They have a chain of command, and at the top is the trading company. They *are* coming back, in force. That's a guarantee."

Ree looked baffled and let go of his shoulders to cross her arms. Her eyes darted around as she worked over it. "You're telling me that the company – a *business* – can overrule their government?"

"That's how their world works, sweetheart," Tan said, more scornfully than he intended. "Hell, ours too, when you get down to it. If you spent more time in it, you'd understand."

"Fine. I get it. They're coming back," Ree snapped, then jumped to her feet, stalking away. Her sudden absence left him cold. He started to reach for her, but clenched his fists at his side instead.

"Your friends in the front may have been through a lot, but it'll all be for nothing if you don't warn them. They have no choice but to answer your call if they want to survive."

"The council agreed to the terms, and that was a risk that they were willing to take on faith."

"So, you're being petty."

"How is that petty?" She whirled back around.

"Risking the future of Suyoram because you're hurt the council didn't put up a fight for you."

"I know it's hard to believe, Prince Tanung…" She stomped in front of him and glared down. By the devas, he did *not* like the way she sneered his name, but damn did she look powerful. Against all odds he felt himself stirring again, until she opened her mouth. "…but I gave myself up knowing full well there might be no other way out. I'm not carrying a personal vendetta. I believe in what I'm doing."

"And you're choosing to believe in the Gris instead of your own people." Tan shook his head in disgust. "You really want to die, don't you? That's it. Back to your deva realm, fuck the rest of us. I think you're afraid of leading Suyoram. You'd rather be a martyr."

"What would you know about serving something greater than yourself?! Of course, a rich royal couldn't comprehend the idea…" She went on, but Tan was not accustomed to being yelled at in anger by anyone he wasn't actively trying to kill. On those occasions, his default was to completely ignore them and focus on his task at hand. So as Ree's voice rose, his attention drifted, along with his eyes, to her bare midriff… and the angry red scar that he'd stitched shut which should have still been bandaged if she wanted it to heal.

How symbolic. She didn't seem to appreciate all the work he'd done for her – all the people that he'd convinced to fall in line with his designs, his crew who were already risking their lives to follow him into uncertainty. She didn't understand the tireless mental labor that went into bending, breaking and rebuilding people without raising their suspicions. She was naive, but pure in a way. He gazed up at her with a sudden rush of affection, seeing her in a new light, and she abruptly stopped her tirade.

"I'm serving *you,* aren't I?" he said, and rose to his feet. This was a woman who'd gone beyond death in search of purpose. He seized her face between his hands and pulled her roughly against him. She sucked in a breath, but her glare softened when he said, "Fuck the council. You're right. We don't need them."

"Tan–"

He kissed her gently, delighting in how she melted back into his arms. After she softened, he wrapped his arms around her, and whispered in her ear, "All I need is you."

"And the throne," she muttered, sighing.

"And the throne," he said, peering down at her with a deadly serious stare, "but only with you at my side."

She scoffed at the line, but Tan didn't flinch. He wasn't being facetious. Under normal circumstances someone like Ree would not be permitted on royal grounds, but nothing about these circumstances were normal. Win enough of the public opinion, and you could get away with murder.

"Is that… seriously… a fucking marriage proposal?"

"It's a promise of whatever you want it to be," Tan said. This was not in his script, not by a long shot, and he felt somewhat possessed, but it spilled out of him without hesitation. "Queen, consort, adviser, general, court jester – I don't care. Whatever you want, you'll have it. So long as you stay with me."

Just then, Simo's warning knock came at the door. Good on him to give them a few extra moments.

"We're out of time," Tan said, feeling as if he were standing on the edge of a cliff. "What's it going to be?"

Ree studied him, seeming to weigh his worth. It felt like ages passed before she said softly, "Enough with the romantic bullshit, Tan. I don't need empty promises."

That wounded him more than a little bit, how cavalierly she cheapened his affections. But he noticed that her face told another story – she was intrigued at the possibility of an ending beyond a blaze of glory. Perhaps… the seed was planted.

"None of my promises are empty," he snapped. "Tell me what you need, and I'll go to the ends of the earth to see it done."

"We don't need the rebels, and we don't need to trick Rimes," Ree said. "Bring me to Jinburi. We'll win the war there. And for that… we need a new kind of army."

Chapter 42

The Ghost Legion

The work must continue. The work was all that mattered.

Homdee hummed her song as she slid through her masterpiece, adjusting any imperfections with any one of her many appendages. Once a thread was laid and dried, her visions were gilded in eternity. She had little thought for the imperfect meat within that would wither with each necessary feeding, eventually rotting into rattling bones. Feeding did not bring her joy – it was only a necessity. Her joy, and torture, derived from the work itself.

The work was all that mattered. But somewhere along the way, the work had changed.

From the beginning, her life as an artist had been more than a mere interest or impulse. It had been a calling. And in her existence as an... what was the word Owun had used... accursed? Yes, even as an accursed, that had never changed. Her motivations had always remained pure in both states of being. But as an accursed, it transcended.

In life there had been so many distractions, so many demands from society in order to simply exist. You had to eat, and to eat you had to pay, and to pay you had to sell, and to sell you had to participate in the never-ending cycle of supply and demand. The art becomes supply, becomes commodity. She had to acquire patrons – the artist becomes commodity. And the commodities did not end at what was produced by her hands, no, they were also required of the hand itself and all that belonged to the flesh. A woman's own flesh, the whole of her body. The cycle requires workers, and to make more workers, she must reproduce, and to reproduce, she must marry, and to marry, she must sacrifice her own wants, needs, and desires to satisfy her husband's.

As an accursed, she could exist without the constant demands to *contribute*. In death, she found peace, and in her art, purity.

And then came the Gray Walker, and everything changed.

Even though Homdee had agreed to comply under a certain level of duress, she soon realized how efficient it was. No longer had she needed to leave her lair to hunt for supplies. She could concentrate on her grand masterpiece, which had been neglected in favor of smaller works.

Of course it wouldn't last. As her patrons had once done in life, the Blood Patron asked for more. In exchange, they would bring her more supplies. Better supplies. All that she needed to do was sacrifice a little of her time to complete a menial task. One that she was particularly good at and could do very quickly – displacing earth and reinforcing tunnels with her threads – but menial nonetheless.

But after one labor was completed, there was always another. And then the tasks became larger and more complicated. The problem began to manifest when she would finish her day's work and return to her lair. Now, the living bodies given to Homdee by the Blood Patron crowded the floor. They were undesigned, noisy, waiting in limbo to become. A body was only good for so long before it became unusable. Now, Homdee had too much supply, and not enough time.

To solve this problem, she built another area for holding them, using the skills she'd started to perfect in constructing the underground living spaces for the Blood Patron and their ilk. But now these supplies, these living bodies, needed to eat and drink to remain fresh, and needed soft things to sleep on, so Homdee requested new types of payment from the Blood Patron, who seemed puzzled, but did not ask questions.

There came a night when Homdee returned to feed her supplies, and gazing upon the cowering huddle of bodies carefully distributing bowls around the curry pot, she realized she had been so busy that she'd not made a single work of art in months. Aside from the one she kept to drain out of necessity when she needed to feed, the others tried to speak with her now, as if she were not their goddess of creation here to usher them into a perfect rebirth, but their landlord. They demanded things like light and tools, and offered their labor in exchange for freedom, or at the very least, to keep living.

Homdee wasn't sure what to do. Her Blood Patron had specified these were the bodies of grave sinners, and if returned, they would be executed. It seemed a waste. So she kept them.

Years later, the Gray Walker returned, this time her blindingly bright aura carrying the authority of Indrajit, and everything changed again.

The Blood Patron's requests grew exponentially as their conflicts in the world above escalated. To relieve this, the Gray Walker sent other accursed to assist Homdee in her tasks. But they were simple-minded, and many were not especially skilled at digging. So Homdee decided to employ her ever-increasing supply of the living to work, with the accursed overlooking them.

And now she realized that she had not made her art in a very long time indeed, because of all these obligations. There was satisfaction in seeing her labors completed, but there was no joy, no communion with the greater mind, no purity. With horror, she realized she was right back to where she'd started her fall in life, trapped in a cycle of supply and demand and this time, not a hapless victim caught in the churn of circumstance, but the architect of her own hell.

Just as she realized this, the world of mortals changed again. For now, the labor was finished. Excited, Homdee crept into what had once been a pen, now a nicely furnished complex, where her living bodies slept, and ate, and lived, in search of the perfect materials. Now she had the supply and the time, and was relieved to finally finish her endless masterpiece.

And as she drew her claws over one of her slumbering workers – Tomas, the others called him – there was something she hadn't anticipated.

She didn't want to use him. Not just him, *any* of them. They were no longer base materials. Their existence had value, even beyond their labor. And try as she might, she could not detach that new value from their bodies and make anything from it. Her art would be impure, uninspired, rendered worthless.

So when the message came that the Gray Walker requested an audience, Homdee dropped everything. She dug her way through the mountain until she arrived directly under the Gray Walker's prison, and with a renewed fury.

It was the Walker who had started this mess to begin with, it was the Walker who needed to solve it.

I am suffering. Homdee curled in the darkness, blanketed in the earth she'd burrowed through, her face pressed against the stone foundation between her and the Walker. *Without the work, I suffer.*

I don't understand. I thought the work could never end. You stopped killing people?

The work has been damaged beyond repair by nature of its supply. The supply... has been tainted by value.

What?

I will show you. Homdee began to hum, and her song filled in the gaps that she hadn't the words to explain. By nature, the Walker was different than the Blood Patron. Through senses, Homdee could paint the picture of her experience and have that seen and felt. She showed her the labors as they grew, along with the tributes. Her living supply and their expanding needs. How they'd become something almost like pets or working animals, and though she had as much affection for them as any weaver would for their fabric, she felt the crushing weight of responsibility for their continued survival.

The Walker viewed all of this with the same emotion that Homdee had. She stopped humming the song, and the Walker returned to her own emotions, which apparently were not the same.

What the fuck, Homdee?! You built a slave village in your underground lair?

They are volunteers. I am not forcing them to work. But the ones that work receive more accommodations, as they expend more energy, thus most want to.

You... you need to let them go.

But if I let them go, the Blood Patron will kill them. They are condemned.

That's not your problem, Homdee. You've done your part, and you aren't responsible for Minh's, I mean... your patron's actions. The Gray Walker paced, her footsteps tapping above. *I know you weren't trying to make them suffer intentionally, but people can't live like this. Even if they've been condemned. This was not what I intended when I sent phi to assist you.*

You initially brokered this deal, Walker.

Ah, so you think it's my responsibility to fix it. Fine. Here's my solution: have them dig a tunnel far away from your patron, and let them go free. Or kill them and continue your work. But you can't keep them imprisoned like that. It's torture. It's inhumane.

Homdee did not feel any better. *I'll consider this. But that will not ease my suffering. The work has changed. My inspiration... gone. If things went back to the way they were before...*

Nothing will be the way it used to be, because you've changed. The Walker stopped pacing. *It's hard to accept, I know, but this is what it means to be human.*

I have no desire for redemption, Walker.

Maybe not, but redemption has found you. It's time to let go of the darkness, Homdee.

Her many eyes leaked with tears. *Why did you summon me?*

Because I have a great task to do, and it requires one who can speak with both the living and the accursed. Serve me as the others do, and after we're victorious, you will be released from your suffering. Are you ready?

Homdee's work had changed yet again.

I'm ready.

Agira had not once stopped flying since he'd left Isaree at the water. He didn't shapeshift often because it made him hungry, and he hated being hungry, but he elongated his wings from bat to bird to easier glide, curling through the air for miles and miles, and days and days, deep over the Kalashas, to Qinseng, and back. He pondered the things she'd said and the things he'd heard and what he'd seen and done and how he fit into all of it.

Forgiveness. It shouldn't be that easy.

But why not?

If one genuinely repented for their sins, then why should they suffer arbitrarily, indefinitely? How did thirty years of hunger equate to taking one life? Or ten? Or a thousand? Or being murdered? Or dying in childbirth? How did digging a tunnel, or carrying a message, or killing Isaree's enemies equate to taking one life? Or ten? Or a thousand? Or...

Too many questions, and he had no one to speak to. All he had was the constant hunger and overwhelming loneliness. His mind kept returning to that riverside temple, with the shining gray ones, the dead-alives, the Ashukari, and all the other mortals, while just across the way, a horde of the accursed, not celebrating and not communing but at the same time together, in community, united in their determination to serve.

Amazing, he thought, shuddering so hard that he was forced to land. A group so beautiful and impossible, and they would have their humanity restored at her will. Agira longed to take part. But he'd seen the dried human blood on the cloaks of the taihong – he'd seen the hunger simmering in their eyes. He couldn't condone violence... but he could be helpful.

Agira returned to that riverbank but found it empty. The temple was empty, no sign of the Ashukari. The underground tunnels full of hiding rebels, also empty. Where had they gone? Had they all died? Agira flew to the city, Kohkiem, but saw no sign of battle. In fact, the city was bustling with a new energy. Then he noticed that it was much fuller, and it smelled less like blood... the Grisi ships that had once crowded the port were all gone.

If the rebels had won, where was Ree? Agira lurked and listened from the gutters and the rooftops and the trees. He heard many things – *thank the devas the Protectorate is gone. Is the Liberation Front going to conscript us? I heard so and so got tied up and thrown to the Weaver for collaborating. I'm scared this peace won't last, we should save up, leave while we can… we should have left for Jinburi when they took the Ghost Princess.*

Ghost Princess? That must be a new name for Isaree. Agira flew south down the Duram, retracing the steps he'd traveled with Ree to arrive there. He lurked through the village that they'd stopped in to find passage north, making himself small again to scurry around.

And then he heard overheard two men sweeping the streets, arguing about going to Jinburi. Why? Because the Savior of Rami is calling upon all to expel the Grisi threat once and for all. Savior of Rami? One of the men had a piece of paper, neatly stamped with writing on it in two languages, and a portrait of Isaree! Someone very skilled carved that image of Isaree's face into a wood block backwards, along with all those words, and ran it in ink and stamped it on papers and handed them out. Agira had done this in life, a long time ago.

These posters were getting passed around everywhere, the man said, all throughout the provinces. Some of the ferrymen already left, after her ship passed by, they're going to join her army. The other one shook his head, saying, no, no, the king has declared her an enemy of the crown, it must be a trap to catch sympathizers because she's going to be executed down there. Don't be stupid. If you go join her army, you'll lose your head.

Agira gasped, then took to the air, faster now. They mentioned her having a ship, so he flew south along the river until morning, stopping only once to watch the sunrise.

Eventually the moon came out, and he started to hear some whispering, started to smell something very strange for the second time. It was the accursed and the stink of spirit magic, but also the stench of humanity. Fire and food and sweat. Steel and gunpowder and leather. It was that beautiful and impossible gathering of mortal, phi, and spirits and he swooped down through the forest, chasing that feeling, eventually pouring out onto the Long Road.

Fluttering to a stop, Agira landed on one of the mile-marker signposts standing on the side of the roadway and stared out in awe over the gathering. There were so many people! They were camped out in loose groups around small fires, some with tents, others on bedrolls. They carried all manner of weapons. Swords, spears, polearms, crossbows, guns... and flags. There were banners attached to many of the pole arms, and on the banners there was a symbol and writing above and below: "United Rami People's Army" and "The Ghost Legion."

Beyond the mass of people crowding the Long Road, he saw the accursed on every side. They stood some ways from the nearest mortals, and remarkably, seemed to be standing watch. In the woods nearby, there were the winged spirits he'd seen before, and beneath them were other fearsome creatures, an entire herd of them. Agira wasn't sure if the humans even knew the spirits were there, but they did know the phi were, and didn't seem to care.

Little one.

Agira heard the Weaver's voice carry over the wind. He peered around, then flew toward the sound. She was further away from the Long Road but within human sight, her massive insect abdomen buried beneath the dirt so only her torso stuck above. She wore a cloak of multicolored silk tribute scarves over her body and arms, expertly woven together, and a black, sheer veil over her forehead where her many eyes would be. It made Agira sad that she chose to obscure her full form, but even he, a fellow accursed, knew it would be disturbing to most humans.

Weaver! You remember me?

Of course I remember you. The day we met changed everything.

Agira hovered, then plopped down. *I didn't expect to see so many here. Not you, either. Are you... what are you doing here?* Nervously, he stared at the disturbed earth where the rest of her body was buried.

My work is to speak between the living and the accursed. It is not so easy for some of us. And, when it is time, I will build. The Weaver tilted her head. *Why are you here?*

I'm looking for Isaree.

She's not here.

Isn't this her army?

Yes.

Um, well... if she's not here, w-where is she?

I don't know.

Would anyone know?

Try her patron. The Weaver pointed a long claw arm back toward the Long Road. *He would know.*

Chapter 43

What One Cannot Forgive

Something was wrong.

Without the sun or sky, Ree couldn't tell how much time had passed, but she knew it had been too long. If she had to guess… three or four days. By now, she should have been on the river, en route to Suyoram, in the custody of the prince.

The nature of what that "custody" looked like had played out in her mind. The memory of Tan's brazen advances still made her cheeks flush, and she hated that she couldn't stop thinking about the way he'd made her feel that first visit. His words were a sweet poison, telling her how much he believed in her, staring into her eyes with a devilish satisfaction as he stroked the very core of her. So maddeningly sure of himself. She longed to cut him down for size, make him grovel and beg for her attention.

But during the second visit, he could have been another person entirely. It wasn't only his strange haircut, shorn on one side like a Kutsu pirate. Though she'd grown accustomed to his rapidly shifting moods, this was extreme. His aura was discolored and distracted, his energy tasted like iron and mercury. She had an abstract urge to staunch the bleeding, as if there were raw, open wounds all over the inside of his head. He was vulnerable, unguarded, and the way he looked at her, well, the first prince might get her off with the heat of a thousand suns but the second one made her want to destroy every higher realm just to ease his suffering.

Which was the real Tan? Could she trust either one?

She had given him very specific instructions on what to tell the Ashukari. Send the Weaver to speak with her. Tell the Ashukari to march south.

Dama's warnings came back to her, but for whatever reason Ree had stopped suspecting that he was lying to keep her complacent. He'd admitted that he wanted the throne, and even if the prince wasn't infatuated with her, he was at least lusting for her. In satisfying her needs, he could be useful too.

The silence started to bother her. And the confinement. And the monotony. She paced the cell, chains clinking. She meditated, recalling some of the Ashukari chants, even some of the phi hunters' guild exercises. Ree was sure that she'd prefer death to imprisonment like this.

Without the sky, time started to drift in circles.

Every little noise from the outside had her starting at the door, hoping that her devoted prince would sweep in and take her away, only to be disappointed. It was the guard changing again. Or a nervous steward come to replace the shit pot and her untouched bowl of plain rice porridge. Disgusted, Ree felt like a dog waiting for its master to return, and her resentment grew, then simmered, then began to fester.

A loud clap startled Ree out of her slumber. She blinked up at the uniformed man standing over her. Six others stood behind him, all watching her with ready weapons. Their uniforms were different than the lighter material the Protectorate wore. These were heavy, straight from Grisland, closer to what she remembered the soldiers wearing in Jinburi.

"So *this* is the witch they call the Heretic," he said in Grisi, scowling. "This dirty little thing? You gotta be shitting me."

Ree met his hateful stare evenly, then looked past him and slowly rose. Behind the row of soldiers, Rimes leaned against the door frame.

"I assure you it is her, general," Rimes said, his skin sweaty and gray. He stared down the hallway while he smoked a cigar. "She's been cooperative thus far."

"How cooperative?" he said with a grotesque leer, eyes lingering on her bare midriff.

General Elleman. Tan had mentioned him being the one in charge of the military. The one who would make the decision on whether or not to break the ceasefire. If he was here… that meant the reinforcements had arrived or were very close.

"Well… I haven't questioned her personally," Rimes dabbed his forehead with a dotted handkerchief, looking more than a little uncomfortable. "Didn't seem necessary."

Elleman grunted, then in broken Suyo said to Ree, "You speak Gris?"

Ree shook her head. Of course she could. She could read and write it as well, thanks to Havan, but they didn't need to know that.

"Tell her that I've taken your advice to heart, and I agree. This land is cursed, forsaken by the Grand Patriarch. We do not belong here, and I have no intention of letting any more of our brave men waste their lives so far from home."

Ree forced herself to keep her face blank, but even Rimes seemed somewhat taken aback. "Sir?"

"Tell her!"

Rimes translated into Rami, though he changed "cursed" to "unagreeable." Hearing it again in Suyo cemented what he said, and now she allowed herself to react with a curt nod.

"The ceasefire stands. The contract made under the eye of the Father will remain intact," Elleman said, casting a stern look over his shoulder to Rimes. The governor-colonel must have made his suggestion, only to be shot down. "This war between our people is too costly."

Tan had been partially right, but so had Ree. She felt elated, holding back a smile until Rimes translated again. She nodded, then said in Suyo, "What about your trading company? Will they agree?"

In Gris, Rimes said, "She wants to know if the company will object."

Elleman scoffed, clearly irritated, and crossed his arms. He turned to the side, the light from the hallway casting a halo on his broken nose. It reminded her of someone, but she couldn't place it. "I don't give a fuck what Burrows says. They can take it back to the grand minister himself, but I won't commit another Grisi soul to this conflict."

Rimes raised his eyebrows in a way that clearly said, *your funeral.* "You… want me to say that, or…?"

Elleman turned back to Ree, speaking in his terribly accented Suyo, "Yes. Company will."

"Good," Ree said, then wondered why they were even telling her this. In their eyes, she was a captured terrorist, a dangerous criminal who supposedly wasn't their hostage. She was supposed to be shipped to the Capital for punishment. Maybe they were even more afraid of her than she realized. "When am I leaving?"

After Rimes translated, Elleman grunted. "She isn't. Let her know the trading company's approval was contingent on this agreement." He reached into his coat pocket to produce an official looking document and handed it to her.

Cautiously, Ree took the paper to inspect, recognizing the seal of the crown of Suyoram. As she began to read, she felt the world start to spin.

"As a gift of friendship, King Sarvupun has granted us, the Grislandi government, full custody of you to pass judgment as we see fit. You are to be burned at the stake for your unholy crimes against the sons of the Grand Patriarch, and in doing so, answer for all the others in the Liberation Front."

Ree blinked a few times as Rimes did his translation, her eyes struggling to focus on one particular signature and seal under King Sarvupun I's name. Crown-Prince Varunvirya IV, Commander of the Wild Cobra Brigade.

"Huh," Ree said thoughtfully, and handed the document back. She swallowed a lump in her throat and leaned back against the wall to keep from falling over. Well, at least she could stop wondering how it felt to get thoroughly fucked by the prince.

"Get those chains back on her," Elleman said to his men, walking out. "Let's get this over with and get the fuck out of here."

An early death had always been a real possibility from the beginning. Ree grew up thinking she would become a phi hunter, one of the most dangerous trades one could learn. And then she became a rebel, also not the safest working environment. Ree liked to think that she had always been prepared to give her life for a cause. If the devas were to be trusted, she'd seen her past lives do the same thing. It seemed to be written into her soul, this karmic cycle, the lesson she was drawn to over and over again, yet could not seem to grasp.

Even now as she was marched out of the half-finished fort on the Kohkiem hill, spotting a huge silver ship shining in the sunlight just beyond the Lotus bridge, she struggled to understand where she had gone so wrong. Or was she wrong? Why didn't this feel like victory?

It wasn't enough.

She was missing something. Tan was not the heir to the throne, yet he'd signed the change of custody order with the title. Had her capture been contingent on a reward from the king? It didn't add up. Once she'd surrendered herself, he had no reason to further deceive her.

He must have been placating her, leading her on, dangling hope to make sure she didn't try to escape. But she'd already told him that if her life was what it took to ensure peace, so be it. She'd been adamant about it, frustrating him.

Perhaps he decided she was right the first time.

Two rows of six Grisi soldiers surrounded her on all sides, with Rimes and Elleman leading the procession. It seemed like Kohkiem had been informed of the event, as the streets were full of people waiting to watch them pass by. They weren't just locals either – she spotted faces she recognized from the Liberation Front. They'd already begun to move in, now that the Protectorate had departed.

The square had been set up with a scaffold, alongside a pillar surrounded by wood. She thought back to her pyre in the Ashukari temple, and tried to tell herself that this was no different.

But as they drew closer, the procession abruptly halted. A wall of people had come to block their path to the scaffold with linked arms. They weren't all rebels either. Many were, but there were also locals, civilians, children, monks, and oddest of all, Grisi missionaries. None of them were armed.

"What is the meaning of this?" Elleman demanded, then nudged Rimes to translate. "Tell them to disperse!"

Jun stood in front, alongside Khim and Bird. Ree searched around for Minh, but didn't see her. Notably absent were any of the Wild Cobras. Damn that coward. The least Tan could do after throwing her to the wolves was show up for her execution and look her in the eye.

"This isn't your city anymore," Jun announced, in Grisi. "If you go through with this, you will be under arrest and charged with murder."

"What?! She's answering for the crimes of your entire rebellion–"

"We committed no crimes!" Jun yelled, jabbing a finger toward him. Ree couldn't remember a time she'd seen him so angry. "You trespassed in our lands, you slaughtered our people, this was an illegal occupation from the start. How dare you."

Astounded at the display, Ree's eyes began to water.

"Tell them to move, or we'll open fire," Elleman said to Rimes, who only shook his head, finally at a loss for words.

"Sons of the Grand Patriarch!" One of the Grisi missionaries stepped forward, holding up his arms. "The eye of the father sees you, and your dishonest ways. The Heretic Whore may be the scion of The Profaned One, but this city has been transferred in peace. You must honor that peace! Or you doom all our souls to eternal hell."

"For the fucking love of…" Elleman muttered. More of the crowd began to shout, while Rimes tried to call for order. The soldiers around shifted, their fingers nervously sliding to the triggers of their rifles. Elleman turned around and stomped toward Ree, shoving them aside. She braced herself, but he only stood before her and leaned down to hiss, "I know you can understand me, you little shit. Remember what I said. The company wants your fucking head, or they will make us burn this place. Maybe not now, but soon. And if I am forced to come back here, trust that it will be a wasteland when I'm through."

Ree stared into the man's eyes, now seeing how bright green they were in the sun, how orange his beard was, how broken his nose had been...

And then it snapped in place.

He was there, in Jinburi that night. Laughing in the guest house of the governor's mansion, Kit's blood on his hands and boots. He must not have been a general back then, or maybe he was, and that was why he'd suffered no consequences for his cruel actions. Just a slap on the wrist for crippling a sweet, talented young boy who had a real future ahead of him.

"Do you understand what I'm saying?"

The blood pounded in her ears as Ree ground her teeth. This piece of shit was the man in charge of all operations in Loram and Suyoram? If she needed any more proof that there was no justice in the world but the one you delivered yourself, here it was. She could melt his face right now. And what would anyone be able to do? Shoot her?! They were about to burn her alive, death by gunfire sounded far more pleasant.

Elleman must have sensed the rage cascading from her, because he cringed, and the red flare of light in his eyes meant hers must have been glowing like coals. She could kill him right now, like she should have killed him back in Jinburi all those years ago. Killed him and all his friends, hell, every one of them must have played some part in strong-arming her country into helping the Gris slaughter their cousins across the river.

And if goddamn apasmara-having arrogant fucking Prince Tanung hadn't interrupted her, maybe none of this would have happened the way it had.

"The hell is wrong with you?!" Elleman said. "Tell them to get out of the way."

She could kill him right now... Ree took a deep breath. It wouldn't solve anything. And now she knew, beyond all doubt, that there couldn't be any half-measures.

That was what she kept screwing up, over and over again. She'd never gone far enough. Someone or something always held her back. If she wanted to win everything, she needed to be ruthless. And to be ruthless, she needed to cut away her emotions and stop being so reckless.

"If you kill me now, you won't make it out of here alive," Ree told him in Grisi, with genuine conviction. His eyes darted around, searching for what he was missing. Snipers? Hidden demons? Suicide bombers? All was possible. "The company wants me so bad? Take me to them, then. Let them take my head themselves."

Chapter 44

Glory Is a Godless Dream

In Kohkiem, Tan had been overseeing some final details before *Lady Mo* would embark, but the unexpected arrival of General Elleman changed everything. Rimes had already sent word to him by one of his "talking birds," the sneaky bastard, and the ornery Grisi general showed up on a twenty-oared galley, carrying a sealed order from King Sarvupun.

Elleman summoned him to the courtyard of the trading company headquarters for a drink and a chat. After some stilted pleasantries, he set his drink down and cleared his throat.

"I'm sorry to tell you this way, but I've news from the Capital. Your cousin's dead," the general said.

"Which one?" Tan asked. He had dozens of cousins.

"Little Sarv."

Of all his royal cousins and half-brothers, that one was the least expendable. Sarvupun II was heir to the throne, the only child of the queen. The king's other children by consorts were female, and the only sons had born from concubines...

"How?" Tan leaned on the table, shaken. He took a big gulp of wine.

"From what I heard, he fell while playing with his dog. And he had that bleeding disease..."

Even though Tan was aiming to usurp his uncle's throne, he still harbored a familial fondness for the man. It truly wasn't personal. Mostly, his sadness stemmed from thoughts of his mother who attended the queen, and thus often took care of the crown-prince. No doubt both women would be devastated by the loss of the little boy.

"It's a shame. But here's some good news, at least." He handed Tan two letters. The first was the order from the king. Tan read it over, fighting to keep his face neutral. The last line was blank, where his name was expected to be signed.

"He made a gift of her," Tan said, struck numb, and let the order drop on the table. Of course he would, it had always been expected, but… it was never supposed to get to that point.

"Don't look so disappointed," Elleman sat back in his chair, taking a sip of his wine. "Less work for you, same amount of glory."

"No, it's…" Tan gulped, then nodded, and feeling his hand tremble, shoved it in his pocket. He forced a smile. "It's perfect. A perfect gesture of friendship between our two countries."

"I heard she killed half your crew," Elleman said, side-eying him. "I was expecting there to have been an… accident at the fort."

"We're professionals," Tan bristled underneath his dismissive manner. "My orders were to return her to the capital for sentencing. Are you taking her to Suyoram or Grisland?"

"Neither," Elleman said, a smug smile showing under his thick red beard. "She'll be executed here in Kohkiem."

Tan clenched his trembling hand into a fist. "Huh. Interesting." He inwardly braced against his rage, which culminated in an intrusive vision of pulling his pistol and shooting this bastard in the face. Instead, he plastered a thoughtful look across his own. "Will you hang her Grisi style, or a traditional beheading?"

"She's a witch, so under the Grand Patriarch's Book of Vows, the punishment entails burning at the stake."

"Is that so." Tan had read the Book of Vows twice throughout his various studies, and he was one hundred percent certain that there was nothing in it about witchcraft, including punishment for such things. In fact, magic was not mentioned at all. Therefore, he was one hundred percent certain that the man before him had not read it and was one of those "Chosen Sons" that believed in all the cultural supremacy rhetoric and a contradictory mess of superstitions – a relatively new interpretation of the religion that had nothing to do with what was in the original holy text.

"Need to set at least one good example. Between us, I'm not happy with how many concessions Rimes made, but I am pleased about one thing. Getting the fuck out of here."

Tan felt the world spinning out of control, but held on by his fingertips. He asked careful questions about the details, and the reasoning behind it. However, Elleman was just as careful with his answers.

"One piece of advice," Tan said. "I'd be cautious of executing her on Loram soil."

"They won't break the ceasefire on one rebel's behalf. Not with the *Pale Evening* here."

Indeed, the general's support ship had arrived after the fast-moving galley, sitting sentinel in the middle of the Duram. The ironclad ship was only one of the many reinforcements arrived from Grisland, and at Elleman's orders the rest had remained at their base in Jinburi. One was enough; the Liberation Front had no defense for the two rows of cannons in range of the city.

"I'm not talking about the rebels," Tan said. "It's the Ghost Legion you need to worry about."

"The what?"

What indeed. Tan had literally come up with the name at that exact moment. "Some have called it the demon army, but that's misleading. We've read the reports, and now I've seen them firsthand. There's more than monsters that can shred the thickest armor like custard. There are powerful spirits, fierce beasts great and small, all of them fiercely protective of her," Tan glanced around, then leaned closer. "And they have eyes everywhere."

"I've had my fill of ghost stories," Elleman's scoffed, then he eyed the ground. "What is this about the soil?"

"The soil and the Duram are the flesh and lifeblood of Loram. As you've said, this land is cursed, but to them, it's sacred. Somewhere like… Jinburi is safer. It's the home of the phi hunters' guild, so the demons don't dare venture near," Tan said. "And now that Loram has been decided, wouldn't it be more useful to make an example to those who could use a reminder of what's at stake? It is her hometown, after all."

"Huh," Elleman's eyes widened. "That's an unexpected insight, coming from another Suyo."

"I'm a simple servant of my uncle's designs," Tan said. "And he often says, the friendship between our people is crucial to the future."

"I'll think about it," Elleman leaned back in his chair. "Anyway, I'm sure you'd love to see that bitch burn for what she did to your crew, but I suspect you'll be on your way to the capital immediately."

"Sir?"

"You should open your second letter."

Tan hadn't given it a thought, he'd been so wracked with stress from the first. He opened the letter, this one sealed with the emblem of the crown. It was short and written in the king's own hand.

Dear Nephew,

Deepest congratulations on your successful efforts in the Protectorate. You have truly ensured the friendship between Suyoram and Grisland, which is imperative for the future of our country. Your quarry will be transferred to General Elleman to serve as a symbol of our continued alliance. This victory has come at a time of great sorrow, but I take this as a sign from the Awakened Lord. As a gesture of my gratitude, return to court immediately to be restored with your father's title as Crown-Prince Varunvirya IV and my named heir to the throne.

Elleman slid the change custody order toward him, then removed a pen from his pocket and set it on the table. "Congratulations, Crown-Prince. Now, why don't you test out that fancy new title?"

There was nothing he could have done. With just over seventy Wild Cobras scattered around Kohkiem, even the last of the Protectorate far outnumbered them, not to mention the *Pale Evening*'s reinforcements. The *Lady Mo* was a marauder and sorely outmatched, and they simply didn't have the numbers to make a move.

The Wild Cobras were expected to leave the next morning, and him and Simo plotted the entire day. They set up a secret midnight meeting with the Liberation Front war council. Now that the rebels had moved into the city, it was an easier process, yet still dangerous. If anyone spotted them, it would all be over. The meeting took place in a relatively busy part of town, in a cellar of a lively public house.

Understandably, they were hesitant to trust him, even after his well-practiced, impassioned speech on why only Ree and her Ghost Legion could defeat the Grisi. How she was the key to the longterm survival of the Rami people. They were hesitant even after he showed them the propaganda he'd finalized, and after his artisan finished, would soon have reproduced en masse and distributed throughout the disenfranchised Suyo countryside. Still, they remained unconvinced, and he started to get pissed off. And a bit too personal.

"You saw what she could do and decided to cultivate the demonic image of the Heretic, because you knew it would scare the living shit out of the Sons of the Grand Patriarch," Tan said. "And because at the end of it all, you knew she'd be the one to take the fall. It was always in the plan to sell her to the Protectorate, wasn't it?"

"How dare you say that!" Minh snarled, with an extra glare to her comrades. "It *wasn't* the plan! Ree's my *friend*."

Tan recognized the guilt in her eyes. Who was she trying to convince?

Khim's face told another story. "Not the primary plan," he amended, with the detached air of a philosopher, "but it was always an option." Before Minh could explode, he quickly said, "But that's true for *any* one of us, should the Protectorate demand. She just happened to be the one they wanted."

"You're a pigeon, doctor," the soldier, Jun, scoffed. "Don't pretend to be a hawk." Until then, he'd mostly remained quiet, even though Ree had said he'd been her loudest critic. "Look, I was always against spreading this Heretic nonsense from the beginning. Now see where it's got us? We've given them a martyr for the cause, and she's not even *from* here." He shook his head in disgust. "You really think they're going to kill her here? In Kohkiem?"

"I don't know," Tan admitted. He couldn't wrap his head around Elleman. On one hand he seemed brash enough to do it, on the other, highly superstitious. Despite championing peace, it was not out of love for Loram.

"But if they don't, they'll take her to Jinburi."

Finally, he showed them the letter from the king granting him the title of crown-prince, a detail he'd kept to himself. Tan cast Simo an apologetic glance, and his second looked rightfully irate.

"I want you to know that I have everything to lose by asking for your assistance," he told the council.

"If you're truly so concerned about Suyoram's freedom, why not do this the easy way?" Khim asked him. "This may be crass, but we're all thinking it. Why not forget about Isaree, accept the appointment, assassinate your uncle in secret, and lead the country as you see fit, benefiting from this established position of friendship with the Gris?"

All eyes turned to Tan and waited.

It was a good question. And he should have had a good answer, something about honor and patriotism, and being the force of will for the people. He could talk for hours about how the only way to expel the colonizers was to fight, not rely on the power of bureaucratic paperwork and meticulous diplomacy – he'd had endless debates on that point for years and could argue either side with complete conviction. Or he could insist that he couldn't bear the dishonor of coming into power under such treacherous means – but that wasn't true at all.

So he told them the one true thing he knew, without a doubt.

"I just can't let her die." With that simple statement, Tan sat back on the couch, exhausted. He wanted to say more. The same conclusions that he came to while holding a knife to her neck: it would be such a waste. Whether it was true or not, her legend had already begun to spread. She'd gone to the realm of gods and returned with their blessings. The land itself welcomed her into its hidden passageways. Letting her die would be a crime against nature.

But his head was throbbing at that point, and he felt nauseous from neglecting to eat all day. All he wanted was to crawl into a dark room and never come out.

It was quiet between the five of them, the only noise creaking floorboards and muffled rabble from the crowd upstairs. And then Minh slapped her knee and said, "I can't either."

And to his surprise, Jun agreed. Khim nodded as well, with the caveat that they should do it how she'd want them to and ensure that the ceasefire remain intact.

Minh would officially split from the Liberation Front with the Ashukari and all those who wanted to follow. Apparently, there was a large faction within the front that were loyal to Ree, many of whom she'd freed from the clean villages, and others within the ranks who'd been inspired to join the Ashukari. With the Ashukari came the Ghost Legion, as Ree had directed her phi allies to protect them. Tan knew they were the key to winning a battle against the Gris, but the only way to command them was through her.

Minh would follow the Wild Cobras to Jinburi, and help recruit the discontent masses along the way, forming the United Rami Peoples Army. It was imperative to maintain a separation from the Liberation Front. Meanwhile, Jun and Khim would remain here in Kohkiem to see to its reconstruction and defense, but they pledged to block Ree's execution on the chance Elleman hadn't been convinced by Tan's warnings.

It wasn't ideal, especially the possibility of Ree's execution, but it was the best he could hope for. They agreed on a rendezvous point at the ruins of the Orchard Bridge, where the Duram met the Namleng river, and treacherous rapids could sink even a beast like the *Pale Evening*. Tan would use the expertise of his Wild Cobras to run the ship aground and board her. If they managed that, they'd likely suffer heavy losses during the raid due to the sheer number of combatants aboard the Grisi ship, but it had to be done. They'd rescue Ree, then turn their sights on the garrison.

For now, there was no point in planning further than that. If he failed, then they were doomed.

Tan and Simo left the meeting via a hidden passageway, walking in silence through the darkened streets to the harbor. Everyone was already aboard the *Lady Mo*, ready to depart at first light. They lingered on the docks, looking over the glittering city, and the behemoth ironclad quietly looming before it.

"He named you his heir," Simo finally said. "And it's not enough."

"It's not enough."

"It's never been just about the throne, has it?"

"No," Tan admitted. "It's about proving I deserve it."

To her.

If the creature had smashed into the side of his tent five seconds later than it did, they might have been mopping Tan's brains off the wall in the morning. He startled at the thud of whatever it was, jerking the barrel of his pistol away from his lips with a racing heart.

Shit, what was he thinking? He wasn't. Or perhaps thinking too much. He was so incredibly tired and ashamed and desperate for some peace. The episodes were getting worse. Since sending the *Lady Mo* onward to do recon in Jinburi, and joining the main host of the People's Army, he'd had three. Two had resulted in losing consciousness, and he'd had to be picked up and put in a wagon to ride along with the supply chain. It was humiliating, but his head hurt so badly after each episode that walking or riding proved impossible.

At night, he was exhausted, but he could never rest. He wanted to rest forever. He sat in his darkened tent, and stared at nothing, feeling numb, and alone, and pathetic. Then he dropped his pistol on the floor and put his head in his hands.

The precious few hours he had managed to sleep had not been kind. The Stranger came to him in fury and vengeance, all bloody eyes and gnashing teeth to rip out his jugular for betraying her. On his hands and knees he begged, pleaded, groveled that he had no choice, none that would lead him back to her, and she spat on him, and lord, he couldn't take it anymore. He reached for his pistol to try again.

A tiny, gray bat-like creature stood next to it, staring up at him with wide, glowing eyes. Same bright green as the phi in the Ghost Legion, lurking about the edges of the host. This one looked far too small to be of much use, though Ree herself proved that looks and size were deceiving when magic was involved.

"What are you doing in here?" Tan mumbled, peering curiously at it. Its tiny mouth dropped open and it panted, then it wrung its hands in a weirdly human way. Without warning, it fluttered into the air like a moth, landing on the table. It waddled over to one of the leftover propaganda posters, then scratched at Ree's portrait with its foot.

"Are you looking for her?"

To his surprise, the little creature nodded vigorously. Even though he'd grown used to seeing the phi, he'd never tried to communicate with any of them. He hadn't thought it was possible. Minh was the point of contact when he needed to tell them something. From what he understood, there was one in particular that could speak like a human, and it had assisted the rebels for years. It was a deal that Ree brokered, she told him, before she joined the cause, back when she was just a runaway phi hunter novice. Minh didn't elaborate on how or the details of this deal exactly, and Tan wasn't sure that he really wanted to know.

"I am too," Tan said with a sigh, and ran a hand through the shaved side of his head. "Just hope it's not too late."

Chapter 45

The Price of Survival

Now that she'd seen two prisons in the last few days, Ree found herself comparing.

Unlike her solitary underground room in Kohkiem, there were six barred cells in the brig of the *Pale Evening,* three on each side of a narrow aisle. All were empty but for hers. The only light came from dim lanterns in the passageway, where two guards stood outside the room on either side of the doorway, armed and motionless.

She had no visitors, unless she counted a casually uniformed crewman who'd come twice a day to refill her wash basin, switch out the shit pot, and set down a tray of onion bread and watered-down goat milk, perhaps some of the most unappetizing food she'd ever tasted. At least she could tell time by the movement of the ship. When it rolled to a stop she knew night had fallen, along with the deafening swell of insects and frogs that clouded the banks of the Duram.

Two long days passed in relative peace.

She wondered if she'd be able to recognize Jinburi by sound alone. It felt like she'd been gone for decades. It had changed so much while she was growing up, how much more could it have changed since? Ironically, the possibility of seeing her parents and Kit appealed to her, even if it might be a fleeting glimpse of their ashamed faces before a public execution.

How long had Tan planned this? If he was named the crown prince, that meant the king's heir had died. Ree hoped he hadn't planned the child's death as well. He'd said he had many friends and associates in the capital, including known criminals and outlaws. Now that she knew how ruthlessly ambitious he truly was, she wouldn't put it past him.

* * *

The door to the brig shut for the first time, waking Ree from her slumber. It usually stood open; the guards only needed to glance over their shoulders to make sure she was still breathing. Three soldiers walked down the aisle, out of uniform, reeking of alcohol. It must have been early in the morning, as the ship had just started to move, when the echoes of the working sailors on deck were loudest and most active.

Ree watched these three trudge toward the bars of the cell, her blood boiling. She'd heard many harrowing firsthand accounts from Lo women about the depraved treatment they'd endured under Protectorate rule. She'd been left alone in Kohkiem, likely a benefit by her reputation. But the soldiers on the *Pale Evening* were fresh from Grisland and probably uninformed about the threat she posed.

A curly-haired one set a lantern on the ground, casting sinister shadows on their faces. Unlike any of the other sailors or soldiers she'd seen aboard thus far, these men wore the extra ropes on their unbuttoned jackets that denoted officers.

"By the fuckin' matron, she's downright... unnatural." The one with the thin mustache looked her over with a grimace.

The blond, bearded, and bespectacled one waved his hand dismissively and shrugged off his unbuttoned jacket. "It's just a costume. Some bullshit demon witch hogwash they used to scare all those son-buggers."

"Scared them enough to give up the whole country," Mustache said. "I don't like those red eyes."

"Who cares, as long as she has parts that matter." Blondie grabbed the bars and leaned forward, wiggling his tongue at her.

"Are we going by rank? Who's going first?" Curly said impatiently. He was the only one armed, a knife on his belt.

"Let's let her pick." Blondie then said in terrible, barely decipherable Rami, "Want make fuck?" He grabbed his manparts and shook them. "I think she wants me, boys."

"Don't be nasty," Curly said, taking a keyring from his pocket and started to unlock the door.

"Elleman's a shit for keeping her all to himself. My brother did a tour here and said they were all fair game."

"I don't know about this one," Mustache said. "She's got black magic."

"What are you, a pansy? Come on, witch girl, show us some–"

Ree smiled, which stunned them into silence, and then she pointed at Blondie.

"Told you!" Blondie guffawed, slapping Curly on the arm so hard he almost dropped the keys. The lock clicked, and he yanked open the door.

"No, no, she's not normal. No, this is a bad idea." Mustache took a step back.

"What exactly do you think an unarmed nine stone girl is going to do to three grown men?" Curly snorted in disdain. Ree stood as Blondie sauntered over to her. Curly followed him in, but Mustache stayed at the door.

She hadn't decided exactly how she would kill them, only that she would. Men like this were a scourge upon humanity.

"Hey there, little lady..." Blondie said softly. "Ready for a real man?" Then he lunged for her.

Ree threw the Star of Yessun in his face. A blinding flash lanced across the cell, and Blondie staggered back with cry of outrage, clutching his eyes. Ree slipped past him and front-kicked Curly in the gut, grabbing his knife.

She grabbed Blondie by the hair and yanked his head all the way back. His eyes rolled wildly, streaming with tears, his lips blubbering with spit. In Grisi, she said, "Too bad you're not a real man." Then slammed the knife into his neck. Hot blood splashed across the deck as he sputtered, choking, and she ripped the blade free to stab him twice more, this time in the center of his chest.

Curly tackled her, screaming curses and beating at her with his fists. One of them caught her in the jaw, fuzzy stars exploding in her vision. Ree fell against the bars and he grabbed her throat with both hands, trying to throttle her. She shoved the Smoking Palm of Anewan directly on his face, the white-hot burning spell sizzling through his flesh and bone.

He squealed like a pig gone to slaughter and tried to pull away, but she pushed harder, sent another burst of power into her hand and curled her fingers into claws. He batted at her desperately as his skin melted, the muscles on his face cooking to blackened crisps. His scream broke down into a gasping, hissing whine. With a growl, she shoved him over into the rapidly expanding pool of blood and then set her sights on Mustache.

Mustache had done nothing but piss himself, staring at the unraveling of their failed assault in abject horror. In a few breaths, two of his mates had gone from walking talking pieces of trash to dead or soon to be. She snatched the knife out of the corpse's chest and strode toward him.

"W-w-wait," he stammered, holding his hands up in surrender. "I didn't want to do it! They made me! Please, have mercy!"

As if being complicit to attempted rape made him any less guilty.

"Fucking coward," she grabbed him by the collar.

Luckily for him, the two guards posted outside must have finally realized the screams were not hers and rushed in, rifles drawn.

Ree had a split second to decide whether she wanted to back down, or take on the entire crew. This would surely interfere with her plans to assassinate the trading company officials in Jinburi. If she returned to her cell, what was to stop them from riddling her with bullets? Three men underestimating her was one thing, but what if there were ten next time? Twenty?

She spun Mustache in between her and the guards, pushing him to walk backward.

"Stop!" one of the guards yelled. "Stop or we'll shoo–"

"Wait, wait, wait!" Mustache cried, panic breaking his voice. He waved his arms. "Don't shoot, don't shoot!"

The knife hit the first guard dead in the eye. He fell to the floor with a thump.

"Shit!" With a gasp, the second guard panicked and pulled his trigger. The bullet thudded into the back of Mustache's head and the exit wound sent a fresh burst of blood across Ree's face. He crumpled. The guard rushed to reload the packet, hands shaking, and judging by his age it might have been the first time he'd seen action. If he'd known better, he would have drawn his sword.

Chapter 46

Treachery Laid Bare

In Ganu Sia's classic book *The Anatomy of Victory*, the legendary Baghani commander wrote "In art, love, and war, timing will always triumph over desire." It was a quote Tan reminded himself of often, especially when he teetered on the precipice of an impassioned decision.

The Mae-Duram was a deep, wide, slow moving river fat enough for seaworthy ships to sail, while the Namleng was winding and treacherous. At the confluence, the tides collided in billowing swirls of color that remained divided for a few miles, until uniting eventually under the name Namleng. In spirit, she would have kept the name Duram, for that river's characteristics were what dominated the mainstem, but this was Suyoram. The energy from the Namleng aggressively eroded the point between, especially during the flood waters, creating a treacherous stretch of narrow rapids that required a careful hand when piloting. It forced ship traffic into a narrower channel, which was perfect for an ambush.

Another landmark and well-known hazard was the remains of the Orchid bridge. A remnant of the same civilization who constructed the Lotus Bridge at Kohkiem, the Orchid was a massive, ancient structure that had once spanned across the whole confluence. It would have been three times larger than the Lotus, but most of it had been long destroyed. The western approach remained intact up to the first pile, where fifty feet of the platform jutted out over the Duram.

That humid, foggy morning, when sentries signaled that the Grisi ship was coming down the stretch, Tan felt a cold calm settle over him. His nights had been restless, his thoughts dark, his nerves frayed with all the minute decisions on how to prepare a rapidly swelling, disorganized host of veterans, rebels, civilian protesters, cultists, ghosts and spirits to attack and take down one of the iron-sided flagships of a superior military force. He'd worked with the leadership to distribute the army where they'd be most useful.

That meant the peasant army would continue on the Long Road toward Jinburi, led by Minh's captains who were also training them for battle. That was the visible host of the movement, while the Wild Cobras and Ashukari would deal with Ree's rescue.

Tan had always been the type to hedge his bets. The first, which was the most likely: Elleman would hesitate to fire upon a Suyo ship without first trying to communicate. Tan was now the crown-prince, and that would be considered an act of war. They'd signal, assuming Tan was here to talk for whatever reason.

The flipside to this possibility was that they might suspect Tan's betrayal. In that case, once *the Pale Evening* spotted the much faster *Lady Mo* approaching them, they would fire their stern cannons or attempt to deliver a devastating raking broadside. There would be casualties, but once they caught up, Tan was brashly confident in his boarding party's chances.

If they timed their chase exactly right, considering the range of the Grisi cannons, the speed of the approaching *Lady Mo,* and where in the channel the *Pale Morning* would be, turning the ship for a rake would result in running it aground on the unseen ruins below the waterline, right below his snipers.

Desire was well and good, but timing was everything.

The *Lady Mo* sat hidden behind the point on the fast-moving Namleng, deep green trees on the gentle, sloping hill blocking the Duram from view, branching mangrove roots like twisting fingers in the bicolored water. The Wild Cobras wore their battle black and golds, and by sporting their tell-tale armor Tan would finally declare his treachery for all of Suyoram.

Simo stood on the weatherdeck with a spyglass, watching the western approach of the Orchid Bridge where Yelu could see both ships. Her sharpshooters were posted alongside the Ashukari, who carried grenades. "Signal for the captain! Mark's passed the first action!"

"Cut the line!" Tan called from his place on the quarterdeck. Immediately, two sailors released the tow line, as they'd fastened the *Lady Mo* to shore rather than using the anchor for a quick release. They started to drift with the current, their pilot expertly navigating through the churning Namleng and picking up some speed.

After a minute or so, Simo yelled, "Signal, sir! Mark's passed the second action!"

"Make sail!" Tan called, the crew echoing the order and the sails snapped on the wind.

It felt like they were going too fast, the Grisi ship nowhere in sight. If they revealed themselves too early, and the *Pale Morning* came up aside or behind, it would be a disadvantageous position. Tan stopped himself from ordering a correction based on pure instinct. They'd already taken the measurements and made the calculations, triple and quadruple checked. He had to trust in their work.

He muttered a curse, then a prayer.

And just before they emerged from cover, the *Pale Evening* drifted into view from behind the point, a ghost in the fog. The *Lady Mo* slipped quietly behind.

"Beautiful!" Simo cried, then blew a kiss to the pilot. "Someone remind me to give that man a raise."

Flawless. He strode down to Simo and snapped open his own spyglass to watch the stern of the Grisi ship, checking for activity at the rear cannons. They hadn't seen them yet. No movement. The world blurred as he checked the deck. Odd, the crew looked rather distracted as well, a few groups of soldiers were milling amongst the deckhands as if they were searching for someone...

"Mark's moving fast to the kill zone," Simo said. "Shall we run up the colors?" That would be Yelu's signal to proceed with the engagement as planned.

There was a commotion. Someone ran up onto the deck of the *Pale Evening* in a panic. They weren't in uniform... the nearest group of soldiers ran over to them, saluted, and after a few seconds, immediately ran below. An officer then, out of uniform. Then the officer grabbed one of the crew members, dragging them over to the rowboat and pointing frantically.

"What the fuck," uttered Tan. "Are you seeing this?" Simo was supposed to be watching Yelu's signalman but quickly checked the target. It looked like the officer was climbing into the boat, along with a few others in civilian clothes... those were Protectorate officials. Then he recognized the mannerisms of the undressed officer. "That's Rimes. What the hell is he doing?"

"Huh. Dunno, cap," Simo said. "Three minutes until they're under the bridge."

Whatever that junkie was doing, it didn't matter. They'd been supremely fortunate so far and it was time to take advantage. The fifty guns on the flagship remained undeployed, and the *Pale Morning* was going too fast into the channel.

Chapter 47

All Bloody Eyes and Gnashing Teeth

That was the worst part of it, Ree thought, as she kicked the weapon from his hands, then punched him in the throat. *The old men in power send the young ones to die.* He staggered, and she snatched his rifle off the ground, spinning about to smash him with it. She knocked him senseless, and kept going until she was sure he wouldn't get up again.

"And for what?" she panted, dropping the gun onto the wreckage of his head. Useless in close quarters fighting, too slow to reload. She took his sword instead, doubled back for Curly's set of keys. Then she ran down the passage, in the opposite direction of the thudding boots coming to investigate the sound of gunfire. At the back of the ship, she found the storage rooms, next to a ladder well leading down into the pitch-black bowels of the hold.

What a waste. What a waste to send these kids to die so far from home. What a waste to normalize the dehumanization of women, who could have been their mothers, sisters, wives in another life. What a waste to indoctrinate them into believing a whole nation of people were inferior, a poisonous lie that did nothing to enrich their own culture.

Minus the five dead in the brig, Ree had no idea how many soldiers were on the ship. And of those, how many were workers, how many were skilled fighters, and how many were children in uniform? The normal thing to do would be to escape, swim for shore, and then figure something out.

The larger problem lay in that she didn't want to escape. Fucking devas, she wanted to go to Jinburi, as she thought everyone had agreed. Even if she was going to her own execution, was it too much to ask to arrive unharmed and unmolested?

In one hand, she considered the sword, spinning the steel cutlass to reflect her gaze. Hiding in the darkness of the cramped hold, she could put all her phi hunter training to use and take them out one by one. It would be exhausting and near impossible and wouldn't get her any closer to Jinburi.

Who was she kidding? There was no way out now. Might as well try and sink the ship somehow, take as many of these bastards with her as possible. All this wood in one place only needed a spark. Or even better… her eyes drifted to the heavy, reinforced door of one of the storerooms, and the Grisi plaque on the wall next to it: *Grand Magazine*. Another small metal medallion hung from a nail, engraved with the likeness of a Grisi woman. She was unveiled, her eyes and hands raised toward the sky, pale hair a blur in the wind, a lightning storm raging behind her. Only the Daughters were depicted like that – they were something like saints. With a deep inhale, she caught the scent of gunpowder. This must be the powder room, where they kept their ammunition for the cannons and shot.

In the other hand, she considered the keys.

Maybe… just maybe… she could make this work after all.

It took about five minutes for them to find her. She waited patiently, listening to the officers' barking orders as the sailors and soldiers frantically but methodically searched throughout the labyrinthine hold of the ship. Finally, someone spotted the ajar door to the grand magazine, where no sane person with any shred of self preservation would hide. Cautiously, the six soldiers crouched, their weapons aimed at the darkened doorway while a sailor lit the lantern in the adjacent room. A light shined through the glass porthole and illuminated the most sensitive area of the ship, where several shelves were loaded with cloth bags stuffed with gunpowder for the cannons, barrels of loose powder stacked and secured with leather straps, and one pissed-off Suyo woman sitting on top of an open barrel. She'd shoved the head of an unlit torch to stick out of the powder, and next to it, held a flint dangerously near a stolen steel cutlass.

"I want to talk to Elleman," Ree called out in Grisi to their stunned faces. "Unless all you cunts want to burn with me."

Not long after, Elleman came storming down the passage, Rimes trailing behind, along with another uniformed man who by the brass on his cap, must have been the ship's captain. He stood behind the six soldiers still aiming at her, his face bright red with fury.

"Holy fucking father!" the captain gasped and clutched his chest when he saw where she was. "At ease! Put down your arms, boys, for the love of vows if any one of you fires–"

"Belay that," Elleman said, crossing his arms. "If she wanted to, she would have done it already. What do you want?"

Ree let the silence hang between them, staring critically at him. He was large and burly, would have been a giant compared to Kit when he'd beaten him. His hair was disheveled, and he looked hastily dressed, only wearing the base of his uniform. He'd probably been asleep when his men informed him of the incident.

"I want a guarantee," Ree said.

"Murderers don't get guarantees."

"What about rapists?" Ree sneered. "What do they get?"

"Sir," Rimes hissed, already backing away. He was even less dressed than Elleman, in a sleeping robe. "Surely, the circumstances–"

Elleman held up a hand to silence him. "I know you're not a naive little girl," he said. "You're on a wartime ship with three hundred men who haven't seen even a bare ankle for weeks. They were weak against my explicit orders to leave you alone. Satisfied?"

"Not really," Ree admitted. "They were officers."

"And now they're dead," Elleman said. "What do you want?"

"I want to get to Jinburi and secure the ceasefire for good. Unmolested."

"That's what I want too."

Strangely enough, she believed him, at least about the ceasefire. He obviously didn't give a shit about her welfare. She wouldn't have been surprised if he was the one to authorize it. At the least, he turned a blind eye. There'd been plenty of accounts on how soldiers would kidnap defenseless villagers to use them this way, systematically. That didn't happen unless the structure in place allowed it.

But nothing she could say, even while threatening to kill everyone on board, was going to change any of that.

"The food sucks. I want better food."

"That can be arranged. Anything else?"

"Maybe one of those hammocks to hang in here."

"You can't stay in there."

"Why not?" Ree shifted her position to a more casual lean, purposely careless with the flint glancing near her steel. The entire ship seemed to flinch as they watched her every moment. The captain hyperventilated as he paced behind the general, clutching his head. Ree smiled. It felt like having the beast by the balls, and it was deeply satisfying. "This room is better. Think I'll move in until we get there."

"It's against maritime law to have any flammable items in the magazine," Elleman said. "We can't operate the ship with a safety hazard–"

"Is rape against maritime law?"

"Of course! I would have had them all flogged, then court martialed. But you saved us the trouble."

Ree doubted that, but pretended to consider. "All right, say I come out. They were *your* officers. How do I know there won't be retaliation?"

Elleman's eyes narrowed, and he uncrossed his arms, holding his hands out, open palms. Wise to switch tactics. "I had my doubts before. But it's clear to me now that you're an honorable warrior who wants to see the contract stand. You want peace, but you won't tolerate indignity. I know because I'm the exact same way..." *Bullshit,* she thought, but let him go on uninterrupted. "...I will fully swear on the Book of Vows that we will secure your accommodations, and unauthorized personnel will not be allowed anywhere near..."

By this time, there was a whole crowd standing aways back, though the narrow passage did not allow for many viewers. The anxiety was palpable, the sour of their nervous sweat thickening the air with bright yellows. As Elleman rattled on, she caught snatches of the whispers beyond, and the overwhelming sentiment was confusion. She had the chance, why didn't she escape? What could they do? This condemned prisoner was being taken to die... and was now demanding that happen. They were unsettled to say the least.

The ship was still moving, a benefit of the river current. They hadn't dropped the anchor.

Though she felt weak by the shit dreadful, Ree was certain she could keep this up until Jinburi. But she didn't know how long that would be, and if they'd figure out a way to storm her in the meantime, flood the room with water somehow.

Elleman cursed under his breath, shaking his head, then barked at his riflemen. "Fucking stand down!" They slowly lowered their rifles, and the general then gestured to her sword. "If you're going to insist staying in there, then at the very least, put down your weapon. We both know if this ship goes down the ceasefire will be considered broken."

"I'm not so sure about that," Ree said. "I'm alone here, acting in self-defense. Accidents happen."

"You really think..." He chewed on his words, and for a moment she thought he might charge in there himself just to call her bluff. Thing was, she suspected he could see in her eyes that she wasn't bluffing. Ree spun the steel sideways, idly, prompting another groan from the captain. She'd never felt more Ashukari before than she had right then, and wished Havan could see her now. He'd be proud, she thought. "You think they'll believe your word over mine?"

"You'd be dead," Ree said, but all the bitterness suddenly overwhelmed her. "Just like last time, huh?" When he only looked at her puzzled, she said. "Jinburi. Ten years ago. You assaulted a boy at the Sabai Five and crippled him for life. You almost killed him. You ruined his life and it cost you nothing."

"I don't know what you're talking about," he said, though his tone had grown stilted. He swallowed, a vein in his sweaty neck twitching. He knew.

One of the sailors came running up to the captain, and started speaking in jargon too fast for Ree to follow.

"What?!" the captain gasped then stomped away, presumably to continue running the ship. "Snipers?! This is fucking madness! General, we're going to need that powder!"

"What's the situation?" Elleman demanded, but the captain had already gone, shouting orders. If he needed that powder, that had to mean the ship was under attack. The crowd of sailors and soldiers quickly dispersed, reporting for duty.

The captain was right. This was madness.

A huge crash came from the upper deck. It sounded like a building had collapsed. Shouts of surprise and outrage rang out while the whole ship shuddered and groaned, lurching abruptly to the side. Ree was thrown off her seat and banged into the shelf of powder packets, and then everything erupted into chaos.

Chapter 48

A New Kind of Army

"Run up the colors! Beat to quarters!" Tan ordered, the call repeating down the ship, his signalman beating the drum. The newly made United Rami People's Army flag unfurled from the mast, a red circle on solid black, representing the blood moon with two silver swords crossed behind it. His marines poured onto deck and into position. He couldn't help the swell of pride when he looked them over, fierce and sleek in their Wild Cobra black and gold, red scarves, armed to the teeth with multiple pistols, rifles, axes, and blades.

He peered into the spyglass again, and finally, the crew of the *Pale Evening* had noticed them. Even Rimes and the Protectorate officials were staring at the fast-approaching Suyo ship as they were being lowered into the water in the rowboat. He wondered what was going through their heads. Did they recognize Tan's ship? Or did they think they were river pirates?

"One minute!" Simo said.

The Grisi deck crew was alarmed now, and Tan watched the gunports. Finally, he felt a shudder of sick excitement as the two back-facing gunports on the stern opened, but they weren't being loaded. The intimidation tactic would normally work, considering how unmatched the two vessels were, but this wasn't the open seas. And besides…

"Mark has entered the kill zone," Simo said, and just as the *Pale Morning* came into range of the western approach, shots rang out across the water. Tan watched through the glass, heart thudding. Like clockwork, ten sailors crumpled, falling out of the rigging, onto the deck, or overboard. The others ducked behind cover, but the Orchid bridge's only intact platform stood but a few feet above the crow's nest. A vicious, nasty execution to a good chunk of the *Pale Morning*'s deck crew. There was nowhere to hide.

He checked the gunport again, no loaders still. What were they waiting for? Some of the Grisi crew had managed to man the swivel guns, and now soldiers had come up to support, taking shots toward the bridge. The thick, stone railings provided ample cover for his sharpshooters. They were slightly exposed when the *Pale Morning* came directly alongside but responded to the assault with a volley of grenades. A few men managed to jump overboard before the deck blasted with a row of small explosions.

"Boarders ready!" Tan called as they drew closer, and his crew pulled their grappling hooks and readied the long planks. Simo put away the glass in favor of his sword. Tan had his pistol, but like some of his other marines, he carried three more guns across his chest, a sword on his hip. Trying to reload a gun on a moving ship slick with blood and cluttered with debris was near impossible. "Back off the sail, easy – *easy*! Pull us up, come on!"

The big gunship loomed before them, deck smoking from the grenades, men still taking fire from Tan's snipers, and more soldiers coming up through the hatches. They cut her speed, the creak of ropes and whip of sails as they adjusted to match.

A railing exploded in a shower of splinters. Grapeshot from the *Pale Evening*'s swivel cannon cut through a sailor and a marine, another injured by the splinters. Tan yelled for the deck cannons to open fire, retaliating with the same type of small, fixed guns. The chaos was building, and everyone was yelling now, the Grisi reinforcements engaging with Tan's crew, where they had the advantage.

They were close enough to spit across, and soon the ships would move out of range of their snipers.

"Boarders away! Give 'em hell!"

"Boarders away!" Simo yelled. "For the Storm Prince!"

A rousing cheer accompanied the swarm of grappling hooks that clattered onto the Grisi ship, wrapping around posts and railings and rigging. Tan rushed to grab the end of one of the ropes alongside his sailors and pulled. Gangway planks heaved up and over. They smashed down onto the *Pale Evening* at an upward angle.

The soldiers trying to repel them fell back when the first marine landed, which happened to be Simo, swinging across the berth like a madman. He landed in a spinning flash of steel, a master of the daab sword technique, that utilized a high rotation speed, and complex flowing movements. A wave of Wild Cobras followed.

Adrenaline surging, Tan climbed onto the rail and hopped over, a pistol in each hand. No thoughts then, only action. He shot anyone in a blue uniform or bearing a Grisi face, until he ran out of bullets, then he drew his blade and dagger and cut through them. The edges blurred as they pushed forward, and for all he felt he was back on the open sea, hunting pirates, storming sloops and gunships and–

"Captain!" Simo came up beside him, panting, as the crew took up positions around the hatches and ladders, some of them reloading their guns if they still had them. From the inside, Protectorate and Grisi soldiers fired from the safety of the ship. "Decks ours, ready to go below…" he trailed off, peering through the smoke at the starboard rail, and Tan followed his line of vision.

A dozen cloaked figures stood in a row, their glowing eyes furrowed into angry slits. His guts felt cold and his face hot, and suddenly he could feel the lick of rain and smell the stink of carnage that night in Loram. One of his marines screamed and rifles were pointed at the phi.

"No! Hold your fire! Hold your fire!" Tan ran out in front of them, a hand up. He slowly turned to face the Ghost Legion, and recognized the one Ree had called Owun. In the daylight, if it shut its eyes, it could have even been mistaken for a human's poisoned corpse, with its grayish-green skin, and broken black veins around its eyes and lips. They stared at one another silence, until Tan forced himself to say, "You're here for her."

The phi lowered its head, but did not respond. Then it walked past Tan, the others following, straight toward the open main hatch. His men who'd been surrounding the sides of the hatch backed away, eyes wide. Tan felt oddly helpless as the Ghost Legion entered the hold, and even though he knew they were on the same side, it still felt…

Wrong.

The panicked shouts of the Grisi floated up from the interior after their barrage of bullets had no effect. The crew could only listen as those shouts turned to screams of terror, only to be cut off seconds later.

"By the lord," Simo murmured, staring at Tan. "Is this what… the village?"

Tan could only nod, throat suddenly parched.

"What should we do?"

His natural response was to run. To return to his ship, and get as far away from these cursed things as possible. Sail straight down the Namleng past Jinburi, past the Capital, into the open ocean and keep going.

But he'd come this far. He needed to get back to her.

"Wait here," Tan said, and then he followed them inside.

Chapter 49

The Anatomy Of

"Get her out of there, you worthless shits, or we're all fucking dead! Get! Her!"

Ree shoved away the pieces of a collapsed shelf as three of the six soldiers charged, unarmed. She reached for the flint but a boot kicked her hard in the gut, another in the side of the head. She curled up, gasping, then her scalp burned with pain as they dragged her from the magazine by the hair.

Ree thrashed her arms, then reached out her foot to catch the side of the doorframe. She reared back and the strands tore out at the root. The men moved to seize her arms and she cast the Blind Eagle's Eye, the momentary camouflage confusing them. She bit a hand, punched a dick, wriggled away, found the sword. Whenever Ree fought in close quarters, the ingrained phi hunter instincts took over – the first strike usually lethal. She sliced two of the three men through the neck and one in the femoral artery before the spell dropped, then turned to face Elleman, who'd gone ashen-faced and moved to draw his sidearm.

Two of the riflemen charged, affixed bayonets aimed at her heart. She swatted the first to the side, and spun with her blow, using her momentum to push the man heavily into the other one. He screamed as the bayonet pierced him in the side. The second man tried to pull back and Ree stepped in, shoving the cutlass up and under his chin.

"That boy you hurt?" she said to Elleman as she kicked the soldier's body away, "that was my brother."

He said, "So what?"

Then he lifted his pistol, aiming at her head.

She stared at him in disbelief. He wasn't really going to shoot at her when she was standing directly in front of the–

The blast seemed to stop time. The bullet whizzed past her cheek, skin burning, and clanged. Elleman's eyes grew wide as saucers, and she braced herself for the explosion.

Nothing. Ree glanced over her shoulder, expecting to see something fizzling before a fireball engulfed them. But somehow the bullet had lodged right into the forehead of the saint's medallion, which had been knocked slightly askew during the fight, just enough to have blocked it from entering the magazine.

Huh. If that wasn't a miracle, Ree wasn't sure what was.

When she turned back to Elleman, the handle of his pistol smashed into her nose. Ree flinched in pain, and he swung again, the solid wood knocking her in the temple, sending her vision spinning about the room. His self-righteous anger flooded her senses with a sickening, suffocating blanket of entitlement, as if screaming *how dare you judge me.*

"So what?!" he yelled again, and cracked her collarbone in two, and kept swinging. "So... fucking... what!?" Sounded on the verge of hysteria. Ree reached for the voiceless chant to cast something, anything, but had trouble finding the words. This had happened before, and it was never good. "I beat your brother, and I'll beat you worse. So! What!"

He screamed in her face, and ripped her sabai, his fingers taut around her neck, and she felt very far away from her body. Like it was all a play, and she was in the audience, and when the men came for Sira, she'd unfocused her eyes, and pretended their words were the birds the sheets were the wind and she was standing on the hill, overlooking the deep red Duram, that first day she'd walked out of the Serene Way with a freshly severed finger and thought, I don't have to be anywhere. I don't have to do anything.

I can just sit here for a while, and be a part of eternity.

"I don't want to fade away," Sira whimpered, sitting next to her. Tears flowed down her cheeks. "I just wanted to live... and love... why did it happen to me? Why me?!" She began to sob, slow, chest-heaving cries. "What did I do to deserve this?"

"Nothing." Ree wrapped an arm around her shuddering shoulders. "You did nothing to deserve any of it."

"Why do they get to ruin our lives... and – and – and then flourish!? When will they *pay*?" Sira grabbed Ree by the throat with both hands. "Promise me. You'll make them pay."

The pressure released, and the peaceful clouds burst away, sucking Ree back into reality. She gasped for breath, staring up at gloomy wooden beams, pain lancing through her face and chest and ribs. When she forced herself to sit up, she saw Elleman a few feet away, kicking his legs.

Prince Tanung stood above and behind him in black-and-gold armor glistening with blood, holding one of the Gris rifles taut against Elleman's neck. His boot was against the back of the general's head as he pulled, the Grisi general's face was all kinds of wrong colors – black, blue, red, and purple. Elleman desperately clutched at the weapon cutting into his jugular.

Ree tried to speak, tried to stand, but fell over. Blood poured from her face and splattered on the floor.

Tan snarled in Grisi, voice calm, but beneath bright with anxiety. "You're no Chosen Son. Piece of shit, you're going to hell." Then he let go, and Elleman slumped over, wheezing. Tan spun the rifle and took aim at the back of the general's head.

"Wait…" Ree gasped, crawling to a sit. "Don't–"

The point-blank shot shattered the man's face into a mess of blood and bone. His body plopped over.

Of course, the world was better without that bullying asshole, but Ree was stunned to find no satisfaction, no relief, even knowing that Kit's suffering had been avenged.

She shuddered, fighting the urge to vomit. It disgusted her, but unlike Rimes, Elleman wanted to end the war and seemed willing to oppose the trading company to do so. He would be replaced, likely by someone subservient to them.

Tan rushed to Ree's side. He helped her stand, and she stifled a groan. "Come on, I'll bring you to the surgeon."

"No," Ree said, wiping blood from her face, doing her best to hide her disappointment. "Let him work on the others. I'll be fine." She allowed Tan to steady her as they walked, and she cast one last look at Elleman's body. What a waste.

"Did you seriously lock yourself in the magazine and threaten to blow up the ship?"

"Didn't lock it," Ree said with a cringe. "You heard?"

"The captain told me. After they surrendered. After the phi showed up and…" His voice went hoarse, and he cleared his throat. "The ship's ours." Tan laughed then, a manic chuckle. "I swear, you're a girl after my own heart."

The fur-lined blanket felt divine on her aching, bruised body. After a long wash in a cool stream, Ree laid naked in the setting sun to dry, hiding away from the many eyes at the camp.

Yelu and the *Lady Mo* had escorted Ree and the injured to the host for treatment and recovery, while Tan and others stayed behind to deal with the prisoners and the *Pale Evening*. He would return by tonight, he promised her, and they'd discuss everything then.

She hardly remembered the trip, she'd been so exhausted. And then the raucous cheers that erupted when she'd stepped off the *Lady Mo*, the huge crowd gathered, waving their banners, pumping their fists in victory.

Ree's mouth had fallen open, and in her silence, Yelu grabbed her wrist and held it up in the air. The resounding cry of victory could probably be throughout the entire province. Ree forced a smile as she looked over the people and their adoring, misguided eyes.

She hadn't wanted this. A slaughter awaited. From what Yelu told her, there were four other flagships like the *Pale Evening* at the harbor, and three more gunships. Ree had asked her if the prince thought they could take them all on, and the woman had only laughed.

Was his madness infectious?

Isaree.

Ree rubbed the tears from her eyes, and stared up at a nearby branch, where Agira perched, holding his knees to his chest.

Hey, Agira.

What... what's wrong?

Just... feeling the pressure. She sighed, closing her eyes. *Did you change your mind?*

Yes, but... I still don't want to hurt anyone.

That's fine. You don't have to.

How does it work? You just... decide when you've won? And poof?

It's the Severer of Sorrows. Ree tapped the hilt to the dark sword. Before attending the parlay, she'd placed it in a wooden box and charged the Ashukari with its safekeeping. Now safely returned, it laid next to her on the blanket. *When it's time, I'll take their heads with it. Their karma will be eaten and dissolved, and they will be reborn with a clean slate.*

What?!

There's a chalice that he uses too. I guess I could have grabbed that instead, but... the sword was calling to me.

You kill them? They all know that's how it works?

They all know. Ree gazed at the little creature, and smiled gently. *If you want, I can do it now. You've waited long enough. You've earned it.*

Agira's big eyes blinked, and he seemed to consider. *No, no, I've earned Indrajit's amnesty. But yours is different. It's not fair to the others. I want to help you. How can I help you?*

Hmm… I'll think about it. You want to try the blanket? It's soft.

After a few moments, a soft thud next to her, and Agira laid spreadeagled in the fur, his wings outstretched. He shut his eyes, panting, and made a strange cooing noise. *So sofffffttttt.*

Sooooooft. Ree laughed.

You usually speak out loud to me.

Yeah… I guess I missed you being in my head, old friend.

Chapter 50

Timing and Desire

On a tributary off the Namleng, the pyres were built for the fallen.

Four Ashukari and Fifteen Wild Cobras died during the attack, and the entire brigade was there to see them off as well. Minor losses, due in large part to the intervention of the phi. Four marauders had arrived upriver from the capital a few hours prior. Though they were smaller than the Gris ships, it would slightly even their odds.

Ree caught a glimpse of Tanung moving around his crew, making speeches, paying respects to each of his fallen soldiers. She caught his eye few times, but stayed next to the Ashukari's pyres for the most part. It was a somber affair, but the accompanying victory and new arrivals gave the night an air of excitement, and the attendees stood around sharing stories about the departed deep into the night.

Minh had also come to see them off, along with a bottle of whiskey and a large group of her Khrapong province fighters. She embraced Ree like an elder sister, and Ree hung an arm around her shoulders, grateful for the company.

"Still feel like a mascot?" Minh asked, raising the bottle. "Did you see that crowd?"

"Yeah, it was... overwhelming."

"Now you're gonna be humble?" Minh chortled. "Remember when we first met up after your little nap?"

"I remember. You called me a cult leader with a god complex."

"It was savior complex. And my opinion hasn't changed."

"Oh, fuck off." Ree laughed. Her gaze drifted to Tan again, where he stood with Simo and some other foreigners. It felt like he always knew when she was watching him, the way he'd slowly smile and briefly meet her eyes before returning to his conversation. Ree took a swig of the bottle.

"That man is in love with you," Minh said, matter-of-factly.

Ree choked on her drink and started coughing, much to Minh's amusement. "He just thinks he is."

"Oh, come on… you could do worse than a crown prince. He's a handsome, rich, ambitious young man. If I was fifteen years younger, and into, that, you know," she made a cuckoo bird sound. "You really have no interest?"

Ree found herself blushing and bit her lip, and Minh erupted into laughter. Then she ahemed, tilting her head toward Tan, who was walking over with Simo. "Ah, shit, here comes his royal majesty."

"Ladies," Simo respectfully wai'd. "May your fallen warriors rest in eternal glory."

"And for yours," Minh returned the wai. "But I heard the maneuver was… how did Yelu put it? Fucking *disrespectful*. How'd you learn to sail like that?"

"I'm Baghani, ma'am," Simo smiled. "We're born in the water. Fancy a stroll?" He offered her his arm.

"Well, don't mind if I do," Minh handed the half empty bottle to Ree without even looking. "When's the briefing again?"

"Dawn," Tan said, an amused look on his face as he watched the two flirt. Ree deduced this had been going on for a while now.

"Aye aye, captain," Simo said, and then he led Minh off as they strolled down the riverbank. Ree had to admit, they cut a handsome, strong profile.

Like Ree, Tan had cleaned the blood off himself and found some new clothes. Unlike Ree, he wore formal attire, the Gris-influenced cut of miltary dress-uniform, but patterns and details traditionally Suyo. He'd combed the long side of his hair back, and his face looked freshly shaved, a scrape on his jaw still healing. As for Ree, no one would have guessed she'd been beaten half to death earlier that morning, but she still felt the seams freshly aching, especially the collarbone.

The sultry, measured way he looked at her, coupled with his highly controlled, manicured appearance, led Ree to believe this was the first Tan – the one that knew exactly who he was and what he wanted and would stop at nothing to get it. She had so many things she wanted to ask, or yell. How had he done this? How long had the king been planning to name him heir? Did he have something to do with the child's death? How dare he turn her into some kind of folk hero?

Did all these people know they were doomed?

But the longer she stared into his eyes, the less she wanted to know about his unquiet mind. The longer she appreciated the way he looked at her, the less it mattered. The sense memory of his touch set her stomach flipping about, and that knowing smile on his lips… she licked her own, waiting for him to say something.

He slowly took her hand, then leaned down to whisper in her ear. "Let's get out of here."

The luxurious captain's cabin on the *Lady Mo* was indeed impressive, and Ree slid onto a maroon, Qinsengi-velvet chaise that looked stolen from a palace. Nestled against the bulkhead, its priceless ebony wood legs were bolted to the floorboards. Tan turned on a lantern, then offered her a glass so she didn't have to drink straight out of the bottle. He poured one for himself, then leaned against a table where various maps, books, and papers lay scattered, along with a few copies of the manifesto she'd seen, stamped with a likeness of her face.

"How did you make that?" Ree lit a kageleaf rollup with a burning Anewan fingertip.

"I drew it," Tan said. At her impressed expression, he added, "Sketched it. A real artist finished it onto a wood block."

"It couldn't have been that bad."

"It wasn't bad," he said. "It was terrible."

"Let me see the sketch then."

He actually seemed to blush, and shook his head, smiling. "No, those are private."

"Those? Multiple? How many did you make?"

"Um," he laughed. "I lost track. Couldn't get the nose right."

"You wrote everything too?"

"The drafts. Khim helped with the final."

"Artist, writer, manhunter," Ree said, her exhale framing him in a haze of smoke. "Sailor, schemer, usurper… is there anything you can't do, Prince Tan?" He tilted his head in response, as if trying to guess her angle. "Your uncle will surely catch wind of your treachery soon. And after naming you his heir…" Ree shook her head, not bothering to hide her disdainful awe at his hubris. "He legitimized your claim and in response you made a fool of him. He'll lose face in front of the world. It's unforgivable."

"He'll understand that it's not personal," Tan said. "But make no mistake, the full force of the royal army is coming for us. I expect a forward regiment may meet us in Jinburi."

"They'll slaughter the people's army," Ree said, growing sullen. "They have war elephants, for devas sake."

"I have some ideas on how to deal with them," Tan smiled. "I'll tell you in the morning." Her jaw dropped at his forwardness, and he added, "At the briefing."

"Right... there's still time to turn me in and throw yourself upon his majesty's mercy."

"I have no regrets."

"None?" Ree leaned forward, astounded. "Because not a day passes that I don't contemplate some of my own."

He held a hand to his chin, then shook his head. "The missteps, the mistakes, the compromises made in desperation, all of it has led to this moment. I think this is the moment... it's... it's not just about expelling the colonizers, Ree. It's about changing the world. We might feel alone and isolated in our struggles here but make no mistake, eyes around the world are focused on the Rami people, from lands we haven't yet seen, and what we might achieve against insurmountable odds. An inspiration for the oppressed and a warning to all would-be oppressors. And I'm grateful, even if the burden at times feels... unbearable."

Ree had hardly noticed she'd risen, drawn like a moth to a flame, seduced by this grand vision, now only a breath away. Tan started to say something, but flinched, and the frayed nerves of the Storm Prince buzzed in his aura, clawing through the cracks, begging to be seen. The liquid in his glass trembled, and he quickly set it on the table, then clenched his hand into a fist.

She searched his face as she gently touched his hand. He resisted at first, averting his gaze... then he sighed and let her take it in her own, tremors and all. "Why is making history so important to you?" she asked.

"Because all of this struggle has to be for something greater than my own desires." The way he said *desires* told her that he despised himself for them.

"It does mean something, Tanung," Ree said, unfurling his fingers into hers. "It's your soul's journey through karma, and it's a mysterious path."

"No, Ree... I don't believe in karma, or reincarnation, or the devas," he gazed at her sadly, as if he were afraid to admit this. "I mean, I don't believe that we, humans, could ever truly understand what exists beyond our own reality."

Ree found that hard to believe, but only because it contradicted her experience. There was no lie in his eyes. "I've seen their world.

You've seen the sword, the phi, the spirits… our entwined fates. You still doubt it all?"

"I'm not saying that you didn't see the face of the divine. Our subconscious creates meaning, finds patterns in the unexplainable, and manifests that understanding into reality. But we make reality. *You* made reality."

She couldn't quite wrap her mind around what he was saying, but it did reflect a suspicion she had about magic, the possibilities beyond human imagination, whose arbitrary laws by those in power attempted to control it. His hand tightened around hers, shaking worse now.

"The truth is, I know this illness is going to kill me sooner rather than later, one way or another. And you were right when we first met. I'm… fearful of fading away. I've always desired a more glorious end. Or at the very least, one made on my own terms."

The thought ached her heart, echoed across Sira's, and she wanted to hold him.

"I understand." Ree smiled, somewhat awkwardly. "Sorry, I'm not much of a romantic with my words." And she grazed against him, guiding his hands to either side of her waist. As his breath quickened, the shaking in his right hand lessened, as if stirring his arousal blocked the pain. "You said we make reality from our desires." Her skin tingled pleasurably where he touched, and she gazed up at him through her lashes, hanging her arms on his shoulders. "Want to know what mine are?"

Taking the hint, he pulled her against him. He leaned down to kiss her, but stopped just short of her lips. "Oh, I know what they are." Enticed, Ree moved in, but he pressed his forehead against hers, wickedly keeping her at bay. "But I need to know something first, love."

A blanket of warmth cascaded over her, shifted deep in her belly to an urgent need. *Love.* "Go on," she whispered, her body pressing into his in a demanding way. He closed his eyes, smiling.

"I believe in you. I believe so much that if I live through this, I swear on my grave I will build you a monument worthy of a goddess." He touched her cheek, stroking her bottom lip with his thumb. "I just need to know one thing. I need to know if…" His breath hitched as she licked the tip. Then he opened his eyes, pinning her with a searching stare. "I need to know if you believe in me too."

Ree wasn't prepared for the question. And he would be even less prepared for her answer. What did it mean, to believe in someone? That they exist? Obviously, he was very real. That they'll be successful? He'd proved to be a cunning leader. Believe they're honest?

Trust them?

He'd certainly proved he wasn't honest. At least, not in a way she could say, with full conviction, that she trusted him. Especially this version of him, the seductive, prideful, shunned heir who would, in his own words, go to the ends of the earth to get what he wanted, damned be the consequences. No, she didn't believe in this one.

But she'd seen the other, the Storm Prince, and his vulnerable desperation, the ragged, raw edge of his psyche teetering on the verge of self-destruction. He was never just one or the other, but both, like the dark and light side of the moon. One could not exist without the other, and despite how much it tortured him, he needed that phantom to challenge the worst parts of himself. And that was what she trusted. Trusted so much she felt her eyes watering.

"Yes, Tanung. I do believe in you."

Her words barely escaped before he pressed his lips against hers. His rush of relief, and elation, and deep-seated desire flowed into her like a whirlwind, and she let herself flow with it, sighing contently when he picked her up with one arm, and with the other scattered all the books and maps and papers. They fell onto the table together amidst the battle plans, the strategic maneuvers, and those romantic promises of death or glory…

All of that could wait until morning.

Chapter 51

An Undeniable Thing

"I can't believe this shit," Raj said, which was the overwhelming sentiment reflected by everyone in the room. Outside, the rain lashed down on the ancient bricks of the Phi Hunters guild hall, leaks trickling into buckets hastily placed by the young scribes.

Esha hadn't seen Raj since she'd convinced him to leave Loram, leave the Wild Cobras and their inspired yet doomed pursuit of Ree. He hadn't wanted to leave, arguing vehemently against it. Esha soon realized he couldn't care less about the mission. He'd found a place with the brigade, and longed for that comradery again. She understood that longing for purpose. But it wasn't the point she pressed.

Ree had become corrupted with some kind of power stolen from the devas. He could be a part of the brigade but the brigade wouldn't be a part of the world for much longer. Raj was shaken by her account of their conversation and her description of the sword.

They weren't hunters anymore, Esha told her friend, but it was their responsibility to inform the masters on how far Ree had broken their vows. Esha and Raj had both come from the streets. Without the guild, they would have no skills, no education, and would probably have ended up like their parents. They owed the guild that much, she said. And you owe your wife and kids a future with their husband and father alive.

They made the long trip back to Jinburi and went straight to the guild to speak with the masters. To their surprise, Elder Nokai, Master Arei and Master Seua weren't there. Their old friend Falah was, however, and informed them that the masters had been summoned to the governor's palace for some kind of "summit," along with Ex, Ree's father.

"The fuck is a summit?" Esha asked.

"Sounds serious," Raj said. "In a bad way."

Falah promised to call on them when the masters returned. Weeks passed before he contacted her, and she was astounded to see that they hadn't summoned only her, but every former phi hunter still alive.

It almost felt like old times at the hunters' meets she'd always remembered fondly. The masters sat on the floor with the others gathered in a circle around them. The great feasting hall table was pushed back against the far wall under the mural, set with some food bought from the local market and drink. Utilitarian, not festive, as this would be a long discussion.

It seemed like a scene from another world. These men had all since departed from the guild for one reason or another, and were dressed according to their new lives, haircuts included. They were now fishermen, blacksmiths, trappers, cooks, fieldhands, a few bounty hunters like Esha and Raj, all working-class trades.

Except for the one last phi hunter, Ex, who hadn't yet showed. His absence was palpable.

What Raj was responding to was Master Arei's summary of this summit, and one of the main points that resulted from it.

"We've all been conscripted by the crown to fight against the United Rami People's army and the Ghost Legion," Master Arei said. "Specifically, as phi hunters."

The scribes trudged through the group, handing every former phi hunter a personally addressed letter, stamped with both the seal of the governor and the king.

Many of the older hunters were illiterate, and one of them, now an out-of-work carpenter with thinning hair to his shoulders, only stared at the official document in awe. "What does that mean?" he said.

"It means that all of you poor sods have to brush off your chainblade, find your mask, and get ready to kill some phi for crown and country," Master Seua said, and Esha caught a glint of excitement in the old man's eye. The group murmured, their responses mixed. Most were confused about why this was happening now, after all the efforts of the crown to make their trade obsolete.

"The fuck is the Rami ghost army?"

"Heard that was Ex's girl's thing. She's a rebel leader, I heard."

"Thought she was dead."

"How much are we getting paid?"

"But Master Arei, isn't this illegal?" Falah said, and the murmuring died down. "By the Sacred Stone decree, the crown can't interfere with our traditions, and harming our fellow man is against our tenets."

"Tell that to the Rising Sun decree," said Master Arei, her voice dripping with disdain. "Any nationally recognized guild can be conscripted to perform their trade during times of war, superseding all other decrees."

"What?" Esha said, appalled. She glanced at Elder Nokai, who sat in a chair by the hearth, gazing into the fire with milky eyes, wrapped in a blanket. He was so old now that his wizened face was a mask of wrinkles, and Esha couldn't tell if he was listening. "I've never heard of the Rising Sun decree."

"That's because the king just made it," Master Arei said.

"You can just *make* decrees?" Raj gaped.

"He's the king," Master Seua said. "They do these things."

"And they want to pretend like it's water under the bridge," an older hunter said, crumpling up the paper. "Destroying our livelihood until it suits them? My family lost our fucking house. I used to kill demons, and now I'm scraping shit stains off barges for coins."

"I don't even know where my chainblade *is*," mused the one next to him, who was closer to Ex's age. He took a drink out of a flask. "Ohhh, wait, that's right. I sold it to a collector so my daughter could go to school." He laughed, then immediately flinched at Master Seua's one-eyed glare.

"Excuse me," said another hunter, "but could someone explain what this Ghost Legion is?"

"The Ghost Legion is a part of the rebel army being led by the Storm Prince Tanung, Captain of the Wild Cobra Brigade. You may have heard his name in the news recently, as the king had just named him crown prince… *before* he attacked a Grisi ship and raised a peasant army in the Nahkong province." Master Arei then turned her eye to Esha. "Esha, you and Raj were hired by him to hunt down the Abyssal Heretic in Loram. Would you please tell us what you witnessed?"

As everyone slowly turned to look at her, Esha felt acutely self-conscious. She cleared her throat, then sat up straighter, rising to her knees. To the best of her ability, she summed up what happened. How the prince suspected the Heretic was a former phi hunter, how she and Raj determined that Ree had been using the Serene Way to wage war against the Grisi Protectorate, and what Esha had seen when she confronted her. It flashed before her eyes as she relived it, fighting through her emotions more than a few times. The way Ree looked that night, so different, so distant.

And the things she'd said – a pact with the phi to bring them redemption, claiming to have been given powers by the devas, the spirits being on her side, indeed, a spirit had been there, gave Esha more than a few broken bones to boot… the guild listened, enraptured, and once she was done, Master Arei thanked her and asked if she believed what Ree had said to be true.

"I believe she thinks what she's doing is right," Esha said. "But she's broken our vows before. My face is proof enough."

"What I think Master Arei wants to know is, do you really think she walked in the deva realm?"

Esha whirled around to see Ex, leaning against the wall near the entrance, in the shadows of a statue of one of the First Hunters. He must have been lurking somewhere in the guild the entire time, listening in.

"If it weren't for that sword, she called it… the Severer of Sorrows, no, I wouldn't," Esha said. "But there was something true about that thing. It shined through in the Everpresent. It was… undeniable. But all that shit about redeeming phi, I don't think that's real."

"That *is* real," Ex said, sending everyone murmuring again, and he stared past Esha toward the masters. "Ree's auntie Narissa was a krasue. She refrained from killing humans for many years, and received amnesty from Indrajit. Became human again. You've all met her before. She's family to us now."

Master Seua audibly sighed, squeezing his forehead. This was all news to Esha, and the rest of the hunters, but it seemed that Ex and the masters had this conversation before, more than once. Yet he was the only one who still hunted these creatures when they were troubling people.

"The world of devas is a great mystery, but Isaree..." Elder Nokai's whisper was so faint, Esha thought at first she'd imagined it, until everyone turned to him. "…Isaree has always been uniquely connected to the Everpresent."

"She has, yes," said Master Seua, "but that doesn't mean the kid should be running around disrupting the cosmic order."

"That's beside the point," said Master Arei. "What a phi hunter does after they leave the guild is not our business. We decided this when it became clear that the guild would not continue to exist as it once had. By the old ways, when a hunter left the guild, they were to return their gift to the First Hunters."

"So… die?" Raj asked.

"The ritual is similar to the one that you went through as a child," Arei smirked. "But the results aren't as favorable. We found it to be a bit… antiquated."

"Hey, uh... I don't know about any of this redemption stuff," said the hunter with the flask. "It sounds like the king wants to pay us to hunt phi. That's one thing, but also, to kill Ex's little girl? Doesn't feel right."

"This isn't a request," said Master Arei, glowering again, it seemed, at the situation. "This is a decree. An order. Yes, we will be compensated monetarily for our services, but if we refuse, we'll be branded traitors, which is punishable by execution."

"And your kids, and wives, and husbands, will literally be branded," Ex said, with a scoff. "This is fucked."

Esha glanced at Raj, appalled and confused at the turn the conversation was taking. She thought everyone would immediately agree to help stop Ree, but even the guild masters seemed like they didn't want to get involved. It sounded like they might even... believe her?

Had she been wrong? Had she let her emotions get in the way of helping her friend?

"Master Arei," Esha said, "What are we going to do?" She sounded like a child then, looking to the adults for comfort as the world fell apart around her.

Yet, this time, Esha realized that what she believed, what she was promised, and the adherence to that identity no longer served her. It was finally time to believe in herself despite what others thought, and follow the beat of those tumultuous, unexplored regions of her heart.

Chapter 52

Between Chaos

Thick clouds rolled over the night sky, heavy with rain, but the storm held back, only allowing a steadily hissing drizzle. Blanketed over the fields outside of Jinburi, surrounding the Grisi Fort Mierna, the forward regiment of the king had arrived. By dawn, the United Peoples of Rami would hoist their banners and march to meet them, sorely outmatched and outnumbered, yet fueled by the unrelenting conviction of true believers.

But tomorrow was forever away. Tonight, the Wild Cobra Fleet and the Ghost Legion would strike the first blow. If all went according to plan, perhaps the inevitable slaughter at dawn might be rewritten.

From the shadows, Ree scanned Fort Mierna, the impenetrable structure standing sentinel on a bluff overlooking an expansive basin of the Namleng. Anchored in the center, the five Grisi warships bobbed and swayed in the rough flood waters, lights blinking in the black. The fort hadn't been built when she lived here. It was about a mile south of the city, attached to the Long Road, boasting cannons more powerful than any ship could carry.

She pulled a note from her bag. Over the last week and a half, she'd been impressed with the way Tan commanded the war table, listened to his allies and oversaw training of the peasant army, somehow inspiring everyone with his confidence. He stayed by her side when she anxiously walked the camp, meeting her new followers, and she stayed by his side when he'd collapsed, more than once, shaking and incoherent.

Their blossoming kinship felt naturally companionable, despite moments of passionate disagreement, which more often than not was resolved, vigorously, in private. One afternoon, Simo pulled her aside to say that he'd had his doubts at first, but he firmly believed the two of them made one another that much stronger.

She believed that. Despite the coming battle, she'd thoroughly enjoyed their time together. And as for their nights... *well.*

Give this to Prince Tan, Agira. She slipped the paper into a small vial, then tied it around Agira's neck.

I... Agira clutched the vial to his chest, then peered at the cloaked taihong waiting in a row behind her. *I have a bad feeling. Maybe I should come with you...*

No, it's too dangerous. It'll all be okay, I promise.

Okay. Be careful, Isaree. He lingered, seemed like he didn't want to leave.

Ree drew him into a hug. His body was cold and slimy, but when she felt his little arms clutch her shoulder, she smiled. *Thank you for everything, friend.*

Agira sniffled, then jumped into the air and sped off over the river to find the *Pale Evening.*

Ree opened a pouch around her neck and smeared the collected ashes of the fallen Ashukari over her eyes. Then she nodded for the Ghost Legion to follow. They descended into the dark passage and walked underground in the pitch black until it began to incline. Up they went, Ree sensing the way with her footfalls, trusting that the Weaver had done her work just as well as she had before. Finally, she heard the clicking of Homdee's carapace, and her green eyes lit up in the darkness.

"Walker, the passage is ready."

"Thank you, Homdee," Ree said, hand on the hilt of the Severer of Sorrows. She couldn't help but think back to the first time she'd done this, when she'd resorted to the Trance, untrained, just to get through it. She'd vomited after killing that first Lo boy... Ree let out a long breath, wishing that she'd still felt as sick as she had that night.

While Homdee dug away at the last bit of stone, Ree said to the taihong, *Remember, don't attack unless attacked. If a man surrenders, leave him be. Any questions?*

They never had questions. She'd already gone over it, several times. If something went wrong, it was her fault Half of the phi would go to the gate, where they would open the way for the fighting Ashukari. Half would help her clear a path to the battery, then the Ashukari would man the guns and assist the Wild Cobras' naval assault.

"I have one." Ree felt a smooth claw on her arm. *"This work has been completed, and I... am tired. May I receive my amnesty now?"*

"Not yet," Ree said. "I may still have use of you."

"But your enemies will be repelled should you triumph. That was the service."

She speaks true, Owun added.

"Yes, but they haven't been yet," Ree said, growing impatient. "There's still five ships out there. Once those are ours or gone, then we'll have won."

"Will you have won? Or will you win when your Storm Prince is on the throne?"

Ree hesitated, shooting a glare toward Homdee, despite not being able to see her face. "I won't ask the phi to hurt Rami people. Once the Grisi are repelled, your service ends."

"Very well."

There was a scrape, and then the sound of a stone moving. The air changed, and there was just enough ambient light from the hallway to see a room shaped like the cell she'd stayed in Kohkiem. Same floorplan, after all, but this wasn't used as a prison since the Gris weren't occupying Jinburi. This was being used as a storage closet.

The phi flowed past her like dancing shadows, and while she followed the route to the battery, she hadn't heard any screams, no gunshots… which had to be a good thing. The Grisi must be surrendering.

Then the deep boom of cannon fire echoed over the water, followed by the sound of an explosion, which meant Tan and the Wild Cobras had begun the night assault on the Grisi ships. Ree only needed to cross the courtyard to access the artillery, but the moment she stepped out into the empty field, she knew something was amiss.

Owun, wait. Ree raised her hand to halt them as she peered around. It felt unnaturally silent. Then movement on the ramparts. A man stepped from the shadows. He was wearing an armored coat, and an opaque white and red khon mask carved in the visage of a snarling wolf.

Her father's mask.

And then it hit her, just as the deafening shot of cannon exploded from up on the ramparts, an answer from the fort. She was too late.

It was a trap.

When the *Fathers Truth,* a 52-gun Grisi warship, ran aground on a sandbar, her massive bowspirit clipped into the main mast of the *Promised Son,* and brought all the fluttering sails and rigging down with it, Tan felt, deep in his heart, that they would win the night.

The two Wild Cobra sloops that had harassed and outmaneuvered them closed in for the kill, their marines howling for blood when the gangplanks smashed down on the decks.

The *Pale Evening* cruised full speed ahead to spar with the *Morning Star* and her sister, the *Widowed Wife*, three ships mirrors of one another, both black flags, with one red, two blue. Meanwhile, the last two Wild Cobra ships closed in to harass the remaining three Grisi ships that remained clustered in formation, defending the fort.

Come on, Ree. Tan gripped the rail as he commanded his crew, peering at the distant fort and their devastating artillery, which had not yet joined the fight. *What are you waiting for?*

"Did those ash-covered freaks forget to bring a fucking match?!" yelled Simo as he ran by. As the *Pale Evening* rapidly flew into range of the two Grisi flagships, and Tan wondered if these were his last few moments, the blaze of cannon fire lit up the fort, and his despair shifted again to elation.

She'd done it, he thought, the Ghost Legion had torn through the garrison, the Ashukari manned the cannons, pointed them at the main contenders... he realized a second too late from the direction of the flicker over the water that his joy had been premature.

"Incoming!" he screamed, running down the deck and shoving sailors over as he went. "Down! Get down–"

The explosion shattered the night into fragments.

Hunters! Owun hissed as a chainblade cut through the air. He dodged but the phi next to him did not, and the chain whipped three times around her neck. The hook lodged into her throat and she tried to run, but a phi hunter slammed into her and continued stabbing. Another squealed as his legs melted off in a flare of Anewan, the phi hunter systematically crippling him. Ree felt struck numb, her hand on the hilt of her sword, but she could not bring herself to draw it.

"Stop!" she yelled at the hunters, but they didn't acknowledge her. She recognized some of their masks – these were the old generation, the class of hunters that her father had grown up with, though he was ten years younger than the youngest. She spotted Falah's dad, the one with the teal hawk-modeled mask fighting with Owun. Ree lunged forward and grabbed his arm. Without hesitation, he backhanded her, sending her staggering. And then he went right back to yanking on the chains around Owun's torso as the phi snarled and thrashed.

"Isaree!" Her father yelled, then jumped down from the rampart.

"Tell them to stop, Pa!" Panic filled her voice, and suddenly, she felt like a helpless child. The taihong could survive lethal wounds, thus the hunters crippled then secured them with chains rather than wasting energy with death blows. They were the most remarkably similar phi in anatomy to human form, thus most valuable if their organs remained intact. Which meant… they needed to be harvested while still alive. "Please, tell them…"

"They can't see us," Ex said, walking through the courtyard. "They're in the Trance."

Ree stared at the hunters with a sinking despair. Unlike her, they'd all passed the Kang-Fye ritual, and therefore, she supposed, had the clarity of mind not to chop her in half. As she'd done to Tian.

Ree's eyes watered, hating herself for being this weak. If these had been Grisi, not hunters… if they'd been *human*, not hunters, she wouldn't have hesitated. She would strike them down as she would any other enemy. She hung her head, staring at the stump of her missing finger, her hand still clenched around the sword.

"Isaree… by the devas…" Ex paused to remove his mask, voice catching in his throat. He held a hand to his chest. "It's really you. Devas, you're all grown up."

The shouts of Grisi artillerymen could be heard from the battery, ordering a reload. She needed to stop them, had to stop them *now*, before Tan and his fleet were pummeled into splinters.

But her father stood between her and the battery, only a sword's-length away.

All was quiet but for the ringing in his ears. Tan groaned, then moved each limb to check if they were still attached. When he opened his eyes, it was all smoke and splinters, screaming men, broken men in pieces. Blood poured from a gash across his forehead. His other pieces were present, but his right forearm sported a nasty bulge where it shouldn't have. Broken. The crew who'd survived the barrage threw sand on the fires and dragged the injured aside.

"Captain!" Simo hauled him to his feet, shaking him. "The fucking Ashukari hit the wrong ship!"

It couldn't have been, unless they'd also aimed for the *Lady Mo* that had moved to flank and support their attack with boarders. She was now sinking in a blaze of fire.

No, that was a perfect hit on two targets. Purposeful, professional, and no doubt executed by the highly trained Grisi artillery men. Ree had been delayed, or she had failed. He couldn't bear to think of anything worse.

"No, Gris have the guns!" Tan said, screaming to be heard above the chaos and ringing in his ears. Too much time had passed, there was no time. The fort gunman had waited until the *Pale Evening* was not only in range, but in the right position. They had very little time to adjust before rolling right through the broadside of two flagships. And if they survived, and cleared the *Widowed Wife*, then the fort would have reloaded, ready to sink them when they emerged. "Back the sails and heave to, keep the *Morning Star* between us and them!"

"Aye, cap!" Simo went forth shouting orders while Tan yelled down the ladder to his master-gunner for a report: they'd lost several men but the focus of the barrage had been the top deck, going for the throat.

"Fire as you bear, we're settling in here!" As their deck shook with cannon fire, he braced for impact. The chaos mounted, and the three ships sparred toe to toe, but mostly, the *Pale Evening* took a vicious beat down. The adrenaline started to ebb, making room for the throbbing pain in his fractured arm. Tan hissed and shoved it under his bandoleer of pistols to minimize damage, on the off chance they made it through the night.

Ree hadn't seen him for seven years in the Blinds, twice over in her existence, and yet she couldn't bring herself to look at him. Behind him, the screams of her warriors might as well have been the rain, as far as the hunters were concerned.

"Isaree, please, sweet girl, would you look at me?"

She shook her head, but the tears fell anyway. Here she was, expelling a colonizing world power from her country after a long and bloody campaign, after liberating a nation... and she felt like her parents had caught her wearing shoes in the house. No, that wasn't quite right. She felt like the parent, having been caught wearing shoes in the house, by a child who couldn't see all the scorpions scattered around his feet.

"Okay. Please, just listen. There's no time before they..." Ex sighed, and she could tell he wanted to close the distance. "The king made a new decree and forced the guild into service. He sent us here to hunt phi, but I didn't go into the Trance because I needed to see you. I needed to tell you–"

"Pa, stop."

"–how much we love you, Ree. Your mother and I, Kit – no matter what you've done, whatever little shitty thing you think is unforgivable, none of that changes anything. You'll always be my little girl."

The phi had started to groan, begging the hunters for mercy, that they were mistaken, they were only serving the shining one, the Walker that would grant them redemption… that they did not kill out of vengeance or rage as they had as the accursed… that this was only the work… the service…

"You must not have heard," Ree managed to choke out. "About some of the things I've done."

"What? Joining a rebellion? You know I'm branded, Ree! My parents were rebels. I don't fucking care how many Gris you've killed."

How could he mean that? At Fort Nestor, there'd been over a thousand Protectorate soldiers, Lo servants, and an Ashukari girl she loved. She'd lost track at the amount of labor camps. Ten on the *Pale Evening*, a few hardly out of their teens.

And she'd come here, ready to send another thousand.

Finally, Ree forced herself to look at him. She saw her own eyes in his, but he still carried that youthful, earnest vibrancy about him, even if sporting a few more wrinkles. It was more his scent that called to her. When he'd left home for his hunts, she'd sneak into her parents' room and hug his pillow when she missed him.

"I searched everywhere for you, sweetie." Ex reached out to her, then clutched his own head. "I stayed in the guild, just to keep looking. I even went to Kohkiem, and they told me you were dead... and Arinya, she…"

He started to break down then, and she wanted to tear her own heart out.

She had to tear her own heart out, if she wanted to break the cycle.

The crash of iron through wood and steel rang out through the night, and the Ghost Legion began to fade away, then a transcendent sense of déjà vu captured her. Ree knew she'd been here before. In other lives, as other people, the same soul connection, but here all the same.

"I cut my finger off," Ree said, her voice growing numb. "A tribute for the guardian, just so you couldn't find me."

"A finger? Devas, I would have given my whole arm just to tell you that you weren't alone! You were never alone…" Ex's eyes darted to her hand, which was slowly drawing the Severer of Sorrows.

"You need to leave now, Aswin," Ree said, and she couldn't say where the name had come from, but he recognized his own, before he took one of the First Hunters' names.

"How do you…?" He still hadn't looked away from the sizzling black blade, the energy radiant in the Everpresent.

"If you don't leave now, one of us has to die."

"What are you talking about?"

Ahead, the battery. Break the cycle, save the prince, and the world.

Behind, the harvest. The hunters, the phi, and their promise… her promise.

Ree took a deep breath. "I love you, Pa," she said, "but I need to do this. If you truly love me, don't try to stop me."

She spun away from Ex, strode three paces, and severed the head of the nearest hunter. His mask bounced off the ground. Ree kicked the body over, which had been in the midst of harvesting Owun's heart. She crouched to gaze into the pained eyes of her faithful servant.

We failed you, Walker, I'm sorry I'm sorry.

No, you didn't. Ree smiled. *It's time. I'll grant you your redemption.*

At last. Thank you. The blade came down, and when it touched the phi, a blinding light echoed between worlds. The accursed was no more, dissolved, sent home with a clean slate, forgiven. She moved to the next one. Another mask fell. Another curse lifted.

If it was the last thing she did, it would be this.

There were no guarantees in life or death, but she could keep her promise. The next one. Forgiven. Redeemed. The hunters were locked in the Trance – a slave to their singular mission of killing phi, and they didn't see her. At least she could send them to the First Hunters, give them that glorious hall they thought had been lost to history.

She laughed as she sobbed, and the sword drank deep. Somewhere, beyond the veil of the world of men, Indrajit smiled. Another promise kept.

You make your reality, Tan had said.

She wished they had more time. He'd made a proposal to her, and in her message she'd answered. Bad timing, this life

I'll find you, again. In every lifetime.

The next one fell.

And she kept going until he finally stopped her.

Chapter 53

And the Divine

As their hull sprouted with rushing water and their masts splintered, Tan searched for a semblance of hope. At least the rain had started to pelt down, dousing the fires, and perhaps helping their marauders escape once they realized the night was lost.

Thunder and lightning synchronized as the storm fell relentlessly upon the Namleng.

"Won't hold much longer," Simo limped over, his left leg bloody and blistered from hip to foot. "The *Widowed Wife* is moving to cross our bow for a raking shot and the ships taking water faster than the pumps can go."

"How many guns have we got left?"

"None. Magazine's flooded. We're defenseless. Orders?"

Abandon ship was the order he was waiting for. Perhaps a few of the uninjured could get to the bank before the *Widowed Wife* cut them off, trapping them in a watery grave. He knew his marines were better than theirs. If they could board...

He cast Simo a hopeful smile. "Can we close distance, bring her aside?"

"Tan," Simo shook his head sadly. "We're dead in the water."

Tan stared out over the fight, and the monsoonal storm that he couldn't help think was downright unnatural at this time of night. Fitting, he supposed. Come into the world with a storm, go out with one.

Tan looked back to his second mate. "Well. Guess that's it, then."

Simo's eyes softened. "Guess that's it."

They walked to the rail of the quarterdeck to watch the Grisi gunners reload for the next barrage.

* * *

The confusing shapes and sounds blurred and shifted as Ree thrashed hopelessly against her glass prison. Without a body, she burned with internal rage. Full images flashed and retracted – explosions over the river, a burning black-and-red flag. They were burning and drowning and dying, all because she had failed.

Despair opened a chasm, and she let herself fall, endlessly.

Then a familiar face appeared.

Elder Nokai. He looked splendid from here, with two hundred and fifty heads, one for every year he'd seen. He smiled kindly as a youth, as a strapping young hunter, as the old master who saved her. His mere presence calmed her, and Ree's descent slowed. She steadied from volatile, hissing mist into a slow whirl of energy.

Slowly, child. Breathe. Just be.

Without lungs there was no breath, but Ree deflated, flattened, expanded. Until she was a straight plane. A blank sheet.

Good. Now, become. Transcend.

Reflections became memories. Ree gave into it. Formlessness could be helplessness. Or... without the constraints of physical form, one could find freedom! One could become a being of light, and that light could shine and travel through these endless refractions, through space and time and beyond.

Ree realized with overwhelming rapture that her awareness, without form, could go anywhere that her eternal soul had ever touched.

You see, child? There was never anything to fear.

Anywhere. To the hill overlooking the Duram, where for the first time, she felt completely at peace. Night had fallen, but the heavens were clear, the milky stars and full moon shining bright over the land.

To the *Lady Mo*, where Tan held her face close while she melted in his embrace and he offered her a kingdom. The table was burning, all the carefully laid plans blazing into ash, the manifestos drifting like lilies in the rapidly flooding waters.

Back to where she'd taken her first breath. To where Arinya sat awake, candles lit before the house shrine, and the Awakened Lord, praying for her husband to return with their little girl. Narissa, Esha, and an unfamiliar man sat next to her, faces solemn.

Kit. He looked... well. Handsome. Strong, his wheeled chair not a deficit but a personal throne. And he played a well-worn phinpia, the same lullaby that Arinya hummed by his bedside when he teetered on the brink of life and death. Her heart swelled with love – unconditional. Endless. How she yearned to stay there.

Arinya paused in her murmuring, and stared toward the doorway, eyes full of tears.

… Please, Isaree. I love you. We love you. Please come home…

Oh, Ma, I know. I always knew. I tried. I really did.

And of all these places, Ree chose to go to the one where she could still manifest.

She flowed into the Swamp Guardian's sanctuary and settled into her long-rotted finger bone. Fingers had no eyes, so she could only sense the electricity of glowflies as they danced in the fog above the mirror-still pond. The stillness, the quiet, the serenity – it was a sacred place. A good choice.

But she did not come here to rest.

I was wondering when you would return, Walker. The Guardian of the Swamp rumbled from deep beneath her pond.

As promised, to offer something of value.

A wayward soul in the fragment of a tribute?! The naga scoffed.

All the trespassers of the land, great one. Those who would destroy our way of life and exterminate your children once and for all. I have brought them all here to you, ripe for harvest.

A deep growl boiled the water. *You'd have me lower myself to appear before man?! I should eat your soul for the mere suggestion.*

They aren't worthy of your presence. But, oh, think of the divine terror you'll invoke when you appear before them in all your resplendent glory! Great one, prove to the faithful waiting for a sign that they are vindicated. Bring low all the nonbelievers who doubt your existence. Cast out these trespassers who have no reverence for the spirits and would deign to strike you down.

These trespassers have been here but for a blink of the eye. It was your people who killed the Pale Mother and Lord Chalawan. Your people slaughtered the Crocodile kingdom.

History has been written, but you, great one, know the future. The swamp will shrink year by year, and even faster with their technologies, accelerated by machines. They'll take your power piece by piece, scale by scale, until your great body has withered away to the size of a mere snake, slinking in the grass, hunting rats. Why fade away when you can burn bright as a dying star? Let's purge the rats now.

The naga had risen from the pond and glared down at the tiny finger bone. She was interested. If Ree had a body attached to that finger, she would have raised her arms in reverence.

And to the faithful, she continued, *remind them of the power and beauty of all they continue to destroy. It will be a legend for as long as man walks the earth, the vision of you, great spirit. Become the fang of the devas and take vengeance. Man will never forget and perhaps, someday, your children will return.*

As Ree spoke, she imagined the rolling river, the flaming ships, the eyes of the royal army watching from the bank with keen interest, the People's army, the citizens of Jinburi who had wandered down to the river to witness what war had brought them.

The Guardian hissed. *This place you wish to reach falls beyond my lands.*

Then take me with you to lead the way. Let us ride together.

The guardian considered for what felt like ages. It was hard to know. Finally, she decided, but with a warning. *If I take you from your remnant, Walker, you cannot return to your vessel.*

I know

When we fall, we will return to the higher realm.

I'm ready.

Ree caught one last glimpse from her vessel – Ex, clutching the necklace to his chest, determined to deliver her back to her mother… again. Then for Esha to take her somewhere far beyond the wrath of the crown and maybe, maybe she could find happiness… Ex reached to open the door, but paused, staring down into the gem with a heartbreaking realization. Esha would make that journey, seeking new fortunes, but she would do so alone.

Okay, he said, voice breaking, but finally, accepting her choice. *It's okay, sweetie. I understand.*

And the guardian inhaled Ree's ethereal being. The entirety of her soul rushed through the nostrils of the naga, swirling and rising to settle behind her eyes as a passenger.

The guardian sunk deep into her pond and surged through the Serene Way, the land cascading around her. The rain sensed the god beast and followed, stirring the clouds to bring forth lightning and thunder. The naga grew larger and larger as she absorbed all the magic of her domains, stronger and stronger. In essence, Ree felt the same exhilaration as when she'd rode upon Dama's back, the Voice of the Valley.

Attachments peeled away, leaving only pure, endless love in their wake. That which connected them to one another throughout space and time. A little piece of eternity

She felt free. She felt at peace.

And if an ethereal soul could smile, the Walker was smiling now.

The *Morning Star* was thirty seconds away from firing a deathblow to their port and the *Windowed Wife* a deathblow to their stern when the rain abruptly petered off, and the clouds parted for a rare glimpse of the stars.

Something broke the surface. It spun like a wheel rising a few feet above the waterline. Of massive size, and patterned strangely, Tan could honestly say he had no idea what the hell it was. He wiped the blood out of his eyes to peer closer.

"Scales," Simo said, in complete awe.

Indeed. Gleaming blue-green scales, keeled, with gold trim. Another instance rose further off, spinning between the trio of Grisi ships in formation and the Wild Cobras marauders. Tan peered into the depths where a glowing crimson eye twice his size gazed back.

And then the water displaced as a gleaming crest of armored plates flared like sails in the wind, and a massive naga rose from the river, its head as wide as the deck.

Tan grasped the rail with his one good arm to keep from fainting. Simo only pointed, struck silent. The crews from every ship stopped to gawk as the naga continued to rise up and up and up, until she loomed over the highest mast. Some of his crew cowered in fear, while others dropped to their knees and raised wais in respect for this most revered spirit of sailors.

Did he lay dying, and was this a magnificent hallucination? The naga exhaled, and spouts of water blew from both its nostrils. Framed by the full moon, it glared indignantly down at them as its black tongue flickered to taste the air. It must not have liked what it tasted, for it opened its jaws and displayed its enormous fangs.

Then it stared directly at Tan, and he froze, couldn't even take a breath. He stared into the creature's eyes, and an image came to him.

He saw Ree, gazing at him from the dark, the moon shining behind her like a halo. Then she smiled, her glistening gold skin transforming. Transcending.

The naga hissed, and the voiceless words were witnessed by all.

I believe in you.

Tan gasped and clutched his mouth, choking back a sob. A crushing ache shattered his heart – he knew then that she was gone.

Suddenly, cannon fire erupted from the *Morning Star* and explosions burst along the side of the naga's snake body. Sailors on the *Pale Evening* cried out in dismay, and the naga turned its head toward the Grisi ship to let out a deafening roar. Tan's men cowered and clutched their ears.

If this were a battle between Rami powers, it would have ended here out of respect for the most revered of water spirits.

But somehow, the Grisi had looked upon this divine creature and saw only a monster.

"By the fucking devas!" gasped Simo. "They're trying to kill it!"

The *Widowed Wife* fired next, smashing scales off its crested back, followed by the other three ships. Shimmering silver blood oozed from the naga's wounds. These spirits weren't like the phi who were impervious to bullet and blade unless wielded with the power of spirit magic. Spirits were living, breathing creatures, a part of the earth, and like all creatures, subject to the violence of other ones, which included the murder and destruction conducted only by man.

But it would be a grievous mistake to think that this grand being was anything like man.

It struck like a bolt of lightning, head shooting forward to dive through the hull of the *Morning Star*. The ship broke in half. Another segment of the naga's body rose up directly under the *Widowed Wife* and tossed it aside like a toy. It smashed into pieces when it hit the water sideways. As for the other three boats, the naga's tail rose from the water, coiled around them, and clenched. The Gris ships cracked and then burst in a fiery jumble of wood, steel, and blood.

Then a half barrage from the fort hit the naga directly on the tail, blasting a good chunk of it completely off. It roared in pain and swayed. With panic, Tan feared it might fall. But it set its sights on the fort and dove into the lake, its submersion sending a rolling wake that almost flipped the half-sunk *Pale Evening*.

Moments later, it burst directly in front of the fort in a cascade of water, mud, and stone, looming above the building with its back arched and fangs extended like a threatening viper.

"No," Tan said softly. The second barrage emptied directly into the naga's throat at point blank, tearing it almost in two. It wavered, teetering... but a snake's head could still bite even when severed from its body. The naga's enormous head fell like a falling star and crushed the face of the fort into pieces. Its body slipped back into the water, and all was still.

By dawn, Field-Marshall Priyut of the Royal Army of Suyoram would send a message to his half-brother, the Storm Prince. All had witnessed the great naga spirit rise from the Namleng and destroy all its offenders. And all had witnessed it speak to Tan, and Tan alone. If the naga believed in him, then so would the entire country.

* * *

The Wild Cobras celebrated in Jinburi for days. Despite their heavy casualties, they were not the type to take victory subtly. The United Rami People's Army joined in, and the atmosphere on Sing-Sing Street was downright rapturous. Most of the Grisi population fled promptly, though some citizens who'd long assimilated remained, as well as missionaries who quickly declared that using the Abyssal Heretic to refer to Isaree was now sacrilegious.

Simo and Minh tried to drag him out but Tan retreated to his tent, where the people's army still lingered outside Jinburi. On his desk, a stack of messages had arrived from the capital. The official, impersonal letter from his uncle that outlined the transfer of power – once Tan returned to the capital, the abdication would be made official, as the coronation ceremony planning was already underway. The man was under no illusions he would be able to maintain power after the royal army had pledged their support for the Storm Prince.

He read the letters from his mother, Arinya, and Somatra. The others he left unopened – his betrothed, the queen, five different cousins, three concubines, and a lot of other people he didn't give a shit about.

On the other side of his desk, he contemplated the small pile of jewelry, clothes and trinkets, a hunter's knife… the few things that had been in Ree's possession. Tan picked up an embroidered white scarf and brought it to his face. Still smelled like her.

Her body hadn't been found anywhere. Rumors circulated, and Minh still held out hope that she would miraculously stroll back into town, but Tan knew, in his heart, that she was dead. He no longer saw the Stranger in his waking visions or his dreams. When Ree came to him, it was his memory of her, as the true love that had slipped through his fingers: his muse, his wild, savage queen that would have never been content to sit in court–

He put the scarf down, and gazed at his pistol strewn amidst the unopened letters. He wondered…

"Ahem."

Tan startled at the intrusion. Standing at the entrance to his tent was a ten year-old child wearing the saffron robes of a Sangha monk. He was skinny, even for a child monk, with large, wide-set eyes and shaved head that seemed on the verge of being too large. The child-monk blinked those big watery eyes at him, while he wrung his small hands.

"Who let you in?" Tan said, and quickly lowered his pistol. There was something strangely familiar about him, but he was sure he'd never seen him before.

"A-Apologies, my prince," the boy stammered, pressing his hands into a wai and bowing. "But I have a message for you."

"My mailbox is full," Tan said, but the child walked up to him and held out a small vial. He felt his pulse race, and his voice came out in a hoarse whisper. "Where did you get that?"

"I tried to deliver it that other night, but I'm sorry. There was so much fire in the air," the kid said, grimacing. "I wanted to let you know, sir, that what you're feeling now... it will pass. I can't say for certain that you will end up accursed if you... give up. B-but I don't think she would have wanted that. She'd say that people need you right now. She'd say that... you'll meet again."

Tan stared at the child, then the message vial, and placed his pistol on the table. "You're right. Thank you." And he took the message, rolling out his last note from Ree. His heart swelled with fondness as he read her answer to his proposal, and he couldn't help his bittersweet smile.

So she had been a romantic, after all.

We Are Eternal

King Varunvirya IV, the Storm Prince, the Rightful Heir, Chosen of Sarvapun the Wise, Banisher of the Invaders, Admiral of the Wild Cobra Brigade, Favored Champion of the Great Jinburi Naga, and Devoted Servant of the Walker would become one of the most celebrated kings in Rami history, however short his reign.

His court reflected the spirit of his brigade, employing voices from far and wide. Simo took over as commander of the Wild Cobras, with Raj as his second. The king modernized the military and put in place measures that would see Suyoram protected from foreign powers for decades to come. They officially allied with Loram, as well as the Baghani Republic, and improved relations with other countries within the region and abroad. His distaste for the Grisland Trading Company inspired him to pass regulations on businesses and trade so any company could never become as powerful as a nation. He brought the printing press to Suyoram. He married his betrothed as arranged, and fathered two children by her, and a few more from his consorts, as was required.

He did many things in that short time, but the most important to him wasn't any reform or royal decree. Laws changed to suit their times, reforms could be undone. But a precious few things might outlast even human civilization.

On the banks of the Namleng river, a mile outside of Jinburi, the king built a monument. It had been five years since the great naga had "blessed him" and fallen, leaving a snakehead-shaped imprint that remained long after its body dissolved into light and vanished. His advisers strongly urged him to build a statue for himself, a naval tribute to his legendary victory.

But he was the king. He built the monument for her.

It wasn't obnoxiously large. She wouldn't have wanted that. But it was a beautiful shrine, surrounded by gardens. A lovely celebration took place on its opening, during which he decreed a national holiday dedicated to Isaree, the Walker. People traveled from far and wide to witness the unveiling of the "Ghost Princess" folk hero from Jinburi who helped to save two countries from subjugation. The leaders of Loram arrived with an entourage, including Minh, who introduced him to man who'd been instrumental in the war – a roguish Grisi dressed as the other generals, but with ashes smeared over his calm, distant green eyes.

Eventually, people from around the world would travel to see the Suyo legend who inspired nations under colonial rule, across the sea and beyond, to fight back.

Her brother performed on his phinpia, his voice haunting, beautiful. Arinya, surrounded by her daughter-in-law, grandchildren, and Narissa, looked on from the front row, with a bittersweet smile.

During his speech, Tan's breath caught when he gazed beyond the crowd, and spotted a lone figure on horseback. Her face, her eyes… her father, Ex.

They stared at one another long enough for the crowd to begin to murmur, and Ex dipped his head ever so slightly to acknowledge the king. Then the last phi hunter tuned his horse and headed off the road, into the wilds.

It may have been his imagination, but Tan swore he saw a large black beast lurking impatiently in the shadows.

After the ceremony, the king and the royal family returned to their accommodations in the governor's mansion. He smiled fondly at his young children playing in the house, then sat alone in the garden looking over the edits for his latest work. He'd already finished his memoir, but realized his words for her could be its own volume. So he'd started on the biography of Isaree the Walker, working on it since he'd met Agira, who found more people they could interview for a complete story. Now it was almost finished, and she could have her place in history.

"Hey, rich boy!" a voice called from the yard. Tan startled. He knew that voice anywhere.

"Ree?" Leaping to his feet, he ran into the yard, beyond the rose bushes, heart in his throat…

And there she was, waiting for him. She smiled, and he marveled at the sight of her shaved head and fresh sak yant tattoos. Funny, he felt the virility of youth again, his body still fresh and undamaged from his years of hard work and violence, not to mention the illness consuming his mind more and more, every day.

He smiled back, his chest aching at the sight. He did what he would have done so long ago, were he in his right mind, and smoothly snapped a rose off a bush, striding up to her. "Where have you been?"

"Oh you know me," Ree said with a sly shrug. "Looking for trouble."

"In search of the next lost cause to uplift?"

"No, I think I'm past that," she chuckled. "I'm ready for something new."

"Sounds like fun," Tan said. "May I come with you?"

Her smile faded, ruby eyes drifting behind him. Tan glanced over his shoulder to see the body of Varunvirya IV on the ground, papers fallen around him. The king shook and seized as the fire of apasmara burned through his mind, for the fifth time just that week. A trickle of blood dripped from his nostril.

"You could hold on a little longer," she said. "I'll wait for you."

Yes, he could rip a few more months out of this fading vessel. Perhaps a year if he were really careful. But he'd already lost his visions of her. He'd forget his children's names, but he could ensure the right advisers were in place before his hands shook too much to hold a pen, pass another few decrees before he lost his words, the remains of his memories...

Oh, but to let go. To let go of the desire to control. Let go of the exhausting push to grasp as much as quickly as possible before it all slipped from his fingers.

To transcend. To become something new, with the one he'd longed to be with for countless lifetimes.

He turned away and saw his love as he had last, framed in moonlight, her pale hair cascading around her shoulders, beautifully strange with her golden skin and ruby eyes. "I think we've done enough," he said, and tucked the rosebud behind her ear. "I want to stay with you. Longer this time."

The Walker reached out to him. He took her hand, and they returned together.

Acknowledgements

To Desola Coker, editor extraordinaire and her finely honed suggestions, the edit comments that sent me as I manically raced to shape this fever dream of a story into a novel I'm terribly proud of. (And despite what she tells you, she can hang with the best of em.) Sam Farkas AKA the best agent, with the wisest council and spot on feedback, translating my rambling braindumps into tactful advocacy. Andrew Hook, Paris Ferguson, Hayley, April, Raeesa, Caroline, Gemma, and the whole crew at Angry Robot for making this a reality. Reza for the amazing cover, and Alice Coleman for the beautiful design.

The DC Speculative Fiction Writers Group – special thanks to Patricia for beta reading and workshopping with me for hours. Brandi Shaddick, my bestie and ride or die. Poet Laureate Rita Feinstien for helping with the verses. My rock and roll friends here in DC and beyond – Jacky, Hana, Fkin Richard, Dora, Neil, Vero, Curt, Lauren, Jon, D.Rob – y'all got endless space in my heart. My family – Mom, Dad, Sheamus, and Teddie, who've always been supportive and inspiring.

To my dear friend Derek Salisbury, who was a rock through one of the darkest times in my life, who encouraged me wholeheartedly when I first told him my dream about becoming an author, who read some of my earliest crap and gave it to me straight, who recognized my voice when I finally found it and told me, "fuck yeah, this is you." I know you told me you were proud of me for making it this far already, but I swear I'll make you prouder too. Till we meet again, homie.

And finally, thank you, dear reader, for going on this journey with Ree. I hope that you found something here to take with you. And to all those who dream in the dark, I see you. Never give up or give in, the world needs your light.

About the Author

SALINEE GOLDENBERG is a speculative fiction writer and multimedia artist who lives in Washington DC, and is drawn to outsider perspectives. A biracial, bisexual, diaspora writer, Sal often explores themes of identity, obsession and alienation in her work. A gaming industry veteran, Sal has created narrative trailers for titles such as Skyrim, Fallout 4, Dishonored, and Minecraft. When not writing, she likes to paint, listen to records, and play in punk bands.